Horror and Dark Fantasy Stories
Volume 1

Praise for Kevin J. Anderson

Horror and Dark Fantasy Stories
Volume 1

Kevin J. Anderson

WFP
WordFire Press

EBook ISBN: 978-1-68057-714-3
Trade Paperback ISBN: 978-1-68057-715-
Dust Jacket Hardcover ISBN: 978-1-68057-716-7
Library of Congress Control Number: 2024937269
Cover design by Janet McDonald
Cover artwork by Tithi Luadthong "grandfailure"
Ornamental Image by Freepik.com
Kevin J. Anderson, Art Director
Vellum layout by CJ Anaya
Published by
WordFire Press, LLC
PO Box 1840
Monument CO 80132
Kevin J. Anderson & Rebecca Moesta, Publishers
WordFire Press eBook Edition 2024
WordFire Press Trade Paperback Edition 2024
WordFire Press Dust Jacket Hardcover Edition 2024
Printed in the USA
Join our WordFire Press Readers Group for
sneak previews, updates, new projects, and giveaways.
Sign up at wordfirepress.com

Contents

Introduction

Creepy-crawlies, ghosts and goblins, things that go bump in the night or slither in the shadows ... Monsters have always been a big part of my life. I don't get scared. I don't have nightmares. But I do enjoy a good horror or dark fantasy story.

As a kid I was enthralled with monster movies. This was before such the availability of vast entertainment libraries on streaming services, or before that DVDs, or before that VHS cassettes. In order to watch a particular monster movie, you had to find when it was broadcast on a local TV station, no matter what time of day or night.

In the small Wisconsin town where I spent my childhood, we could pick up the Milwaukee stations, but our house also had a high TV antenna with a rotor that could turn it to different angles. If I got it set just right, I could catch a weak independent Chicago station that ran "Creature Features" late Friday night and "Sci-Fi Cinema" on Saturday afternoon.

I didn't differentiate between alien monsters, or werewolves, mummies, and vampires. The nuances between science fiction and horror were unimportant to me. Monsters were monsters. And special effects didn't matter either, because my flexible young imagination got just as excited by the most absurd-looking rubber monster as if I had seen a real monster.

Introduction

I owned and assembled all the plastic Aurora monster model kits, the ones with separate glow-in-the-dark components. I saved my allowance, and any time my dad would take me to the hobby shop in Racine, Wisconsin, I spent my money to the next one on the list. The Phantom of the Opera, the Hunchback of Notre Dame, the Creature from the Black Lagoon, the Mummy, King Kong, Godzilla, the Wolf Man. My bedroom was filled with them.

My dad was baffled by my obsession with monsters, and he wanted to throw a baseball back and forth in the front yard. (I was terrible at it, not only being a scrawny, uncoordinated kid, but also one with thick bifocals, so that the ball's position jumped whenever I looked up through a different part of the lens.) He set up a slot car racetrack in our basement, and we would race the little humming cars around and around ... which was fun enough, I suppose, but I didn't get the point, any more than my dad understood why I would rather stay inside and watch *Attack of the Giant Leeches* rather than go outside to play on a nice Saturday afternoon.

My favorite magazine was *Famous Monsters of Filmland*. I would sometimes get hand-me-down copies or find a new issue on a newsstand. I made lists of all the movies I hadn't seen. I read the commentary by "Uncle Forry" (Forrest J. Ackerman, who was like a cool, surrogate uncle to me).

But horror and dark fantasy wasn't just about monsters. As I grew older, I loved the works of Ray Bradbury, especially *Something Wicked This Way Comes*. I watched reruns of *The Twilight Zone* every afternoon and learned that sometimes the monsters are in your own mind, that sometimes your assumptions are more frightening than any real enemy.

I also believe that intensity is best tempered with a sigh of relief, and so I wrote many horror stories designed to make a reader laugh instead of scream. I edited three Blood Lite anthologies that mixed humor and horror, and then launched an entire series of adventures featuring one of my most popular characters, Dan Shamble, Zombie P.I.

In these stories you might fidget nervously, or jump at a

sudden surprise, or snicker out loud. In all cases, I hope you'll be entertained.

—Kevin J. Anderson
Monument, Colorado
May 2024

I knew I wanted to be a writer since I was five years old. At that age, since I didn't yet know how to read or write, I drew pictures and told stories aloud. I didn't embark on writing my first novel until I turned eight.

I remember sitting down at my dad's manual typewriter in his den and rolling in a page of pink scratch paper. Then I started typing.

Over the course of three days, I wrote my "novel" about a mad scientist—and monsters, of course. "The Injection" is that first story. And since I was sure it would be my magnum opus, I rewrote it again and again over the next couple of years, trying out different plot lines, different side adventures, even changing the main character. I eventually expanded "The Injection" (retitled as "The Life Serum") into a whopping ninety-seven-page draft by the time I was ten or eleven. Surprisingly, it was even double-spaced and in proper manuscript format.

While searching through many archive boxes to find previously published stories for this collection, I discovered a box of my old school records and childhood memorabilia that my mom had kept. Buried there were two bright pink pages stapled together. My original copy of "The Injection"!

It's published here for the first time ever, and it's surprisingly epic, with multiple characters and storylines ... and lots of monsters, reflecting my love for the old Universal movies.

If I wrote this today, I would probably be sent into therapy.

The Injection

I 've done it!" cried Jerimy Dorman. He was a mad scientist. "I've created an injection that will make anything dead, alive again." He ran into the museum. There he gave the injection to some old Tyrannosaurus bones. Quickly they came alive. (It didn't kill Jerimy because he was his master.) He ran into the mummy room and gave a mummy the injection. "Now I can conquer the world!" he cried excitedly. "But I am still not finished; I still have the wax museum and the graveyard." So Jerimy ran with the monsters behind him. He ran into the wax museum. There he gave the injection to Frankenstein's Monster, the Wolf Man, and Count Dracula. They came alive. Then Jerimy started off to his final destination, the graveyard! When he got there, he dug up his old grandmother. (She had been dead for a year, so she was a skeleton.) He gave her the injection. Then he went to his brother's grave. He dug up his brother. He gave him the injection. "Go my pets, go and kill!" Jerimy said slyly. Wolf Man went into the woods and hid in the tree. The mummy and Jerimy's brother went to the swamps. Jerimy's grandmother went to the mountains. While Jerimy and the Tyrannosaurus went to the city. At the swamp, Jerimy's brother scooped up a big fish. He was just about to eat it when the mummy grabbed his arm and threw him in the swamp. This started a fight of course. They looked like they were ripping each other apart. But they didn't know that they were fighting in quicksand! They kept sinking faster and faster. Until they couldn't be seen. While at the woods, Wolf Man was just about to spring upon a man that was under the tree. Wolf Man jumped.

The man quickly pulled out a gun and shot Wolf Man in the heart. (It was a silver bullet, so it killed Wolf Man.) The man stepped back as Wolf Man slumped to the ground. Up in the mountains, Jerimy's grandmother was chasing a mountain climber. The mountain climber ran behind a boulder. He shoved it off a cliff, and it came crashing down on Jerimy's grandmother. And Dracula was charging a carpenter in a darkened room. The carpenter pulled out a spike and slammed it into Dracula's heart. Dracula dropped to the floor. While Frankenstein's Monster was carrying a girl to drop off a cliff. When he tripped over a vine, both he and the girl went plummeting over the cliff. Now only Jerimy and the Tyrannosaurus were left. The Tyrannosaurus was picking up Bairds Hotel. He threw it on the street and it crashed to pieces. Then the army came and they shot their bazookas and threw their hand grenades. Finally Tyrannosaurus started to tip. Then it fell on top of Jerimy. The terror was over. But who knows? Maybe some other scientist may again discover the secret of life and death ...

As you can tell from "The Injection," I was fascinated with the Frankenstein Monster from a very early age, not just from countless movie incarnations, but from reading and rereading the Mary Shelley novel. In 2006, my mentor Dean Koontz asked me to work with him on a modern retelling of the Frankenstein story, which was published as Dean Koontz's Frankenstein: Prodigal Son. It sold a million copies in its first year.

As part of my work for that novel, I developed a back story of where all the monster's pieces came from. The hands, the heart, the body, the brain ... and how did Victor Frankenstein come to possess them?

We didn't end up using any of the material in the novel, but all the components came together in a wonderfully braided story. Dean graciously gave me permission to publish this story as an original work of my own, something I just stitched together ...

The Sum of His Parts

Lightning turns the castle tower into a silver silhouette. Energy collects in metal rods, floods into crackling apparatus. Sparks fly from wires connected to a bandaged figure composed of cadaverous tissue assembled with thick sutures.

The doctor studies his creation, the mismatched parts, the thick sutures.

Spiderwebs of electricity flow like white-hot blood into the patchwork body, awakening the components like embers under an insistent puff of breath. The reattached hands twitch, the fingers flex. Transplanted lungs expel fetid air, unleashing a flood of memories.

He drew a deep breath of the open air. The snow-capped Alps framed the fragrant meadows where his sheep roamed. He preferred to be alone in the mountain vales, away from his brother Stefan and his flock; he didn't like the sound of talking. In fact, he didn't like sounds at all.

The wind spoke to him with breezes that whispered in his ears and taunted him like the hot breath of a wolf. The waving grasses hissed and rustled.

One afternoon during a thunderstorm, he huddled next to a rock, wrapping his hands around his ears, but the thunder made his head ring. The wind was all around, plucking at his clothes, gasping, wheezing, *shrieking*. He abandoned his flock, ran to his hut, and slammed the rickety door. The wind moaned through the cracks, slipping inside to get him. Plugging his ears with beeswax only amplified the sounds of his own breathing, the blood pounding inside his head. There was no escape....

When it was time for the two brothers to join their flocks and take them to market in Ingolstadt, he and Stefan climbed a pass that separated their grazing fields from the valley. His brother was lonely, loquacious, and pestered him with constant conversation, to which he received no reply. As the two hiked up the steep slope, Stefan began panting, louder and *louder*, breathing so heavily that he could not even keep up his inane patter.

The shepherd squeezed his eyes shut but couldn't block out the sound of the awful heaving breaths. Each loud inhalation and exhalation was like the thunder, until he could stand it no more.

He spun and wrapped his hands around Stefan's throat. His brother struggled frantically while he squeezed, but the shepherd focused only on stopping the noise, smothering it. When he let his brother's limp body tumble down the steep path, the world was peaceful for a time. A few moments of blessed silence. Then the wind picked up again.

He fled toward the valley. When the shepherd reached Ingolstadt and left his sheep in the market pen, he passed an old woman sitting in front of her candle shop. She coughed incessantly, hacking, wheezing; she spat a mouthful of phlegm into the gutter and started coughing again. The sound was like hammers pounding on his nerves. The old woman breathed and coughed and wheezed and coughed and *breathed*—until he knew he had to silence her as well.

She stood on creaking legs and tottered into the dimness of her shop, still coughing and coughing. Without hesitation, the shepherd stalked after her. She turned, no doubt thinking him a customer, and before she could speak, before she could cough again, he wrapped his callused hands around her thin throat. His muscles were strong, and he clamped down harder and harder until her struggles stopped, and the silence came back.

When he reeled outside again, the streets of Ingolstadt were a storm of people, a constant din, far too much *noise*. He had to escape back to the high mountain meadows, but before he could run from the square, a town crier began to bellow at the top of his lungs, announcing a tax that old Baron Frankenstein had imposed. The crier's words broke through the air like cannon shot.

The shepherd wanted to scream for silence. He needed the crier's mouth to stop opening and closing, to stop spewing words. Unable to control himself, the shepherd threw himself upon the man, shutting off the breath and the voice. It took four grown men from the astonished crowd to pull him away. The crier squawked and gasped, but his throat was so damaged he could no longer speak.

After the strangler was dragged before the magistrate, he was convicted of killing the old candle shop woman and his brother Stefan, whose body had been found by another shepherd. In addition, several children around Ingolstadt had disappeared over the years, and (since he was in custody) he was accused of killing them as well, though he denied that. He did not, however, deny the rest.

While the shepherd sat in his cell, the mocking wind stole through chinks in the wall and laughed at him. One blustery night, he watched the Baron's son, Victor Frankenstein, come to talk to the jowly jailer. From where he huddled sullenly in his cell, he could overhear the conversation. Victor had an edginess and a calculating intelligence. "I am here on behalf of several medical students from the University. We are woefully short of cadavers for dissection."

When the jailer's breathing quickened, it set the strangler's teeth on edge. Victor looked at the pot-bellied and splotchy-skinned jailer;

distaste was clear on his face, as if he dismissed him as a potential specimen. "If we are to become physicians, we must have material with which to practice." He indicated the miserable prisoner. "This madman is penniless and without family. He will be hung tomorrow. I would like to purchase his body afterward. At present, I have a particular need for a pair of hands and a set of lungs."

The jailer pretended to be offended. "That's highly illegal, sir!"

"But quite commonly done—as you well know." Victor pulled out a pouch of gold coins. "Perhaps this will salve your conscience?"

The jailer looked at the coins, looked at the Baron's son, then sneered at the strangler in his cell. "Done." Victor's breathing was calm with satisfaction. Outside, the wind scraped past the walls. It never stopped....

The following day, when the shepherd was brought to the gibbet in the town square, he heard the mob shouting, *breathing*.

As the rough noose tightened around his neck, the strangler realized that the loudest sound that had haunted him all his life came from air passing through his own throat from his own lungs. Every waking moment he had been forced to listen to each breath whistling in and out of his mouth and nose. Finally, that noise would cease too!

When the hangman hauled on the rope, lifting him into the air to dangle under the gibbet's crossbar, the noose squeezed off the sounds he made. All of them. The straining pulse grew to a roar in his head—and then he fell into blessed, total silence....

Until now.

Storm electricity floods the muscle tissue. The bandaged legs twitch, as if remembering how to run.

"Just nerve impulses," Victor says, checking his apparatus. The

legs spasm again, trying to break free and bolt from this hellish place....

He loved to run. As a servant in Castle Frankenstein, he preferred being sent to town to perform errands for the old Baron. He was fleet as a deer, and his muscles sang with the satisfying ache of tired legs after a long and glorious run.

His main duties were to tend Baron Frankenstein's menagerie of exotic animals on the castle grounds: peacocks, a wildebeest, an aardvark, a spotted ocelot, even a lemur. The Baron's noble friends marveled at the private zoo, while his son Victor studied the creatures with a scientist's eye. The Baron also indulged the boys and girls from Ingolstadt who sneaked onto the estate to look at the animals.

The runner was a happy-go-lucky man with many flirtations, and the young women did not mind his attentions, especially the innkeeper's plump daughter. The old Baron paid his servants well enough, but coins did not stay long in the servant's purse. He cheerfully bought food, wine, and friendship for his companions, though the generosity usually went only one way.

The innkeeper's daughter chided him for his spendthrift ways, especially in the evils of gambling, but he simply laughed her off, then pinched her substantial bottom. He frequented the dicing tables, invoking the name of his master to gain special privileges or to increase his line of credit.

Unfortunately, his luck was never good, even in the best of times. Finding himself out of money and in debt, he assumed that his fellow gamers (who had been happy to accept his coin when he bought food or bottles of wine) would be sympathetic to his plight. But his supposed friends vanished like smoke, and the gambling house proprietors demanded repayment.

Twice in the past four months, the old Baron had lectured him to be careful. "Because you work for the House of Frankenstein, you have a responsibility not to cause shame and scandal." So, the servant knew he could never ask his master for a loan. Baron Frankenstein was a hard man, not unjust, but not softhearted either.

Owing so much money, the runner didn't know what he could do. Collectors had cornered him in an alley, describing in great detail what they would do: First they would tie a gag around his mouth to stifle his screams, then they would beat his boots with iron clubs until his ankles shattered. Afterward, they would slowly pull off his boots, drawing out the pain. Once his broken feet were bare, they would take a set of curved tongs stolen from the local blacksmith, and twist his toes one by one, bending them backward and up until the bones snapped. He would never run again.

He could not allow that to happen. He couldn't! Therefore, when the old Baron went off to be alone in his isolated hunting lodge deep in the forest preserve, as was his habit, the runner slipped into Castle Frankenstein. He bundled up four silver candlesticks and hurried out the servants' entrance, beyond the squawking and grunting creatures in the menagerie, and ran down the path to Ingolstadt as fast as his legs could take him.

The candlesticks were more than enough to pay his debt, but his tormentors showed no sympathy. They accepted the stolen silver and looked at him as if they knew he would gamble again, that this was only the first theft he would be forced to commit. But they had their money, and the servant was free of his tormenters. Relieved but not at all interested in the pleasure of running, he stayed the night with the innkeeper's daughter, who did not know of his troubles. In the morning, shaky with both relief and guilt, the runner went back up to the castle, glad to have a fresh start.

When he arrived, the household staff members were distraught, and young Victor Frankenstein glared at him with angry eyes. His voice was cold. "We know what you've done. Those candlesticks were my mother's heirlooms, fashioned out of the purest silver from the mines of Transylvania."

"I ... I did nothing. I didn't take them."

"You were seen!" cried the head housekeeper, her face streaked with tears. "I saw you, and so did two others!"

Victor said, "You are hereby discharged from service."

The runner stood aghast. "I will make up for it, sir. I'll pay you back. Please don't tell the Baron!"

"I am in charge while my father is away. You cannot repay this debt. You have stolen from us. You have betrayed people who trusted you. Leave Castle Frankenstein, before I call the magistrate."

The runner went dejectedly to town. Hearing of his disgrace, all those who had laughed and played games with him, all those who had delighted in his generosity, now did not wish to be seen in his company. Very hungry, he begged the innkeeper's daughter for food, and she scolded him for gambling despite her warnings. She slammed the door in his face.

As he left the inn, the runner turned into a narrow, dim street where he hoped to curl up and sleep undisturbed. At first, he didn't see the shadowy man following him, but once in the alley, the stranger came close. He had sharp eyes and a broad face with a thin dueling scar on his left cheek. The man said, "I have a gift for you from Victor Frankenstein."

The runner felt a sudden irrational hope. Perhaps he was forgiven after all! Then he saw a long stiletto with an ivory hilt. With a swift jerk of his arm, the other man slashed his throat. "There, not a scratch on the rest of the body, especially the legs. Exactly as ordered."

The runner gurgled, feeling hot blood pumping onto his skin, his shirt, and the cobblestones. The assassin leaned over him with a feral smile. "Now Victor says your debt is paid."

The heels of the young runner's boots beat an erratic drumbeat on the ground. His legs stuttered, then stopped running forever.

The thump is faint at first, then louder. Stronger. No other sound is such a powerful symbol of life. Victor lifts his head from the bandaged chest, raising his triumphant voice to the storm. "One of the hearts is beating!"

Thump. The blood begins to circulate through quiet blood vessels. Thump.

With a loud thud, the silver smile of his sharpened axe bit deep into the trunk. Pine chips sprayed as the woodcutter swung again, using his mighty biceps. The impact rang through his hands and wrists, up to the shoulders, absorbed by a sturdy chest. His heart was pumping heavily.

His old clothes carried the healthy smell of sweat earned through hard work. The axe handle was stout oak polished by the sweat of his palms, smoothed by years of use. His muscles ached after a day of such labor, and it was a good soreness.

Five more swift strokes, and the gouge had gone to the core. The woodcutter checked the angle, judged where the tree would fall, then struck again. Splinters flew. With a groan of wood and a whisper of scraping boughs, the pine toppled. He stood back with satisfaction, then guided the old horse and cart around fresh stumps to the site of the felled tree. With a saw and a hatchet from the cart bed, he trimmed the branches, then cut the trunk into smaller pieces. He could sell the load in Ingolstadt. He would never become a rich man, but he had a cottage in the forest, food to eat, and a beautiful wife, Katarina. She was the most important part of his life.

He'd been gone from home for weeks, chopping wood in the dense and untraveled forests near Baron Frankenstein's isolated preserve. The loneliness of the forest only made the time sweeter whenever he went back to Katarina. When he was home, he liked to carve little animals out of scraps of wood. Since he and his wife had not yet been blessed with children of their own, he gave the toys to girls and boys in town. The woodcutter loved children.

As night fell, he saw the glow of a nearby fire. Wanting company, he came upon a clearing where another man had stopped his wagon and built a camp. "Y-y-you are w-w-welcome to share my f-f-fire," the stranger said, his words slurred both by a severe stutter and a foreign accent. "I h-h-have vegetables, but no m-m-meat."

The woodcutter offered some smoked venison that was chewy but edible. "I can add this to the pot."

The other man was a tinker named Goran, from Budapest. His wagon was full of oddities, pots, tools, trinkets, and five cages of birds (three doves, two songbirds). A gray wolf circled the campsite, making the woodcutter uneasy, and Goran introduced his pet, named Odin after a Norse god.

As they ate their stew, the woodcutter talked wistfully of Katarina. "I met her in Ingolstadt, a dark-haired beauty. Her eyes are the color of roasted chestnuts, her lips as full as fresh berries, and they taste as sweet when I kiss them. I don't understand how such a beautiful woman could have married a man like me. But one does not spit in the face of good fortune."

"N-n-no, my friend," said Goran.

The lonesome woodcutter inspected the tinker's wares, hoping to find a special treasure for Katarina. His eyes settled on a fabulous gold medallion etched with a wide-armed cross and trimmed with ruby and sapphire chips. Making up his mind, he went to his cart, where he had two stout axes, both of the finest manufacture. They had served him well. He gripped the wooden handle of his best one, lifted it from the cart, and stepped toward the tinker. "I can trade you this for the medallion. To give to Katarina. It's not gold but made of sweat and wood and iron."

The tinker smiled but shook his head. "N-n-not for s-s-sale. A special k-k-keepsake." Goran explained with halting sentences that a kind priest had recently given him the jeweled cross as a reward for driving off a robber in the woods. The tinker could never part with his treasure.

Downcast, the woodcutter returned his axe to the cart. He knew that the forest was not safe from highwaymen and assassins.

While the wolf prowled around the campsite, the woodcutter slept, dreaming of Katarina. He wished he could find some way to show her how much he loved her. The quiet cottage life did not suit a fancy woman like her. While he was away, Katarina spent most of her time in Ingolstadt with her best friend Greta. He didn't begrudge her that. He wanted his wife to be happy....

After he and Goran parted company, he spent two more weeks cutting and piling wood that he would sell throughout the winter. When he returned home at last, calling Katarina's name, the empty cottage only answered with silence. It took him only a moment to guess that she had gone to stay with Greta in town.

Grinning, he decided to surprise her. His horse pulled the loaded cart down the rutted trail into Ingolstadt, where he sold his load of wood in the square, ignoring the jeers and catcalls from the gibbet, where a mad strangler was being hung. Earlier, there had already been a beheading. The woodcutter didn't care about such spectacles. He used the money to buy all the supplies they needed and found he had enough left over to purchase some sweet pastries he could share with Katarina.

He tied the old horse and the now-empty cart in front of the half-timbered town home where Greta and her husband lived. With a spring in his step, he went to the door, surprised that the windows were shuttered even in the warm afternoon.

As he approached the loose shutters, he heard laughter, muttered conversation ... and the sounds of exertion, groans, a gasp. His brow furrowed as he identified Katarina's sweet-husky voice and Greta's musical timbre—and the thin nasal voice of Greta's husband. He heard rhythmic sounds, heavy breathing, a wooden bedframe creaking under strain.

The woodcutter's blood ran cold as he peered through a crack. He saw a crowd of arms and legs on the bed, naked flesh, a patchwork of intertwined bodies. He recognized both Greta and Katarina cavorting with a lean man: Greta's husband. He had long dark hair, a wide face, and feral eyes; a thin dueling scar traced his left cheek. His lips were drawn back in a smile so deep it was almost a grimace. In the candlelight, all three were sweaty and panting, as if they'd been exerting themselves for some time. By the coordinated way they moved together, shifted positions, and pleasured each other, they seemed quite well practiced at their ménage a trois.

The woodcutter couldn't feel his arms or his hands, the muscles that had ached from swinging the axe and lifting heavy wood. He realized he wasn't breathing. Before he could tear his gaze away, he saw something else: Next to the candle on the fine lacquered nightstand lay the beautiful cross medallion fringed with sparkling chips of sapphire and ruby. Two weeks earlier, the tinker had refused to sell it to *him*, but somehow Greta's husband had gotten it.

The woodcutter's heart dissolved, leaving only a cold vacuum in his chest. Conscious and rational thoughts vanished with an inaudible pop like a bubble bursting. He walked leadenly back to his cart, where he selected his sharpest and stoutest axe. He lifted it in one well-muscled arm; for good measure, he took the second axe in his left hand. Holding both, he strode back to the door.

With a single blow, he smashed the latch and the crossbar. Sparks and splinters flew. The sounds abruptly stopped. He kicked the ruined door inward, then stepped inside, raising both axes.

The two women scrambled backward on the crowded bed. With just a flicker of his conscious mind, the woodcutter realized how beautiful Katarina was, her pale skin flushed, her dark and sweaty hair thrown back behind her shoulders. Her lips—yes, as red and full as fresh berries—were now open in a faltering scream.

Greta's husband sprang off the straw mattress and into a crouch, not caring that he was naked. He grabbed a long ivory-handled stiletto from the nightstand, knocking the medallion aside in his haste.

Katarina and Greta continued to cry out as the woodcutter waded forward, one axe in each hand. As he swung them, their sharp silver smiles whistled through the air. Greta's husband danced with the knife, twirling the tip in the air as if performing some sort of embroidery. He seemed as familiar with his stiletto as he was in fornicating with Katarina. He didn't even seem afraid.

But the woodcutter had no need for knife play. Without finesse, he swung his axe, and a single blow severed the man's forearm, which fell to the wooden floor, fingers still clutching the knife. A second broad sweep decapitated him more cleanly than he deserved. The head fell to the floor, eerily undamaged, and rolled so that his wide-open eyes could watch the rest of the spectacle.

Then the woodcutter turned his axes upon the two women until they were no more than red kindling.

Drenched in blood, he stood with both axes leaning against him. His muscles ached as they did after a day of hard work, and it was a good soreness.

The screams had drawn a horrified crowd, many from the strangler's hanging. The woodcutter did not resist as the constable and the town guards came to arrest him. He did not explain his horrific actions, though the answer was obvious for anyone who could piece together the myriad body parts.

He did not speak a word in his own defense. In fact, he never uttered another sentence throughout his trial, sentencing, and swift execution.

Bandages shroud the broad, firm face. Victor touches the creation's head like a lover's caress, placing both hands on the stranger's cheeks, one of which is marred by a thin scar from a knife fight.

"Can you hear me? Are you there?" he says in a voice full of hope.

His head hurt from sharing one-too-many bottles of wine the night before, and the thin scar on his cheek throbbed again, as it often did ... but if the wine and fine food kept Greta and her friend Katarina happy, he would gladly pay the price.

The thrill of the crowd in the town square buoyed him up. Two executions in a single day! He was particularly interested in the beheading of the foolish stuttering tinker. He stood close to the block, one woman on each arm, all three of them watching with intent amusement.

The mad strangler's hanging would take place later in the day, but by that time, he expected that the two lovely women would be entertaining him in bed, enjoying their good fortune. Life was good.

More than a simple cutpurse or highwayman, he took any job that paid well enough. He was known in local taverns as a man who could accomplish difficult tasks that must remain quiet: eliminating debtors, traitors, spies ... even rich old uncles who needed to die so families could have their inheritance. Recently, Victor Frankenstein had hired him to slit the throat of a servant who had stolen some family silver to pay off a gambling debt. In his work, he had been cut in knife fights, slashed in the face, even endured the pain of a lead musket ball in his ribs. Thus, the ache of a hangover was nothing.

He had a fondness for good wine and brandy, dice and cards, stylish clothes, and especially women. Greta was as lusty as he was, and both of their appetites extended to her friend Katarina as well. For appearances, Greta's friend had married an unlettered and oafish woodcutter, who was gone most of the time. Doting on Katarina, the oaf gave her trinkets that were small in comparison to what Greta's husband provided.

One time, a month ago, as a masked highwayman, he had waylaid a plump and red-faced priest who carried a jeweled medallion among his treasures as he traveled through the forest. The medallion would have fetched an excellent price, but before the highwayman could complete his robbery, a meddling tinker and his pet wolf had come upon them and driven the robber away.

Some days later, dressed as a fine dandy, he encountered the tinker again and learned that the red-faced priest had *given* the stuttering foreigner his medallion out of gratitude!

Incensed and wanting it for himself, the now-undisguised highwayman tried to buy the medallion for Katarina and Greta, who were both with him. They ogled the treasure from the tinker's cart, but the stuttering idiot wouldn't part with it. So, they had gone back to Ingolstadt with a concocted story. Weeping, Greta reported that the stranger had stolen her dear aunt's jeweled cross, and then raped her and her friend. The constable and town guard rushed out to arrest the tinker straightaway.

Once the medallion had been "returned" to them, and the tinker got the punishment he deserved, Greta and Katarina went back home with the handsome highwayman, arm in arm, where they all engaged in an afternoon of celebration. Everything was going so well.

No one had expected Katarina's husband to find them, or his axes to be so swift.

After his head fell to the floor, the highwayman's vision faded swiftly. He couldn't feel his body, which lay much too far away. Thoughts, and blood, drained out of him.

Once the second heart begins to beat, the creation is close, very close to real life. Another jolt, and the muscle clenches, pumps, stutters to life. Stutters ...

The memories flow smoothly, without the logjam of words that had always caught in his throat.

As a tinker, he loved to make pieces fit together, to fix things that were broken. He owned a wagon full of pots, pans, prisms, swatches of bright cloth, and assorted treasures from foreign lands. Though alone, he had animal friends to keep him company. He whistled to his caged doves and songbirds; his pet wolf followed the cart like a dog. None of them cared about his stutter.

Once, he and his wolf had driven off an evil highwayman who was trying to rob a priest on the forest road. In gratitude, the kindly priest had given the tinker a jeweled cross medallion, one of the tinker's most prized possessions. Not long ago a muscular woodcutter wanted to buy it as a gift for his beloved wife. Another insistent would-be customer was a well-dressed man with a dueling scar; the man was accompanied by his wife and her friend (both of whom clung to him so adoringly it wasn't clear which was the wife and which was her friend). With halting, tangled words he tried to sell them something else, but the three had stalked angrily down the road.

A day later, to his astonishment, the constable and a group of guards came to arrest him. Sensing danger, the pet wolf attacked, trying to defend his master—and the guards shot the beast dead. The tinker wailed in grief for Odin, unable to find words in any language.

He was thrown into jail, appalled to learn that the scar-faced man and his two female companions had accused the tinker of stealing the medallion *from them*; both the wife and her friend wrung their hands and swore that the tinker had raped them. His denials were vehement, though inarticulate. With growing terror, his stutter became worse.

Distraught parents, including the town's blacksmith, came forward to point fingers of blame, suggesting that the stranger must be responsible for Ingolstadt's missing children. A baby had vanished only the day before, and ten other young sons and daughters had disappeared in as many years. A mad strangler had also been recently accused of the crimes, though no one truly believed him to be the criminal. Now, despite the fact that the tinker could not possibly have been in the area for that amount of time, the poor man was a convenient scapegoat. Once someone in the crowd voiced the suspicion, many others took up the cry.

Since he had been seen talking to birds and consorting with a wolf, the tinker was convicted as a warlock. He had stolen a holy artifact, no doubt to be used in some Satanic ritual (which must involve the blood of the babies or innocent children). The townspeople demanded that he be burned at the stake. The loudest voice came from the blacksmith's young apprentice, whose family had perished in a forest fire years before. The boy seemed hungry to smell the smoke of burning flesh.

Oddly enough, Victor Frankenstein begged for mercy. "Ingolstadt is a civilized town and should not bow to superstitions." But the crowd wanted some medieval touch of justice for such heinous crimes, and they already had an upcoming hanging. Very reasonable and persuasive, the Baron's son suggested, "Perhaps the headsman's axe should be brought out of retirement? The chopping block could be set up in the town square, as in olden days."

This sated the bloodlust of the people. And so, the old executioner's axe was sharpened by the vengeful blacksmith, who fervently believed the tinker had stolen and killed his daughter Maria.

Hands tied behind his back, the falsely accused tinker was brought out and forced to his knees. As his neck was stretched across the bloodstained block, his frantic gaze caught a last glimpse of one man in the crowd. Victor Frankenstein looked intensely interested, a scientist studying a specimen. The tinker felt the ripple of a completely different kind of fear. Why was the Baron's son looking at him so ... hungrily?

Because the headsman's axe was razor-sharp, and the cut exceedingly swift, the flash of pain seemed as gentle as a feather. The stutter of his heartbeat stopped.

Victor checks the machines, adjusts the electrical flow, then hurries back. He presses down on the cloth windings of the sturdy chest.

"Live!" he shouts, as if the dead parts will hear him and obey his command. "Live!"

Victor hammers his fist down on the sternum. The torso is thick, muscular, like a suit of armor around the two implanted hearts ... a blacksmith's chest.

His broad chest was always smeared with soot and smoke from the forge, his hair singed from sparks and cinders. His arms were strong from pounding on an anvil, pumping the bellows.

He had a good wife and fine children, whom he loved more than anything else. But his oldest daughter, Maria, had disappeared a year ago while picking mushrooms in the woods. Many boys and girls had vanished around Ingolstadt—yesterday, even a baby had gone missing! When Maria had been lost, the blacksmith and his wife spent agonized days combing the hills, calling the girl's name, praying for her safety ... and then, resigned, weeping for her soul.

To fill the emptiness, the blacksmith adopted a new apprentice, an orphan boy whose parents were killed in a forest fire. Though the boy worked hard in the smithy, no one else's son could make up for lost Maria.

A traveling tinker had been arrested and charged with the crimes. The blacksmith and his wife were both convinced he had abducted their little girl. Even next to the blistering heat of the forge, the blacksmith shuddered to imagine the things the stuttering foreigner must have done to Maria....

Sparks flew from the grinding wheel as he sharpened the headsman's axe. The monstrous criminal would pay the price the following day. The bitter but unsatisfying taste of vengeance bubbled like bile in the blacksmith's throat.

He closed his eyes, quoted scripture to himself, and prayed for forgiveness. His wife often came to sit with him in the smithy, to comfort him by reading aloud from the Bible while the apprentice boy continued the daily work, hovering close to the blazing fire.

Lately, instead of words of consolation, he was more interested in stories of demons, how the darkness of Satan was a shadow over the land—such as the rituals the guilty tinker no doubt performed with the blood of children while his wolf, his demon familiar, watched.

The blacksmith could not get Maria's musical laughter out of his head. She had loved to ride on her father's broad shoulders as he walked down the streets. She had played with other children, plucking flowers from the meadows, even running up to Castle Frankenstein where the old Baron showed them the exotic animals in his menagerie.

Now she was gone. The damned tinker had done terrible things to her!

When the blacksmith saw the fiery forge and the sparks flying from the grinding wheel, he thought of Hell's inferno where this razor-sharp axe would send the evil tinker. He intended to stand so close to the chopping block that the hot and satisfying blood would splash onto his face.

Finished, he lifted the sharpened axe from the wheel, but it seemed very heavy all of a sudden. The blacksmith tried to stand. His apprentice came closer, looking worried.

Though his chest and arms were strong, the blacksmith's heart was weak. The thudding sounded hollow in his chest, the slowing blood flow faded to a faint roar in his ears. He found himself falling. As the executioner's axe dropped to the ground, his last thoughts were of his wife, his daughters. How would they survive without him?

Then he clung to the vision of lost Maria, her large blue eyes, her laughter. He collapsed dead to the smithy floor, unable to watch the execution after all.

At last, with the bandages removed, the dull yellow eyes open. The lids flutter, the transplanted eyes flick from side to side, seeing the grandeur of the lightning storm outside, the frenzied apparatus in the laboratory. Flashes, sparks, little fires.

He liked to stare into the flickering flames and watch the hungry elemental spirit devour wood. His eyes had an unhealthy yellow tinge, as if part of the fire's glow hovered there.

He had lived with his family in a cottage near old Baron Frankenstein's hunting preserve. The summer was dry, and a lightning strike started a nearby fire, which raged in the night. He awoke, smelling bitter greenwood smoke in the air, then crept outside to watch the swift fire come like a marching army. He went far from his house, to a high rock outcropping where he could sit and watch. The hypnotic flames enraptured him so that he did not even think about his family trapped inside the cottage as the fire engulfed it. He had never seen the house look so beautiful, so bright and cheery and ablaze.

Then the flames curled in a different direction—maybe the wind changed, or maybe the fire simply chose to avoid him. When the villagers found him later, they considered it a miracle that the boy had survived, while his family was overcome by smoke.

Though an orphan, he was old enough to be taken in as the blacksmith's apprentice, where he loved to toil near the blazing heat of the forge. When he pumped the bellows, he made the heat blossom like a flower. He was accepted by the blacksmith and his family, who were grieving over their missing daughter. They thought they understood the boy's "loss."

The young apprentice went alone into the forest—an excuse to build secret fires, some of which (not unintentionally) got out of hand. One of his blazes nearly burned down the Baron's hunting lodge.

Later, he was the loudest voice demanding that a tinker,

convicted of being a warlock, be burned at the stake. The apprentice wanted to see a person tied to an upright log, the flames consuming clothes and flesh. He was furious when Victor Frankenstein insisted that the man be beheaded instead. Why did the Baron's son have to meddle? The fire would have been so glorious, a spectacle he could have remembered for the rest of his life!

It was either irony, or divine justice, that the vengeful blacksmith had died while sharpening the headsman's axe. Now, the apprentice did not know his future. He was too young to work the forge himself, and he feared the distraught widow would sell the business and turn him out into the streets.

The future did not concern him. The apprentice saw one way to make everything right. On the night after the tinker's head was chopped off, he lit a flaming brand from the blacksmith's forge and set the smithy building on fire.

But that was only a start. He went to the jail and then the magistrate's home, setting them alight as well. It was sure to be the greatest fire in the history of Ingolstadt. The apprentice made no attempt to hide what he was doing. While the alarms rang, and people rushed out to help douse the fire, angry men chased after him.

The arsonist ran. One of them shot him in the back with a musket, and the ball lodged just beneath his shoulder blade. The pursuers were coming closer, shouting for his blood, carrying torches as they hunted him down. He staggered into the Baron's hunting preserve, until he reached a swollen, fast-flowing stream. He tried to cross it, but he was too weak. When he stepped into the icy, rushing water, he could barely keep his footing.

The pursuing mob shot at him again. Another musket ball shattered his leg, and he fell into the water. As he was swept downstream, he caught a glimpse of Ingolstadt and the smoke rising into the air. He hoped his fire would burn for a long time.

His head was dunked under the fast current, and he couldn't breathe. As the musket shots drained the life's blood out of him, the apprentice gulped frigid water, praying for fire, yet the spark within him was extinguished. The darkness was cold and wet, but finally his eyes saw a spark again, lights ... life.

The mosaic of a monster is alive, functioning, but without a mind it does not truly live.

Victor attaches an electrode, unleashes a flood of condensed lightning. A sharp shock pours into the head, like a musket touching off a flash of gunpowder, the last surge of memories. A mind adrift, separate. Thoughts run like raindrops down an uneven pane of glass.

Despite his wealth and bloodline, he had never been a strong man, the runt of the litter. His younger brothers—even his sister—spurned him, though the noble title was his by birthright. Years ago, as a boy, he had turned his feelings of inferiority against small animals—secretly killing cats, clubbing puppies. The young, helpless ones were the most gratifying.

Copying the more eccentric European nobles, he had purchased exotic animals from foreign lands, darkest Africa, South Sea islands, the Americas. He kept a menagerie on his estate, and though the miserable creatures did not live long, he replaced them with other specimens as fast as they died. His son Victor delighted in having so many dissection subjects for his medical studies.

The Baron's fondness for strange animals made him popular among the children. Generous and benevolent, he would let them stare at the creatures, even pet the tame ones.

Most of the time he could control his urges. Most of the time.

And when it became imperative that he follow his obsession, he had a special private hunting lodge deep in his forest preserve with secure doors and stout shutters. After he lured the children out to the cabin, just like in the story of Hansel and Gretel, he would lock them in so he could have his way with them over and over; then he would kill them and bury them out in the forest.

All the servants at Castle Frankenstein were familiar with their master's habit of slipping off for solitude. No mere peasant would dare to accuse, or even suspect, Baron Heinrich Frankenstein. A wandering band of gypsies or a suspicious stranger could always be blamed for the latest disappearance. Over the years, many were arrested; a shepherd had been hung and a tinker had been beheaded that very day, both accused of the same crime, providing a convenient excuse for the little "lamb" he had just stolen....

Back at the Castle, he regularly told the cook to prepare veal, suckling pig, a fine tender lamb, or fresh kid spitted over a fire. Innocence seemed to give the flesh a better flavor. Thus, once a new idea had occurred to him, he couldn't drive it out of his head. What might be the taste of another sort of tender flesh?

Only two days ago, he had wandered the streets of Ingolstadt in a filthy disguise, until he saw the chance to snatch an infant, still breast-fed. After roasting all day over a slow fire, the flesh would be succulent, better than veal.

Now, as the forest darkened around the hunting lodge, the Baron was glad to be away. The meat was still on the spit over the fire, almost ready for an evening feast, when he heard the shouts of searchers outside, musket shots. From the window of his cabin, he looked down the steep slopes to Ingolstadt. The city itself seemed to be on fire!

Alarmed, the Baron went to the door and threw it open just as the constable and six guards rushed up the path. "My Lord Baron, beware! There is an arsonist in these woods. We are hunting him—"

Then the constable saw what was on the fire. One of the guards cried out in horror before he began to retch. The old Baron could not slam the door quickly enough....

Locked in the jail—the same cell that had held a strangler only two days before—the Baron confessed. Despite his admission, the torturers still wanted to break his arms and scourge him. The townspeople howled for his blood, ready to lynch the old Baron, and only a contingent of guards reluctantly prevented them from doing so. His noble rank would not save him. The magistrate had no choice but to sentence him to death by a slow garotte in the public square.

Victor—now the new Baron Frankenstein—came to see him. Oddly, the intense young man showed no revulsion at his father's crimes, no greed for the position of power he now held. He looked at the older man clinically, as if he was already making plans.

Victor turned to the jailer. "It is a pity what my father has done. He always had such a fine mind."

The beating hearts grow stronger. "He's alive!" Victor cries. "Alive!"

The yellow eyes are open, the patchwork body twitches and trembles. Victor unwinds the gauze to reveal the scars on cadaverous flesh. He unstraps the restraints binding the arms and legs. The creature is awake now, aware.

"I made you. You will be greater than the sum of your parts!" He looks at his creation with pride. "Can you hear me? Do you know who you are?"

Yes, the pieced-together man knows who he is: the hands and lungs of a strangler, the legs of a thief, the head of a hired assassin, the torso of a vengeful blacksmith, the eyes of an arsonist, one heart from an axe murderer and the other from a wrongly executed man, the mind of a child molester and baby killer.

Voices clamor through him, so many identities roiling in a single body. Fusing the cacophony into a consensus, he remembers the Bible he read in his blacksmith persona, a particular verse from the Gospel of Mark. The other converging memories and lives know it as well, and they all agree.

His voice crackles out like a dry wind. Victor, face shining with perspiration, leans closer to hear.

"My name is Legion," the creation says. "For we are many."

He grabs Victor's throat with the hand of a strangler. With all the lives inside him, he finds it very easy to squeeze.

I grew up in rural Wisconsin, with all the nostalgia, repression, and cultural baggage that entails. If you've seen A Christmas Story, that was my existence. It was a wonderful place and time to grow up, but it also had its own nightmares for an "odd duck" kid who liked to dream, to read comic books and science fiction novels, a young man who wanted to be a writer someday.

Over the course of my career, I have returned again and again to the fictional town of Tucker's Grove, Wisconsin, with its dark history and even darker happenings. This is the first story, chronologically, in the Tucker's Grove sequence, with the members of the Tucker family staking their claim in the untouched farmlands of southern Wisconsin in the 1800s.

You'll see that things don't always turn out well.

Bringing the Family

B oth coffins shifted as the wagon wheels hit a rut in the dirt road. Mr. Deakin, sitting beside his silent passenger, Clancy Tucker, clucked to the horses and steered them to the left.

The rhythmic creak of the wagon and the buzz of flies around the coffins were the only sounds in the muggy air. Over the past three days Mr. Deakin and Clancy had already said everything relative strangers could say to each other.

Clancy rocked back and forth to counteract the motion of the wagon. A sprawling expanse of prairie surrounded them, mile after mile of green grassland broken only by the ribbonlike track heading north. Clancy looked up at the early afternoon sun. "Time to stop."

Mr. Deakin groaned. "We got hours of daylight left."

Clancy made his lips thin and white. "We gotta be sure we get those graves dug by dark."

"Do you realize how stupid this is, Clancy? Night after night—"

"A promise is a promise." Clancy pointed to a patch of thin grass next to a few drying puddles from the last thunderstorm. "Looks like a good place over there."

With only a grunt for an answer, Mr. Deakin pulled the

horses to the side and brought them to a stop. The rotten smell settled around them. Clancy Tucker had insisted on making this journey in the heat and humidity of summer; in winter and spring, he said, the ground was frozen too hard to keep reburying his Ma and Dad along the way.

Clancy grabbed a pickax from the wagon bed and sauntered over to the flat spot. By now they had this ritual down to a science. Mr. Deakin said nothing as he unhitched the horses, hobbled them, and began to rub them down. These horses were the only asset he had left, and he insisted on tending them before helping Clancy on his fool's errand.

Clancy swung the pickax, chopping the woven grassroots. His bright, bulging eyes looked as if someone with big hands had squeezed him too tightly at the middle. He slipped one suspender off his shoulder, and a dark, damp shadow of perspiration seeped from his underarms.

As he worked, Clancy hummed an endless hymn that Mr. Deakin recognized as "Bringing in the Sheaves." The chorus went around and around without ever finding its way to the last verse. Over the hours, between the humming and the stench from the unearthed coffins, Mr. Deakin wanted to shove Clancy's head under one of the wheels.

When he finished with the horses, he pulled a shovel from between the two coffins and went over to help Clancy. To make the daily task more difficult, Clancy insisted on digging two separate graves, one for his Ma and one for his Dad, rather than a single large pit for both coffins.

They worked for more than an hour in the suffocating heat of afternoon, surrounded by flies and the sweat on their own bodies. Mr. Deakin had run out of snuff on the first day, and his little pocket jar held only a smear or two of the camphor ointment he kept for sore muscles, which he also used to burn the putrid smell from his nostrils.

Mr. Deakin's body ached, his hands felt flayed with blisters, and he did his best to shut off all thought. He would work like one of those escaped slaves from down south, forced to labor all day long in the cotton fields. Clancy Tucker's family had kept a freed slave to tend their home, and she had spooked Clancy badly, filling his head with strange ideas. Or maybe Clancy just had strange ideas all by himself.

A month before, Mr. Deakin would never have imagined himself stooping to such crazy tasks as digging up coffins and burying them night after night on a slow journey to Wisconsin. But an Illinois tornado had flattened his house, knocked down the barn, and left him with nothing.

Standing in the aftermath of that storm, under a sky that had cleared to a mocking blue, Mr. Deakin had wanted to shake his fist at the clouds and shout, but he only hung his head in silent despair. He had worked his whole life to compile meager possessions on a homestead and some rented cropland. It would be months before his harvest came in, and he had no way to pay the rent in the meantime; the tornado had crushed his harvesting equipment, smashed his barn. After the storm, only two horses had stood surrounded by the wreckage of their small corral, bewildered and as shocked by the disaster as Mr. Deakin.

His life ruined, Mr. Deakin had had no choice but to say yes when Clancy Tucker had made his proposition....

"Make it six feet deep now!" Clancy said, throwing wet earth over his shoulder onto a mound beside the grave. Fat earthworms wriggled in the clods, trying to grope their way back to darkness. Mr. Deakin felt his muscles aching as he stomped on the shovel with his boot and hefted up another load of dirt. "What difference does it make if they're six feet under or five and a half?" he muttered.

Beside him, standing waist-deep in the companion grave, Clancy looked at him strangely, as if the answer were obvious. The floppy brim of his hat cast a shadow across his face. "Why, because anything less than six feet, and *they could dig their way back up by morning!*"

Mr. Deakin felt his skin crawl and turned back to his work.

Clancy Tucker either had a sick sense of humor, or just a sick mind....

Only a day after the tornado had struck, when things seemed bleakest, Mr. Deakin stood alone in the ruins of his homestead. He watched Clancy Tucker walk toward him across the puddle-dotted field. "Good morning, Mr. Deakin," he had said.

"Morning," Mr. Deakin said, leaving the "good" off.

"You know my brother Jerome recently founded a town up in Wisconsin—Tucker's Grove. Can I hire you to help me bring the family up there? You look like you could use a lucky break right about now."

"How much is it worth?" Mr. Deakin asked.

Clancy folded his hands together. "I can offer you this. If you'd give us a ride on your wagon up to Wisconsin, my brother will give you your very own farm, a homestead as big as this one. And it'll be yours, not rented. Lots of land to be had up there. In the meantime, we can loan you enough hard currency to take care of your business here." Clancy held out a handful of silver coins. "We know you need the help."

Mr. Deakin could hardly believe what he heard. The Tuckers had no surviving family—Clancy and his broad-chested brother Jerome were the only sons. Who else would they be taking along?

Clancy nodded again. "It would be the Christian thing to do, Mr. Deakin. Neighbor helping neighbor."

So he had agreed to the deal. Not until they were ready to set out did he learn that Clancy wanted to haul the exhumed coffins of his recently deceased mother and father. By the time Mr. Deakin found out, Clancy had already paid some of Mr. Deakin's most important debts, binding him to his word....

It was deep twilight by the time they had two graves dug and both coffins lowered into the ground with thick hemp ropes. They finished packing down the mounds of earth, leaving the rope ends aboveground for easy lifting the next morning. Mr. Deakin built a small fire to make coffee and warm their supper.

He felt stiff and sore as he bedded down for the night, taking a blanket from the wagon bed. Now that the cool night air smelled clean around him, with no corpse odor hanging about, he wished he had saved some of that camphor for his aching muscles.

Clancy Tucker lay across the fresh earth of the two graves. Mr. Deakin grabbed another blanket and tossed it toward him, but the other man did not look up. Clancy placed his ear against the ground, as if listening for sounds of something stirring below.

One of the townspeople had used a heated iron spike to burn letters on a plank. *WELCOME TO COMPROMISE, ILLINOIS.* The population tally had been scratched out and rewritten several times, but it looked as if folk no longer kept track. The townspeople watched them approach down the dirt path.

The flat blandness of unending grassland and the corduroy of cornfields swept out to where the land met the sky. On the horizon, gray clouds began building into thunderheads.

"Don't see no church here," Clancy said, "not one with a steeple anyway."

"Town's too small probably," Mr. Deakin answered.

Clancy set his mouth. "Tucker's Grove might be small, but the very first thing Jerome's building will be his church."

Mr. Deakin saw a building attached to the side of the general store and realized that this was probably a gathering place and a saloon. Some townspeople wandered out to watch their arrival, lounging against the boardwalk rails. A gaunt man with bushy eyebrows and thinning steel-gray hair stepped out from the general store like an official emissary.

But when the storekeeper saw the coffins in back of the wagon, he wrinkled his nose. The others covered their noses and moved upwind. Without a word of greeting, the storekeeper wiped his stained white apron and said, "Who's in the coffins?"

"My beloved parents," Clancy said.

"Sorry to hear that," the storekeeper said. "Not common to see

34

someone hauling bodies cross-country in the summer heat. I reckon the first thing you'll want is some salt to fill them boxes. It'll cut down the rot."

Mr. Deakin felt his mouth go dry. He didn't want to say that they had little to pay for such an extravagant quantity of salt. But Clancy interrupted.

"Actually," he looked at the other townspeople, "we'd prefer a place to bury these coffins for the night. If you have a graveyard, perhaps? I'm sure after our long journey"—he patted the dirt-stained tops of the coffins—"they would prefer a peaceful night's rest. The ground is hallowed, ain't it?"

The storekeeper scowled. "We got a graveyard over by the stand of trees there, but no church yet. A Presbyterian circuit rider comes along every week or so, not necessarily on Sundays. He's due back anytime now, if you'd like to wait and hold some kind of service."

Mr. Deakin didn't know what to say. The entire situation seemed unreal. He tried to cut off his companion's crazy talk, but Clancy Tucker wouldn't be interrupted.

"Presbyterian? I'm a good Methodist, and my parents were good Methodists. My brother Jerome is even a Methodist minister, self-ordained."

"Clancy—" Mr. Deakin began.

Clancy sighed. "Well, it's only for the night, after all." He looked at Mr. Deakin and lowered his voice. "Hallowed ground. They won't try to come back up, so we don't need to dig so deep."

The storekeeper put his hands behind his apron. "Digging up graves after you planted the coffins? If you want to bury them in our graveyard, that's your business. But we won't be wanting you to disturb what's been reverently put to rest."

Mr. Deakin refrained from pointing out that these particular coffins had been buried and dug up a number of times already.

"You wouldn't be wanting me to break a sacred oath either, would you?" Clancy turned his bulging eyes toward the man; he didn't blink for a long time. "I swore to my parents, on their deathbeds, that I would bring them with me when I moved to Wisconsin. And I'm not leaving them here after all this way."

Seemingly from out of nowhere, Clancy produced a coin and tossed it to the storekeeper, who refused to come closer to the wagons because of the stench. "Are you trying to buy my agreement?" the storekeeper asked.

"No. It's for the horses. We'll need some oats."

Though the graveyard of Compromise was small, many wooden crosses protruded like scarecrows. The townspeople did not offer to help Mr. Deakin and Clancy dig, but a few of them watched.

Mr. Deakin pulled the wagon to an empty spot, careful not to let the horses tread on the other graves. As the two of them fell to work with their shovels, Clancy kept looking at the other grave markers. He jutted his stubbled chin toward a row of crosses, marking the graves of an entire family that had died from diphtheria, according to the scrawled words.

"My parents died from scarlet fever," Clancy said. "Jerome caught it first, and he was so sick we thought he'd never get up again. He kept rolling around, sweating, raving. He wouldn't let our Negro, Maggie, go near him. When the fever broke, his eyes had a whole different sparkle to them, and he talked about how God had showed him a vision of our promised land. Jerome knew he was supposed to found a town in Wisconsin.

"He kept talking about it until we got fired up by his enthusiasm. He wanted to pack up everything we had and strike off, but then Ma and Dad caught the fever themselves, probably from tending Jerome so close."

Mr. Deakin pressed his lips together and kept digging in the soft earth. He didn't want to wallow in his own loss, and he didn't want to wallow in Clancy Tucker's either.

"When they were both sweating with fever, they claimed to share Jerome's vision. They were terrified that Jerome and I would leave them behind. So, I promised we would bring them along, no matter what. Oh, they wanted to come so bad. Maggie heard them, and she said she could help."

Clancy didn't even pause for breath as he continued. "I could see how bothered Jerome was, because he wanted to leave right away. Our parents were getting worse and worse. They certainly couldn't stand a wagon ride, and it didn't look like they had much time left.

"One day, after Jerome had been sitting with them for a long time, he came out of their room. His face was frightful with so much grief. He said that their souls had flown off to Heaven." Clancy's eyes glowed.

"He left the day afterward, going alone to scout things out, while I took care of details until I could follow, bringing the family. Jerome is waiting for us there now."

Clancy looked up. He had a smear of mud along one cheek. His eyes looked as if they wanted to spill over with tears, but they didn't dare. "So, you see why it's so important to me. Ma and Dad have to be there with us. They have their part to play, even if it's just to be the first two in our graveyard."

Mr. Deakin said nothing; Clancy didn't seem to want him to.

The sun began to rise in a pool of molten orange. Mr. Deakin dutifully went back to Clancy Tucker, who had slept up against a wagon wheel. Mr. Deakin's head throbbed, but he had not gotten himself so drunk in the saloon that he forgot his obligations, bizarre though they might be.

He and Clancy set to work on the dewy grass with their shovels, digging out the loosened earth they had piled into graves only the night before.

Mr. Deakin looked toward town, sensing rather than hearing the group of people moving toward them. Clancy didn't notice, but Mr. Deakin halted, propped the shovel into the dirt where it rested against the coffin lid. Clancy unearthed the top of the second coffin, and then stopped as the group approached. He went over to stand by the wagon.

The people carried sticks and farm implements, marching along with their faces screwed up and squinting as they stared into the rising sun. They swaggered as if they had just been talked into a fit of righteous anger.

At the front of the group strode a tall man dressed in a black frock coat and a stiff-brimmed black hat. Mr. Deakin realized that this must be the Presbyterian circuit rider, just in time to stir up trouble.

"We come to take action against two blasphemers!" the circuit rider said.

"Amen!" the people answered.

The preacher had a deep-throated voice, as if every word he uttered was too heavy with import to be spoken in a normal voice. He stepped close, and the sunlight shone full on his face. His weathered features were stretched over a frame of bone, as if he had seen too many cycles of abundance and famine.

The bushy-browed storekeeper stood beside him. "We ain't letting you dig up graves in our town."

"Grave robbers!" the circuit rider spat. "How dare you disturb those buried here? You'll roast in Hell."

"Amen!" the chorus said again.

Mr. Deakin made no move with his shovel, looking at the group and feeling cold. He had already lost everything he had, and he didn't care about Clancy Tucker's craziness—not enough to get lynched for it.

Clancy stood beside the wagon, holding Mr. Deakin's shotgun in his hands and pointing it toward the mob. "This here gun is loaded with bird shot. It's bound to hit most everybody with flying lead pellets. Might even *kill* someone. Whoever wants to keep me from my own parents, just take a step forward. I've got my finger right on the trigger." He paused for just a moment. "Mr. Deakin, would you kindly finish the last bit of digging?"

Mr. Deakin took the shovel and went to work, moving slowly,

and watched Clancy Tucker's bulging eyes. Sweat streamed down Clancy's forehead, and his hands shook as he pointed the shotgun.

"I'm done, Clancy," Mr. Deakin said, just loud enough for the other man to hear him.

Clancy tilted the shotgun up and discharged the first barrel with a sound like a cannon. Morning birds in the outlying fields burst into the air, squawking. Clancy lowered the gun toward the mob again. "Git!"

The circuit rider looked as if he wanted to bluster some more, but the townspeople of Compromise turned to run. Not wanting to be left behind, the circuit rider turned around, his black frock coat flapping. His hat flew off as he ran, drifted in the air, then fell to the muck.

Clancy Tucker shivered on the seat of the wagon, pulling a blanket around himself. He had cradled the empty shotgun for a long time as Mr. Deakin led the wagon around the town of Compromise, bumping over rough fields.

"I would've shot him," Clancy said. His teeth chattered together. "I really meant it. I was going to kill them! 'Thou shalt not kill!' I've never had thoughts like that before!"

Mr. Deakin made Clancy take a nap for a few hours, but the other man seemed just as disturbed after he awoke. "How am I going to live with this? I meant to kill another man! I had the gun in my hand. If I had tilted the barrel down just a bit I could have popped that circuit rider's head like a muskmelon."

"It was only bird shot, Clancy," Mr. Deakin said, but Clancy didn't hear.

As the horses followed the dirt path, Mr. Deakin reached behind to the bed of the wagon where they kept their supplies. He rummaged under the tarpaulin and pulled out a two-gallon jug of whiskey. "Here, drink some of this. It'll smooth out your nerves."

Clancy looked at him, wide-eyed, but Mr. Deakin kept his

face free of any expression. "I traded my little silver mirror for it last night in the saloon. You could use some right now, Clancy. I've never seen anybody this bad."

Clancy pulled out the cork and took a deep whiff of the contents. Startled, stinging tears came to his eyes. "I won't, Mr. Deakin! It says right in Leviticus, 'Do not drink wine nor strong drink.'"

"Oh, don't go giving me that," Mr. Deakin said, pursing his lips. "Isn't there another verse that says to give wine to those with heavy hearts so they remember their misery no more?"

Clancy blinked, as if he had never considered the idea. "That's in Proverbs, I think."

"Well, you look like you could forget some of your misery."

Clancy took out a metal cup and, with tense movements as if someone were about to catch him at what he was doing, he poured half a cupful of the brown liquid. He screwed up his face and looked down into the cup. Mr. Deakin watched him, knowing that Clancy's lips had probably never been sullied by so much as a curse word, not to mention whiskey.

As if realizing that he had reached his point of greatest courage, Clancy lifted the cup and gulped from it. His eyes seemed to pop even farther from his head, and he bit back a loud cough. Before he could recover his voice to gasp, Mr. Deakin, hiding a smile, spoke from the corner of his mouth. "My gosh, Clancy, just pretend you're drinking hot coffee! Sip it."

Looking alarmed but determined, Clancy brought the cup back to his lips, then squeezed his eyes shut and took a smaller sip. He didn't speak again, and Mr. Deakin ignored him. Morning shadows stretched out to the left as the wagon headed north toward Wisconsin.

Mr. Deakin made no comment when Clancy refilled the metal cup and settled back down to a regular routine of long, slow sips.

By noon the sky had begun to thicken up with thunderheads, and the air held the muggy, oppressive scent of a lumbering storm.

The flies went away, but mosquitoes came out. The coffins in back of the wagon stank worse than ever.

Clancy hummed "Bringing in the Sheaves" over and over, growing louder with each verse. He turned to look at the coffins in the back of the wagon, and giggled. He spoke for the first time in hours. "Can you keep a secret, Mr. Deakin?"

Mr. Deakin wasn't sure he wanted to and avoided answering.

"I don't think I know your Christian name, Mr. Deakin."

"How do you know I even have one?" he muttered. He had lived alone and made few friends in Illinois, working too hard to socialize much. The neighbors and townsfolk called him Mr. Deakin, and it had been a long time since he'd heard anyone refer to him as anything else. Clancy found that very funny.

"Yes, I can keep a secret," Mr. Deakin finally said.

"Promise?"

"Promise."

Clancy dropped his voice to a stage whisper. "Jerome lied!" He paused, as if this revelation were horrifying enough.

"And when did he do that?" Mr. Deakin asked, not really interested.

"When he came out of my parents' room and said that their souls had flown off to Heaven—that wasn't true at all. And he knew it! When he went into that room, after Ma and Dad were sick for so long, after he wanted to go found the new town so bad, Jerome smothered them both with their pillows!"

Mr. Deakin intentionally kept his gaze pointed straight ahead. "Clancy, you've had too much of that whiskey."

"He did Dad first, who still had some strength to struggle. But Ma didn't fight. She just laid back and closed her eyes. She knew we had promised to take them both to Tucker's Grove, and she knew we would keep our word. You always have to keep your word.

"But when Jerome said their souls had flown off to Heaven, well, that just wasn't true—because by smothering them with the pillow, he trapped their souls *inside*!"

Clancy opened his eyes. Mr. Deakin saw bloodshot lines

around the irises. "What makes you say that, Clancy?" Mr. Deakin asked. He wasn't sure if he could believe any of this.

"Maggie said so." Clancy stared off into the gathering storm. "Right after they died, our Negro, Maggie, sacrificed one of our chickens, danced around mumbling spells. Jerome and I came back from the coffin makers and found her inside by the bodies. He tried to whack her on the head with a shovel, then he chased her out of our house and said he'd burn her as a witch if she ever came back."

"And so Jerome left while you packed everything up and made ready to move?" Mr. Deakin asked. He had no idea what to make of killing chickens and chanting spells.

"I'm the only one who didn't see the vision. But Ma and Dad wanted to come so bad. Maggie said she was just trying to help, and it worked. That's why we have to keep burying the coffins—so the bodies stay down!" Clancy glanced at Mr. Deakin, expectant, but then his own expression changed. With a comical look of astonishment at himself, he covered his mouth with one hand, still grimy from digging out the graves at dawn.

"I promised Jerome I wouldn't tell *anybody*, and now I broke my promise. Something bad's bound to happen for sure now!" He closed his eyes and began to groan in the back of his throat.

In exasperation, Mr. Deakin reached over and yanked on the floppy brim of Clancy's hat, pulling it over his face. "Clancy, you just take another nap. Get some rest." He lowered his voice and mumbled under his breath, "And give me some peace, too."

Clancy slept most of the afternoon, lying in an awkward position against the backboard. Mr. Deakin urged the horses onward, racing the oncoming storm. He hadn't seen another town since Compromise, and the wild prairie sprawled as far as he could see, dotted with clumps of trees. The wagon track was only a faint impression, showing the way to go. A damp breeze licked across Mr. Deakin's face.

The first droplets of water sprinkled his cheeks, and Mr. Deakin pulled his own hat tight onto his head. As the storm picked up, the breeze and the raindrops made a rushing sound in the grasses.

Clancy grunted and woke up. He looked disoriented, saw the darkened sky, and sat up sharply. "What time is it? How long did I sleep?" He whirled to look at the coffins in the back. The patter of raindrops sounded like drumbeats against the wood.

Mr. Deakin knew what Clancy was going to say but maintained a nonchalant expression. "Hard to tell what time it is with these clouds and the storm. Probably late afternoon ..." He looked at Clancy. "Sunset maybe." A boom of thunder made a drawn-out, tearing sound across the sky.

"You've got to stop! We have to bury the—"

"Clancy, we'll never get them dug in time, and I'm not going to be shoveling a grave in the middle of a storm. Just cover them up with the tarp and they'll be all right."

Clancy turned to him with an expression filled with outrage and alarm. Before he could say anything, a *thump* came from the back of the wagon. Mr. Deakin looked around, wondering if he had rolled over a boulder on the path, but then the thump came again.

Out of the corner of his eye he saw one of the coffins move aside just a little.

"Oh, no!" Clancy wailed. "I told you!"

An echoing thump came from the second coffin. Another burst of thunder rolled across the sky, and the horses picked up their pace, frightened by the wind and the storm.

Clancy leaned into the back of the wagon. He took a mallet from the pack of tools and, just as the first coffin bounced again, Clancy whacked the edge of the lid, striking the coffin nails to keep the top closed. The rusted and mud-specked nailheads gleamed bright with scraped metal.

Mr. Deakin had his mouth half-open, but he couldn't think of anything to say. He kept trying to convince himself that this was some kind of joke Clancy was playing, or perhaps even the townspeople of Compromise.

Just as he turned, the first coffin lid lurched, despite Clancy's hammering. The pine boards split, and the lid bent up just enough that a gnarled gray hand pushed its way out. Wet and rotting skin scraped off the edge of the wood as the claw-fingers scrabbled to find purchase and push the lid open farther. Tendons stuck out along yellowed bones. A burst of stench wafted out, and Mr. Deakin gagged but could not tear his eyes away.

The second coffin lid cracked open. He thought he saw a shadow moving inside it.

Clancy leaped into the back of the wagon and straddled one of the coffins. He banged again with the mallet, trying to keep the lid closed; but he hesitated, worried about injuring the hands and fingers groping through the cracks. "Help me, Mr. Deakin!"

A flash of lightning split across the darkness. Rain poured down, and the horses began to run. Mr. Deakin let the reins drop onto the seat and swung over the backboard into the wagon bed.

Clancy knelt beside his mother's coffin. "Please stay put! Just stay put! I'll get you there," he was saying, but his words were lost in the wind and the thunder and the rumble of wagon wheels.

One of the pine boards snapped on the father's coffin. An arm, clothed in the mildewed black of a Sunday suit, thrust out. The fingers had long, curved nails.

"Don't!" Clancy said.

Mr. Deakin was much bigger than Clancy. In the back of the wagon he planted his feet flat against the side of the first coffin. He pushed with his legs.

The single rotting arm flailed and tried to grab at his boot, but Mr. Deakin shoved. He closed his eyes and lay his head backward —and the coffin slid off the wagon bed, tottering for an instant. As the horses continued to gallop over the bumpy path, the coffin tilted over the edge onto the track.

"No!" Clancy screamed and grabbed at him, but Mr. Deakin slapped him away. He pushed the second coffin, a lighter one this time. The lid on this coffin began to give way as well. Thin fingers crept out.

Clancy yanked at Mr. Deakin's jacket, clawing at the throat and cutting off his air, but Mr. Deakin gave a last push to knock the second coffin over the edge.

"We've got to turn around!" Clancy cried.

The second coffin crashed to the ground, tilted over, and the wooden sides splintered. Just then a sheet of lightning illuminated the sky from horizon to horizon, like an enormous concussion of flash powder used by a daguerreotype photographer.

In that instant, Mr. Deakin saw the thin, twisted body rising from the shards of the broken coffin. Lumbering behind, already free of the first coffin, stood a taller corpse, shambling toward his wife. Then all fell black again as the lightning faded.

Mr. Deakin wanted to collapse and squeeze his eyes shut, but the horses continued to gallop wildly. He scrambled back to the seat and snatched up the reins.

"This weather is going to ruin them!" Clancy moaned. "You have to go back, Mr. Deakin!"

Mr. Deakin knew full well that he was abandoning a farm of his own in Tucker's Grove, but the consequences of breaking his agreement with Clancy seemed more sane to him than staying here any longer. He snapped the reins and shouted at the horses for greater speed.

Lightning sent him another picture of the two scarecrow corpses—but they had their backs to the wagon. Walking side by side, Clancy Tucker's dead parents struck off in the other direction. Back the way they had come.

With a sudden, resigned look on his face, Clancy Tucker swung both of his legs over the side of the wagon.

"Clancy, wait!" Mr. Deakin shouted. "They're going the other way! They don't want to come after all, can't you see?"

But Clancy's voice remained determined. "It doesn't matter. I've got to take them anyway." He ducked his head down and made ready to jump. "A promise is a promise," he said.

"Sometimes breaking a promise is better than keeping it," Mr. Deakin shouted.

But Clancy let go of the wagon, tucking and rolling onto the wet grass. He clambered to his feet and ran back toward where he had last seen his parents.

Mr. Deakin did not look back, but kept the horses running into the night.

As he listened to the majestic storm overhead, as he felt the wet, fresh air with each breath he took, Mr. Deakin realized that he still had more, much more, that he did not want to lose.

I like to hike, and I am particularly fond of the Utah desert. The area around Moab—Canyonlands and Arches National Parks and other more obscure Bureau of Land Management sections—are breathtaking, clean, isolated. If you pick the right trails, you can avoid seeing people altogether, for days. Those canyons are where Aaron Ralston famously went hiking alone, got his arm pinned by a falling boulder, and had to amputate it with a jackknife and stagger back to civilization.

I know exactly where I would go to hide during a zombie apocalypse.

When Jonathan Maberry asked me to write a story in his V-Wars monster post-apocalypse series, I decided to write about what I knew: Hiding in the desert while the world falls apart. What could be better than that?

It was also a good excuse for me to take a "research" trip out to southern Utah, where I wrote this.

Solitude

The monsters hit the RV in the middle of the desert—three hairy beasts, howling, drooling, snarling. Their bodies were bloated with an overabundance of muscles and fangs; their skin bristled with shocks of black fur that would have made a porcupine seem cuddly. As they tore at the metal side of the vehicle, their claws made an awful fingers-on-chalkboard screech. The walls of the big RV didn't offer much more protection to the people inside than the perceived weak spot of the spiderweb-cracked windshield.

The overlapping chorus of screams was such a loud racket that I couldn't tell how many victims were inside, but if I had to guess —judging from the make and model of the recreational vehicle—it was probably Mom, Dad, a boy, a girl, and maybe even an obnoxious yap-yap dog. I doubt this was the family vacation they had expected to have.

Yeah, another example of the American Dream falling short. Been there.

The recreational vehicle was one of those big palatial monstrosities, the kind retired people call a "camper," but is basically a spa on wheels. It was decked out for state parks and fishing trips, not boulders, washouts, and other typical desert undercarriage-killers. This one looked new, with a good paint job, although smeared with the reddish dust from the canyonlands.

I don't know how the hell they had gotten the RV all the way out here in the deep desert. In this part of southern Utah, a person should know where he's going. The scenery is bleak but spectacular; the sky is wide and clear and blue, as if washed clean, except for crisscrossing vapor trails of jets going to and from the Air Force bases. The "roads" are faint dotted lines on the map, and in actually they're little more than ruts and suggestions across the landscape. It's not a place for blundering amateurs.

As I rolled up on my ATV, in which I don't feel any obligation to follow roads—dotted lines, or otherwise—I could see the lopsided way the vehicle sat on the rutted desert road. A flat tire, probably a broken axle or universal joint, too.

This was by no means an off-road vehicle; it didn't have the suspension or clearance to go on roads like this. What was the idiot thinking, driving all the way out here? The only unpaved road that sort of vehicle was rated for is the gravel parking lot of a Good Sam Campground.

Sometimes you have to wonder what people are thinking. Definitely contenders for the Darwin Awards, if anybody still keeps track of those.

In a national park like Arches or Zion, you expect lowest-common-denominator tourist yahoos who don't know what they're doing, but here in isolated Bureau of Land Management territory, you almost never see anyone else—and that's the way I like it.

I love the desert, and I feel I belong out here. The tough and unforgiving environment makes a person strong and self-sufficient, gives you the time and silence to figure out things, or just to have a little bit of peace. The desert rewards those who understand it and punishes those who don't.

The three monsters—werewolf types, if I had to put a label on them—rocked the RV back and forth, which only increased the terrified screams from inside. I heard a gunshot, and a bullet hole punched through the side door of the vehicle, then another shot blew out the passenger-side window.

At least somebody inside had the good sense to carry a firearm with them; unfortunately, the shooter didn't have any skill. Both bullets missed. Bad luck.

With the passenger window shattered, I could hear the screams even louder. The three monsters let out a victorious howl. With the passenger-door window shot out, which was clearly a stupid tactical move from the people inside, the werewolves could get a good grip. They tore the door right off its hinges. The racket was deafening.

If I wanted this much noise in my daily life, I could have stayed in Afghanistan.

After coming back from over there, I couldn't leave my nightmares behind, but I could leave everything else. I threw in the towel, turned my back on civilization, and came out into the isolated Utah desert, where I hoped to find a little solitude. There's a lot of emptiness in these hundreds of square miles of BLM lands. Once every few months, I'll make the long trip into Mexican Hat to load up with supplies, and then I head back out. That's all the contact with people I need or want. I have no TV, no radio—no interest and no cares.

Now it looked like I was going to have to head even deeper into the desert. Why is it so difficult just to be left alone?

My ATV engine is loud enough, especially in the desert silence, but the three werewolves were so intent on their victims, they wouldn't have heard a full brass band. I roared up to the stranded vehicle, grabbed my weapons from the back—and combat training kicked in.

The monsters were like a comedy routine as they all tried to pile in through the open door at the same time. The victims were trapped inside like fish in a barrel. I heard the tearing of skin and muscles, the sucking and cracking of limbs being torn from torsos, screams of terror taking on a different note of despair and agony.

The third monster lagged behind his buddies, and I killed him as he was trying to climb inside the vehicle to share in the Winnebago banquet. I kicked the carcass aside.

Sensing something wrong, the second werewolf smashed out the whole spiderwebbed mess of the windshield, popping it onto the hood. He sprang out onto the RV's hood and glared at me with blazing yellow eyes, curling his black lips back to show off his fangs—which might have impressed a dentist or a taxidermist, but I didn't care. His muzzle was splattered with blood; torn ribbons of flesh and muscle dangled from his mouth. He flexed long, curved claws and coiled his muscles as if he was auditioning for a "don't let this happen to you" steroid-abuse commercial. He let out a roar and sprang at me.

The monster might have been big and ferocious, but I'm not a soft pink family from the suburbs. I'm used to defending myself. I know how to fight, and I know how to kill. I've done it often enough. Sometimes in Afghanistan they were faceless enemies; sometimes they wore terrified expressions. Sometimes they pleaded with me in a language I did not understand; sometimes they spat their hatred at me in the same language. Even without understanding the exact words, you get a feel for what they meant. Regardless, all those enemies ended up dead in the end.

Just like the second werewolf did. Adrenaline, training, and instinct can work wonders.

I tossed his carcass next to his companion's, then climbed through the gap in the side of the RV where the passenger door had been.

The vehicle's interior was a bloodbath, limbs strewn about like discarded chicken bones on all-you-can-eat wings night back at the mess hall. At a quick glance, I could see enough body parts to make up a little boy and a little girl, lying about like the pieces from a Mr. Potato Head. There was even a mass of bloody fur— yes indeed, the family yap-yap dog. Do I know how to call it, or what?

I heard a loud crunch and saw the third werewolf bite down on the head of a woman—Mom, I supposed. He crushed the skull as if it were the shell of a hard-boiled egg, then slurped out the brains. I thought zombies were the ones with a fondness for brains, but judging from the bloody mess and the mangled corpses, werewolves were not picky eaters.

He looked up, startled to see me there, with blood and gray matter oozing from his fang-filled mouth. His black fur bristled, his hackles rose; he challenged me as if I might be competition, someone intent on stealing his fresh kill. But I wasn't interested in his meal, and I wasn't his competition in the natural order of things. I was a threat, nevertheless.

After all my time out here in the desert, I've come to think of this as my territory, and I don't like anyone intruding on my territory, whether it's unprepared families in large RVs or big hairy monsters.

I killed the third werewolf and was done with it.

I drank in the sudden blessed silence for a few seconds before tiny background noises intruded: blood dripping from where it had spattered on the walls, the hum and low drone of voices and static from a poorly tuned radio station ... then the whimpering groan of one of the victims, not quite dead. The father.

I saw that his forearm had been torn off, noticed a detached hand lying on the floor, still gripping a pistol. The weapon hadn't done him much good. Dear old Dad was twitching and mangled, half-dead from blood loss and fear.

On the radio, an announcer whose voice had an edge of urgency spoke with breathy words beyond the usual gravitas of a "trusted news anchor."

I frowned. Ever since I isolated myself in the desert, I haven't exactly kept up on current events. The world was a cesspool before I left, and it didn't sound as if it had gotten any better. Good riddance.

The dying father looked up at me, his mouth open and trailing blood. His eyes were glazed. As I leaned over him, he obviously didn't know where he was. His face buckled in terror, and he lifted his arm to fend me off—but he didn't have much of an arm left, and the stump wasn't much of a threat. He gurgled and coughed. Dying people aren't much for conversation.

The radio continued to talk about an invasion of vampires, werewolves, strange hybrids from dusty old folklore books, but it was all nonsense to me. I switched off the radio so the pure, beautiful desert silence could return. Why ruin it with talk radio?

The father died as I leaned over him, which was a relief for both of us. I didn't want the responsibility, and he didn't want the pain.

I climbed back out of the blood-soaked RV under the blue Utah sky. No wonder people came out here for vacation. I could just stare at the surrealistic landscape of red rocks for hours. Despite the similarities of rugged terrain, this did not look at all like Afghanistan, nor did it feel like that place.

Upon closer inspection, I saw that the RV did indeed have a broken axle as well as a flat tire. The driver must have been hauling ass, pursued by the hounds of Hell (which wasn't far from the truth, I guess). A driver has to exercise care and caution on rugged roads like this. I suppose they had learned their lesson.

Looking at what was left of the dead family, as well as the carcasses of the three werewolves, I pondered driving all the way to Mexican Hat to report what had happened. I didn't own a sat-phone or CB or any other way to make contact—on purpose. In the end, I decided it was none of my business.

I was pleased to discover that the RV had plenty of supplies, canned and dried food, containers of water, even toiletries. The suburban family had packed up and rushed out to the wilderness to get away from the horrors and complexities of the world. Right idea, lousy execution. Amateur survivalists!

But the RV wasn't going anywhere, and somebody may as well make use of their stuff. Why look a gift horse in the mouth? I loaded up my ATV with all their supplies, even unwrapped the dad's dead fingers from the handgun to add it to my own arsenal.

When I had secured the packages, I spun the ATV around and rolled off. I glanced over my shoulder at the wrecked RV, the mangled bodies strewn about. I considered giving them a decent burial or a funeral pyre, or ... hell if I know. The Taliban liked to leave dead bodies around as a warning for others to see. Since this was far enough from my camp, I decided to let the desert take care of it. The circle of life and all that. La, la, la.

Even the engine of the ATV grated on my nerves as I rolled off. This wasn't at all how I'd expected my day to go. It was going to be a long time before I could feel the silence settle inside me again.

On a clear black night without a moon, the stars shine down like a billion bright eyes—and it's creepy to think about all those things watching you.

Heightened sensitivity, paranoia, PTSD—the military has developed plenty of handy labels, but not many cures. They like to package their cases up in neat categories and write prescriptions for the drug of the month, pat you on the back, assign you a counselor, and applaud themselves for the great job they did.

After Afghanistan, I found my own cure. Solitude works better than any number of pills, no matter what color they are. People, in fact, are the problem—with their noise, hatred, emotions, jealousies, ambitions, vendettas. For me, the best way for a full body-and-mind cleanse was to turn my back on the world, let the VA seal my file, mark it "Case Closed," and worry about other things.

I know the feel of raw wounds, torn flesh. I've seen IEDs up close and personal, watched a buddy get blown apart by a rocket-propelled grenade right when he was in the middle of telling a joke, and I never did figure out the punchline.

I even saw the flash of white teeth in a suicide bomber's last ecstatic smile before he detonated his vest and headed off to his version of Heaven, some assembly required. And I remember those pearly whites flying at me like projectiles along with gobbets of flesh and blood. It wasn't bullets that injured me, but the sharp and jagged teeth of a terrorist.

But the Army decided the injuries still counted, so I earned my Purple Heart.

I didn't just get wounded in Afghanistan; I was *changed* there. That place, that war, changes everybody, one way or another. I don't think I'll ever get back to the way I was, but you gotta do what you gotta do.

I have my place out here in the desert, a shack made of corrugated metal reinforced with wooden walls, set into a natural alcove at the base of a canyon wall. My own private little lair. A long time ago, some uranium prospector or Navajo shepherd had abandoned it, and I fixed it up. I've got my sleeping bag, a cot frame, some clothes, plenty of supplies (thanks to the fortunate encounter with the RV today), a folding chair, and my fire pit. That's all I need.

And solitude.

The dark night smells clean, and the desert has few enough insects to make a bothersome noise. The burning mesquite logs send up tiny sparks like tracer fire, but that crackle is the right kind of sound, and it only adds to the silence. I can spend hours here alone, hands folded, thinking hard and *not* remembering.

After a while, you get attuned to the desert; you can sense things. I perked up, sniffed the air. I heard movement, something furtively pacing in the darkness beyond the ring of firelight. I heard a skitter of pebbles, claws moving on the ground, then a snuffle.

I levered myself out of the folding chair, which creaked. I stood, shoulders squared, hands loose, ready to flex. I inhaled deeply and let all of my senses broaden. I could sense beasts in the shadows out there, like Taliban. They were circling, probing, exploring ... but this was *my* territory. They could sense that.

They probably knew what I had done to the three werewolves in the RV. They were assessing me, and I stood facing the darkness without a flicker of fear—not provoking them, but letting them know that it wasn't in their best interest to come closer. I put my hands on my hips, refusing to budge. I stood by my fire and saw muscular, bestial shadows moving out there. I waited, defiant.

Eventually, the beasts went away.

The dawn stillness in the desert is crisp, clear, and with a biting chill. It's like glass, so intense and transparent that it magnifies the surrounding world. And like glass, it can all too easily shatter.

I woke from a deep sleep that might have been classified as a coma. I had eaten well, rested well, and enjoyed the warmth of my sleeping bag and my extra blanket in my alcove. I boiled water for the morning coffee, rummaged in the supplies I had taken from the RV, and found packets of something called "cinnamon dolce latte mix"—what the hell was that? Amateur survivalists, indeed! It was sweet and not at all like anything I would have called "coffee," but I had learned how to adapt.

I moved about my camp, hoping for a quiet day. I thought I might explore the canyons before the day got too hot, or maybe I'd just stay here and watch the world, look at the red rocks, admire the endless kaleidoscope of sunlight and shadow on the formations. I didn't even need to move to get a good show.

Swallows were nesting high up on the slickrock cliff, and I could hear desert mice pattering around in the rock field. Most of all, the *stillness* had its healing effect on me, and I just drank it in. I was feeling calm and settled enough that I even endured a second packet of that powdered cinnamon dolce latte.

I saw the tiny human figure, a backpacker, making his way across the desert, stumbling through the bed of the wash and heading up into the deeper canyon, straight for my camp. He lurched along, clearly exhausted and in a hurry, but the enormous load on his back made him ungainly.

There used to be a certain camaraderie among hikers and backpackers. Out on the trail for long periods, you rarely saw anyone, but when you did cross paths with another hiker, you were expected to say a polite hello, share information about trail conditions, maybe exchange supplies if you needed anything. It was a brief and tolerable interaction.

This man, though, came directly to my camp. I could hear his breathing from a long distance away, hear the stutter-stumble of his footsteps. A shame. The day had started out so quiet, so pristine. This intrusion was as grating as a dentist's drill.

I waited for him, wary but resigned, not knowing what to expect but convinced that I didn't want his company, didn't want what he was selling. I was not interested in a "backcountry buddy."

As he came close, I could see he was bearded, dust-streaked, gaunt, as if he'd been living on the run and in constant fear for a very long time. I'd seen that look on the faces of some comrades back in Afghanistan, especially the ones who had served three or four tours.

Some say that when you get that haunted, you'll never recover. I disagree. Solitude can even a person out. Uninterrupted solitude.

He was bedraggled, sweating, ready to drop as he staggered to my camp. "Thank God!" he said. "I saw your fire last night and I marked where you were, but ... I don't travel at night. I found a safe spot, barricaded myself, and just hunkered down to wait. Did you hear the howling?"

I just looked at him, cold and silent, then finally answered, "I heard."

"As soon as the sun came up, and it was safe, I made a beeline here. I hoped you wouldn't leave your camp."

"This isn't just a camp, this is my home," I said. "I'm not going anywhere."

The backpacker looked around, studied my shack, my supplies, my chair. "So ... you're safe here? It's secure? They leave you alone?"

"Nothing bothers me out here—until recently." I only have one chair and I sat in it. To make a point.

As if I'd invited him to join me, he unclipped the front straps, groaned, and swung around as he dropped the bulky frame off his shoulders. The backpacker didn't seem to understand subtleties.

"I see you had the same idea," he said. "It's sheer hell out there, and I decided the only way to survive that holocaust was to head out into the middle of nowhere. Be self-sufficient. It's monster against monster back in the real world, a menagerie of vampires—civilized ones and barbarian ones, all at each other's throats ... and at our throats! We're just fodder to them—some of them at least." He shook his head, and, seeing no other chair and receiving no invitation from me, he hunkered down on his pack.

"I try to stay away from all that mess," I said.

"Me, too! Hole up out here in the deep desert, someplace where no one will find you, and let all those *things* sort it out back in the cities. Then we can come back when it's settled down."

"I'm not going back," I said. "I'm here for the peace and quiet."

He unzipped one of the front pouches of his pack, pulled out a sealed envelope of jerky. "I've got supplies. We can share. But it's not safe—some of those monsters have come out here, too. You and me, though ... safety in numbers, right? The two of us could stick together, join forces. I'll watch your back, you watch mine."

I cut him off. "No thanks."

He looked crestfallen, then grew more desperate. "You're dead meat out here if they come. And I can make myself useful. Honest! Let's just try it for a week or so." He extended a grimy hand, pleading. "By the way, my name is—"

"I don't want to know your name. I don't want to know *you*. I don't want you here." I could feel my blood boiling, my hackles rising. I hate it when someone provokes me to anger. "You don't understand solitude," I said. The words sounded rough, like a growl.

The backpacker was slow to realize what was happening, and only in the last instant did he have fear in his eyes.

I dragged his body far from my camp. No need to have the smell of blood and death near where I live.

It took me half the morning to dig a grave deep enough in the rocky, sandy soil so that I wasn't worried about scavengers. I didn't mark the grave—what would be the point?

After all that, I was jittery and stressed. I had an edge to my mood. I don't like being disturbed; I don't like having my solitude shattered; I don't like all this nonsense. I went back to my camp, stretched out on my cot, closed my eyes, and just *breathed*, listening to the air, feeling the silence.

Far overhead I heard the roar of fighter jets, saw the vapor trails of dark aircraft racing across the sky ... chasing after some other war. But it wasn't my war. I've already done that, and I left it behind.

I worked hard to calm myself, opening my hands, flexing fingers, making the claws retract. I felt as if I could just *wring* the silence out of the air, but it eluded me. No matter how long I stay here in the empty desert, it's hard to control the beast inside me, the one that's been there since Afghanistan.

At first, I tried to crush it, kill it ... but that wasn't going to happen. Now I revel in the wide-open emptiness, the beautiful red rocks, the deep canyons with guillotine shadows, the painted terrain and the hardy plants and animals that know how to survive in a world that doesn't make it easy for them.

I like to let the beast out sometimes, but on my own terms, when I can be free to lope for miles, run across the desert and hunt whatever I like, stop and sleep in whatever lair I choose.

In the distance, even during the daylight, I could hear a bestial howl, a call of some other monster. It sounds ... lonely. I hope it doesn't track me down. Kindred beasts or not, I wish they'd just leave me alone.

I recently spent a year taking online classes to earn my Master of Fine Arts degree. At age 56, with 150 published novels under my belt, it might seem strange to dedicate the time and expense to getting a degree, but having an MFA is a bureaucratic requirement before I could teach grad-level classes at the university that had already hired me.

While completing "busywork" writing to fulfill the MFA requirements, I took every opportunity to write flash fiction that I could publish somewhere. This brief, fun story was written for a Flash Fiction class.

Age Rings

Out in front of Grandma's farmhouse, the long-handled axe rested on the stump, its blade firmly embedded in the wood. The stump was wider than Aaron's arms could encompass, but he was only eight. A grownup might be able to reach all the way around.

It was an ancient box elder tree, much like the others in the yard, with drooping branches and knobby bark. This one, though, had been cut down when their own father had been a boy on the farm. The wide stump had served for decades as a chopping block, all of the wood split and stacked up against the farmhouse wall.

His twelve-year-old brother Nate stood looking down at the wide trunk, the weathered gray wood, the numerous scars and notches from the axe. They were both bored, and Nate liked to explain things. Aaron was a captive audience.

"How old do you think this tree was when Grandpa cut it down?" Nate asked.

"I don't know," Aaron said. "A hundred years?"

"There's a way to tell," Nate said, bending down. "Look at the stump. You can count the age rings. All of those circles. Each one marks a year."

"Really?" Aaron bent down, saw the concentric rings tightly packed at the center from when the tree had just been a sapling, then spreading outward all the way to the last shreds of bark. "One ... two ..."

"The thick rings are from a good year, when the tree grew a lot, and the thin rings are from bad years. Each one leaves a mark, and you can just count."

Aaron studied the lines, fascinated by this clear method. So many of them! "This tree was really old." He eventually lost count and gave up.

"Nate," he asked, "how old do you think *Grandma* is?"

His brother considered. "I don't know. Let's go find out." He yanked the axe out of the chopping block and headed for the house.

I remember watching the classic science fiction film The Thing from Another World *and loving the creepy, claustrophobic fear of an alien monster rampaging through an isolated Antarctic base.*

I saw the John Carpenter remake of The Thing *when it debuted in theaters. The Carpenter version was much closer to the original John W. Campbell novella "Who Goes There?" Then, of course, I had to find the original story and read it.*

I think all three versions are masterpieces.

John Gregory Betancourt, who has been my friend since we were both seventeen years old, announced a new anthology from his Wildside Press: original spinoff stories based on the original "Who Goes There?" Of course, I was in—and it gave me the opportunity to rewatch the movies and reread the Campbell novella.

"Cold Storage" is the result.

Cold Storage

Being assigned to an ultra-secret government warehouse deep in the Nevada desert wasn't as exciting as it sounded, but nobody chose a civil service job for the excitement. That was exactly the way Malcolm Hobbs liked it.

The work was interesting and engaging, especially on days when a new object landed on his desk. After he passed through the guard gates and security fences and entered the small cinderblock Unusual Object Intake Office, Malcolm found a plastic-wrapped package waiting for him.

The sturdy government-issue desk was painted seafoam green, and he had his own rolling chair on the linoleum floor. A metal file cabinet stood like a sentinel with gray fireproof drawers locked with combination dials and marked with classification tags. He glanced at the Uncle Sam calendar hanging on the wall, May 1950. Before considering the new package, he X'ed out the previous day with a black marker, as if it had been redacted and locked away. For the sake of national security, Malcolm did his best to forget everything he had seen, but some things he could never forget. It all went with the job.

He regarded the rectangular package, about fifteen inches on a side, wrapped and wrapped in several layers of plastic with hazard stickers on each layer. A standard Unusual Object Intake

Form, in triplicate, was attached with cellophane tape. The form listed serial numbers and a chain of custody, but—as usual—gave very little real or useful information about the item in question.

Up and down the chain of command, no one did the slightest bit more than they were authorized to do. Malcolm was just a small cog in a very large machine, and he was on his own to figure this out.

He sat in the swivel chair, pulled a new government-issue notebook from the side desk drawer, and opened to a clean page. He sharpened his pencil, then began to record his observations. Malcolm would fill many pages with a thorough description of the item, and the logbook would then be stored in the fireproof, floodproof, and atomic-bomb-proof drawers of his secure file cabinet. After he was finished, the object itself would be locked away inside the gigantic government warehouse complex, where it would remain safe.

Once he finished his external observations, he took a box cutter from his top desk drawer and sliced the packing tape to unwrap the first sheet of thick plastic, only to find another layer of equally thick plastic and more hazard stickers beneath.

The warnings made Malcolm uneasy, but he was a loyal civil servant, and the government was here to help him. They had assigned him this job, and he knew they would never expose him to undue risk.

After making a few more notes, he cut through to the third layer, sawed through the thickest layers of tape yet, and finally exposed the actual object inside—a bound journal, a scientific notebook that was burned at the edges, battered and crimped as if it had been dropped out of a low-flying bomber. The broken spine had been taped to hold together the charred and bent pages. The bitter tang of soot rose from the book.

Gingerly, Malcolm lifted the cover with a creak of exhausted binding. The front page, marked in clear, confident handwriting, identified the journal as from "Antarctic Research Station, 1939," written by someone named Blair.

"What did you get today, Buddy?" said a voice that was

altogether too loud for the hushed confines of the small office cubicles. "I sure don't want to trade with ya, though. I got cattle mutilations. Those are always fun!"

Flinching, Malcolm looked up to see blustery Glenn Romano, his lone coworker in the intake office. Instinctively, he covered the journal with the flat of his hand. "None of your business, Glenn. This is classified. Eyes only."

"Sure, but I've got eyes." He poked a finger at his face as if he meant to gouge out his orbs. "Were you expecting some bug-eyed monster?"

"I was expecting you to respect boundaries." Malcolm leaned protectively over the journal. "I take my security clearance seriously."

"Of course you do, Buddy. Nobody ever confused you for a fun-loving guy, but you're all the company I have in this dungeon."

In previous years, the Unusual Object Intake Office had employed many more workers. During World War II, even before the testing of the atomic bomb down in Alamogordo, New Mexico, the giant desert warehouse had been used to store dangerous and important items, including weapons stolen from the Nazis—the Spear of Destiny, some biblical ark, spell books, magical artifacts, and numerous technological prototypes. One entire wing of the warehouse held super-secret materials from the Manhattan Project, as well as the far more destructive and even more super-secret Brooklyn Project. During the War, Malcolm often received as many as five mysterious artifacts in a single week. The work was dizzying and exhausting, not at all what he'd expected when he'd taken his civil service exam.

After the end of the war, they had begun to catch up, until the Roswell Incident in 1947 threw everything into turmoil again, forcing the intake offices to bring in an army of extra staff, with desks crammed together, diligent clerks filling drawers with classified records, and entire file cabinets rolled out and locked away forever. Now, three years after Roswell, the world had settled into a relative calm, and the Unusual Object Intake

Office had only himself and Glenn Romano to work on the backlog.

He hated Glenn.

The man had no personal boundaries, asking pesky questions, always snooping into Malcolm's work under the guise of "friendship," but Malcolm didn't want to be friends. This was a top secret installation, and Malcolm didn't even know who his immediate supervisor was.

The intake office building was no larger than a bunker and as secure as a bomb shelter, with thick cinderblock walls, no windows. His desk and Glenn's were at opposite sides of the main room. The only human touch was a little kitchen area with a refrigerator and a hotplate. Employees were allowed to socialize there, which Malcolm avoided whenever possible.

In the middle of the cinderblock wall near his desk was a large red button, prominent but untouched. Stenciled letters admonished NEVER CALL FOR HELP. Both he and Glenn knew that the red button was to be used only in extreme circumstances and would result in the termination of their employment and the revocation of their security clearance.

Though Glenn Romano was extremely annoying, Malcolm doubted a personality conflict warranted pressing the red button.

"I've got this new intake. You're interrupting my work."

"Sure thing, Buddy." Glenn slapped the painted wall with the flat of his hand. "Maybe we can meet at the commissary after hours, have a beer, let your hair down?"

Self-consciously, Malcolm touched the short and receding stubble on his head. He liked his hair just the way it was.

Finally, he couldn't control his annoyance any longer. "You took my sandwich from the Frigidaire yesterday! Ham and cheese, just the way I like it. I went without lunch because of you!"

Glenn snickered. "I didn't eat your sandwich."

"It wasn't there. I looked."

The other man kept grinning. "Aww, I was just pulling a prank on you. Lighten up! Look in the bottom drawer. I kept waiting for you to say something, but you spoiled the joke." Glenn strolled over to his own desk to enjoy his new photos of cattle mutilations.

Malcolm turned back to the burned journal, wondering what had happened to the 1939 Antarctic Expedition. He'd never heard about it, which didn't mean anything. That was the whole point of this government installation. The journal had remained here, wrapped and untouched in the intake office for more than a decade. He would read it, cover to cover.

Before starting, he went into the kitchen area, pulled open the heavy door of the Frigidaire, and looked at the empty shelves where he had placed his sandwich yesterday. Determined not to go hungry again, he had brought a fresh sandwich this morning, sliced ham, Swiss cheese, and bright yellow mustard on white bread, wrapped up in butcher paper. Malcolm pulled open the bottom drawer designed for fresh produce, which was never used because here in the Nevada desert fresh produce was as rare as a UFO sighting.

Yesterday's sandwich was exactly where Glenn had hidden it.

In frustration, Malcolm snatched up the wrapped package and went back to the desk. He would eat the sandwich while reading the mysterious journal. Munching on the cold ham and cheese, he paged through the damaged book, careful not to get mustard on the paper.

Blair was the expedition's biologist at the Antarctic station, serving with dozens of meteorologists, geologists, engineers, radio men, support crew. Malcolm read with widening eyes about the discovery of an enormous alien spacecraft buried deep within the ice. From the description, the ancient ship sounded vastly larger than the more recent flying saucer found near Roswell, New Mexico.

During excavations, the team had found a hideous, blue creature with three red eyes, also frozen in ice outside the ship. The alien inhabitant was certainly dead, especially since one of the diggers had accidentally cleaved its head with an ice axe when they chopped it out of the ice. When they had used thermite bombs to clear more of the ice sheet, they unintentionally vaporized the entire alien vessel.

A shame, Malcolm thought, since the ship would surely have been brought back here to Nevada to be stored inside the warehouse.

"You've got to see this, Buddy!" Glenn stalked over from his desk holding up a manila folder. He pulled out glossy black-and-white photos of mangled cattle, their bodily organs strewn across fields in Montana. "It looks like a combination of Dr. Mengele and some insane barbecue chef."

"We've already processed all the Mengele records." Malcolm looked up from Blair's engrossing journal, but quickly averted his eyes. "Hey, I'm not supposed to see that! It's not my project."

"Sure, sure," Glenn said as he wandered back to his desk. "Thought you'd find it interesting."

Malcolm went back to reading, turning one page after another as Blair described how the supposedly dead alien had thawed from the block of ice and come alive again ... but more than alive. As the research crew studied it, they found that the alien organism was somehow infectious, a cellular chameleon that was much more than the three-eyed, blue monster they found in the ice. The "alien" itself had infected the expedition members like a plague, taking over and mimicking one man after another. Something as small as a cell could spread the inhuman presence like a virus.

Malcolm kept reading, amazed. With all those expedition members crowded in tiny huts, shoulder to shoulder with no privacy whatsoever, how could they possibly remain in quarantine for an entire Antarctic winter? There would be no stopping such an insidious extraterrestrial invasion.

He was suddenly reminded of how he and Glenn were sealed inside a cinderblock office building in the middle of the desert, forced to work under conditions that were far too close for comfort. Malcolm shook his head, tried to get his thoughts back on track.

The journal described how the monsters subsumed one member after another, while Blair himself, a suspected alien, had been locked away in his own hut, isolated from everyone else. He had written this account, thinking that he was the safe one, while the crew turned on one another both through genuine alien violence but also with all-too-human paranoia.

Blair had huddled in his shack day after day. As his account grew more erratic and less rational, Malcolm thought the biologist might be suffering from cabin fever, slowly going insane. Then the writing itself became illegible, no longer the clear and concise letters from the opening pages, following the neatly ruled lines in the scientific ledger. The writing degenerated into scrawls and, chillingly, into a different language entirely—undeniably alien symbols conveying a message that no human was ever meant to read.

Malcolm swallowed a mouthful of ham and cheese and wiped mustard from the corner of his lip.

According to Blair's account, the alien presence was amazingly infectious. One little germ could transform a man into an extraterrestrial monster. At least the bubonic plague had required rats and fleas, but this silent invasion passed from person to person through nothing more than a touch. It was terrifying.

Self-consciously, he wiped his hand on a napkin, then froze, looked down at his fingers, at the pages he had been touching. He swallowed hard.

If Blair was contaminated when he'd written this journal, how long would the germs endure? Many disease organisms could not survive in the open air and stopped being contagious after only a minute or two. But this thing from another world had been frozen under the Antarctic ice for thousands of years, and it had thrived as soon as it was exposed.

Malcolm tossed the rest of his sandwich into the wastebasket, no longer hungry. He scrubbed his hands on his slacks and hurried to the lavatory to wash his hands, again and again, with hot water and soap. Finally clean, he heaved a sigh of relief. Next time he would wear gloves.

The following morning, Malcolm passed through the guard gate and thick vault door, eager to finish documenting Blair's journal so he could be done with the unsettling story. He would fill out the Unusual Object Report and lock away this case once and for all. Flying saucers and little green men were far more palatable than a shape-shifting alien plague.

He went straight to the kitchen area and opened the Frigidaire to verify that his uneaten sandwich was still there from yesterday. Good, he was set for lunch. Just to be cautious, he slid it into the bottom produce drawer, hiding it. Maybe Glenn wouldn't notice.

When he entered the main room, he caught Glenn at his desk hunched over the charred journal, reading intently. His face bore a lascivious expression like a man staring at a pornographic pamphlet.

Malcolm squawked, "What are you doing? That's a breach of security!"

The other man had the decency to look embarrassed before he laughed it off. "I won't report it if you won't."

"I just might!" Malcolm snapped. He would have done so if he knew exactly where to file a complaint. He glanced at the red button on the wall—NEVER CALL FOR HELP—and sighed in frustration. "You're not supposed to be looking at my cases."

"I'll show you mine if you show me yours."

"No!"

Glenn offered a disarming grin that did not work on Malcolm. "We're coworkers, Buddy. We both have the same top-level security clearance." Trying to change the subject, he pointed down at Blair's journal. "That's an amazing story! I've been pawing through the pages, trying to get more information. You think it's real? Pretty hard to believe!"

Malcolm crossed his arms over his chest. "Think of all the things we've cataloged and placed into storage. *Everything* here is real."

With his bare hands, Glenn flipped the pages again, then closed the cover of Blair's journal. "That story reminds me of hoof-and-mouth disease, which I've been researching for my report. That's the official government explanation for the cattle mutilations, you know. Hoof-and-mouth disease is so deadly that if one cow gets infected, you can't just cull and quarantine the animal. The only way to be sure is to take out the whole herd." He nodded as if agreeing with himself. "The whole herd."

"Now, of course that's not the real explanation for the cattle mutilations, but the government is incinerating every carcass, burning an entire ranch to the ground and blaming it on wildfires. The ranchers who first reported the mutilated cattle are also suffering convenient accidents."

Malcolm backed away. "You're not supposed to tell me that."

Glenn tapped his finger on the closed cover of Blair's journal. "That's probably what happened to the 1939 expedition, extreme measures to stop the infestation. I bet the whole camp was burned to the ice, no survivors, no bodies, nothing left to salvage. Newspapers back in the day must have reported a fierce winter storm wiping out the station, condolences to the brave scientists, et cetera, et cetera. You know what I'm talking about, Buddy. We've both written stories like that ourselves."

"That's above my pay grade!" Malcolm said. "My job is to document the unusual object, fill out a report, and place it into storage. And you'd be well advised to do your job."

"Whatever." Glenn stepped away from the desk, rubbed his fingers together, then wiped them on his pants before he went back to his cattle mutilations.

Today, Malcolm pulled on a pair of latex gloves and turned the fragile pages with care. He filled half a notebook with his impressions of what he'd read yesterday, determined to make his report as complete as possible. Once Blair's journal went into cold storage, he wanted no excuse for anyone to touch it again.

In the journal, the biologist speculated that the infection rate might progress at different rates, depending on the host. The alien cells could seize and subsume any organic matter, not just the expedition members themselves, but also the cows at the research station, the sled dogs used for transport across the ice. Blair feared that a wandering gull might be infected, copied, and fly off to spread the alien infestation to the mainland.

The second time through, Malcolm read the speculations with increasing interest as well as skepticism. Since Blair had been quarantined and isolated in his shack, he was away from the rest of the camp. Therefore, how had he known the things he described as the camp fell apart around him?

Unless the alien cells that were taking over his body had some sort of connection with the others. Telepathy? An alien biological network? Maybe as he became more and more inhuman, Blair in his quarantine shack did know everything the other aliens knew.

Or maybe he was just a man losing his mind due to the isolation and the howling Antarctic wind.

Yes, that was the best explanation. Considering Malcolm's experience here in the government storage complex, though, mundane explanations rarely turned out to be true.

That night, back in his assigned employee barracks on site, Malcolm locked the flimsy plywood door then barricaded it with the single chair from his dinette table. He didn't want to talk to anyone, didn't want to go to sleep, but he couldn't stay awake.

He lay on his hard bunk, wide-eyed and listening to muted sounds through the thin walls. In the adjacent room, Glenn had a record player and was not shy about sharing his music. He played platter after platter, Nat King Cole, Bing Crosby, Guy Lombardo, the Andrews Sisters. Tonight, the music was at least comforting, and it was *human*. And Glenn himself was human, even though Malcolm didn't want his company.

He was hungry and queasy. That day, he had been so disturbed and distracted that he'd forgotten to eat his sandwich, so he left it in the refrigerator for the next day. Maybe he would have his appetite back then. His head throbbed. His ears had a ringing in them, possibly from the music next door.

Though still edgy, he finally dozed off, but the nightmares that came to him were far from comforting—vile dreams of monsters and spaceships. The cold emptiness of the universe was Earth's only real protection against all the terrors out there. Though he didn't dream in words or distinct images in his fugue state of sleep, Malcolm was overwhelmed by a surging loneliness replaced by intense anger, a need for conquest, a hunger to take over the world.

When he woke at dawn, those strange thoughts persisted, as did the headache, worse than an extreme hangover. He sat alone in the commissary and drank his morning coffee, shaking and confused. For some reason, his body was sluggish and hard to control, but the alien thoughts disturbed him more than anything.

Malcolm Hobbs was a civil servant, a quiet man; some might even call him meek. He had no delusions of grandeur. In fact, he had very few aspirations at all, and he was proud of it. He was comfortable with his role as a tiny cog in a big machine. He was not an emperor. If he took over the world, what would he do with it?

Thus, these thoughts clearly were not his own. They originated from outside his personality. Something alien.

He rubbed his hands together and washed them again furiously with soap and water. Was that sufficient? But if soap and water could kill an alien invasion, then surely the Antarctic research station would never have fallen.

What if the thing was inside him now? What if some alien cells had survived on the pages of Blair's journal? What if they had worked their way through his fingertips, penetrated his bloodstream, then swirled through his body, changing him cell by cell, organ by organ. Would he even know?

And what could the thing possibly want with him? He was isolated in the bleakest desert in the United States, a place as barren and isolated as savage Antarctica.

The answer dropped on him like a meteor falling from

above. This government storage complex was no minor meteorological station. The top secret government warehouses held the most amazing artifacts, extraterrestrial technologies, powerful objects considered too dangerous for anyone but the US government.

What if the thing wanted the Roswell spacecraft?

If the aliens spread among the workers here, they would have access to all the technology and resources they needed—not only to fly home, but to take over the Earth, even destroy it a dozen times over!

According to Blair, the alien organism could easily transfer from host to host without being noticed—not just human to human, but the sled dogs, the cows, everything in the research station could have been infected. The alien cells could take over any organic substance.

What if an infected person got out of this installation? Even if the "human" were killed, the alien cells could jump to a desert rat or a tortoise, a rattlesnake, a beetle. The Nevada desert wasn't nearly as lifeless as it looked. What if the thing got loose?

Malcolm rushed off. He couldn't get through the guard gates, sally ports, and heavy vault doors quickly enough. He needed to get to his desk so he could seal away Blair's journal, along with its fully completed Unusual Object Information Form, forever!

He hoped he wasn't too late.

Malcolm nearly collapsed with relief when he saw the journal still there in the middle of his desk. He had to finish the paperwork so the unusual object could be placed under even higher security deep in the warehouses, where Malcom need not worry about contamination.

He pulled on rubber gloves, then donned a second pair for extra security. The bland scientific journal looked so innocuous, like the lab reports he had written in college chemistry class, but he knew it contained a ticking biological bomb. The ringing in his head was so loud he couldn't concentrate.

He found the original layers of thick industrial plastic and wrapped the journal as tightly as he could, taping and retaping, scribbling *Danger! Hazardous Material! Danger!* in bold black marker. When that was done, he stuffed the bulky package into a lead-lined Top Secret courier packet. On the tag he wrote *Dangerous Material. Do Not Open.*

With shaking hands, he fumbled with the combination lock on the top drawer of his armored file cabinet. Due to his blurred vision, he had to try three times before he finally got the combination settings right. Malcolm stuffed the object inside the drawer, wedged it between thick manila folders about other mysterious artifacts he had worked on. When he slammed the drawer and spun the combo lock, at last he let out a sigh. He swept a hand across his forehead, smearing away beads of perspiration, and swallowed hard. His mouth tasted funny. He wondered if he was coming down with the flu.

Glenn barged in, whistling. He paused to give Malcolm a long suspicious look. "You okay, Buddy? You look like you went on a bender last night."

"I'm fine. It's all taken care of." Inside his head, he heard what sounded like faint and distant fire alarms ringing. He didn't want to talk to Glenn, couldn't stand to be around the man.

What if his office mate was infected? Glenn had smeared his sweaty hands across the pages, maybe contaminating himself. What would he do if Glenn was secretly an alien?

What if Malcolm himself was an alien?

He slapped a palm against his temple as if to jar his brain loose.

"Whoa, careful there, Buddy!" Glenn cried. "Don't hurt yourself."

Malcolm ran to the kitchenette just to get away. His stomach felt queasy, his body was shaking, and with a start he realized that he hadn't eaten since the day before. He had been so engrossed in filling out the report and documenting the terrifying journal that he had left his ham sandwich hidden in the drawer. Maybe that was all, low blood sugar, malnutrition ... Unreasonably ravenous, Malcolm pulled open the Frigidaire, ready to wolf down the sandwich right there. He just needed to eat.

But when he pulled open the produce drawer, he saw that the butcher paper wrapped around the bread had burst open, the paper tape split apart. The top slice of exposed white bread was pulsing and writhing. Startled, Malcolm recoiled.

Exposed to the light and the warmer air, the sandwich twisted, awake now. The neatly cut bread flapped open like the lips around a toothless mouth. The slices of ham churned and became alive.

Malcolm sucked in a breath to scream, realizing that the alien cells could invade anything organic ... like ham, cheese, even mustard!

Before his eyes, the slices of ham grew needlelike fangs. The sandwich became a rabid, chomping monster. Long, thin tentacles flashed out, whips filled with mustard-colored blood.

Malcolm screamed and kicked the refrigerator door shut as the sandwich thing tried to escape from the drawer. The heavy door sealed and locked.

His heart pounding, his pulse racing, Malcolm staggered back. He heard a thump from inside the Frigidaire as the unearthly thing hammered inside its cold prison. He turned and ran.

He was isolated here in the office complex. Malcolm bolted to the main room, gasping for breath and trying to form words. He had screamed in the kitchenette, but now he saw Glenn patiently working at his desk, undisturbed, studying his cattle-mutilation photos as if enjoying them for breakfast.

"There's something weird in the refrigerator. It's trying to take over the world!"

The other man turned to him, and his eyes were strange. "You're acting a little odd, Buddy."

"Odd? The odd thing is in the produce drawer!"

Glenn rose to his feet, letting his swivel office chair turn slowly like a planet in a dying orbit. "Maybe you need a rest. You're not yourself."

"Nothing is the same!" Malcolm screamed.

Glenn took a step closer, consoling. "This is awfully strange behavior."

From the kitchenette behind him, Malcolm could hear the louder thumping and then a crash. The sandwich thing had burst through the seal and the lock, tearing open the refrigerator door. "Can't you hear that? It's escaping!"

"Come here, Buddy." Glenn's expression was unusual, as if he couldn't quite control his face.

Malcolm froze. "You're not acting normal, Glenn. I think you're—"

"Everything's fine, Buddy." Glenn reached out, but as he extended his arm, it kept growing. His fingers elongated into twisted tentacles. His hands split, and his chest swelled, reshaping itself to sprout a third arm that popped through the buttons of his shirt. All the appendages reached toward Malcolm, bursting with claws and suckers. One of Glenn's hands sported three red eyes.

Malcolm squirmed away as the Glenn-thing closed in. The sandwich monstrosity shambled out of the kitchenette, no longer resembling bread, deli meat, cheese, and mustard. It grew in bulk as if absorbing material from the air, and more tentacles lashed out as it approached Malcolm from the opposite direction.

Glenn's face melted, and his mouth dropped open, filled with fangs, yet still moaning in a quiet voice. "It's all right."

Pressed against the cinderblock wall, Malcolm expected to be torn to pieces as the monster grasped him, but the disfigured tentacle hand simply patted his shoulder. "It's all right."

Malcolm looked down to watch his own arm elongating as if the bones themselves had become thorns, as if the cartilage added extra inches. His fingers twitched and twisted with minds of their own, and one sprouted a bright red eye that peered back at his face.

Malcolm couldn't stop screaming.

The sandwich thing thumped into the room, joining them.

Glenn's body split in half, sprouting fangs and claws in all the wrong places.

Malcolm's own throat was changing, his neck stretching. His corrupted vocal cords altered his scream into an inhuman roar.

But he saw the red button on the adjacent cinderblock wall. It wouldn't normally have been within reach, but his arms were freakishly longer now. They flopped about, but he could still control them ... somewhat.

NEVER CALL FOR HELP.

Malcolm didn't care about losing his job or his security clearance. If there had ever been a time to push the red button, this was it.

The Glenn-thing tried to stop him as it realized what he intended to do. The ham and cheese monster lunged, but not in time.

Malcolm hit the big red scary button.

A recorded woman's voice spoke calmly from the ceiling speakers, "Thank you for initiating the extreme decontamination protocol. Please stand by."

Alarm sirens went off along with rotating, magenta danger lights, flooding the intake office with a storm of racket and light. Ignited flame jets dropped down through the ceiling panels, bursting into bright orange fire at the same time as acid nozzles gushed a flood of caustic liquid.

As Malcolm saw a last burst of bright heat and searing chemical pain, he realized he was looking through a dozen additional alien eyes, all of which mercifully went dark in an instant.

Being assigned to an ultra-secret government warehouse deep in the Nevada desert wasn't as exciting as it sounded, but nobody chose a civil service job for the excitement. That was exactly the way Dennis McGann liked it.

He was proud to have his top secret security clearance and glad to serve his country. This wasn't necessarily the most glamorous job assignment, but it would be interesting, no doubt about that.

Dennis was a new hire brought into the Unusual Object Intake Office. He and his new partner, a man named Wilson, had the office all to themselves, each with a sturdy government-issue desk and his own file cabinet. The office had plenty of elbow room, even a kitchenette with a new-model Frigidaire refrigerator. The cinderblock walls had a fresh coat of white paint.

"Nice digs," he said to Wilson. The other man just grunted and took a seat in a swivel office chair at his desk.

Dennis was pleased to see he already had a project waiting for him on his desk, a bulky lead-lined classified courier envelope. It contained a rectangular package, wrapped in layers upon layers of plastic. Someone had handwritten on the package label *Dangerous Material. Do Not Open*—obviously meant for someone at a lower pay grade.

Dennis had been brought in to document unusual objects, study them, and write reports. He intended to do a good job. He cut the layers of plastic and began unwrapping.

"Best get to work," he said aloud, receiving only a grunt from his office partner. Dennis opened the package.

Back to the creepy town of Tucker's Grove, but moving forward to a different time period, the 1950s.

In high school, my parents let me subscribe to various Time-Life libraries, the Nature Library, the Science Library, The Seafarers, The Old West, and especially The Enchanted World, twenty lavish hardcover volumes that showcased myths and legends from around the world. Every other month, a new book would arrive in the mail, and I would dive into it. They were beautifully designed and great to read—that was as exciting as life got in small-town Wisconsin.

One volume of The Enchanted World featured the myths and manifestations of Death, and I was entranced (and horrified) by the French version of the Grim Reaper called the Ankou, who could only be seen by someone destined to die in the next year. The book included a chilling painting that I just couldn't get out of my head.

I knew I needed to use it in a story someday.

A Glimpse of the Ankou

R ay lit another cigarette, but this time he offered it to Betty, taunting. She steadfastly refused and concentrated on her driving. He watched how her lips pressed tightly together, how her hands gripped the steering wheel almost desperately. Betty had quit, all right—hook, line, and sinker. *New Evidence Shows Cigarettes Cause Cancer* all the newspapers and all the newsreels screamed. Too bad they hadn't told him that a couple of years ago —Ray didn't have much to lose anymore.

Wind whipped around the windshield of their brand-new convertible, a baby-blue 1954 Buick Century. They had bought the car just a few months before, back when Ray had his whole life ahead of him, back when everything was fine and normal. The wind seemed to sting Betty's eyes and they glistened, brimming with tears. Christ, she was going to have one of her sobbing fits again. He wished she'd stop being so selfish.

Ray leaned back against the passenger side door, tired and cramped from the long drive. His joints ached most of the time now, and he had long ago stopped trying to "keep a stiff upper lip" about it all.

"Ray, will you *please* put up the top now?" Betty asked.

Grudgingly, he turned around and leaned over the back seat,

fumbling with the canvas top to the convertible. His aching joints protested, sending complaints of pain to grate on his nerves. In the back seat, their baby Scotty fussed and whined in his basket, cranky after spending so many hours in the car ignored by both his parents. Scotty had also recently come down with a low-grade fever, the kind that babies seemed to get regularly, just bad enough that it made him fussy and miserable all the time.

Ray finally managed to pull up the convertible top against the resisting wind, locking the struts and fastening it firmly to the windshield. He felt a wetness below his nose and touched it, not surprised to find blood running out of one nostril. "Oh, hell!" he whispered to himself, biting back a more bitter outburst. He yanked out a stained handkerchief from his trouser pocket and dabbed at the blood. If only he had worried about his nose bleeds sooner ...

He didn't really care how many Communists were abroad in the land—Ray knew now that *doctors* were the ones doing a lot more to destroy the American way of life. Who would have thought that aching joints, a few mysterious bruises, and bleeding gums could come together as *this!*

One day he had come home from work, grinning from ear to ear. The brand-new Vice President of the bank—Betty hugged him and called him "Big Shot" over and over again. He changed his tie, combed his hair back with a fresh dab of hair cream, and promptly swept Betty off her feet. He gave her only time enough to call Shirley, their usual babysitter, before they went out for surf and turf at the "best supper club in Northern Wisconsin." Soon after, they had bought the new car, putting themselves out a little bit with a too-large loan, but the Vice President of a bank *had* to have a new car.

It wasn't long before he stopped sleeping well at night, and found himself taking hot baths more frequently, trying to ease the soreness in his joints. For a while, he kidded himself that the pressure of the new job was getting to him ... and then—

Acute Myelocytic Leukemia

Decreased production
of normal blood
Great excess of
abnormal leukocytes
No Effective Treatment
No Effective Treatment
You're going to die

Everything was a confused blur in his mind, but it all focused down to one fact. And the damned doctor hadn't even been able to offer any hope: one month—at best.

Aminopterin. Methotrexate. Thioguanine. All the chemical names were irrelevant—the doctor insisted that some of the treatments showed distinct promise, but for such an advanced case as Ray's ... He suggested that Ray drive to Rochester, Minnesota, check into the Mayo Clinic, and let them do their best.

The doctor was rather young, but he wore an odd monocle in his eye, reminding Ray of the commandant in *Stalag 17*, which he and Betty had gone to see earlier in the year ... back when they used to spend their Saturday nights at the theater. The last big movie they had seen together was *From Here to Eternity*—and now Ray was on the road to Eternity all by himself, taking an express route.

Before he left the doctor's office, Ray pulled the wallet from his back pocket and took out a picture of his wife and baby son. The doctor pushed the monocle back into his eye, looking at the photograph in silence. Then Ray got dressed, retrieved his snapshot, and turned to leave.

"There's something at the University of Chicago called *krebiozen*," the doctor said before Ray could open the door. "It's very new, but their researchers say it's a painless cure for all forms of cancer. Some other people say they're just quacks, and that krebiozen does nothing. I simply don't know. I can't recommend it. But a man in your position—I can't tell you what to do. I just wanted you to know about it."

Ray was too conservative to be a gambler, but only one of the options had a large enough payoff to make it worth risking everything. With only a month to live, he didn't have time to make mistakes. Krebiozen. Chicago.

They had left early in the morning, taking the convertible out on the web of little country roads in northern Wisconsin, the roads which eventually joined up with Highway 51 and led straight south. They passed through dozens of small crossroads-with-taverns towns, each of which forced them to slow down momentarily before Betty could let the convertible fly down the highway again. The dark woodlands, with their summer-tourist villages and sportsmen's bars, gave way to farmland as they reached the center of the state. North of Madison, when they reached their last chance to turn west and head instead toward Rochester, Minnesota, to the Mayo Clinic, Ray closed his eyes and made himself concentrate on the way south. Chicago. Krebiozen.

"Do you want me to drive?" Ray asked disinterestedly.

Betty shook her head, making her wavy hair bob back and forth. "Not if there's a chance you might pass out again. You just rest."

"I can't stand sitting here much longer. It's three more hours to Chicago." He turned his head to watch the cornfields flicker by. "I think we might have to stop for the night."

Betty didn't answer and kept driving. The road was not busy, though occasionally they found themselves stuck behind a slow pickup truck or some farm machinery. Ray concentrated on the optical illusion of the cornfields, as the car rushed past the individual rows so fast they seemed to flash on and off. The fields of alfalfa had been cut and baled into hay, and some of the land looked naked without a crop. Scattered barns and silos surrounded by the wide fields looked like misplaced modern-day castles. The corn itself was bleached brown from an early frost and stood waiting to be harvested. Ray watched the scenery, letting the monotony and the helpless boredom lull him.

The sun had recently gone down, taking the day's warmth with it as the blue sky faded into burning colors. Ahead, like a black blot on the landscape, one of the cornfields was charred and lifeless. The bronze shadows of sunset fell on the burned field, showing how it abruptly ended against a tree-lined lane that ran straight back into the cropland. The lane was rutted, and partially grown with weeds, and seemed not to lead to any visible house.

Ray sat up to look, feeling a rusty nail of pain in both elbow joints. Where the dirt lane met the road back under the growing shadows of the fence line's oak and wild cherry trees, he saw a dark man standing by a bulky oxcart, as if waiting for something. For a moment, Ray stared at the half-hidden shapes of the two oxen in front of the cart, surprised at how incongruous they seemed. The two animals appeared massive and powerful, very dark in the failing light, but they were turned away from the road, ready to plod back into the fields, and he couldn't make out much detail.

Then Ray focused his attention on the man by the cart. He was dressed all in black, with a tight collar like a preacher's and even black gloves on his hands. The man was gaunt and cadaverous, with his downturned mouth slightly open and showing only a black emptiness, no teeth, no tongue. His nose jutted sharply, twisted, as if broken several times and poorly healed. He wore a wide-brimmed hat that draped a muffled shadow over his eyes, but Ray still could see burning orange slits in the sockets.

Then the man looked directly back at him. Time stopped. Ray suddenly felt a shadow leap out, wrapping around his heart and squeezing it with icy fingers. Ray's eyes bulged, and he felt the ice in his chest thickening. He believed he was staring at a spectre, haunted by a shadow of Death itself. An unreasonable, gibbering terror mounted his shoulders, making him begin to shake. His lungs didn't want to breathe any more. Black spots started to swim before his eyes.

The spectral man slowly reached down to lift something out of the cart, a sharp farming tool.

"Ray!" Betty screamed, he realized, for the second time. "It's Scotty!" The car swerved back and forth on the road as Betty tried to reach to the back seat. Suddenly, Ray heard the little-animal sounds of a baby choking. Scotty was already turning blue in the face, and he writhed with his tiny arms and legs, eyes wide with disbelief and betrayal.

Ignoring the roaring pain in his joints, Ray broke his fascination with the spectral man and snatched Scotty into the front seat, flipping him over his knees, and pounded him roughly on the back. Scotty finally coughed and spit up again, crying and breathing great gasps of air.

Ray pulled a hamburger-stand napkin from the glove compartment and wiped off the baby's mouth. Scotty had apparently spit up and started to choke, unable to turn over in his basket. Betty's eyes were glassy and terrified. Her voice fluttered as she tried to shout. "He's got a fever, Ray. We've got to *watch* him! It only takes a second, and if—"

"He'll live," Ray said, and was surprised at the accusatory tone in his voice. Betty shut up almost immediately and looked as if she were trying to keep her tears back. Ray hated it when she cried.

"Did you see that man?" he asked.

"What man?"

Almost fearfully, Ray turned to look back, but they had passed him by.

The ancient attendant turned the crank on the rust-red Conoco pump, ratcheting the numbers back to zero before he began to pump gas into the Buick. As the numbers slowly turned, he massaged the bugs from the windshield, checked the oil, and performed all the typical service station amenities. The station sat at the intersection of two infrequently travelled roads, but "G. DuBay, prop." seemed to be doing an adequate business with his two gas pumps.

The old man's house was attached to the station building; several automobile skeletons in various stages of decay littered his back lawn. Somehow, Ray expected to see a mongrel dog pressing its snout up against the weathered picket fence around the yard.

"Ready to close up for the night," the old man said, wiping his hand on his stained, gray coveralls. His voice carried the ragged ends of a faded French accent. "You jes' caught me before I started cleaning up."

Ray avoided looking at the man and sat motionless against the passenger-side door. Twilight had plunged deeply into the sky. He kept looking behind him, where a curve had caused the road to be swallowed up in the darkening cornfields. The gaunt man with the oxcart was back there someplace. Ray felt fear begin to swell in him again, a maddening paranoia that refused to admit any explanation for the spectral farmer other than a supernatural one.

Betty stepped out of the car, stretching her legs and ignoring the mud that splashed on her high heels. "Are you Mr. DuBay?" she asked, nodding toward the sign in the window. A red Coca-Cola machine hummed next to a rocking chair in front of the station's door. Old newspapers were stacked beside the chair on top of a case of empty bottles, as if the man carelessly read the papers in whatever order he happened to pick them up.

"Yes, ma'am, I am Gillie DuBay," he answered, grinning at her with a mouthful of perfect teeth, odd in itself for a man his age. He almost held out his hand, but saw the black stains from engine oil, kerosene, and gas embedded into the skin. He tipped a non-existent cap instead.

"Is there any place to spend the night near here?" Ray spoke up, sounding gruff. He didn't want to be out on the open road, in the dark. The spectral man could be waiting for them around any curve, from any side road, beckoning Ray to climb into his cart. Ray realized what he was thinking, then, and became even more frightened, wondering if the leukemia and the unrelenting fact of his own upcoming death might possibly have squeezed his mind into a dark corner where healthy men could never go.

DuBay pointed down the road. "Tucker's Grove is not too far, a couple of miles. Jes' this side of the town you will see one of those motor-hotels, and you may get a room there, sure enough.

They might even have a television for you to look at. Red Skelton should be on tonight ... or is it Tuesday? I know Fibber 'n Molly will be on the radio."

"Thank you, Mr. DuBay." Betty paid him for the gasoline and looked sidelong at Ray, as if to be sure that he wanted to stop for the night rather than continuing for another hour or so.

"DuBay—" Ray sat up and turned to look the old man square in the eye. "About two miles up the road we passed a big burned-out cornfield ..." He paused, afraid he would sound ridiculous. Ray had been dealing with the fear of his own mortality almost constantly for the past week, but this fear of the shadowy man was something he couldn't put a finger on—and that made it much worse.

"That is Sanderson's place," DuBay interrupted. "He is a hothead, yes—heard about how Eisenhower was going to remove price supports due to the farm surplus, so he went out and burned his crop to the ground." He slapped his knee, as if he thought it was funny.

"I saw a man with an oxcart parked in the lane by that field," Ray continued, fixing DuBay with an intense and frightened stare. "He was all dressed in black and wore a wide-brimmed hat. He didn't seem to have any eyes—but he looked like Death himself, like the Grim Reaper or something. I never felt so horrified in my life. Do *you* know who I'm talking about? Does this man live around here?"

DuBay looked at Ray oddly, studying him. Then he laughed a short disbelieving bark. "I think you are pulling my leg, mister!"

Ray began to lose his temper. "Dammit, I asked you a question!"

DuBay frowned gravely. "My *Meme*, my Granny, used to tell me stories. I cannot imagine how you might know them or know me enough to think I'd be familiar with it." Hesitantly, he put a grimy finger to his lips. The black semicircles under his fingernails looked like tiny perplexed scowls.

"She talked about a horrible spectre called the Ankou." His slightly accented voice drew out the last syllable, slurring it. "He is the ghost of the last man to die each year. The Ankou stalks the night, with his scythe in one hand and his demonic oxen pulling a creaky cart by his side; he looks for victims, poor souls to throw into his cart, until the next year brings another Ankou to take his place. Now, I do not mean to scare you none, because it means not a thing. My *Meme* said any person who catches a glimpse of the Ankou is doomed to die within a month."

For just a moment, Ray's blood stopped cold in his veins. Then he snorted at the old man from behind the convertible's windshield. "Tell me something I *don't* know."

DuBay raised his eyebrows, then looked searchingly at Betty. She remained silent for a brief, hesitant moment, and then seemed to draw strength from her own ability to answer. "My husband has leukemia, Mr. DuBay. He *does* have less than a month to live. According to one doctor, anyway. We're going to Chicago for a new treatment."

The old man appraised Ray with such intensity it made him uncomfortable. But the scrutiny didn't make Ray feel pathetic, as many other people made him feel when they wept their crocodile tears for the poor, terminally ill man, the martyr to the terrible disease ("only thank God it didn't happen to Me!"). DuBay came over to the passenger side of the car.

"Maybe you *did* see the Ankou, then. It is possible, you know." He leaned down to look Ray in the eye. Ray wanted to slide over the seat to get away from the old man. DuBay spoke softly, with touching sincerity in his voice. "You'll get used to the dying, mister. I have been doing it for the past forty years."

"Yeah, well, I don't have quite that much time to adjust." Ray caught himself on the point of rebuking DuBay for having had so long to see all the places, to do all the things—He cut himself off before the words started to roll of their own accord. That particular sermon had been building up in him for days, and his nightmare was that he would unleash it at Betty, condemning her for having a life ahead of her, that she'd be able to remarry some *other* bank Vice President, someone else who could watch Scotty grow up, who could go with her to see all the new movies in the cinema, who could hold her hand in the darkness while the Big Screen romance took place in front of them ...

"Do not be too sure I have seen all that much in my life," DuBay said in his mellow way, seeming to understand the anger bubbling beneath Ray's silence. "But, yes, I have learned to be satisfied with what I *have* done and seen. It takes a special kind of trick to sit and look at your own yard every sunset, year in and year out. I cannot remember the last time I have left Rutherford County. Some people want to go everywhere and see everything—but I could stare at that field for the rest of my life and still not see it all."

"Don't stare too hard, Mr. DuBay—you just might catch a glimpse of the Ankou yourself. Then we'll see just how prepared for Death you really are." Unconsciously, Ray flinched and almost looked back over his shoulder again.

"Ray!" Betty cried. DuBay didn't seem to take any offense, though, and rapped his knuckles on the baby-blue paint of the Buick's hood.

"Good luck to you." He smiled with his perfect teeth and pulled at his imaginary cap again. "About that treatment in Chicago, I mean." As if by a silent agreement, he said nothing more about the Ankou. Ray wanted to be safe behind a locked door for the night.

Ray pulled himself slowly out of the steaming bathwater, trying to make the heat work a moment longer on his body's pain. His skin was crab-red as he grabbed a scratchy, bleach-smelling motel towel. While in the tub, he had spent most of his time feverishly thinking about death, and about Death personified, whether it be the Grim Reaper or DuBay's Ankou. The Ankou, the spectral man Ray had seen on a deserted farm lane—Betty said she didn't remember anyone, but perhaps his own nearness to death made Ray able to see things other people could not. Maybe the vision he had seen was the *real* Ankou, the *real* precursor of his own death. Certainly, no ordinary farmer could give him such a case of the creeps.

As he toweled himself off, Ray felt a slow-burning anger grow in him, overshadowing his irrational fear. After all, what did a man like himself have to fear from death anyway? He could not direct his helpless anger at the abnormal white blood cells in his veins, so he lashed out at his wife instead, hurting her because he needed someone to blame for his helplessness. But if the Ankou by the field were *real*, then Ray could confront him, focus his questions, his fear, his outrage.

What did he have to be afraid of? He was going to die anyway.

Betty had dozed off in the motel room chair, and Ray moved quietly as he dressed, not completely willing to consider the plan already forming in his mind. He slipped into his black shoes, picked up the car keys, and dropped the large motel key in his pocket. Ray stared at his wife for a long moment, remembering her, thinking about her. Betty's makeup had smeared, and her hair looked as if it needed the curlers, but she appeared peaceful while she slept. He wanted to kiss her on the cheek, but he knew that would wake her up. He didn't want her to worry about him.

Scotty had also fallen asleep in his basket propped up on the floor. Ray bent over the boy and touched his small forehead. Scotty stirred and squirmed but didn't make a sound. His fever had dropped a little, and he seemed to be getting better. Scotty's immune system hadn't been raped by something it couldn't handle, like leukemia. But Ray would never be getting better— unless, for some crazy reason, he was able to strike a bargain with the Ankou.

He hesitated for a moment at the door of the motel room, staring one last time at Betty awkwardly asleep in the chair, at Scotty lying contentedly on his back in the basket. He wanted to fix the scene permanently in his mind. Then he quietly shut the door behind him.

Out on the open road, he left the convertible top down, letting the brisk knives of night wind buffet his skin. He breathed deeply, looking up at the magnificent arena of stars overhead, and pushed down heavier on the accelerator before he could lose his nerve.

The burned cornfield was several miles down the road, but Ray knew the exact location. The convertible passed by Gillie DuBay's darkened Conoco station; he saw that a light still burned in the kitchen window of the old man's home. Ray kept his eyes fixed on the left side of the road as the semicircle of headlights scooped a path of illumination in front of the car. Soon he could distinguish the short black stubble of the burned field, and he slowed almost to a stop as the trees along the fence line loomed up to block out the stars just beside the narrow dirt lane. The swath of light from the headlights bounced up and down as Ray turned slowly off the road and parked in the middle of the shallow ditch. He switched off the engine and the lights, allowing himself a moment to adjust to the darkness. He heard grasshoppers, crickets, frogs.

Ray suddenly became aware of the spectral man standing in the darkest part of the lane beside his massive oxcart. Ray could see the burning orange of the Ankou's eyes. He stepped out of the convertible and left the door open; the small courtesy light shed a feeble yellow glow into the shadows.

Taking two faltering steps before he finally remembered his boldness, Ray strode up to the dark man and placed his fists on his hips in an absurd gesture of bravery. The night air around him was cold but suffocating, like the air in a sealed coffin; a sickening stench hung faintly around the Ankou, just barely beyond the range of detection. Ray felt mindless horror building up in him again, making him want to cringe, making him want to run back to the car and laugh insanely as he drove off at full acceleration into a telephone pole.

The Ankou said nothing as Ray stood defiantly terrified in front of him. Ray had no more doubts about the reality of the thing; he could feel his mind stretched and distorted by the wrongness of the spectre, stretched *almost* to the point of snapping.

"Look, I know who you are," Ray stammered. "I *know* I'm dying. I know I've got only a month." The Ankou glanced sharply at him with his blazing orange eye sockets, and Ray almost collapsed then. But he kept thinking to himself, *I've got nothing to lose, I've got nothing to lose.* He forced himself not to mumble; he tried to shield himself with thoughts of Betty, of Scotty, of his promotion to Vice President, of the new car that Betty would have to sell once he was gone ...

"Why do you have to take *me*?" Ray realized he had tears in his eyes, and he felt pathetic. "I've got a wife, and a son! He's just a baby—how can you take away his father? And my wife, how can you hurt her? She won't be able to survive without me!"

The Ankou seemed to show no interest whatsoever and turned slowly to stoop over his cart, reaching down inside. The two massive oxen stood in complete blackness, unmoving, facing away from Ray so that he could see only their bulky backs. The Ankou pulled out a long, gleaming farm implement, a scythe, and gripped it in his gnarled hand with enough force to make the wooden handle groan. He held the scythe for a moment, as if drawing power, then stalked toward Ray.

The man stumbled backward in terror and fell to his knees. "*Please* don't take me! Wait! I understand—you have an accounting to make. You have to balance the ledgers, take your proper toll. But if you're really Death, you shouldn't *care* who you take."

The Ankou stood over Ray and seemed impossibly tall. His glowing orange eye sockets were indeed lifeless. He said nothing and raised the scythe.

"But it shouldn't *matter* to you! Take someone else! I can *bring* you someone else! Please—if I bring you someone else, will you promise not to take *me*?"

The Ankou stopped and looked down at him, as if silently considering. Ray pushed himself to his feet, trying to stand on shaking legs. He didn't feel he had control over his own mind anymore; his brain had changed into a nest of shadows slashing at his sanity. He pushed the issue, repeating himself and praying he could sound convincing. "If I bring you someone else, will you promise not to take *me*?"

The Ankou stood rigid like a statue, and Ray backed off one step, widening the distance between himself and the Deadly scythe. The shadows made details of the Ankou's face uncertain, but Ray desperately wanted to believe he saw a smile form on the cavernous mouth, a slight nod of the leathery head visible under the wide-brimmed hat.

Ray stumbled and fled back to the car, breathing great gasps of air. The Ankou made no move to follow him.

DuBay's porch light came on the second time Ray pounded the rattling screen door. The old man opened his door and squinted into the light of the harsh yellow bulb. Ray could hear voices from the radio inside, and smelled kerosene from DuBay's house. "Ah, it is you," DuBay said, blinking in the direct light, smiling with his bright teeth. "I am closed, you know. But what may I help you with?"

Ray stepped back away from the porch, trying to find the edge of the light. "I'm sorry to come so late, Mr. DuBay. But you know I'm ... you know we have to drive all the way to Chicago tomorrow morning. Our Buick's making some strange noises, and I wondered if you could have a look?"

DuBay stood by the door in slippers that had several large holes in them. He seemed reluctant to leave his radio program. "I can give you a minute or two, but I can certainly fix nothing until the morning. It is the light, you know—my eyes are a bit weak, and I will not do your engine much good in the dark."

"But you could tell us if it's something *serious* or not, if we're going to break down somewhere between here and Chicago."

"That I could." DuBay pulled on an insulated jacket, found a flashlight from somewhere near the door, and followed Ray out into the darkness in front of his station.

Ray sobbed and wheezed as he drove, trying to keep the convertible from weaving off the edge of the road and into the ditch. He couldn't see straight. His joints screamed in agony, and he knew it would never get better again until he died. But DuBay, Gillie DuBay, that poor old man, oh, God!

DuBay was crumpled and bleeding in the back seat of the convertible, staining the new white vinyl seat covers. He had wrestled the old man's body there, then tossed the tire iron back into the trunk. Ray's nose had started to bleed again from the exertion. His head pounded and whirled, making him giddy from the leukemia, from his conscience, from the awed abhorrence at what he had just done.

He tried once more to call up the resentment he felt toward DuBay, who had had seven decades to enjoy life ... the frustrating despair that DuBay had all that *time* to see the world, to do anything he desired, and instead he sat on his porch and watched the sun set night after night. Ray focused on creating hatred for the old man, hoping it would help his own conscience. But the anger wasn't there anymore, only a stunned horror.

The baby-blue hood of the convertible had been up, DuBay squatting under it to look at the mechanical mass of the engine. "Yes, and what seems to be the trouble?"

"I'm *dying*, that's the trouble."

Ray prayed he had killed the old man with his first blow to the head. He could hear the *thud* and the *squash* over and over in his ears, like a skipping phonograph record. He felt like a betrayer, a vile and selfish monster. A murderer—he had *killed* somebody. He wanted to squeeze his eyes shut and hide, or scream, or run back to Betty and hold her close. DuBay. DuBay. He had *killed* DuBay.

If I bring you someone else, will you promise not to take me?

It was worth it. Even if it meant he had to face the Ankou again. He kept telling himself that a second chance at *life* would be worth even twice this agony. He was doing it for Betty. For Scotty. For *himself*.

He parked the Buick in the rutted lane again, and made certain to switch off all the lights, just in case someone might drive by. Betty could be awake now, she might be looking for him, growing more and more worried when she noticed the car was gone. *Don't worry yet, Betty,* he thought, *I'm going to have a big surprise for you very soon.*

The Ankou waited by his cart, blanketed with darkness. Ray wiped the wet blood from his nose and got out of the car, breathing fast, shaking his fear away. He wrestled with DuBay's heavy body, dragging it out of the car and dropping it on the lumpy dirt lane so he could get a better grip under the old man's armpits. Feeling anxious, hearing his heart pound like African drums in his ears, Ray heaved DuBay up into a rubbery standing position and draped him half over his back. He stumbled and dragged the dead old man toward the Ankou's cart.

"I brought you someone else, someone who deserves to die more than I do," he said breathlessly. "Fair exchange, right? Now you won't take me, right?"

The Ankou only stared coldly at him, then placed a hand on the rough edges of his cart, and Ray understood immediately. The spectral man watched as Ray shuffled awkwardly forward, pulling the old man to the side of the cart. Ray paused a moment, panting, and then tried to heave DuBay up over the edge.

DuBay let out a loud, agonized groan. He wasn't dead.

Frantically, Ray pushed his shoulder against the old man, heaving him into the cart. DuBay's shining white dentures dropped out of his mouth, clattering against the wood before falling to the ground.

DuBay dropped awkwardly into the bed of the cart, limbs flopping every which way—and he kept falling. With one insane glimpse, Ray saw that the cart had no bottom at all, but was a swirling vortex of bottomless stars, extending infinitely like a gaping mouth that was always hungry.

Ray collapsed in numb shock at everything that had happened in the past hour, sliding against the rough wood of the cart wall until he was kneeling on the ground. The Ankou stood over him, holding another sharp farm implement. Ray sobbed and found he couldn't even try to run.

The two oxen turned toward him at last, and Ray nearly screamed again. Both oxen had grossly distorted human heads wearing idiot expressions, with blunted horns curving out of their foreheads, and blasted eye sockets that had already seen far more than any human eye could bear.

If I bring you someone else, will you promise not to take me?

The Ankou shouldered his scythe and turned away from Ray, letting him get back to his feet. Ray stepped backward, afraid to take his eyes from the spectre as the Ankou dropped the implement back into the cart with finality.

Ray suddenly felt the barbed wire of pain unwind from his joints. His head stopped pounding; his bruises were healed. He ran his tongue along his gums, and they felt whole and healthy again. New energy flowed through his bloodstream, and he felt explosively *alive*. The leukemia fled defeated into the night. Ray laughed out loud until he began to cry, and he kept crying until he managed to get back to the convertible. By the time he had found the keys and started the engine, he saw that the Ankou had vanished. *Of course*, he thought, starting to laugh again, *only* dying *people can see the Ankou.*

And it *was* all worth it. As he drove off, he laughed heartily because it felt so good to *laugh*. He filled his lungs with air, raised one triumphant fist above the windshield, and reveled in feeling his body respond as it was meant to respond, without the claws of cancer surging through his bloodstream.

He was euphoric as the Buick flashed down the highway, and he paid little attention to his speed or his driving. Ray purposely didn't notice DuBay's darkened home or the deserted gas station as they passed. Back at the motel, he left the convertible's lights on and the engine running as he leaped over the door in a boyish gesture he hadn't wanted to do in years. Look at the stuffy bank Vice President now, whooping like a wild Indian! He tossed the motel room key high up in the air and caught it with one hand, then he grinned as he fit it into the lock. Ray was whistling, ready to explode with joy and love for Betty.

He didn't take me! All's fair in love and war—and death. He didn't take me!

As he strode through the door, Ray saw immediately that Betty was not in her chair. Instead, he heard an animal-like sobbing of despair, a heart-torn keening. She hunched over Scotty's basket, and her body shook with spasms of stunned helplessness.

One of the best small press magazines in the horror/dark fantasy field was The Horror Show, *edited by David B. Silva. Alas, it has been gone a long time, but I loved that magazine and published a lot of my favorite creepy stories there. Here is another one of them.*

Sometimes, to do a horror tale right, you don't need a lot of words.

Baggage Check

The suitcase felt like a bag of cement mix as he lugged it up to the baggage counter. It made an unpleasant soft thump as he slid it across the scratched metal threshold.

"Just one bag to Washington, Mr. Danvers?" the airline attendant asked after a cursory inspection of his ticket.

Danvers nodded, directing his gaze at the floor. He didn't dare risk an idiotic smile—he just wanted to keep most of the tension from his face. God, he hoped the baggage compartment would be cool enough to preserve his wife's body during the long flight to Washington, DC.

The attendant punched buttons on her antiquated computer terminal, searching for a place to seat him. "Smoking or nonsmoking? Can I get you a window seat or an aisle today?"

He mumbled back at her, trying to make sure he said the right words. "Uh, non-smoking, please. As close to the baggage compartment as you can get."

She raised her eyebrows, and he inwardly winced at his stupid answer. *Cool it, Danvers!* he thought, *You're going to blow this whole thing.* He motioned nonchalantly at her and made a strained laugh. "Never mind. Just a joke. Wherever you find a spot will be fine."

"You must not fly much, Mr. Danvers," she said with an "understanding" tone in her voice.

"I guess not." He swallowed, sensing his heart thumping. Danvers stared at the TV monitor that listed all the arriving and departing flights. Less than an hour and he would be out of here, escaped, free as a bird ... People bustled around. The scratchy unintelligible voice of the intercom seemed to be calling his name, accusing, every five minutes. It would be good to get out of San Francisco.

"Everything'll be just fine, Mr. Danvers," the attendant said. "Have a nice flight and come see us again." She stapled his baggage claim check to the flap of the ticket envelope, handing it back to him. The attendant grunted as she hauled his suitcase onto the conveyor belt. "Wow, what've you got *in* there? An elephant?"

He swallowed in a dry throat. Lillian? An elephant? "I guess I like to pack everything but the kitchen sink."

Danvers double-checked his gate number again, and as he turned to go, he suddenly noticed the conversation from another traveler at the counter, a man in the Frequent Flyer line.

"We must have 24 hours prior notice, sir," the worn-looking attendant was explaining to him. She looked like a burned-out stewardess. "They have to make arrangements for pressurizing the baggage compartment ahead of time. We can't just put your dog in there."

The other man was thin and in his late forties, with a tweed jacket and *pince-nez* glasses, making him look like a professor. Color rose in his cheeks as he tried to keep his temper in check. A slate-gray poodle paced restlessly in a small cage by the baggage counter, growling and barking every time the man raised his voice.

The man's words seemed cultured but with an edge of annoyance, as if he were explaining things to a small child. "I am sorry, madam, but I telephoned two days ago. I spoke with a woman named Jackie at your toll-free number."

"The number is based in Denver, sir. Sometimes these mix-ups happen."

"Well, then you're in a good position to fix it this time. Rimbeaux and I must get to Washington DC. He has to come with me now, because no one else can take care of him. I think you'd better call someone in higher authority. Call the captain, perhaps. I'm sure he'll understand." He gestured to the telephone, and then impatiently reached over the counter to pick it up, handing it to her. Exasperated, she dialed three numbers.

"We're going to Our Nation's Capitol, Rimbeaux," the professor said to his dog, poking his fingers through the cage. The dog began to lick them.

Danvers cursed under his breath, lightheaded with frustration. No! Bad luck—not now ... everything was going so well! If they pressurized the baggage compartment for that damned dog, then they would have to heat the area, too. A dog would freeze so high up, wouldn't it? He thought of Lillian for a moment, crammed into the suitcase, unmoving—uncooperative, as she had always been. The flight would take only five hours— would that be enough? Would it be too much? Why the hell did the professor have to be on *his* flight? Why did *he* have to own a dog? Why did something have to go wrong *now*!

Danvers felt his heart sink as the other man finally nodded in satisfaction; the attendant reluctantly hauled the barking poodle behind the counter. She called a baggage handler on the telephone as the professor waved to his dog. "Bye, bye, Rimbeaux!"

As if fleeing, Danvers scuttled away from the ticket counter. He didn't want to see, he didn't want to know—he wished all of this would just be *over*. Five more hours ... a little longer, and then he'd be in Washington for a fresh start, a new chance, a slate wiped clean, bright and shining. That's real optimism, isn't it?

He forced the professor and the obnoxious poodle out of his mind. Danvers shuffled uneasily past the generic gift shops, all of them selling inane last-minute "San Francisco" souvenirs. He bought two rolls of antacid tablets and chewed the tablets one after the other, trying to ease his restless stomach.

He looked at his watch. Waiting, killing time. Yes, it had been "killing time" a day ago—that's what had gotten him into this mess. He walked into a coffee shop, stared at the prices on the menu, and left again. Although nobody seemed to be noticing him, he tried to look nondescript, like a businessman or a slightly overweight tourist.

Danvers had let himself get out of shape lately. He and Lillian had often played tennis late at night, having the court to themselves under the harsh sodium lights. But she always beat him—it was another one of her annoying habits, showing off her superiority. She never thought about his feelings, about how much he might like to feel like a winner just once.

Danvers sat motionless at his gate, waiting for the plane to arrive. He twiddled his thumbs, and wrinkled his nose at a fat man smoking a brown-wrapped cigarette in the non-smoking area. He got up to buy a cup of coffee at the bar but stopped himself—he was too keyed up already, no need for more caffeine. He sat down in a different chair, and fidgeted ...

Finally, after the boarding call for his flight, Danvers shuffled down the walkway, finding his seat by the window. He sat back, closing his eyes and breathing through his teeth. Almost gone, almost over.

He rubbed his chin and grimaced at the stubble he found there. Damn! He had forgotten to shave—that was stupid, call attention to yourself, let them all see that something's bothering you. Danvers let out another long sigh and swallowed.

He squeezed his eyes shut and forced himself not to look as two baggage carts wheeled up, driven by one man and one woman —both, apparently, failed race car drivers. Danvers didn't want to watch the rough handling, didn't want to imagine what would happen if his suitcase tumbled off the baggage compartment, if it struck the pavement and split, spilling out Lillian's cold body. Wouldn't that be wonderful? Or, even worse, what if they had mislabeled his baggage, sending it off to the wrong city, where it would be stored in some unclaimed baggage area ... until Lillian began to—

After takeoff, the Bay Area cities dropped away below him at last, and Danvers heaved a huge sigh of relief. The sun and the plane fled in opposite directions across the sky, and twilight fell within an hour. People flicked on their reading lights, but Danvers sat in the dimness, sulking in the chill of his own sweat. He had already thumbed through the in-flight magazines half a dozen times anyway.

In the middle of the flight he heard a strange *thump* beneath him, somewhere under the floor. The baggage compartment? The plane had just passed through some mild turbulence ... in his mind he pictured his own suitcase, piled on top of others, sliding, suddenly dislodged, to come tumbling down. Would the suitcase hold? What if the locks and the zipper broke? Maybe it would fall and squash the professor's gray poodle—ah well, he could hope.

Danvers began to chew his nails.

When the plane finally landed, hours later, Danvers could see the bright lights of the Dulles terminal stabbing out into the darkness, shining on the light snow sifting down from the sky. A rush of gooseflesh crawled up his back. He had arrived safely, so far. Only a few more minutes, then he would get the bag containing Lillian's body. Washington, DC.—far away from all the memories, all the crimes on the west coast.

He tried to push his way down the aisle out of the plane, but the other passengers blocked the way, occupying themselves with tugging too-big suitcases stuffed into overhead compartments, guitar cases, even skis and ski poles. Feeling giddy with impatience, Danvers fidgeted and listened to his heart pound.

At last, he rushed out into the terminal, bustling out of the carpeted security area and onto the worn linoleum tile. Danvers walked with his head craned high, turning where the signs directed him toward the baggage claim area.

He forced himself to slow down, to take a deep breath. He stopped in the men's room and splashed water on his face. In the mirror, his expression looked appallingly haggard, and his skin had a grayish tinge. He swallowed, looked at his watch, and rushed out of the bathroom, still dripping water down his cheeks. God, this waiting was punishment enough for any crime!

Down in the lower levels, he found the baggage claim, and quickly identified the proper carousel just as the conveyor groaned and began to turn. Other passengers crowded around, ready to grab for their luggage, but the conveyor turned for many minutes until suitcases began to emerge pell-mell from some mysterious pit far below. As he stood, cold with anxiety, Danvers saw the professor with his *pince-nez* glasses, clutching a briefcase and waiting by the outside door for the baggage attendant to present his gray poodle.

Other passengers snatched up their luggage, but the crowd did not seem to diminish. Danvers waited, tense, ready to push them aside. Then, almost with a groan of reluctance, the conveyor belt spewed the large suitcase up and out until it rolled over like a dead thing and began its shuttling journey around the carousel.

For almost an entire second, Danvers couldn't move. Painfully apparent in one corner near the zipper oozed a bright patch of thickening blood, staining the fabric of the suitcase, and even leaving a faint smear on the scuffed metal of the carousel. His insides turned to ice. Blood! Surely everyone could *see* that! Didn't they notice?

Apparently not. Most of the passengers gave the large suitcase only a cursory dismissal and then hung waiting for their own luggage. Danvers bit his lip and pushed his way through, chasing the suitcase until he finally grabbed the handle and hauled the bag off onto the floor. He paused, panting for a breath, then heaved again, dragging it after him as he tried to escape. Almost done, almost over. Just get out of the airport, find a nice hotel, reassess everything, get a good day's rest.

He saw the door up ahead, sliding automatically open as people passed the electric eye. Puffing, he pulled the suitcase along.

A keening wail made Danvers stop in his tracks: a man's voice, but high-pitched and twisted into a womanish scream of shock and despair. For an instant, all noise stopped in the baggage claim area. Danvers turned to see the professor standing stricken, his eyes and mouth wide open. Tears streamed down his cheeks, but his expression cried out with shocked disbelief. He seemed ready to faint.

A confused and sick-looking attendant stood holding up something Danvers recognized as the cage that had contained the gray poodle. But the cage had been wrenched open forcefully, destroyed. Blood spattered the floor, and clumps of fur and scraps of torn meat clung to the jagged hinges of the cage.

The baggage attendant said in an inane voice, "I just don't know what could have happened, sir ..."

Danvers felt as if all his internal organs had knotted themselves together. With a great exertion, he yanked at the suitcase and tugged it after him. He had to hurry, had to get away, now more than ever. His knees felt ready to collapse. He was exhausted, and he kept breathing, deeper and deeper. He had to get her out of here.

"Why couldn't you have waited!" he cursed at the bag, low enough so no one would hear him. He made as if to kick the suitcase in anger, but he stopped himself, partly out of fear. "Why can't you ever have any consideration? Do you know how much trouble you're putting me through?"

Danvers gasped, exasperated. The automatic doors slid open as he approached them. "It's a big city. There's *plenty* of other people here—fresh ones. Just learn to control yourself!"

As the commotion grew behind him at the baggage claim area, Danvers pulled his suitcase through the doors and out into the night.

I can't possibly have a horror/dark fantasy collection without featuring one of my most popular characters, Dan Shamble, Zombie P.I. Dan has starred in seven novels so far and a lot of short stories. "Role Model" is one of my favorites, and I have read it aloud many times at science fiction conventions. You'll see why.

SF conventions, comic cons, and pop-culture expos have been a major part of my life, and I know them inside and out. I pulled on a lifetime of experience to get these details right.

Role Model

A Dan Shamble,
Zombie P.I. Adventure

—I—

C ome on, Shamble—it'll be fun," said Officer Toby McGoohan, my best human friend. He acted as if he'd gotten season tickets to his favorite sports team.

I was immediately suspicious, sure that this would not be typical police business. "I don't even know what a cosplay convention is, McGoo."

He had met me outside the offices of Chambeaux & Deyer Investigations, seemingly by happy coincidence as he walked his beat, but we both knew it wasn't an accident. He'd been waiting for me.

"Cosplay—costume playing. It's when people dress up as characters from their favorite movies, TV shows, comics, video games, whatever." He had looked it up online, so he considered himself an expert.

"Oh. Trick or treat for grown-ups." Every day in the Unnatural Quarter, I saw a parade of werewolves, mummies, vampires, zombies, ghosts, witches, and second-string monsters, so I wasn't going to be impressed by a few interesting costumes.

"A lot more than that. These people think they *are* the characters. It gets a little intense. And weird. And fun."

It didn't sound any stranger than my usual cases, and McGoo and I often helped each other out. "So why do they need a zombie detective?"

He seemed exasperated that I was spoiling his fun by being such a hard sell. "They don't *need* a zombie detective any more than they need a beat cop, but the hotel manager is nervous about having such big crowds—naturals, unnaturals, all those people running around in costumes. Thought he might need some extra security." McGoo flashed one of those grins that had, over the years, convinced me to do things that would get us both in trouble. "Besides, he gave us two free passes to the con."

He's a redhead with a round, freckled face and a rough sense of humor (to put it mildly). We've been friends for a long time, even back when I was still alive, and our friendship had survived me coming back as one of the walking dead. If a friendship can survive that, it can survive anything (though he still makes jokes about the unsightly bullet hole in my forehead).

My caseload at Chambeaux & Deyer Investigations was light at the moment, so I shrugged and agreed to go. I had already been to the Worldwide Horror Convention when it was held in the Quarter last year. I assumed this would be the same sort of thing.

So, that was why the two of us found ourselves in the lobby of the Motel Six Feet Under and Conference Center standing next to two clattery silver-armored Cylons from the old *Battlestar Galactica* TV show. They gleamed and hummed, red optical sensors in their helmet visors drifting to and fro.

"CosplayCon security," one said in a vibrating synthetic voice that I could barely understand. He took his helmet off to reveal a young man with dark sweat-plastered hair. "Whew, those things get hot after awhile! Thanks for joining us, but I doubt you guys'll be needed. We don't expect any trouble. Everyone has a good time at the con."

As I looked around the lobby and common areas, I saw Klingons with wicked-looking bat'leths, masked ninjas with curved swords, Star Wars stormtroopers with heavy blasters, Lord of the Rings orcs with large battle-axes.

"How could there possibly be trouble?" I asked. "Nothing looks harmful at all."

"All the weapons are peace-bonded," said the Cylon. When I gave him a blank look and McGoo didn't seem to recognize the term from his extensive Wikipedia research, the Cylon security guard said, "Zip-tied. Everything's strapped down, so the bladed weapons are perfectly safe. And, of course, the blasters are just molded resin props. The Jedi lightsabers are neon tubes." The Cylon put his helmet back on and told us in his monotone robotic voice, "Have fun—and stay in character," then marched off with a clatter of silver armor.

Tables had been set up in the hall with volunteer staff doing their best to register attendees. This was the first year of CosplayCon in the Unnatural Quarter, and they were glad for the added attraction of real monster attendees as well as cosplayers.

A banner over the registration area proclaimed, "We are all someone else inside!" and the program book cover said, "Find your inner YOU!" as if this was a therapy session. Maybe it was—costume therapy.

At the motel front desk, a lone vampire clerk shook his head at all the costumes. He muttered, "Bunch of weirdos," then went back to a magazine he was reading. I didn't see why costumed fans were any weirder than the socially acceptable sports fans who put Viking helmets or cheese wedges on their heads.

Normally on a slow Saturday I might have walked around the Quarter with my ghost girlfriend Sheyenne or helped my lawyer partner Robin Deyer finish paperwork on cases. Like any workaholic, I had "fun" by doing my job—solving cases and helping clients. It was my reason for living, in a loose definition of the term.

More than a decade ago, a ridiculously improbable alignment of planets, coincidences, and real-world events had caused the Big Uneasy—a magical phenomenon that brought legendary and supernatural creatures back to the world: vampires, werewolves, ghosts, ghouls, gargoyles, mummies and, yes, zombies. The unnaturals tended to gather in this section of the city where they were accepted, where they felt right at home.

But they still had problems, just like anyone else. While most unnaturals lived perfectly normal everyday lives, some were criminals; others wanted a divorce; others needed to find lost family members. A detective working in the Quarter had the same sort of cases as a mundane detective on the outside, but the clientele was a little stranger.

Back when I was living, and trying to *make* a living, I'd hung out my shingle and partnered up with young firebrand Robin Deyer. I had a good run, a successful business, before I was killed. But, as I said, I *like* doing what I do. So, when I came back from the dead, I just got back to work.

In the Unnatural Quarter, being a zombie is no handicap to being a detective, though I insist on maintaining my physical appearance, bathing regularly, going for scheduled top-offs at the embalming parlor, even seeing to it that I receive my monthly maintenance spell. I won't let myself turn into one of those slobbering shuffling embarrassments that make polite society turn up their noses at zombies.

I'm accustomed to seeing monsters in my everyday life, but I had to admit these costumes were amazing, even a little intimidating, when I started to think about the obsessive time and effort the fans had put into making them.

A squad of white-armored Star Wars stormtroopers marched past, representing the 501st Legion, led by an impressive black-caped and wheezing Darth Vader impersonator.

A group of Klingons had taken over the motel's woefully inadequate coffee shop and sat around the tables, pounding fists and demanding more coffee. They grew louder and more unruly by the minute, while a harried-looking mummy waitress tried her best to serve them.

A drunk furry fan was coming on to a full-furred werewolf busboy, who didn't know how to react to all the unwarranted and unwanted attention.

"See, told you this would be fun, Shamble," McGoo said. "Look over there, it's the Doctor. How many can you name?"

I looked around, but only saw a random assortment of eccentric-looking men. "Who?"

McGoo rolled his eyes. "Let's not get into the Abbott and Costello routine. Dr. Who. The first one there with short dark hair—he's the David Tennant Doctor. And the one with the scarf —you gotta recognize *him*—it's a Tom Baker lookalike, probably the most classic Dr. Who. And the one with the bow tie—Matt Smith."

Even after all this time, I was surprised to learn something new about my friend. "I didn't know you were a fanboy, McGoo."

"Not to this extent," he said, gesturing around. "But I've got a TV, and I am culturally aware."

One tall beanpole fan peered over the crowd, trying to reach the information table. Finally, he gave up and just yelled, "What time is Van Helsing going to be on stage?" Some of the vampire attendees booed.

"Five o'clock in the main ballroom," yelled an unseen person from behind the desk.

Four skinny guys in clinging red shirts from classic *Star Trek* walked by, and someone yelled in mock panic, "Look out, it's redshirts!" I couldn't see why they posed any kind of threat; in fact, the tight shirts emphasized how scrawny their arms and chests were. If that was the kind of security available to Captain Kirk and crew, no wonder the old show got canceled after only three seasons.

For my own part, I wore my usual sports jacket with crudely stitched-up bullet holes and my fedora—it's my trademark, and what P.I. would be without one? McGoo wore his blue beat-cop uniform, and everyone seemed to think he was playing a part from an old police show. Several fans came up with very clever guesses from obscure programs that I hadn't heard of in years. One fan marched up with a sneer, poked a finger at McGoo's chest, and said, "T.J. Hooker—not Shatner's best," then walked away without waiting for a response.

Suddenly, we heard yelling from the mezzanine open area and the sounds of a growing altercation. McGoo glanced at me. "This is what we're here for, Shamble. Come on."

We ran up the stairs (and I use the term "ran" loosely, since my joints are stiff enough that it takes me awhile to get up to speed). A group of rowdy Klingons yelled, "Star Trek is better!" One heavyset Klingon woman had the loudest voice of all.

Across the room, the 501st stormtroopers, who had made an uneasy alliance with costumed Jedi Knights and Mandalorian bounty hunters, took offense. "Star Wars is better!"

"Star Trek!" insisted the Klingons.

"No, Star Wars!" The intellectual debate continued in that fashion for a few more exchanges before the groups ran forward and clashed in an all-out brawl. The Klingons struggled to draw their bat'leths against the peace-bonding ties. The stormtroopers punched and pummeled with a clatter of white plastic armor. The Jedi Knights lit their fluorescent-tube lightsabers but were careful not to damage them.

Before McGoo and I could break up the fight, the group of redshirts rushed into the fray, trying to drive the combatants apart. Eventually, the Klingons brushed themselves off and the 501sters adjusted their body armor. Somehow, the only ones genuinely battered, bruised, and injured in the fight were the redshirts.

"You're right, McGoo. This is fun." I smiled.

Wandering about to get the lay of the con, we walked past large and small panel rooms, costuming workshops, and autograph tables featuring bit actors from long-canceled programs. One large room hosted a "robot smash" where model-builders pitted a remote-controlled R2D2 against a more ominous-looking Dalek. The two machines clashed, with the Dalek crying in a synthesized voice, "Annihilate, Annihilate!" while R2D2 responded with a series of incomprehensible but clearly rude beeps and squeals.

Primarily, though, people wanted to show off their outfits (or lack thereof, in the case of some of the very scantily clad barbarian princesses).

A hard-faced Asian woman wearing a COSTUME JUDGE

badge blocked my way. As she ran her critical gaze up and down my appearance, she looked as if she'd had her sense of humor surgically removed. In an officious voice, she said, "I've seen one or two of you already at the con, but your costume isn't up to snuff." She clucked her tongue, then tugged on the front of my sport jacket. "Wrong number of bullet holes on the left. That exit wound in your forehead is at least a centimeter off. And that makeup is terrible. It should be blended more."

"But I'm the real one," I said. "I *am* Dan Chambeaux."

She rolled her eyes. "Right, keep telling yourself that. Getting into character is important, but you have to take the costume seriously, too. After a decade as a cosplayer, trust me, I know what I'm talking about. If you're going to be a zombie detective, at least do it right." She walked off muttering.

Loud enough to slice through the background noise came a bloodcurdling scream—and not the good kind of bloodcurdling scream. We hurried toward the source, as did all the other attendees, as if the shriek somehow signaled free beer for everyone.

McGoo and I shoved our way toward a small second-floor panel room, but a crowd had already clogged the door. We tried to jostle people aside, but they reacted as if we were just fellow costumers. So, we got more aggressive and finally made it through the door.

A stormtrooper lay sprawled on his back on the floor—with a wooden stake protruding from his chest. It had been pounded right through the white armor plate.

A burly Klingon stood over him, raising both hands. His bronze skin was flushed, and his mouth drawn back in panic. "I just found him like that!"

A young woman in the back of the room—a motel employee holding a pitcher of water for the next panel—screamed again for good measure, although her first scream had already accomplished whatever a scream could do.

By now, all the formerly brawling Star Wars and Star Trek fans had made their way to the crime scene. The man in the Vader suit came huffing up behind them all, gasping with real exertion that was louder than the sound of his respirator voice box. The stormtroopers reeled when they saw their murdered comrade. One of the troopers looked through the open door and cried out, "Oh, no! It's TK-9399!"

I asked, "You can tell that just at a glance?"

The helmet turned toward me. "Of course, look at the red shoulder pauldron. It's very distinctive. That's TK-9399 all right."

"Yes, I suppose it is." I turned and called out, "Is there a doctor in the house?" The David Tennant, Matt Smith, and Tom Baker Whos arrived, drawing sonic screwdrivers and looking eager to help. I revised my shout. "Somebody call an ambulance."

McGoo drove the spectators away. "Out of the way, all of you. This is a crime scene."

"I didn't do it!" yelled the Klingon, unable to tear his gaze from the body on the floor. "I didn't touch him!"

McGoo turned to him. "I'm Officer Toby McGoohan from the UQPD. I need to ask you some questions. What's your name?"

The Klingon composed himself and said proudly, "I am Ach-gLokh Heqht!"

McGoo had drawn a pad from his pocket, poised to take down the information, but didn't know how to spell it. "Is that a name, or are you coughing up phlegm?"

"That is how I got my name!"

"Ach-gLokh Heqht didn't do it!" claimed a loud and busty Klingon woman. "I was with him at the time."

"No, you weren't," I said. "I saw you in the altercation up on the mezzanine just a few minutes ago."

"You would call me a liar?" The Klingon female strode forward as if she meant to tear my limbs off.

I've already been through having a limb torn off, though, and found it unpleasant. I backed away, trying to be calm. "Just stating a fact, ma'am. It won't do for an alibi."

The Klingons regrouped and tried to come up with something else. McGoo and I bent over the staked stormtrooper.

"Take his bucket off," called one of the troopers in a sad voice. It took me a minute to realize that he meant the helmet.

McGoo shook his head. "Nothing gets removed until the Coroner examines him."

"What if he's not entirely dead?" I asked. "Never can tell these days."

Though it went against normal police procedure, McGoo couldn't argue with that. "Right, Shamble. Better make sure." He and I carefully lifted off the victim's helmet without disturbing any other part of the armor.

Then we discovered an even greater surprise. The dead stormtrooper TK-9399 was a vampire.

—II—

The ambulance and the Coroner's wagon arrived together with a dueling set of screeching their tires in the motel's designated "Coroner" and "Ambulance" parking spot. (The two spots saw frequent use.)

McGoo had called for UQPD backup, and now half a dozen uniformed officers swarmed through the Motel Six Feet Under and Conference Center ... which was even more confusing because some of the cosplayers wore similar—some might say better executed—uniforms, including one dressed up as the T-1000 from Terminator 2.

The Klingons had commandeered the coffee shop again, where they demanded goblets of warm bloodwine to celebrate the life of TK-9399, whose soul had now gone off to some place called Sto-vo-kor ... which sparked a lively discussion as to whether Star Wars fans could even go to Sto-vo-kor, or if that was exclusively limited to the Star Trek franchise.

McGoo and I went to the Con-Ops room, just off the registration area. We met the pot-bellied and balding con chairman named Phil Somerstein. He looked bleary-eyed, harried, and overworked with management details. The murder of one of the CosplayCon attendees seemed just one more hassle he had to deal with.

McGoo said, "This is an active investigation, Mr. Somerstein. I'm going to have to impose a lockdown. The murderer is likely still in the motel, and until we've had a chance to talk to everybody, we'll need your help in insuring that all of your attendees stay put."

Somerstein wiped a sweaty palm across a sweaty forehead. "Officer McGoohan, you don't understand—this is *con weekend*. Nobody's leaving the motel, with or without a lockdown."

The elevator chimed, and the doors slid open to reveal two uniformed trolls from the Coroner's office. They wheeled a gurney on which rested the zipped-up body bag. They had placed TK-9399's white bucket on his chest like a memorial, and as they rolled the gurney past, the other 501sters stood in a solemn honor guard, their heads bowed. Darth Vader also hung his helmet, flicking off the respirator in a sign of respect.

One of the stormtroopers shook his white helmet. "He never stopped trooping."

The crime scene techs had swarmed in with their kits, taking the necessary photos, although many of them spent too much time taking additional photos of sexy Xenas and Wonder Womans (Wonder Women?) who posed for the shots. The police detectives conducted interviews. Off in a quiet area they were taking statements from a Batman and an Indiana Jones.

McGoo looked overwhelmed already. "I may need your help with this, Shamble."

"The cases don't solve themselves," I said. "And you did promise me this would be fun." I was already starting to formulate a plan.

Ach-gLokh Heqht was the obvious suspect, and I've been a detective long enough to know that the obvious suspect usually isn't the guilty one in the end. Besides, if all these cosplayers were really into their characters, why would a Klingon kill someone by pounding a wooden stake through the chest? TK-9399 was a vampire, however, so the murderer's options had been limited. Still, I would have expected a Klingon to, say, decapitate him with a bat'leth and stuff his mouth full of garlic. Then I realized the white bucket would have posed a challenge to the garlic follow-up....

"I can help," said a cheery voice. "It's what I do."

I turned, and faced myself—or at least a reasonable facsimile of me. He extended his hand. "Dan Shamble, Zombie P.I."

I was taken aback—he had the fedora, the bullet hole in his forehead (though shifted a centimeter closer to center than mine was), and his skin was pallid. His sport jacket had prominent stitched-up holes. His facial features even bore a strong resemblance to mine. "You dressed up as me?"

"It's an honor to meet you, Mr. Shamble. I've read all your books."

"They're not actually my books," I said. "Someone else writes them, and they're just loosely based on my actual cases." In fact, I found it embarrassing that Howard Phillips Publishing kept releasing comedic horror mysteries that featured the cases of a fictitious zombie detective, based on me. "Just as long as you remember that I'm the real one." I paused to consider. "I'll call *you* Fanble."

He seemed disappointed. "But I have to believe I'm the real Dan Shamble. It's cosplay. I'm in character. Cosplay means you *are* that character, not just dressed like him. It's all about finding the real *me* inside."

"Right. I saw the program book."

McGoo looked from Fanble to me and back to Fanble again. "Usually one Shamble's enough, but we have a lot of potential witnesses and a lot of potential suspects." He raised an eyebrow, as if about to give a test. "Hey, Fanble, have you heard this one? A skeleton walks into a bar, says to the bartender, 'Give me a beer ... and a mop!'"

Fanble managed to stay in character by not laughing any more than I did. McGoo has an unfortunate repertoire of bad jokes.

McGoo shook his head. "Yeah, Shamble, he's just like you."

He started off down the hall. "Let me talk to the crime scene techs to see what they found."

I nodded. "Meanwhile, I'll go meet with the stormtroopers, learn more about the victim."

"We're on it, McGoo," said Fanble. "The cases don't solve themselves."

—III—

After TK-9399 had been hauled away in a body bag, CosplayCon got right back into swing as if nothing had happened. The attendees waited all year for this event, and they worked on their costumes with obsessive attention to detail. They weren't going to let a simple thing like a murder ruin their fun.

I didn't know what to think about Fanble. He seemed earnest and more serious about being "me" than I was. He took great care to imitate my movements, my mannerisms. It was like having my own portable 3D mirror walking alongside me. I decided to accept the help, though. Two heads are better than one when trying to solve a case.

The 501st troopers were nowhere to be found. I looked around, frustrated. "How do you hide a bunch of fans in identical white armor or a tall man in a Darth Vader suit?"

Fanble responded, "It's our job to find out. We are detectives, after all."

As we walked down the hall, other con attendees gave admiring glances and complimented us on our realistic costumes. When I assessed Fanble again, I realized that the bullet hole in his forehead was in the correct spot after all. I must not have noticed it before. We looked like twins.

But the grin on his face made him appear immature and idiotic. Did I really look like that? "Don't smile so much," I said. "It's out of character." He immediately resumed a stern "I'm a P.I. and I'm at work" expression.

A young man impersonating Edward from *Twilight*—who didn't look like any real vampire I had ever met in the Quarter—

asked us if we knew when and where Van Helsing would be giving his talk. Fanble gave him the Crown Ballroom number, then asked if "Edward" knew where we could find the 501st members. I wouldn't have expected a character from *Twilight* to pay much attention to Star Wars personnel, but the imitation sparkler directed us to an unused panel room that the stormtroopers had commandeered.

Fanble and I looked at each other. "Do you think they're discussing the case? Maybe working out a retaliation against the Klingons?" he asked.

"Maybe they're holding some kind of memorial for TK-9399," I said. We found the door and pulled it open without knocking. In detective school I was taught that it's best to surprise your suspects.

The surprise wasn't exactly what I'd intended, though, because we came upon a group of half-undressed stormtroopers. Definitely not something I'd ever intended to see.

"Oh, excuse us," I said.

Fanble added in a gruff, no-nonsense voice, "We're investigating the murder of a Mr. TK-9399."

The troopers had taken off their helmets and shucked out of their white resin armor. They stood around in skintight body gloves while they adjusted boots, butt plates, greaves, and shin plates.

"Come on in, but close the door," said the troop leader, who identified himself as TK-6370. "We've got an important troop in an hour, lots of exposure, lots of attention. We wanted to check our kits."

"I'm sorry about your fallen trooper," I said. "We're trying to determine who killed him and why."

The stormtroopers grew solemn. "Poor TK-9399. Even after he died and came back as a vampire, nothing changed. I've never seen a fan so dedicated. Star Wars is a way of life." That trooper identified himself as TK-7246.

Another trooper, TK-9754 , said, "I'm going to miss TK-9399. Sure, he was a fan. Sure, he was a vampire. But he didn't let that change who he was. TK-9399 always used to say, 'Star Wars is my life, and now it's my unlife.'" He picked up a piece of white plastic and turned to the person beside him. "Help me with my codpiece, will you?"

The man in the Darth Vader suit flicked his respirator box on and off, fiddled with the sound effects, then unsnapped a compartment on his wide utility belt to remove a roll of menthol cough drops. "TK-9399 caused quite a stir by trooping as a vampire. He was an activist, even wanted to form an Unnatural Quarter garrison. He tried to round up Star Wars fans among the werewolves, mummies, and ghosts." He tugged on his black gloves. "He thought it would be cool to have a real ghost Obi-Wan and Anakin, maybe even a troll dressing up as Yoda. TK-9399 didn't expect to cause trouble by expanding the fanbase."

TK-6370 chimed in (and I was proud of myself for remembering the name/number), "Star Wars is a pretty diverse universe. Think of the cantina scene, or Jabba's Palace. Gamorreans and Jawas, Twi'Leks and Trandoshans, Gungans, Ithorians—even Chiss and Khomms and Dathomiri."

TK-5794 snorted. "Chiss and Khomms and Dathomiri are from the Expanded Universe. I hear even Disney's dumping those now."

"They still count," insisted TK-6370.

"And don't mention Gungans. I want a Jar-Jar free convention," said another trooper; I was starting to lose track of the numbers.

"Point is, everybody gets along just fine. Why can't vampire fans and human fans share a love of Star Wars? But TK-10625 certainly didn't like it. He claimed it was ruining the purity of Star Wars, to which we all said, 'Excuse me, *Star Wars Holiday Special*?'"

"And *Greedo* shooting first? Like *that's* pure?" piped up another trooper, to a general groan of assent.

"TK-10625?" I asked, looking around.

"What really bothered TK-10625 was that TK-9399 had to wear a modified stormtrooper suit and armor once he became a vampire. Added sun protection so he could troop out in broad daylight as long as he wanted," said TK-5470. "But TK-10625 said the modifications made the armor an unofficial variant and therefore non-canon."

Several troopers groaned simultaneously. "Let's not get into the canon discussion again."

"But TK-10625 can be a stubborn and angry man. He didn't like the idea of an Unnatural Quarter garrison at all, and he made no secret about that."

Fanble stepped up. "Where is TK-10625 now? We'd like to talk with him."

"Not here," said TK-6370 with a sigh. "Just after the con started, he and TK-9399 got into a huge argument. TK-10625 stormed off, and we haven't seen him since. I was surprised TK-10625 agreed to troop at CosplayCon in the first place."

I glanced at Fanble, then looked at the troopers. "A huge argument? And TK-9399 was murdered right after that?"

The man in the Vader suit frowned. "Sure, but a lot of things happened right around then. I mean, the con was getting into full swing."

TK-5794 glanced at the wall clock. "Time's tight. Better get ready to troop."

TK-6370 nodded. "Happy to help with the investigation, but we've got to be on stage in a few minutes."

Fanble also looked anxious. "I have to go, too, Mr. Shamble."

"It's Chambeaux," I said. "You should know better. What's so important?"

"Van Helsing is about to take the main stage. Who wants to miss that?"

I had intended to miss it, but I let Fanble go, and he dashed off so he could get a good seat. The 501sters finished adjusting their armor components. TK-6370 said, "Buckets on!" and they all donned their helmets. I was now in a room full of identical stormtroopers (although one of them seemed a little short). The man in the Vader suit flicked on his respirator, seated his black helmet in place.

"What is this important troop you're doing?" I asked.

Between gasping breaths, his words garbled by the cough drop, the Vader impersonator said, "We're escorting Van Helsing in the main ballroom."

"And ... how can you tell each other apart?"

"We *are* supposed to be clones," said one trooper, and they marched out.

—IV—

Out in the common area, a Heath Ledger version of the Joker was comparing notes with a Cesar Romero version of the Joker as the crowds made their way toward the ballroom, ready for the main event.

Since I was alone for the moment, I took a few minutes to call the office—not because I had any important pending cases, but because I wanted to talk to Sheyenne. "Sorry, Spooky, this was our date day," I said. "You would've enjoyed hanging out at this cosplay convention."

I could picture her ethereal spectral form as she sat at her desk in Chambeaux & Deyer Investigations. She would hold the phone, smiling, her sparkling blue eyes lighting up. "You always take me to interesting places, 'Beaux."

"Interesting ... right. This time a murder's gotten in the way. Star Wars fan dressed up in a stormtrooper outfit found dead with a stake through his heart. Turns out he was a vampire. We've got a Klingon as our main witness."

"Oh, another one of those," Sheyenne said. "Are we on the case?"

"I'm here helping McGoo. The motel's on lockdown, but no one seems interested in leaving anyway."

"Let me know if you need our help. Robin and I are here for you."

"I've already picked up an unexpected sidekick," I said, looking around for Fanble, but I didn't see him among the crowds. "I'll explain later."

After I said goodbye to Sheyenne, McGoo came up, red-faced and harried. "I tell you, Shamble, this is turning out to be a full-fledged cluster-frack."

"Cluster-frack? That's a new one."

"From the new *Battlestar Galactica*, Shamble. Get with it." He mopped his forehead. "Ach-gLokh Heqht has gone missing—and the rest of the Klingons aren't talking. He was our only suspect."

"We might have another person of interest." I explained about the internal dispute between TK-9399 and TK-10625.

McGoo looked interested. "All right, let's have a talk with him. Is he with the other stormtroopers?"

"Unfortunately, no. He's gone missing as well."

"How do you lose a Klingon and a stormtrooper in the same day?" McGoo asked, then looked at the chaos of convention-goers and answered his own question.

I said, "I'm going to the main ballroom to see Van Helsing's keynote speech. Since the man's known for killing vampires, it's worth a look."

McGoo, meanwhile, had to get back to the crime scene. The techs had promised some preliminary results.

I entered the Crown Ballroom, where hundreds of chairs were spread out—and every one was occupied. I worked my way through the costumed and uncostumed fans, many of whom were unnaturals: curious zombies and werewolves carrying comic book issues and limited-edition action figures. A burly, bent-over hunchback clutched a pack of *Magic: The Gathering* cards, and a mummy held a first-edition papyrus scroll covered with hieroglyphics that he claimed was the "real" ashcan version of *Action Comics Issue* 0, available only in Ancient Egypt. He was excited at the prospect of getting it signed by one of the ghost comic creators.

Vampires comprised the majority of the seated audience, apparently having a love-hate relationship with Van Helsing.

Over the ballroom PA system, loud music started playing the thunderous notes of the Imperial March. The audience applauded and booed simultaneously as the costumed Darth Vader strode out from backstage, his black cape flowing, boots pounding on the rickety raised platform, respirator chugging. He reached the podium, lifted his black gloves, and waited for the crowd noise to die down. In his best James Earl Jones impersonation, the suited Vader said, "Some consider me a bad guy, a person who took a walk on the dark side of the Force and enjoyed it. But I did get better in the end."

Several fans in the audience grumbled. I couldn't tell if they disliked his original villainy or his epiphany.

"My exploits are nothing, however, compared to the man I'm about to introduce. The greatest villain known to monsters ... the bloodiest serial killer in all of vampire history."

The crowd grew more raucous. They screamed, yelled, and hissed. The vampires in the audience rose to their feet, shaking their fists.

"CosplayCon is proud to present our special guest: For one day only—Honest Abe Van Helsing!"

Vader turned and extended an arm in a dramatic gesture to the curtains at stage left. The vamps screamed and roared, then werewolves joined in, and finally everyone in the audience shared in the hate.

With a clatter of plastic armor, the stormtroopers marched in as an honor guard around a man in a trench coat and floppy hat. He had a narrow face, long dark hair, stubbly beard. I wasn't familiar with this incarnation of the character, but he seemed to exude predatory evil and bloodlust. His eyes were close-set and blazing.

When Vader yielded the podium to the guest of honor, Van Helsing just stood there in silence, spreading his glare across the audience and basking in the anger he provoked. "Thank you for the warm welcome. It makes my blood boil, seeing all of you disgusting creatures out there. You think you're safe. You think CosplayCon is harmless fun."

A ghost in the audience yelled, "Boo!"

Van Helsing parted his trench coat like a lecherous flasher to show dozens of sharp wooden stakes tucked into his belt, as well as long knives and a bandolier of garlic bulbs across his chest. "I've only got an hour, so I'll just hit the highlights of my career. Let me reminisce about some of the scumbag bloodsuckers I've slain over the years. Ah, there are so many.... Good times!"

The vampires howled so loudly they sounded like werewolves.

"Dracula was the one I killed most often, but that guy's like a Timex watch—takes a staking and keeps on sucking!" He laughed at his own joke. A few audience members groaned. Van Helsing rattled off his favorite impalements, beheadings, or solar overexposures.

As the crowd grew angrier, I wondered if they remembered that this was just a guy in costume, a fan playing a character. Van Helsing seemed to be really getting into the spirit of his cosplay. *Find your inner YOU!*

Thinking of that, I looked around for Fanble, since he'd been so interested in the speech, but I couldn't spot him in the packed ballroom. I did see a couple of other Dan Shambles, though not as well executed as Fanble's costume.

Even so, I realized that Fanble's preoccupation with me as an alter ego was nothing more than innocent fun. Van Helsing's role-playing seemed deadly serious. If this guy truly believed his mission was to kill vampires, and if he happened to find a vampire stormtrooper alone in an empty panel room, maybe he wouldn't have been able to resist.

I needed to find out if one of his wooden stakes was missing.

After the hour-long panel was over, the crowd filed out of the ballroom, while a few people rushed the stage to mob Van Helsing with questions and curses. Since I had a few questions of my own, I pushed forward, too. "Excuse me, coming through—zombie detective, coming through! Official business—zombie detective."

When I finally reached the front, fans were pushing program books at Van Helsing for him to autograph while Cylon security guards tried to herd people into an organized signing line. When I was within earshot, I introduced myself, which got Van Helsing's attention. Although he had a grudge against vampires, other types of undead didn't knot his undies quite so much. "Are you aware there's been a murder here at the con, Mr. Van Helsing?"

"*Doctor* Van Helsing."

"Whatever." I decided to let him stay in character. "A vampire stormtrooper was murdered with a stake through his heart."

"Murdered?" Van Helsing raised his dark eyebrows. "If he was a vampire, wasn't he already dead? I'd call that house-cleaning, not murder."

The gathered vamps spewed more hatred, but Van Helsing ignored them. He looked me in the eye and said, "Vampires everywhere are fair game—even at a cosplay convention. They'd better watch out."

His comment was greeted by more venomous ire ... yet somehow his autographing line got even longer.

–V–

The initial report from the crime scene techs did not contain any good news. McGoo let out a sigh. "Whenever I have a case like this, why can't we just turn up a simple clue and an obvious explanation?"

"Whenever you have a case like *this*? When do you ever have a case like this?"

"When I'm around you, Shamble, more often than not."

The crime scene techs had dusted the wooden stake from TK-9399's chest but found no fingerprints. McGoo tried to draw conclusions. "That means it could have been another stormtrooper—they all wear gloves."

"So does the Darth Vader guy," I pointed out, then attempted to remember whether the Klingon Ach-gLokh Heqht had worn gloves as well. "And so do the Cylons. And so do half the cosplayers here. And why limit it to that? Many con attendees are unnaturals, and a lot of them don't have fingerprints at all."

"Yeah, I guess the lack of fingerprints doesn't limit the suspect pool by much."

As McGoo and I talked, two full-furred werewolves walked by, laughing and bumping shoulders. Each wore a Jayne hat, an odd-looking orange-and-brown stocking cap that looked as if it had been knitted by a blind but well-meaning grandmother. The two were immediately adopted by a group of similarly chapeau'ed Browncoat fans of *Firefly*, the long-ago canceled show from which the style derived. I realized that everyone seemed to be part of one big happy fannish family. All fun and games, until someone gets murdered.

The Motel Six Feet Under was still on lockdown, with uniformed police officers at all doors, but the attendees didn't seem distressed, or even interested in leaving. As McGoo and I contemplated our next step, Fanble strutted up, looking as if he had just won some kind of costume contest. "I got a break in the case," he said.

McGoo looked at me. "How did he figure it out before you?"

Fanble adjusted the fedora. "Never underestimate Dan Shamble, Zombie P.I. I had a hunch and, getting into character, I convinced the con chairman to let me see the registration records. He thought I was you." He nodded toward me, then continued his summary. "I discovered that Ach-gLokh Heqht and TK-10625 both registered under the same street name! They're the same person in real life."

McGoo looked at me. "Now that's unexpected."

Fanble nodded again. "Indeed. Crossover fandom doesn't typically happen."

I said, "The Klingon and the stormtrooper were our two most likely suspects. If they're the same person, then it sounds like a slam dunk." I grudgingly added, "Good work, Fanble."

Fanble grinned before he remembered to get back into character. "The cases don't solve themselves."

"So, what's his real name?" McGoo asked.

Fanble showed great pride as he revealed the identity of our likely perpetrator. "John Doe."

Just knowing the suspect's name didn't help much, though. We had no idea what John Doe really looked like, not that anyone really "looked like" themselves at CosplayCon. *Find your Inner YOU!*

If Ach-gLokh Heqht/TK-10625 knew he was wanted for detailed questioning, however, maybe he would hole up where he wouldn't be seen.

"Let's check with the front desk and get his room number," I suggested. "We might find some clues there."

The desk clerk stood behind the front counter, using it as a protective barricade against the costumed fans. McGoo meant business as he strode up and flashed his badge. "UQPD. I need you to let me into a room."

To show that I meant business, too, I held out my official private investigator's ID card. "Zombie detective. I'm with him."

Fanble flashed a fake ID, which, I had to admit, looked pretty good. "Zombie Detective II, Cosplay Edition. I'm with them."

The motel desk clerk, a rabbity little vampire who looked as if he currently regretted his choice of employment, fluttered his hands, mumbled, and turned the computer screen toward him. "And what name is it under?"

"John Doe," McGoo said.

The desk manager keyed it in. "Yes, we do have a John Doe. He's in room 1013. May I see your search warrant?"

McGoo smiled benignly at the officious request. "It's a ... welfare check, not a search. We have information that someone may be injured."

"Oh dear, of course! I'll make you a duplicate key."

The three of us waited for an elevator. And waited. And waited. Each elevator stopped at every single floor. The doors finally opened at lobby level to disgorge a throng of cosplayers.

McGoo waved his badge and said, "Police business, we're commandeering this elevator." I pushed the button for 10, and we began to ride upward, but of course we stopped at every floor on the way up. Soon the elevator was jammed with imaginary characters. It was a relief to get off on the tenth floor.

McGoo pounded on the door of John Doe's room. "Police! Open up." When we received no response, he slipped the magnetic card into the key slot and opened the door. "Okay, we're coming in." Before entering, McGoo drew his revolver, and I pulled out my .38.

I was surprised when Fanble also pulled out an identical .38. "Is that real?"

"Part of the costume, for that added bit of realism."

McGoo frowned. "Shouldn't it be peace-bonded, like they said?"

He looked too much like me when he responded, "It would be if they knew about it."

Together, we entered John Doe's hotel room. The shades were drawn. A suitcase was open on the luggage rack. Clothes lay strewn around the floor and furniture, but the room was silent.

"Looks like nobody's home," McGoo said.

"Records showed that only one person checked in here." I glanced at all the clothes.

"Fans often share a room at cons to save money," said Fanble, picking up a long Dr. Who scarf draped over the back of a chair. "Maybe John Doe is more than one person."

McGoo bent over to inspect a half-open black suitcase that contained all the components of stormtrooper armor. "There's not enough normal stuff here, though. Only one suitcase of street clothes."

I found a complete Klingon outfit tossed roughly in the corner. Behind the chair, McGoo was startled to come face to face with a polished silvery Cylon suit.

Fanble was amazed. "You know, we never did see any of those characters together at the same time."

"How could you tell?" McGoo went into the bathroom and studied the vanity counter—saw only one toothbrush and a set of basic toiletries. "No makeup here, no prosthetics or wigs. How did he manage that whole turtle head for his Klingon outfit, or the mop of hair for Dr. Who?"

As I went to the closet, I felt a sense of dread. Normally in the Unnatural Quarter you might find skeletons in any random closet, but this time I found something else. When I slid the door aside, I saw the complete Van Helsing outfit hanging there—the trench coat, the bandolier of garlic bulbs, the floppy hat, the belt loaded with wooden stakes.

And yes indeed, one of the stakes was missing.

—VI—

TK-9399 had somehow made himself a target for either Ach-gLokh Heqht, or TK-10625, or Van Helsing. An intersection of motives. And if the killer had an entirely flexible murderous intent, then CosplayCon was full of potential victims.

We had to find John Doe—and soon. And among hundreds of disguises.

Fanble had had the bright idea to cross-check the registrations, discovering that the various suspect characters were all under the same street name. I had the equally brilliant idea of flipping that around: we could look up any registrations submitted by "John Doe" and find out what other characters he intended to play. Since we'd already found the Klingon, stormtrooper, Dr. Who, and Cylon outfits discarded in the hotel room, John Doe had to be wandering around the con dressed as someone or something else.

As precious seconds ticked away, McGoo, Fanble, and I waited for the interminable elevator. Each time the doors opened, the car was going up, not down. Finally, when another upbound elevator opened on Floor 10, two of the costumed fans motioned us in anyway. "Dude," said a Star Trek redshirt, "you have to go *up* to go *down*."

So, we rode the elevator up to Floor 14, then back down to the lobby (again, stopping at every floor). When we reached the lobby, McGoo bolted out, and the two of us zombie detectives—both the fake one and the real one—followed him to the con registration desk.

CosplayCon was in full swing, with attendees preparing for the evening's big masquerade, though I couldn't see how an official "masquerade" was any different from the rest of the day here. Natural and unnatural fans were grinning. Werewolves got their pictures taken with Wolverines and a too-scrawny-looking Thor.

We had a case to solve. I could enjoy the con after we captured the murderer.

The registration desk wasn't busy this time of day, since everyone already had their badges and set about to enjoy the convention (at least those who hadn't been murdered or were considered suspects). No one was going in or out of the Motel Six Feet Under because of the lockdown.

A woman sat behind the information table, happily knitting, while a forlorn cat sat in a zipped-up pet carrier beside her. The woman looked up. "How may I help you?"

"We need to cross-reference your database," McGoo said. "One of the con attendees, Mr. John Doe, registered as several different cosplay characters. We need to know the full list, so we can track him down."

She frowned and set down her knitting close to the cat carrier; inside, the feline batted at the sidewalls, trying to catch the yarn. "Our computers are down right now, but fortunately, we rely on a more efficient analog system." She pulled out a large plastic recipe box full of colored index cards. "I have every one of the attendees listed here. I can look up your John Doe and pull out his entries."

I let out a sigh of relief. "How long is that going to take?"

"As long as it takes. I'll flip through the cards and pull them out."

"Aren't they organized alphabetically?" Fanble asked.

"No, chronologically. By date of registration." She began flipping through the cards one at a time, starting at the front. While we waited, I looked at the large banner at the doorway: "We Are All Someone Else Inside!"

Right, I thought. *And one of the people here is a murderer.*

A group of rowdy Klingons stormed through the lobby, chasing after a Captain Jack Sparrow who had insulted them somehow. A Mandalorian Boba Fett bounty hunter sneered at a colorful figure of Kenny from South Park, saying, "He's no good to me dead."

I picked up a spare program book at the registration desk. "Find Your Inner YOU!" Killing time, I flipped through the program listings. McGoo fidgeted, waiting.

Fanble seemed optimistic. "We're on the verge of solving this case, I know it—and I'm proud that I could help. Is there any better way of getting in character?" He grinned, then remembered his serious expression again. I had to admit, he was doing a decent job.

The registrar's fingers must have been nimble from her knitting. She flipped through all the cards quickly, pulling out every one that listed John Doe. "That's all of them."

McGoo, Fanble, and I turned as she spread the cards as if they came from a Tarot deck. "All these were submitted at different times, all registered to a John Doe. He's a very ambitious costumer." She flipped one down. "Klingon, name of Ach-gLokh Heqht." I was impressed by how well she pronounced the name.

"501st stormtrooper, designated TK-10625. And a Dr. Who —Tom Baker Incarnation—oh, we have several of those here at the con." She kept flipping down cards.

"Old series Cylon, toaster variety." She pursued her lips. "Hmm. Honest Abe Van Helsing ... one or two of those at the con as well, but he claims to be the real one." She rolled her eyes, "Don't they all? And ..." She held up the last card, squinting down at it. "This is strange ... he's also dressed as Dan Shamble, Zombie P.I."

McGoo looked at me. "What's that all about?"

A cold dread rose within me as I turned to look at Fanble. "You?"

Startled, Fanble raised his hands. His fedora was askew. "No, not me! How could think it was me? It was one of those other guys!" He shook his head as if having a seizure. "That was someone else! They were all someone else!"

"But you're the one who called attention to John Doe in the first place," I said, though I liked to think I would have figured it out myself sooner or later. "If you're the murderer, why would you put us on the trail?"

"Because that's what Dan Shamble would do."

McGoo pulled out his handcuffs, crouched, and prepared for a fight.

Fanble lurched away. His shoulders jittered, his arms flapped. His bullet-ridden sport jacket whipped about as he thrashed. His face blurred like melted putty, fuzzing, reshifting. He shook his head. "No, not me! Gotta stay in character … all the voices in my head!" He clapped both hands to his temples, knocking off the fedora. "Too many personalities. So many expectations!" His features shifted, twisted.

Ever since the Big Uneasy, just about every form of legendary creature had returned to the world, from basic garden-variety vampires, werewolves, et cetera, to the more exotic mythical beings. I had even solved a case when Santa Claus hired me to find his missing Naughty-and-Nice list. After all my years of investigating in the Quarter, I was beyond being surprised when I figured it out. "You're a shape-shifter."

"That would explain all the different characters," McGoo said. "John Doe, you are under arrest on suspicion of the murder of TK-9399."

Fanble backed away, still twisting and writhing. Somehow, he found the energy within himself to snap back into character so that his features looked just like mine again. He reached inside his sport jacket and drew his .38—which I suspected was very real.

The con chairman, Phil Somerstein, ran forward with an angry and annoyed look on his face. "Hey! That's not properly peace-bonded!"

A large number of cosplay fans had gathered in the main lobby, many in costume, everyone excited for the impending masquerade. They gasped to see Fanble wave his gun. He pointed the .38 at me again.

I took a chance, though. I saw how determined Fanble was, how hard he worked. His features were so eerily similar to mine it was like confronting myself in the mirror. Holding my hands up, trying to calm him, I stepped closer.

Fanble yelled, "Don't come any closer. I'll shoot!"

"I've been shot plenty of times."

Then the shape-shifter swung the gun toward the fans in the crowd. "Then I'll shoot *them*."

I took another step forward. "But if you're truly in character, as me, then you know I'd never shoot innocent people. Not humans, not unnaturals."

The crowd grew thicker around the tableau: redshirts, numerous incarnations of Dr. Who, Klingons, stormtroopers, Cylons, Jedi Knights, Browncoats, Visitors, and countless anime, superhero, and videogame characters, even another faux Van Helsing, whose costume was much less impressive than the one I had seen on stage—the costume John Doe had worn.

And it wasn't just the cosplayers. The unnatural attendees from the Quarter were also caught in the crowd: real vampires, werewolves, even the dedicated mummy fan with his hieroglyphic Issue o *Action Comics* ashcan edition.

Fanble's .38 wavered. He swung it around the gathered crowd, then seemed to sulk like a marionette with the strings cut. "You're right—Dan Shamble, Zombie P.I. would never do something like that." He dropped the .38 on the floor, then shucked the sport jacket, stomped on the fedora—and his features began to morph in an extravagant transformation.

As the flaccid flesh, skull, and facial features reorganized themselves, Fanble shifted through Tom Baker, then into a burly Klingon, thrashed about, and finally settled on a powerful and murderous character, someone who would not hesitate to harm innocent fans: Van Helsing—Honest Abe, ruthless vampire serial killer. His eyes flashed, his dark hair writhed. He drew his lips back to expose his teeth in a snarl. "I'll kill you all!"

But despite his facial features, he didn't have his full costume, didn't have his tools or props.

Before McGoo and I could bolt forward to seize him, though, my doppelganger lunged toward the crowd like a quarterback in a game. The fans yelled, trying to scramble away.

Then I saw where he was headed. Van Helsing leaped toward the other Van Helsing cosplayer, knocking him to the ground and ripping at the wooden stakes thrust into his belt. He drew back, holding up one of the sharp projectiles.

Trying to get away, the vampires in the crowd screamed, "Watch out! He's got a stake!"

Van Helsing's hands blurred as if they were rapid-fire crossbows. He hurled his sharp projectiles at random into the crowd, and somehow every stake struck and injured a Star Trek redshirt, all of whom dropped to the ground, bleeding.

Drawing my own .38, I yelled at McGoo. "As Van Helsing at least he's *human*. We can take him down."

Realizing his vulnerability as a human, Van Helsing blurred and took on a different form, sprouting fur and massive muscles. His face elongated into a fang-filled canine muzzle and he became a powerful bull werewolf.

I hesitated before I fired, but McGoo didn't. He drew one of his two service revolvers. "I'll just wing him," he said.

McGoo's shot struck him in the shoulder, which flung the shapeshifter backward to the floor of the lobby. He thrashed about like an earthworm on a hotplate.

"It's just a flesh wound. I was careful—nothing to worry about."

The shapeshifter didn't react as if it were a minor injury, though. He wailed and spasmed, clearly dying.

"What did you hit him with, McGoo?" I asked.

"Uh-oh. Looks like John Doe picked the wrong cosplay creature this time." He looked down at his service revolver. "This is the one loaded with silver bullets in case I get in a shootout against unnaturals."

The shapeshifter moaned and jittered, shed his werewolf

persona, and lay twitching—a formless thing like a store mannequin whose features had melted away, gasping out of a round toothless mouth.

He said something, and I bent close, still feeling a certain connection to the man—to the *being*—who had known and imitated me so well. John Doe gasped, "I couldn't stand the pressure ... I just wanted to be somebody ... to be *everybody*."

With a last writhing rattle, the shapeshifter lost even its featureless humanoid form and dissolved into a puddle of organic goo that seeped into the StainGuard carpet of the motel lobby.

I stood next to McGoo, and he shook his head. "I didn't mean to kill him. Now there'll be a lot of paperwork." He sighed. "I can honestly say I've never seen a shapeshifter before."

I turned to him. "How would you ever know if you had?"

The Cylon con security guards came forward to help wrap up, and McGoo decided there was no further need for a lockdown. I realized that it was a good thing McGoo had coaxed me here in the first place.

I felt sorry for Fanble. He had been so earnest, wanting to be the best "me" he could be. I often wondered who I really was inside, just an undead guy who liked to solve cases—was that enough? I had a wonderful (if ectoplasmic) girlfriend in Sheyenne, a great partner in Robin, a true friend in McGoo. I didn't have a need to be anybody else. Zombie detective suited me just fine.

Phil Somerstein announced that the CosplayCon Masquerade would take place in fifteen minutes, on schedule. He called out, "Photo opportunities in the side hall."

McGoo looked at me, adjusted his cap, and I adjusted my fedora. Both of us had to remain in character, of course. "I told you this would be fun, Shamble. Thanks for your help solving the case."

"It's what I do," I said. Maybe I'd call Sheyenne after all. She might enjoy this with me. The event ran all weekend.

As people passed, Phil Somerstein handed out pre-registration cards for next year's CosplayCon. Almost everybody took one.

So did I.

I consider myself a pretty straightforward storyteller, more concerned with plot and characters than playing around and showing off with the language. Thus, I don't write many experimental or literary stories.

But when I was deeply immersed in my university creative writing and English classes, I did try something else. "Running Inside" is a strange and, I think, compelling exploration of an alien mindset from the point of view of a possessing demon that hops into the minds of person after person—as it's being chased by an even nastier demon. I liked how it came out.

I gave the manuscript to my sister as a test reader, who was in high school at the time. She read it and pronounced with true sisterly praise, "You're weird!"

As a side note, this story was inspired by a song from the Fixx album Reach the Beach called "Running."

Running Inside

I have trespassed the Dark Passage, and escaped. And now the guardian *Gom* will pursue me evermore, ravening to regain the knowledge that *I* have stolen from him and devoured for myself.

Seeking enlightenment with Darkness, *I* have found more than a mystery ... and taken the power that accompanies it. With the forbidden knowledge still undigested within me, with the furious *Gom* in pursuit, *I* use my newfound power to escape the Passage and flee into the Catalog of Lives, hoping to elude him there.

I switch myself. And *I* am someone else.

I am an old woman, alone in the house that my husband left to me in his last will and testament. *I* withdraw into my memories of him, and of our children who dutifully come to visit every time their crowded calendars tell them another holiday has rolled around. And they always bring with them the grandchildren, reflections of themselves ... images of me, two generations removed. I dearly love the children, for they resurrect my memories of when I was young. And I dearly love to be reminded of when I was young.

My age-worn crucifix hangs in a special place on the wall, and the mass-produced face of the Lord Jesus Christ stares down at the top of my television console which is often polished but seldom used. The clock ticks loudly on the wall. A small pile of *Reader's Digest* sits on the end table next to the telephone. The telephone has a thin layer of dust on it.

I am feeling the power grow as *I* assimilate the stolen knowledge, incorporating it within me. And *I* am beginning to realize that *I* have taken from the *Gom* something far more vital than *I* had realized.

The doorbell rings, and I am momentarily startled, feeling brief trepidation. Will it be those horrible, taunting boys again? It takes me a moment to cross the room. A furtive glance behind the curtain, and my anxiety melts away. I open the door quickly to greet a young Girl Scout clad in a marvelously trim uniform. She extends a box of cookies ... asks me if I'd like to buy some. She smiles as I look into her eyes.

And *I* see the dark smokiness swirling behind those eyes an instant before the light explodes outward, engulfing me, entrapping me. The girl is the *Gom*.

I struggle in panic, ripping myself free from the webs of ignorance the *Gom* had spun to weaken and confuse me. Then *I* am able to switch myself.

And *I* am someone else.

I am a student, a young man caught up in the dream that knowledge—any kind of knowledge—is power. And I enthusiastically take on the task of decreasing my ignorance of all things. I have found refuge in the university library, surrounded by books.

Here, I can hide from the condemnations of my parents, their horror when I told them that I was attending college to *learn* something, as opposed to just "Preparing for a Job." They say I have become "radical"—and it is true that I have taken an active interest in politics and world affairs, but when I see grievous injustices, I must speak out now, rather than let myself grow older and cease to care, as they have.

I sit at a small table in the dim stacks of the library's sixth floor. Around me are rows upon rows of countless books ... but they are not really countless, for someone took the time to number each book carefully, and to arrange them in perfect order. The musty, aged volumes kept in an environment of carefully controlled dampness create an aroma that is not unpleasant, but soothing to me. Here I can hide from the superfluous pressures of the academic world—professors more concerned that their students earn satisfactory grades than that they learn anything ... secretaries who claim the important criterion for graduation is that one knows how to fill out the proper places in the proper forms at the proper times.

I pick up one of the books in front of me and flip to the back— it has not been checked out in over two decades. I take a grim satisfaction in obtaining knowledge that others deem too obscure to bother with. These lonely books give me their knowledge freely, to nourish my comprehension.

I am astonished at how easily *I* have escaped the *Gom.* During our brief conflict, *I* have become aware of the exact nature of the knowledge *I* appropriated from him. In my blind gropings in the Dark Passage, *I* took and devoured that which amounts to the utmost heart and soul of the *Gom.* *I* have access to incredible power ... if only *I* can learn how to use it. And now the *Gom* also knows exactly what *I* have stolen from him ... and he will stop at nothing to rend my being and take back that part of himself which I have digested. *I* fear him greatly.

I look up from my book as someone taps on my shoulder, interrupting my thoughts. It is another student, a young thin woman with dark hair going prematurely gray ... another fugitive hiding in the depths of the library. She asks if she can borrow a pencil, and she smiles at me as I fumble in my backpack to find one. I give it to her.

I cringe, poised and ready to run once more, sure that the *Gom* has found me again, too soon! But then *I* look deeper and find nothing behind her brown eyes. She is merely another Life in the Catalog of Lives. *I* am safe.

I watch as she moves down one corridor of books, a small piece of scratch paper and my pencil clutched in one hand, her other hand running lightly down the spines of books until she has found the one she wants. She copies something out of its pages, then returns to me, handing the pencil back with her thanks.

Even before *I* can see the dark smokiness that has so suddenly appeared behind her eyes, the *Gom* attacks, hurtling upon me with waves of scintillating confusion. He is ravenous, frenzied, and walls off my escape with his blinding lights. He tears into me viciously, consuming parts of my being, but *I* manage to shunt away the stolen knowledge and protect it by sacrificing other parts of myself. *I* try to escape, but *I* cannot. *I* am growing weaker.

I take the pencil and smile back at her before opening my book again to pick up my thoughts where I left them.

As a last desperate effort, *I* find my deepest, darkest hidden secret and thrust it to the fore, breaking it from myself. While the *Gom* is momentarily startled and choking on the horrible knowledge *I* have sacrificed to him, *I* switch myself.

And *I* am someone else.

I am a hunter, crouching in the brush with my new rifle poised on my knee, waiting for the prey to come along. My red flannel jacket and my Day-Glo orange cap are very bright, but the deer will not see them. The air around me is brisk with a late-autumn chill, and I smell the fresh tang of dead leaves mixed with a thin shadow of new-fallen snow. The wind rattles the naked branches above me, only emphasizing the deep, deep silence of the forest. I find it exhilarating—this is the one week of the year when I can escape my mundane life and truly feel alive.

For the rest of the year, I am an underpaid cook in a greasy-spoon restaurant, confined in the hot, bright kitchen where the air is oppressive with the stink of someone else's food. Here I have to tolerate the stupidity and slowness of the high school dishwashers, the smartass comments of the busboys, the illegible writing of the waitresses. But now, for this one week, I can escape all that. I am in control, here in the Northwoods.

I am incredibly weak, cowering inside my new identity, too frightened even to despair. The *Gom* has devoured and taken into his being much of what had been my memories, my past, my Self, so that *I* am left with only tattered remnants of my former existence around the bright core of the knowledge that had once been part of the *Gom*. The knowledge pulsates, filling me, and *I* am finally able to make use of the power ... *I* hold the key. But *I* need time.

I do not know how the *Gom* is able to find me so swiftly. The entries in the Catalog of Lives are arranged in a random order, and *I* am fleeing from life to life with no plan and leaving no trail behind me. But still the *Gom* follows easily in my wake, pursuing me no matter who *I* become.

I wonder if these Lives ever realize that *I* am part of them, hiding within their souls and fighting for my existence. Are they even aware of my presence as a ghostly memory, or are they completely oblivious to the conflict raging between the *Gom* and myself? *I* am inclined to believe the latter, for they are aware of so very little.

I am completely in tune with the forest, fully aware of all that goes on in it. My instincts are heightened to the level of an animal that has to fight every fleeting moment to remain on the razor's edge between survival and death. My muscles are coiled; my reflexes will be incredibly swift. i have crouched in this same position for so long that my body has forgotten discomfort. The cold in the air is just deep enough that my flesh is numb, and I feel detached from it.

The sound of the cracking twig seems as loud as a gunshot in my ears. Another twig snaps, leaves rustle. Footsteps. Someone is coming, but I can see no one. It is probably another hunter, intruding upon my area of the forest.

I am almost extinguished by my panic. Has the *Gom* found me again? Already? *I* have no way of knowing, no method to determine his presence. *I* cannot face him again. Not now. Not until *I* fully understand the stolen knowledge. *I* cannot take the chance. *I* cannot remain here if the *Gom* is waiting to strike. *I* must run again, become another Life, hoping to elude him once more, for just a short while longer. *I* hear another footstep just as *I* switch myself.

And *I* am someone else.

I am running. The damp sand beneath my feet is resilient and rebounds with each step I take. Ahead of me, the beach stretches to the misty distance where it is swallowed up in the veils of sea spray suspended in the air ... where crashing waves make gray hulking shadows of rocks crouching near the shore. Coaxed by the moon, the retreating tide leaves a naked expanse broken only by occasional pieces of driftwood or scattered sea onions that look like limp, rubbery tentacles. Gulls fly overhead, searching for treats abandoned by the sea. Barnacles, clinging to the imagined security of their driftwood homes, are now orphaned and left to gasp outstretched, waiting for the tide to return before it is too late.

The early-morning air is cool and salty in my lungs, and my hair feels damp. I wish I could find time to run every day, and not just on weekends. The silence. The peace. The fulfillment.

I dare not hope that *I* have escaped the *Gom* completely. He is growing weaker through his own missing knowledge—the knowledge that had become mine—but still he has powers *I* cannot begin to imagine. And as the *Gom* grows weaker, he grows more desperate. *I* must be very careful.

I see that I do not have the beach to myself this morning. A tired-looking middle-aged man stands half-watching two young children as they search for broken sand dollars, scattered shells, or foul-smelling crab claws. The man is probably a camper, one of those who drags a huge recreational vehicle larger than my own apartment to the oceanside so he can "Get Away From It All." He doesn't seem to be paying much attention to the children as they throw sea-foam at each other or splash in the retreating waves. He watches me closely and takes a step forward as I run by. Strange.

I can feel the invisible walls spring up around me, boxing me in, stronger than ever before. The *Gom* has come to make his final stand.

The flashing lights bombard me as he attacks, scorching parts of me, leaving the brightness of knowledge scarred by the shadows of ignorance. *I* try to switch myself ... but *I* rebound off the intangible prison walls. They are too strong for me. *I* cannot attack the *Gom*, for my own powers are purely for the purposes of escape. And even that power had failed me.

I retreat, tunneling deeper into this insignificant Life, hoping to find some long-forgotten flight of imagination in this memory that will let me bridge the walls ... or at least a time of past despair where *I* can hide in the labyrinths of confusion.

But the *Gom* follows me down, ravening, closing the walls tighter. He has me trapped. He knows it, and his smoky substance pulsates with glee. He will consume me and return to the Dark Passage to hang my existence as a trophy and a warning to all the others who would defy him as *I* have done.

He and *I* face each other down a long corridor of memory. He wishes to rip the stolen knowledge from me, the knowledge that gives me the power to switch myself ... but *I* cannot breach the walls, and the power is useless. *I* am alone with the *Gom* in a prison of his own construction. His power builds to a raging inferno, just before he launches himself at me.

Then *I* switch myself—to the *Gom*.

I am the *Gom* and he is myself ... and *I* must punish him, for he has trespassed the Dark Passage and can flee no more.

After *I* have swallowed him whole, *I* depart laughing from the Catalog of Lives, for *I* am now the *Gom*, the Guardian of the Dark Passage. *I* have much knowledge to attend to, and my hunger will be satisfied as never before.

Beware, those who would attempt to trespass among the Dark secrets to which *I* alone am entitled. The *Gom* cannot be defeated.

Another exercise for one of my MFA classes, this time for a Romance Fiction course. We were told to write a romance scene centered around a non-apology, beginning with "I'm sorry, but ..."

I like to twist the assignment.

Cupid's Arrow

I'm sorry, but I never claimed to be a perfect shot. You always placed such high expectations on me. There's something gratifying about being adored, about being placed on such a high pedestal, but a man can't always live up to that kind of pressure, and now you're the one suffering for it. Believe me, this really does hurt me more than it hurts you.

I tried to be your knight in shining armor. When we first met, you were the one armed with all the arrows, with your smile, your laugh, your flashing eyes. It was Cupid's Arrow shot right through my heart. We seemed to have so much in common. You listened to me explain all my hobbies; you laughed at all my jokes, even if I did have to explain some of them to you.

You knew how much I loved hunting, even though only twice in my life had I actually brought home a deer with my bow. I knew you understood when I explained about hunting, the process, the outdoors, getting back to nature. It didn't really matter whether or not I killed anything. But then, you never understood fishing either, how enjoyable it is just to sit in a boat with a line in the water and spend the day with your thoughts. Even if I didn't catch a fish, it was still a good day of *fishing*.

Ah, Cupid's Arrow! You seemed to love me. We would walk

in the peaceful forest, just with our own thoughts, my thoughts of love for you. I never guessed that you were thinking about Brad.

But I saw the flirty messages on your phone, the private date you set up on Facebook, thinking I would never look at your account. I'm sorry, but why did you have such an obvious password? Was it because you trusted me, or because you thought I was a fool? I think it was the latter.

You and Brad met for coffee out in the open where anyone could see you ... where *I* could see you. Leaning close to each other over the small table, laughing, brushing fingertips together. That was an arrow straight to my heart! You caught me like a deer in the headlights. Do you have any idea how much that hurt?

What did I do wrong? Wasn't I loving enough? What more could you really ask of me? But you didn't ask—and that's the thing. We could have worked on it, but you didn't ask, didn't try, and that's your fault.

So, when I asked you to go for a walk in the woods with me, as we so often did in the times I believed our romance was real, I carried my bow and the razor-edged, steel-tipped arrows. "Just for target practice," I said, as we had done many times before. You didn't suspect a thing, because you really must have thought I'm an idiot. That still hurts me more than you can imagine.

I'll never forget the look of surprise on your face when I strung the bow, nocked the first arrow, and told you to run. You just stared in disbelief, even laughed nervously. But I was serious. I am a hunter, whether or not I'm any good at it. I told you I would give you a head start, a fighting chance. I didn't have to do that, you know, but I still love you. It means a lot to me.

Finally, you did run, crashing in panic through the underbrush with no plan at all, flailing your arms, yelling and crying. I might not be a very good hunter, but you weren't very good prey.

You gave me a perfect shot, and I let the arrow fly, like Cupid's Arrow. I meant to shoot you straight through the heart. It seemed poignant, even romantic. I'm sorry, but I never said I was a perfect shot.

Instead, the arrow struck to the left of your heart, punctured your lung, hit the spine, so now instead of a quick, sweet death with me cradling your lifeless body in my arms, you're going to die slowly and painfully, bleeding out in the middle of the forest, unable to crawl for help. You made it a lot harder than it had to be, and now I'm going to have to live with that guilt. I feel like I'm the one with an arrow through my heart.

But I'm a strong man, and I'll get over it. Maybe I'll even find love again, with some other lucky woman.

Many people are tormented by night terrors, waking up in a cold sweat from a horrific dream. Not me. I often can't get to sleep because I have so many ideas and stories running through my head, but once I drop off, I'm in a sound, dreamless sleep until morning.

My parents and teachers were concerned about my fascination with monster movies and horror fiction, sure that I would be plagued with nightmares. I think the opposite occurred: the fact that I spent so much time dealing with horrifying things during my waking hours meant that I could be untroubled by nightmares while sleeping. I had already gotten it out of my system.

I almost never have nightmares, but there are exceptions to every rule. "The Circus" is one of my only tales based on a nightmare. I wrote down my nightmare, and eventually fit it into a new Tucker's Grove story.

The Circus

S unset was accompanied by strange shadows, and galloping on them came the black horse, hooves chewing up the dirt main street of town, leaving its imprint bold among the other crowded tracks. A small, ugly figure crouched on the horse's back —a hunchbacked dwarf, dressed in a brilliant blue tunic and a scarlet cap.

The dwarf held a rolled sheet of paper in the crook of one arm as he guided the black horse with his other hand. Past empty storefronts, past the saloon where gas lamps were just being lit, past the three old men who sat on the boardwalk every afternoon at five o'clock to talk about the weather—the dwarf pulled his horse to a halt in front of the old gallows. The gallows had never been used, though every town needed them, if only to scare away the riffraff.

The dwarf unrolled the paper he carried, smoothing out the wrinkles, and without dismounting he tacked it to one of the wooden beams of the gallows, displaying his poster. Finished, he spurred the horse into motion again with his polished black riding boots and was gone.

The sunset continued without him.

People hesitantly began to gather, led by their own curiosity and the three old men whose never-changing discussion had been so rudely interrupted. They circled the gallows-post, pushing closer to stare at the poster as a murmur rippled slowly through the crowd.

Collier and Raven's Traveling Circus

ONE NIGHT ONLY

Bordering the poster were little cameo sketches of clowns, tightrope walkers, trapeze artists, a fire-eater, and a knife thrower. But the center picture held everyone's attention, dominating the poster: a tall black woman, dressed in dark flowing robes, her eyes staring out of the paper, piercing through the ink. Flowing lions surrounded her, snarling at something only they could see, dodging the caress of the whip she held.

"From Abyssinia—Ramonza, Mistress of the Lions."

The crowd hushed, gazing at the poster. A fat man, originally from Boston, muttered, "A circus! About time we had something out this way!"

Isolated in the South Dakota wasteland, the town rarely drew attention. Its founders had named it "Miracle Bluff," although the desolate flatlands made any references to a bluff, or even so much as a hill, just wishful thinking. Some said they could see California on a clear day; others said the Rockies got in the way.

The town was a clump of people who had lost their momentum on the Black Hills gold rush. They had somehow run out of stamina and decided to settle down in the lazy emptiness of monotonous grass and grass and grass. Miracle Bluff was already well on its way to total extinction, asleep, perhaps in a coma.

And now a circus was coming to town.

The tents set up just outside Miracle Bluff. People gathered to watch, almost desperate for something to break the monotony of their existence, but the circus recruited no help. Someone sold balloons; stores closed as if it were a holiday; more posters were tacked up around town, though they were unnecessary; a preacher cried out that circuses were evil, but nobody listened; the dwarf sold tickets; and people smiled. Miracle Bluff had begun to come alive again.

At nightfall the town was empty, but not the circus tents. The townspeople were scattered among rickety wooden benches that had the words "Collier and Raven's Traveling Circus" burned into the boards. It wasn't a very big crowd, but Miracle Bluff did the best it could.

A hushed silence greeted the ringmaster as he stood before the audience and introduced the first act. The people applauded as a fire-eater performed, but always before their imagination was the haunting picture of black Ramonza with her powerful lions that threatened to leap from the poster. Suspense built as the tightrope walkers, clowns, trapeze artists all paraded before the crowd; but they wanted more.

The lights dimmed. The ringmaster stepped into the spotlight again.

"Ladies and gentlemen! Collier and Raven's Traveling Circus is proud to present, from Abyssinia, at the heart of darkest Africa —Ramonza, Mistress of the Lions!"

The ring was dark and filled with shadows; nobody saw her appear, but suddenly she was there, standing in the midst of her lions, light reflecting off her ebony skin. The five lions, two males and three females, flowed around her, unchained, snarling at the audience.

The crowd hushed itself with joyous fear, then began to applaud wildly. Ramonza searched the faces in silence, deeply scrutinizing the people of Miracle Bluff; she reached out to snap her fingers at the lions, and they quickly fell into a neat row.

Turning away from the crowds, Ramonza motioned to the cats, and her lions performed. The people applauded as the animals jumped through a ring of fire, then made a pyramid of themselves. For a time, they rolled large, brightly colored balls about, and chased after clowns; but Ramonza had yet to finish her act. Once again, she snapped her fingers and the lions lined themselves up on the far side of the ring, sitting down on their haunches, warily keeping their slitted amber eyes on the crowd.

Ramonza faced the people, stepping forward as she coiled the whip in one hand. For the first time, she spoke, her voice thick and resonant inside the tent. "For my next and final act, I require a volunteer from the audience."

The crowd fell silent, suddenly frozen in time. Nobody dared move, afraid one of their actions might be misinterpreted. Ramonza stood, running the braided leather of her whip through her fingers.

Grunting to himself, the fat man from Boston lifted a chubby hand and stood up, swinging his girth as he pushed past people to descend the rickety wooden benches. "All right, all right," he muttered. He looked at the faces around him, then walked out to meet Ramonza.

She looked at him with dark eyes, spreading lips in a smile that showed off glistening teeth. "Yes, you'll do fine."

She told the fat man to remain where he stood; then she backed away to stand behind the neat row of lions. The cats tensed, gazing at the volunteer. Ramonza muttered something only he and the lions could hear.

"Kill."

The lions rushed forward, muscles rippling. The smug grin on the fat man's face quickly dripped away; he turned to run; then the lions were upon him.

The crowd hesitated in an awesome silence for a long moment, hearing nothing but the lions feeding; then slowly they began to applaud ...

When I edited the three Blood Lite *anthologies, I demonstrated that horror and suspense could also be funny. In this story, I give a different twist on a standard Hitchcock model—a character thrown into a sudden crisis situation, not knowing what is happening to him. "Who is this guy, and why is he trying to kill me?!" Who can forget the classic Far Side cartoon of the terrified bear hiding behind a tree and trying to figure out why the hunter wants to shoot him?*

Now, try it with a vampire.

I hope Hitchcock would be proud ... if he were undead, of course.

Rude Awakening

I was resting in peace and surrounded by warm red dreams when the lid of my coffin flew open. A madman brandished a pointed wooden stake and a heavy mallet. When I saw the murderous gleam in his eyes, I knew he was trying to kill me.

"Foul demon!" he shrieked with such passion that spittle flew from his lips.

His challenge gave me a fraction of a second, and I snatched a handful of the native soil in the bottom of my coffin and hurled it into the killer's face. The spray of dirt caught him in the eyes, and he lurched backward.

I flung myself out of the coffin on its raised pedestal, careful not to snag my cape. I may be undead, but my heart was pounding. Who was this man? What did he have against me?

No time to think; just react.

As soon as I touched the flagstones of my castle's main vaulted chamber, I sprang to my feet and bounded away from the coffin. My attacker was already rubbing the soil from his eyes, still clutching his mallet and stake. I knew that wouldn't stop him for long.

I felt a chill as I saw several lengths of chain he had curled next to my coffin. My blood ran even colder than usual. He could have chained me up inside, imprisoned me forever.

What a jerk!

As I stumbled away, I felt sluggish, lethargic after being awakened from a deep sleep, made even worse by the fact that I'd fed well the night before. I felt bloated, not as fast as I should be. Damn it!

It had been such a good and satisfying dinner. I had sampled the rich blood of a tavern wench, who unwisely went out after dark to get washing water from the well. I also sipped from a stable boy and a traveling tinker. It was like a sampler platter, and I didn't drain so much that anyone would complain. I knew that my three beautiful vampire brides had also shown restraint, though they were a bit rash by choosing to slip in and feed upon the women in the local nunnery. It had been a fine night, a full moon, a lingering mist on the ground.

And now this nightmare.

"I will send you back to hell, foul bloodsucking monster!" the madman howled. I heard him gathering his implements of death, coming relentlessly after me.

My thoughts spun with panic and confusion. Who was this man? Why was he trying to kill me? How had he found me?

He had broken into my castle in broad daylight, my most vulnerable time. I could never escape outside or I'd be roasted by the purifying rays of the sun. Long black velvet curtains covered the castle windows, blocking the bright sunlight, but I could see the fiery golden lines. It must be noon.

I had only one choice—hide in the lower levels, the dungeons and the catacombs. I ran across the torch-lit chamber to the arched entrances leading into the deeper dungeons. I could escape there. I entered a shadowy catacomb and the shadows deepened, but my night vision intensified.

But when I reached the first of the descending passages, I came to an abrupt halt. My stomach churned, nauseated. The attacker had spread garlic across the threshold—a dozen bulbs blocking my way with a smelly impenetrable barrier!

I spun, raced to another passage, and again I came upon garlic. Then I noticed to my horror that he had draped strands of poisonous bulbs around the windows and the other deep passageways. This killer had left nothing to chance. He meant to stalk me, toy with me. I was trapped—in my own castle!

With a loud whistling sound, a wooden crossbow bolt struck the stone wall next to me and clattered to the floor. He was trying to shoot me through the heart! I swirled my cape to distract his aim, ducked, and bolted away from the garlic, so dizzy I could barely see.

"Today you will die, Count Ordoff!" He fired several more crossbow bolts in rapid succession. Two pierced my cape and one grazed my side. I felt a flash of pain before I rapidly healed, but I didn't waste breath returning his challenge. I needed all my faculties to think of a way I could escape. How was I going to get out of this alive?

Why was he trying to kill me? Think! Think!

But I recalled how many of my closest vampire friends had disappeared over the years. There had been dark and frightening rumors about a serial killer on the loose, an insane stalker who tracked down our safest daytime resting places, who broke into our homes to slaughter us while we slept. So far, he had eluded justice.

Now he was after me.

My castle should have been a fortress, a safe place I could go to ground, have quiet time with my three lovely vampire brides. I had let my guard down. I had been deceived by my pursuit of happiness, my pleasant unlife, my fine home, my fortune.

My brides are exciting women; Ashley, Tiffany, and Sienna—each one carefully chosen. We'd been together for half a century, but it still felt like a honeymoon. We could play card games. Tiffany liked to dabble with watercolors. I toyed with writing my memoirs.

And this monster had shattered our peace! But together, we could fight him off. I had to get to them.

Another chill made my cold skin crawl: my brides had their own darkened chamber with three separate coffins draped with frilly lace—especially Sienna's. She was the youngest, just a teenager when I'd turned her, and she still liked girlish decorations.

Were they all right? What if the stalker had gone to them first? I hurried.

As another crossbow bolt ricocheted against the stone walls, I reached the bedchamber of my three brides. I saw the sickening sight—their coffins were open, and empty. Ashley's had been toppled off its pedestal, as if she had fought back. A stake inside Sienna's coffin protruded from a pile of ashes in the vague outline of a female form surrounded by diaphanous fabric. I recognized one of my favorite negligées.

"No!" I howled.

On the floor another mound of ashes filled the bright red nightgown that Tiffany liked to wear. I clutched at the garment, lifted it up. Ashes trickled onto the flagstones. I wailed again. He had slain my beloved wives, one by one. The bastard!

Anger welled up inside me. Now I didn't want to just survive. I wanted to kill this awful man who had brought such tragedy to my peaceful home. Curling my lips back to show my fangs, I rose up, cast Tiffany's red nightgown aside, and turned to find the hunter standing there, grinning. He was a cruel-looking man with a thin face, a goatee, deep-set eyes, and a crooked nose.

"Aha, I have you!" He splashed an open vial of liquid at me, and I barely dodged in time. Holy water! Several droplets smoked and sizzled on my hand, seeping through the sleeve and burning my arm.

But I didn't care. I looked at Ashley's toppled coffin. "You killed them!"

"And this time they'll stay dead," he said with a laugh. "Next, I'll kill you!"

Using my vampire strength, I hurled Sienna's coffin at him, knocking the serial killer backward. I bolted past, running back into the main chamber where a curving stone staircase led to the upper gallery from which hung my favorite tapestries and the black velvet curtains that masked the windows. My coffin was still down in the main chamber, its lid open ... the place where I had been so peacefully sleeping not long before. It had been quite a rude awakening.

The stalker raced after me, discarding his crossbow with a clatter because he had spent all his bolts. He still brandished his mallet and his stake, though—and no doubt he carried an arsenal of other sadistic weapons.

I bounded up the stairs because it seemed the most likely escape, though it was not a tactically wise thing to do. The madman panted but kept up with me.

"There are many ways to kill a vampire," he said, as if trying to frighten me. "A wooden stake through the heart, that's my preference. I like to watch a vampire writhe and scream as he turns to dust. But there is also exposure to sunlight, to cremate you under the harsh light of day. I could drown you in running water, but your castle is so old, it doesn't have running water. Or, there's my favorite—cutting off a vampire's head and stuffing his mouth with garlic. That's always amusing."

I kept running, up and up, not deigning to respond. My initial conclusion was reaffirmed. This was an evil, insane man.

"Or, in a pinch," he said, "I could just wrap chains around your coffin and trap you inside for all eternity. One of those alternatives is going to work today."

I reached the top of the landing in the gallery only to find that he had placed more garlic up there, blocking my way. I couldn't go any farther—I was trapped at the top of the staircase. I faced him ascending the steps, and the hated garlic cutting me off from the other direction ... and the long drop-off to the flagstones of the main gallery below. I had no place to go. He was closing in.

Pulling out his stake and mallet, he advanced toward me, sure that I couldn't escape. Instead, I fell backward off the bannister and into open air.

Unlike what you've read in stories, vampires can't actually transform into bats. I fell with my cape flapping around me, and I crashed onto the hard flagstones. That really hurt.

From high above, the stalker glared down at me before his gaze flashed to the black velvet curtains. With an evil leer he leaped outward and grabbed the velvet, using his own weight to dislodge the curtain rods, tearing the fabric as he fell away from the castle windows. Blazing streams of golden sunlight poured in, and I scrambled out of the way, blinded. The air itself turned into an unbearable oven.

I crawled out of the direct beam, but I could still feel my clothes and my skin smoking. My coffin sat open on its pedestal in the middle of the room. I wasn't thinking straight, but I knew it was shelter, the only protection I could see. Trying to avoid the direct sun, I staggered around the edge of the room, looking for a way to the coffin.

But by the time I reached it, the killer had gotten there first. He stood in front of the open lid holding up a heavy wooden crucifix like a shield. Blocking my way.

After all my years of being an undead, though, I was for the most part an agnostic, and such symbols didn't have the effect on me as they once did. The fact that I was blinded by sunlight and could barely see the crucifix made it possible for me to resist.

I knew what I had to do. With this serial killer on the loose, I would never be safe in my castle again, even if I found a hiding place. I had to get rid of this bloodthirsty man who had murdered my three brides and likely dozens of my vampire friends over the years. No one would be safe until this man was destroyed.

I bent low and charged forward fast enough that the sunlight wouldn't sear me too much. The killer looked startled as I struck him in the center of the chest with my lowered head, driving him backward. He squawked and flailed, dropped his wooden crucifix. Out of his pockets the wooden stake and a heavy mallet also clattered on the floor. I didn't care about those.

I knocked him backward into the coffin. He fell, sputtering, startled, and I slammed the lid down, trapping him inside. The ambient sunlight scorched my skin, but I endured the pain. I had to stop this madman before he struck again.

I could hear him pounding, struggling. He tried to push up the coffin lid, but he couldn't fight against my strength. I could only endure the sunlight for a few more seconds, but I had to make sure. I seized the lengths of chain he had left on the floor. The killer had intended to trap me, but instead I wrapped the chains around the coffin, one loop, then another, and I secured it.

The killer struggled inside the coffin—*my* coffin. He pounded and shouted, but his muffled voice sounded as if he had a lump of dirt in his mouth. Maybe he did. But he was secure for now, trapped and out of the way.

The sunlight was too bright, and I had to get out of there. I staggered away from the main gallery and into the blessed shadows. Thankfully, he hadn't put garlic on my secret, hidden passageways, and I made my way toward a small secondary crypt where I always kept a spare guest coffin, just in case a friend stayed over for the day.

I could rest and recuperate there in healing darkness. After my terrifying ordeal, I would be safe at last, and I could recover from my terror ... and deal with my grief over the loss of my loved ones.

Come nighttime, though, when I was strong again, I intended to go back to the chained coffin and deal with this stalker. Poetic justice. I was sure a stake through the heart, or the decapitation with a seasoning of garlic—would be just as effective on a human monster.

And then we could all sleep easy.

This is one of the first really ambitious stories I ever wrote, a Lovecraftian modern horror story inspired by a family vacation out to the Black Hills of South Dakota. In structure and tone, it's a lot like a Stephen King story.

The original draft of this came out of my typewriter (yes, a typewriter!) when I was 23 years old, and I've rewritten it several times since, publishing versions of "Family Portrait" in small press magazines and even using the core storyline as the basis for a two-issue X-Files comic story.

I think I'll stop revising it now. I like this version.

Family Portrait

Henry Franklin's testament, recounting the events of February, 1944:

"Finding the mysterious camera was no accident, and it wasn't luck. The camera found me.

"The war sounds outside began to die down. I had hidden in the corner of a ruined building during the bombing raid, and now I could smell the smoke of fires outside. I would dearly have loved to warm my hands over one of them. Snow started to fall in the night, and that made the silence seem deeper. I could hear an occasional moan from wounded people still trapped in the rubble.

"Then I saw a very odd thing. An old man dressed in a baggy gray business suit came striding over the broken debris in the street, with an ancient camera on a wooden tripod tucked under his arm and carrying a black leather satchel in his right hand. His left arm dangled by his side, and the left half of his face sagged in paralysis, his eye squinted shut—like he'd had a stroke or something. Despite the partial paralysis, though, the old man moved surprisingly well with his awkward burden. *Agile*—that's the word I'm looking for.

"As I watched, he set down the camera box and his leather case, snapping open the tripod with a flick of his wrist. The camera was one of those old monstrosities where the photographer has to hunch under a cloth and take pictures on heavy glass plates. Despite its age, the camera was in beautiful condition, a lovely antique ... and I had always had more than a passing interest in photography.

"Then the photographer bent over several bodies, some of them crushed beyond hope of life and others still quivering and moaning. Then the man adjusted his camera and took a photograph of the victims—like a parasite, a ghoul, trying to capture the death and pain around him on film. For his scrapbook? Christmas cards, maybe? Something in me thought it was one of the most disgusting things I had ever seen. I was very naive then.

"I lifted my rifle, lining him up in my sights. I was supposed to shoot Germans, and looters—that would make me a good soldier. I was already hardened to the many horrors I had seen ... but something else repulsed me about this old man. I *wanted* to kill him. That feeling made me hate myself, and I had a sudden terror that I was becoming one of those 'combat barbarians,' like Sam, who actually enjoyed the war and found it exciting. I didn't want that to happen to me.

"The camera came into focus in my rifle sights, and I could see how beautiful it was—a Stradivarius of cameras. I wanted to have it, badly, and without any discernible reason. I didn't know what I was doing.

"A few scattered shots bounced around the night from fighting in the streets—and I fired my rifle. The old man jerked and fell backward to the rubble, clutching at the camera for protection. The camera wobbled on its tripod but regained its balance. Sweat broke out on my forehead.

"Silence returned, and I crouched low as I ran from my hiding place to the camera. In the sparse light of the dying fires, I looked like no more than a flickering shadow, a cat stalking a downed bird. I smelled the blood, the dust, the snow. I licked my lips.

"The old photographer sprawled on the ground next to one of the wounded. The expression on the dead man's face—the frozen left side an emotionless mask of rubbery skin, the right side twisted into an impossible expression of surprise—was so unnatural that it made my skin want to crawl off my bones and go back to where I had been hiding.

"All of the victims on the ground—the old man's photographic subjects—had died. They had been alive only moments before when he'd taken a picture of them.

"The camera itself called me, and I ran my fingers over the wooden veneer on the box. Strange symbols had been etched around the lens. In the leather case at the foot of the tripod I found a stack of coated glass plates wrapped in black paper and some jars of chemicals, one of which glowed with a sickish warmth, like a fever. The old photographer's equipment was more desirable than anything I had seen before. When you're fighting a war, the animal instincts come closer to the surface, and rational thought doesn't always enter into the making of decisions. I was trapped, and such a perfect trap that I didn't realize it until decades later.

"Suddenly, I felt naked out in the open. I snatched up the camera and the leather case, scurrying into one of the ruined buildings. Already I began thinking of how I could bring the camera and the equipment home with me.

"Why did I ever see the cursed thing in the first place?"

Will Steiger stared at the five framed photographs on the wall of Uncle Henry's cottage, raising his eyebrows in appreciation. The photographs seemed so real, hypnotic, so lifelike despite the blurred sepia tone. Will had seen many antique pictures in old family scrapbooks, the faded brown-and-white portraits where nobody ever smiled and everybody dressed up in funeral costumes. Like for Uncle Henry's funeral.

Three of the five framed photographs showed gruesome detail of wounded World War II soldiers. Uncle Henry had been in Europe during the War—had he taken pictures of people lying in the rubble of a bombed-out street? The photographs seemed to ooze pain and suffering, striking at a gut level. Will felt uncomfortable just looking at them.

Nancy would take them down, without a doubt, when she packed and sorted through all the old photographer's things—the pictures wouldn't bother their young son Chet, with his macabre interest in such things, but she would insist it was a "bad influence on the children."

The other two framed photographs were portraits. One showed an old, elaborately dressed woman, decked with gaudy jewels and wearing a sour expression on her face. The portrait next to hers showed a thin, middle-aged man dressed in a chauffeur's uniform—he seemed to be gazing toward the old woman's photograph with something like lighthearted tolerance. But Will could see much more in the photographs: satisfaction from the chauffeur, but a gnawing hopelessness of knowing he'd never do anything else in his life; the rich lady seemed to be lonely, and not happy that she was forced to wear a stern mask in front of the chauffeur with whom she wanted to be friend as well as employer.

Will was delighted. Though he knew a little about photography himself, he could not discriminate how Uncle Henry had captured so much "depth" in the pictures. He'd had an incredible rapport with his camera.

"Dear Mr. Steiger, We regret to inform you that your uncle—" the letter had read.

Imagine dying all alone. Isolated in a cottage deep in the Black Hills of South Dakota—with a heavy wooden beam fallen across your back. Waiting, paralyzed, without a friend in the world to come look for you ... it must have taken a week for him to starve. And how many more weeks before someone found him? And what had Uncle Henry been thinking about all that time?

Will put it out of his mind. Again. But the gruesome death kept echoing in his head.

The fireplace stood cold and empty next to a wall full of bookcases. Will ran his index finger along the spines of some of the books, bemused. The origins of things intrigued him. Now with Uncle Henry's estate, maybe he could afford to go to grad school, get his Master's in history. Nancy had already begun to talk about how she wanted to plant a garden and make pickles and learn to quilt and sew and raise her children. All that from an uncle Will had never known because his mother refused to talk about him.

Dropping everything to pile in the car and drive across country to the Black Hills had made his whole family run ragged. A mile back in deep forest they found the deserted cottage surrounded on all sides by tall dark pines.

Baby Beth slept through their breathless exploration of the rooms, content simply to be out of the car for the time being. Nancy had changed her diaper, propped Beth's basket against the diaper bag, and left her to coo happily into a deep doze. Nancy found a brown grocery bag and dropped the disposable diaper in it, then set the bag outside the screen door. Will watched her do everything in an efficient but rushed manner, as if she were anxious to get back to inspecting the cottage.

Chet had made a quick trip to the bathroom before dashing back outside to go "exploring." Will almost went with his son, but ultimately decided he didn't have the energy to go bounding around the yard. Nancy automatically called, "Be careful," but Chet gave no indication that he heard.

One entire wing of the cottage had been converted into a photography studio. As he entered the sparsely furnished room, Will noticed the massive wooden beam fallen from the rafters, lying in a hulk on the floor. An ancient camera stood poised and erect on its spindly tripod, staring with its Cyclopean lens at the hardwood floor.

Will moved forward in grim fascination—Uncle Henry had died here, trapped and immobile, all alone. Henry had stared at these barren walls, at the camera, for a week. Had he even been able to blink his eyes? Will swallowed the thickness from his throat. The eight-inch-thick oak beam had snapped cleanly for no apparent reason. Impossible. On the phone, the lawyer called it a "freak accident."

The fallen beam had barely missed crushing the antique camera. Will forced himself to stop looking at the floor—there didn't seem to be any blood—and felt a strange attraction from the camera. He smiled as if seeing a new toy. It was in such beautiful condition. The lens pointed down, perhaps waiting to take a snapshot at the moment of Uncle Henry's death? Beside the camera rested a black leather case containing two glass plates, each wrapped in black paper.

The old camera couldn't be too difficult to use: complicated photography attachments had not been invented until after this one's time. It looked so easy—focus the lens, place the plate in the camera, open and close the shutter by hand. Perfect.

The darkroom entrance waited on the other end of the studio. Will flicked the red-light switch on the outside before he zigzagged his way through the light baffle—three black wooden partitions staggered so that light couldn't get through. Inside the shadowy room red light flooded all the corners but washed out most of the detail. A narrow shelf ran above the developing tanks, cluttered with jars of chemicals—more than just the materials needed for developing and fixing the photographs. Will realized that Uncle Henry would have needed to coat his own glass plates, too.

As he disturbed some of the jars on the shelf, Will thought he noticed a sparkling glow in one of them, scintillating in the red light. But it vanished quickly, and he convinced himself that the darkroom had been playing tricks on his eyes.

He found his way back out of the light baffle and blinked his eyes in the harsh light of the studio. Nancy was calling him from the kitchen to come eat a lunch she had pieced together from their leftover camping supplies and Uncle Henry's canned soup. Beth still slept, but Chet had come in, messed up and flushed from running around outside. But his hands were clean—Nancy had seen to that.

"Well, Chet, find anything interesting?" Will pulled up a chair across from the boy and met him eye to eye, man-to-man.

Chet's eyes sparkled. "I found a secret hiding place! With two mummies inside—they were real ugly, but it was neat! And they were dressed up in funny clothes. And I found some Bigfoot tracks in the woods, and a giant spider in a tree!"

Nancy shot Will a sharp look, scowling, but he refused to meet her gaze. He knew what she was thinking, and they had had the "discussion" over and over again about Chet's obsession with monster movies and creepy-crawly things. Nancy insisted it was unhealthy for her son to have such morbid preoccupations, but Will reacted strongly to parental quashing of anything in which the boy showed an interest, as Will's own parents had tried to do to him. The argument still simmered, unsettled, but Will was too tired now to make a comment. Besides, their tempers were both short from the wearying trip and they might end up saying too much. Will began to eat his soup with careful concentration.

Henry Franklin's testament, recounting his photography business in Deadwood, South Dakota, 1948-1968:

"My studio was an enormous success, but they could all see I wasn't happy. Thank God nobody cared enough to find out why. All alone in the shop, I had only the camera—I made and developed the glass plates myself. Sarsaparilla Studios always got popular in the summer. I could prey on Black Hills tourists coming to see Mount Rushmore, or the mines left over from the Black Hills gold rush, the old west, Boot Hill, or the saloon where Wild Bill Hickok got shot. The tourists look so petty, so unhindered by care or conscience, so *defenseless*. I can't remember the last time I enjoyed myself like they do.

"My prices were high, but Sarsaparilla Studios was more than just a photography place. Look what you got for $29.95 and a little piece of your soul! With the camera I could capture their portraits on old glass and print them in sepia tones so that the pictures looked like antiques. The tourists thought it was great fun.

"Physically, I haven't aged since that day decades ago when I shot the half-paralyzed photographer—I feel energetic, but my vitality doesn't do me any good. I have no friends (for my own protection and theirs) and I've become hardened. The pathetic victims didn't even *know* they've had their souls assaulted, part of their lives sucked away. But I *do* have a conscience, no matter how many people call me a bitter old grouch. They'd be bitter too. My conscience just isn't strong enough to fight the incubus.

"The hardest part was severing all ties with my family. Imagine trying to convince them that I had grown grim and cold, that I was smugly successful and didn't need them anymore. It's easier to keep away from people who think they hate you. Dear Addie, my sister, used to forgive just about everything I did—but what relief I felt when she finally refused to speak to me unless I changed back to my old self. But that was already impossible ten years ago. At least Addie stopped threatening to come out and visit me. What if she had asked me to take her photograph with the camera? I don't know if I could have stopped myself.

"That sort of thing gives me nightmares.

"I couldn't help but feed the incubus. It uses the camera as a tool to suck out the life energy of its victims, taking little sips from the soul, a bit here and a bit there, so none of the customers knows. The incubus and I seem to have a symbiotic relationship: I feed it by taking photographs with the camera, and it gives me health and success in return. But I can see now that I was manipulated from the first moment I saw the camera. I thought I was using its powers to advance myself—it's laughable to think that I didn't even see the puppet strings on my own arms.

"Meanwhile, my customers came and went, a steady stream, paying a much higher price than any traveler's cheque. And with each photograph I took, the incubus grew stronger and stronger. I couldn't do anything to stop it."

"Chet, can you move a little closer to Mommy?" Will crouched under the tent-like cloth behind the old camera, watching through the lens as Chet tried to squirm closer to Nancy. Baby Beth bawled her lungs out in the crook of her mother's arm.

"This is going to be great!" Will kept fiddling until he felt satisfied with the focus.

"Hurry up, Daddy!" Chet called from between his teeth clenched into a forced grin. Will removed one of the black-covered glass plates and pulled it up under the dark folds of cloth. He had only the two plates Uncle Henry had left behind—no margin for mistakes. He had checked the darkroom and found the chemicals he needed to develop his first shot. "Family Portrait #1" by Will Steiger. He'd had to insist that Nancy refrain from changing her clothes, making herself up, cleaning the children.

Unfortunately, Will resigned himself to being excluded from the picture. This camera was from before the days of devices to trip the shutter automatically. Offhand Will wondered why he'd never seen a photograph of his Uncle Henry.

In the dimness, Will peeled the black paper from the coated glass and slid the plate into the camera. "Ready ... hold very, very still now—"

Beth let out a loud yowl, as if to spite him. Will opened the shutter by hand, waited an instant, then closed it again.

Beth fell silent, as if someone had snipped her vocal cords.

Both Chet and Nancy winced simultaneously as if a cold claw had hooked into their stomachs, tearing something from them. Will fumbled with the plate under the dark cloth covering and didn't see them.

"Is that all, Will?" Nancy asked, sounding exhausted. She looked down at Beth and smiled. "Look at this—she's sleeping like a rock! All that yelling must have pooped her out."

Chet yawned and stretched with almost comic seriousness. "I'm tired, too, Mommy."

Nancy stood up off the bench, pulling Chet to his feet. "Of course you are, honey. You've had a rough day."

Will poked his head out of the tent cloth. "I think you could use a nap, kiddo." Chet didn't object, which Will found odd, since the boy *always* hated taking a nap.

Nancy rubbed her eyes. "I'm going to lie down, as long as the house'll be quiet. Wake me up when it's finished."

Will nodded and went into the darkroom.

Henry Franklin's testament, recounting the end of his photography business and his resultant seclusion, 1968-1979:

"For nineteen years I watched the incubus feed on the souls of others. I guess that made me a parasite, too. But then the incubus grew bolder, greedier.

"A young girl, all bright-eyed and full of tourist awe, sat down in front of my camera, *the* camera, while her parents stood back and watched, amused. I remember the girl wore a little western outfit, a miniature Calamity Jane. Let's have a big smile, little girl, for your *special* portrait. Parents always need to have something for their scrapbook. She smiled into the lens. I opened the shutter and closed it, like the wink of an infernal eye. The girl shuddered and collapsed, deathly pale.

"The parents urgently took her back out to get some fresh air, babbling to themselves about 'too much excitement.' I put the 'Closed' sign in my window and padlocked the door, vowing never to open the shop again.

"I couldn't destroy the incubus, not then or now—even if I were strong enough, I didn't dare risk it. Now, at least it is *contained* in the jar—I can't take the chance that I might set it free.

"But I *refused* to keep feeding it!

"Clammy chills broke out on my skin, and my head pounded. My hands shook as I turned to leave. All my nerves were going off like firecrackers. But I had seen the little girl's eyes through the lens, and I kept holding that memory up like a shield—and I won my first test of strength. I managed to turn my back from the shop. I took everything with me into seclusion, deep in the Black Hills.

"I fell violently ill for days—but the incubus couldn't let me die. We needed each other too much, especially now that I had taken away its prey. In the following years, I began to lose the unnatural health I'd had for so long. But I wondered if I was getting my own soul back, if the incubus was releasing me in disgust. I realized with a kind of terrified joy that if my health was fading, the incubus must be dying. It had to be. I had a chance— imagine the ecstasy that simple idea brought to a man who has been without any real hope for thirty years!

"And then I felt cheated, outraged, in despair, when the old woman and her chauffeur arrived. Like misguided sacrificial lambs.

"The wealthy old lady had seen one of my Sarsaparilla Studios photographs and sought me out. She insisted that I take her portrait, as a surprise gift for her husband. She had secretly come out to South Dakota while he went away on business. How convenient. Nobody knew she had come, nobody could trace her here. I should have denied her, thrown them out of my house, anything. I refused to photograph her. I insisted that I would never stand behind the lens again. But she would not be turned away, and the ravenous incubus stole my will like a rug out from under my feet.

"As if watching from a distance, I saw myself become a cordial man in front of the victims. I insisted on taking a free photograph of the chauffeur as well, a gift for such a devout fan who would come so far just to find little old me.

"The incubus was ravenous. In the tourist-filled photography shop, it could feed many times each day, like a spider with so many insects in its web that it needs only a drop of blood from each. Then, it could afford to sip a bit from each victim and let them go, none the wiser. But now the starving incubus dug in its psychic fangs, forging a permanent link through the camera. The incubus sucked up the life force of the old woman and her chauffeur like a glutton, draining them dry.

"They were both dead in hours, shriveled and empty. And to my horror I found that I felt nourished, too—vibrant and alive.

The thought made me physically sick. If the incubus has discovered a taste for killing, then it will never end."

The glass plate was still wet, but in the dim red light Will could tell his family portrait had come out even better than he'd hoped. He used a squeegee to wipe off the excess water, dabbed the plate with a soft cloth, then zigzagged his way through the light baffle and out of the darkroom. He held the edges of the plate with his fingertips and grinned, proud of himself.

He strutted to the bedroom, eager to show Nancy the photograph. Will paused at the door, frowning first and then smiling. She lay sound asleep on the bed with Chet curled up next to her, looking as if they could sleep through the end of the world. They had forgotten even to take off their shoes. Will shook his head fondly, then glanced in the other bedroom to see Beth sleeping peacefully in her crib with one small hand curled around her nose.

He set his still-wet photograph on the nightstand and moved closer to the baby. A nightmare skittered up and down his spine. His eyes focused with tunnel-vision on his baby daughter's face, her mouth.

Beth didn't appear to be breathing. He watched her in petrified silence for a brief moment before he let the words "My God!" fall one after the other out of his mouth. Beth's skin looked dry and lifeless, and Will was unable to stop his hand from reaching out to touch his daughter's forehead. The skin was rough and stiff, like a dry leaf; her eyelids seemed to be cracked, as if about to shatter.

"Nancy!" His voice twisted in his throat like a stinging bullwhip. He felt Beth's chest with his fingertips, frantically trying to find a small heartbeat. *"Nancy!"* Why the hell wasn't she answering?

He stumbled into the other bedroom. Nancy and Chet still

slept undisturbed. "Nancy!" Will began shaking her. Her skin felt strange to his touch, stiff instead of pliable. She began to respond, groggy, listless, like a record player switched down to a lower speed. Her eyes opened, milky and confused.

"What is *wrong* with you?" He took her limp arms and hauled her into a sitting position. She tried to shake her head to clear cobwebs from her brain, but she could not. Will wondered for a paranoid instant if his family had been drugged or poisoned. He tried to slap her on the cheeks, but she did not respond ... and her pasty skin didn't even show a red blotch where he struck her.

Time moved in slow motion for him. None of this could be real. It was impossible, simply impossible. Things had been going too well only an hour ago. He ran back to Beth's room, hoping he had somehow been mistaken, *knowing* that Beth was alive. She had to be alive.

The baby had changed, and Will halted himself in horror. She had collapsed in on herself, withered away, shriveled up to leave only a dried and empty husk of skin behind. Her face was puckered and folded, like one of those hideous dried apple dolls he had seen at country fairs ... or like a mummy.

A mummy? Hadn't Chet said something about mummies?

Then he was back in the other bedroom shaking the boy, all the time muttering things that didn't make sense even to himself. Nancy had fallen back into unconsciousness on the bed.

"Chet! Where are the mummies? Chet!"

The boy woke more easily than Nancy had. Will scooped him up in one arm and ran to the bathroom, turning on the cold shower. He pulled his son with him under the icy water, letting the cold shower blast at his pores and making his head pound. He shook Chet, praying for him to wake up, and laughed out loud when he saw the boy's teeth begin to chatter.

"Chet! Tell me where the mummies are! It's important!"

The boy had trouble working his mouth, forming the words. But he sensed Will's urgency and he genuinely tried until his voice finally came out in a brittle whisper. "In back, Daddy ... by the dump ... there's a trapdoor."

Will propped him up against the back of the bathtub and let the cold water continue to spatter down on him. Will jumped out of the shower and sprinted across the floor, leaving slops of water from his dripping clothes and soaked tennis shoes. He dashed out of the house, flinging water out of his eyes.

The afternoon was filled with hulking shadows thrown by the steep bluffs and the old pines and Will confused his bearings for a moment. In frantic impatience, he looked around and finally saw a pile of garbage in back of the cottage where Chet would have wandered during his explorations. Will ran to it, seeing the trash Uncle Henry had collected during his years of seclusion: rusted cans, decaying paper packages, broken jars and bottles.

He had no intention of calming himself. He felt adrenalin now and did not want to let it peter out before he could find something to help him, to help his family. What would Chet's vivid imagination call a "trapdoor?" He found some old boards set into the ground and held together by three thin crossbars nailed to the top.

Will snatched at the construction and yanked it upward so forcefully that some of the boards splintered and pulled away from the rest of the door. Below, he found a pit that must have been a root cellar. He saw shapes inside and dropped down into the shadowy pit without hesitating. Beth was already dead; Chet and Nancy were dying—he didn't dare risk being cautious.

Musty smells of earth and mold, and something else, hit Will's nostrils. But he ignored them as his eyes adjusted to the gloom. Chet had been telling the truth—two "mummies" were propped up in the small dirt cellar, withered and dry, as if their lives had been sucked out of them.

Will had no time to gape in horror—this was no match for the horror that was happening to his own family. From the photographs in the library, he recognized the shriveled chauffeur and the rich old woman. They both looked dried and empty, like baby Beth.

And suddenly, like a battering ram in his head, Will connected the family portrait he had taken, the photographs of these victims, even the strange old camera with the symbols etched around the lens. "What the hell!"

Then he noticed a sheaf of papers on the lap of the rich old woman, lying on the mold of her dress. He snatched at it and saw in the dim light that it was something of Uncle Henry's. Will needed answers if he was going to help his family. Nancy! Chet! What's wrong with the camera? He leaped back out of the root cellar and sat down on the ground, tilting the handwritten papers into the slanted afternoon light, feverishly skimming page after page.

Henry Franklin's testament, final entry:

"I don't care anymore what happens to me. I don't have much left inside to fight the incubus with—so I had better make my stand now. The worst that can happen is that I'll die. At least I hope that's the worst.

"I've been planning this for a while now, getting up my nerve, writing everything down in this ... confession? Testament? The incubus doesn't seem to be able to make the connection between cause and effect, and it does not stop me from writing everything here. Maybe I should mail this stack of papers to the police? No, I certainly don't want to risk having others come up here looking for proof. What if I lost my challenge? What if the incubus made me take a group photograph of the police? God, no.

"Why don't I just leave this paper on the kitchen table, out in plain sight? If I could think of a valid reason, I would state it here. But I can't think of anything, except that I can't *leave* it in an obvious place. Maybe the incubus is stopping me. Perhaps the sight of the shriveled husks here in the root cellar will make a reader more likely to believe my crazy story.

"No, I don't know where the incubus comes from. Did the half-paralyzed war photographer summon it, looking for a way to regain some of his vitality lost in the crippling stroke? I had no chance to ask questions before I shot him. What if some lost deer hunter out in the hills right now is aiming his rifle at me, urged on by the incubus looking for a new caretaker?

"I'll have to stay away from the windows.

"I don't know how to destroy the incubus. I've searched in old archives, dug through pop-culture paperbacks on black magic, but nothing tells me what I need. My only clue is the camera. It doesn't live in the camera—but uses it as a tool, a point of contact to form a link with its victim, like a straw to siphon off life energy. A soul vampire?

"But if I can destroy the camera, break the link, then the incubus will no longer be able to feed. I'd be taking away its fangs. It can't escape from its glass prison, and it can't get any new victims. The thing will starve slowly on its shelf ... and I hope I can control it in the meantime."—Henry Franklin."

Will flipped through the handwritten pages, skimming some parts again, then scattering the papers into the dim root cellar.

"So, what the hell *is* an incubus?" he shouted. His words refused to echo from the damp earth walls. "And where is it if it's not in the camera?" He glared into the dim shadows of the pit as if the mummies inside could tell him. "On a 'shelf' somewhere?" A rock ledge on one of the bluffs? And what the hell was a "glass prison?"

A jar? A jar on a shelf? In the darkroom!

Will sprinted back to the cottage, cold and clammy in his soaked clothes. To the studio, the darkroom. His eyes blazed. Will's adrenalin was going to run out soon—he knew it. He didn't dare stop even for a second because then he might realize how tired he was.

Will staggered through the light baffle, back and forth, until he confronted the eerie contrasts of the red-lit darkroom. "All right, where the hell are you!"

He snatched jars from the upper shelf, dropping some in the water-filled sink, shaking some, opening some. He had almost cleared the shelf when he noticed one jar half-hidden in the shadows of the back corner, glowing out of his reach. Will showed his teeth in a half-smile, half-snarl of triumph. He stood on his toes, grabbed the jar with his fingertips, and drew it toward him. "Gotcha!"

The dark brown glass felt heavy, warm to the touch. He tried to peer through the side and saw dimly swirling sparkles, like a thousand incandescent lights spiraling in nothingness. The glow brightened as Will watched—it was feeding on Chet and Nancy, drawing strength. It had already killed Beth. And Uncle Henry.

"Go back to wherever it was you came!" With both hands Will hurled the jar at the cement floor of the darkroom. But as he released it, half-skimmed words from Henry Franklin's testament flashed across his mind—"Now at least it is *contained*."

The glass jar struck the floor and erupted in an explosion of fire and blinding light. The incubus let loose an unearthly roar just beyond the range of Will's hearing as it burst free from its long imprisonment, seething and filling the darkroom with its presence.

Will found himself lying on the floor, staring up at the incubus as the dazzle faded from his eyes. The thing was a throbbing cloud of fire and smoke, writhing tentacles of gas strewn with random arcs of blue lightning. The air felt charged with static electricity, like a thunderstorm ready to burst. One tendril of flaming smoke touched the darkroom shelf with a violent discharge of lightning that blasted the wood from the wall. Then the incubus began moving forward, toward Will.

On his knees, he scrambled to the light baffle, to escape. His movement triggered something in the incubus and it rushed forward. Will stumbled through the black partitions of the light baffle trying to move faster through the maze. He burst into the bare studio, but he didn't know where to go.

Behind him came an explosion, and he turned to see shards of black-painted wood blasting outward from the darkroom as the incubus cut a straight path *through* the light baffle. Some of the wood caught fire. The incubus paused for a moment. It hovered and pulsed in the air as if glaring at Will. It came at him again.

Will threw papers and boxes at it, but they incinerated on contact with the thing. He stumbled backwards over the beam that had fallen on Uncle Henry ... trapping the old man, paralyzing him. The incubus had somehow caused that to happen, too.

Then he saw the camera pointing like a specter at the wreckage the incubus had caused. If he destroyed the camera, as Uncle Henry had attempted, the thing would be unable to feed—in fact, it would break the thing's contact with Chet and Nancy, stop it from sucking away any more of their lives. The incubus would eventually starve—but Will didn't have quite that much time.

On an inspiration, Will leaped for the camera. The thing rushed at him roaring like all the tornadoes in Kansas. He snatched up the one remaining glass plate in the leather case and ripped off the black paper casing as he rammed the plate into the camera. The incubus hesitated a moment, giving Will time to focus, then it charged forward again.

"Say *cheese!*" Will thought of the paradox, the contradiction, the infinite loop, the incubus forced to feed on itself. He opened the shutter on the old camera with the strange symbols etched around the lens.

The incubus gave an unearthly shriek as it was sucked into the camera. Will leaped away from the wooden tripod. The incubus died into echoes and glimmers of light as it vanished inside the lens. Trapped. Paralyzed.

Before he could let the fear overcome him, Will reached under the dark cloth and yanked the glass plate from the back. The glass was burning hot in his hands, but he held onto it, gritting his teeth against the pain. His legs felt like lead as he ran back into the ruined darkroom. He dropped the plate into the tank of developer and gasped, stumbling backward and coughing as the developing fluid began to boil and steam.

An image appeared on the plate, but Will couldn't bear to look at it: a horrible smoking, writhing thing. He was afraid it would be moving, even when trapped on the glass emulsion. The image darkened, grew more intense like a frozen roar, and then Will looked again, watching the blackness creep in from the edges. The developer continued its work, finally turning the glass plate completely dark. The acrid smell of photo-chemicals burned his eyes and nostrils. He waited an extra minute, then plunged his fingers into the developing tray, pulling the dripping plate out. The glass was still hot and weirdly black all the way through, like obsidian.

Careful not to drop it, he stepped through the wrecked light baffle and into the light of the studio. Moving like an automaton now, Will removed the lens from the camera and threw it with all his might, watching the glass shatter against the cinderblock walls of the studio. He didn't know if the incubus was dead, or inert, or just trapped in the black plate. But it could no longer feed. He tipped over the camera's tripod, then stomped on the wooden box, crushing it to splinters.

Later, he was going to take a long walk, deep into the forest out back; Uncle Henry must have a shovel somewhere, and he would bury the glass plate far down under the sandy Black Hills soil.

Will's legs refused to support him any longer, and he collapsed in an awkward position on the cement. His skin turned white, tears and terror came to his eyes, and he couldn't stop his hands from shaking.

Sometime later he forced himself to his feet and fearfully went to see Chet and Nancy. The shower still pounded down. The boy was sound asleep in a puddle of water on the bathroom floor—but it seemed to be a natural sleep of exhaustion and nothing more. The incubus had been tied to itself, forced into a psychic moebius strip—Will hadn't dared to hope, but apparently the thing's other ties, to Chet, Nancy, had been broken. His wife and son would be weak ... but they would recover.

Will picked Chet up and carried him to the bedroom, laying

him neatly beside Nancy. He shook her, and she came slowly awake, looking alarmed but too tired to show it much. "Will? What happened?"

His throat refused to respond to the words he had to say. It was too soon. He couldn't tell her about the incubus, about Beth ... it was too soon.

"Just rest now, Nancy." She closed her eyes and seemed perfectly willing to comply. Will sighed and stood looking at her for a long time before he finally sat down in a chair and fell asleep.

In high school I never much liked history, which was dry and boring, but in college I discovered professors who had a genuine passion for ancient times and places. They made it interesting, and I was hooked.

Though I was a Physics/Astronomy major, I grew so interested in history courses that I ended up with a minor in Russian History, which is reflected in several stories in these collections. In one of my Russian History classes, I discovered a few references to horrific work camps that were established during the time of the Napoleonic Wars. These camps were run by the brutal General Arakcheev, with the blessing of the normally gentle Tsar Alexander I. Immediately, I had the spark for a dark fantasy story, and when the professor handed out a term paper assignment, I used that as an excuse to do my research.

Unfortunately, Arakcheev's workcamps were so obscure that virtually no books or scholarly articles had been published on the subject. Nevertheless, I uncovered enough material for a great horror story. When I delivered the term paper, the professor was quite pleased, saying that he had learned a great deal about the obscure concentration camps.

I smiled and quipped, "Then I should make up my information more often."

He was not in the least amused.

In any event, as accurate as I could make it, here is my story of what might have happened in those harsh Russian encampments....

New Recruits

April 28, 1825

My dearest Tania,

In the military colonies of our beloved Tsar Alexander I, circumstances do not often grant me an opportunity to write you a personal letter—a truly *personal* letter which none of them have read beforehand. Things are still in a state of confused shock here after the tragedy—some of the buildings are still smoldering, and Lieutenant Goliepin has assumed temporary command; but he has not had us drill for two days now—and I am taking these precious moments of solitude to write you what I fear will be a rather lengthy letter.

Perhaps you may understand the reason for my prolonged silence once you realize the daily routine we undergo here. General Ursov, who was our commanding officer, believed that perfect discipline is the highest achievement any man can hope to accomplish in his lifetime. Thus, we spend three days a week in intense military drill from 6 AM to 11 AM and then again from 2 PM to 10 PM. But then, Tania, you are not accustomed to the slavery of clocks, so these numbers probably mean nothing to you. On alternate days we erect new buildings since Ursov insists that "building is the best means of ensuring that one's name will be remembered after one is dead." We also drain the land, dig ditches, and clear the stumps and stones ... and we attempt to reclaim the swamp near which our colony is situated, which turns into a deathtrap mire every spring when the snow melts.

I believe the peasants, though, have it even worse than we soldiers do. They must rise two hours before us to care for the cattle, wash down the sidewalks, sweep the streets, sand the paths, or clean the latrines. And they must also drill with us in the morning, before going out into the fields to till the soil, *in uniform.* Even their six-year-old boys are required to drill. If only the Tsar knew what it was like—surely, he'd change things.

Tsar Alexander said that he wanted these colonies to be places where we soldiers could settle down in times of peace, grow our own food, and live with our families. All I know is that I have been here almost a year—and you, dear sister, and the rest of my family are still not with me. It almost brings tears to my eyes when I think of the day I was conscripted. How you and Mother wept, how the rest of the village already mourned me as dead. Twenty-five years of military service! I might as well be dead. I remember how Father and I drank too much vodka, for it was expected that I overindulge on the last night of my freedom. And then the next morning, riding in the lurching wagon along the muddy, pitted road, my head throbbing and my insides churning, and adding my own groans to those of the other new recruits riding in the crowded back of the wagon. I remember it rained that day—a light, misty rain ... a gray rain.... That was over a year ago.

I am writing this letter myself, Tania, for I have perfected my knowledge of how to read and write here. I am hoping you will know to take this to Father Paniskii—how is he? Is he still alive?—and he will read it to you. Father Paniskii always liked me—he was always so kind. I first learned from him how to read, remember? He was going to send me to one of the church schools, but I was taken into the army before I had finished my lessons from him—barely enough time for me to learn to manage by myself. Old Endovik says that I am lucky to have a priest that I love, for he says the only priest he remembers from his village was a mean, unfriendly man. Endovik has been in the army so long.

Endovik is the man I live with—*lived* with; I still cannot believe he is dead. But his death was the means for me to get this letter to you—you shall see. I must tell all this in order, lest I lose my sanity by going off on too many tangents. You know me, Tania, as does Father Paniskii, so you know I am not a liar or a storyteller. And I sincerely hope that you will show this letter to no one else, for they will surely not believe me—especially after the "official statement" of what happened here is released. You must believe me—you will see.

It was spring, and wet, and miserable—perfect for the outbreak of cholera which struck our camp. Over one quarter of our population died from the disease, in throes of vomit and diarrhea which brought about the exhaustion which killed them. The peasants suffered worse than the soldiers did—and while both Endovik and I escaped the sickness, both of our peasant hosts died within hours of each other. They were a childless peasant man and wife, who had been kind to us and looked on their two soldier "lodgers" as the children they had never been blessed with. When we weren't drilling, Endovik and I helped them with their chores. They died, with the last words of each asking how the other had fared. "Regaining strength," we had said. "Coming along nicely."

We were taken to new, hastily erected barracks which were crowded with all the refugees from other cholera-stricken households. Every home which had encountered cholera was abandoned, and due to the strict, almost vicious measures of General Ursov, the epidemic was contained within one section of buildings.

No one can say what Ursov intended to do with the abandoned buildings. In all sensibility he should have burned them to the ground—everything a cholera victim has touched or even gazed upon should be destroyed as a precaution against further spread of the disease. But the General's stubborn ... one could almost call it *worship* of the things he had accomplished, which would not allow him to destroy the buildings erected under his command.

The houses are symmetrically arranged along the main road—a watchtower stands for observing the fields; the chapel and the fire station are in the center of the village, surrounded by the officers' quarters and other administerial buildings. One entire block of houses along the road stood empty, waiting for new occupants.

General Ursov had ordered new recruits from the Tsar in St. Petersburg, and he worked us survivors harder to make up for the loss of workers—and still he did not relax our military training. "Discipline is more important than rest," Ursov had said. I'll add my curse to all those others who have cursed him at one time or another, for one reason or another.

Even before it seemed possible—only four days after Ursov had sent his request to Tsar Alexander—the new recruits arrived. It was not possible that a message could have reached St. Petersburg, that the Tsar could have arranged for new troops and sent them to our colony in only four days. Yet they were here, and we looked on them as a blessing. A blessing! At the time we did see them as such. I think of them differently now.

The rain had stopped in order to make way for the heavy fog which had rolled in, wet and gray. The soldiers were standing in ranks for our military drill which had already gone on for several hours. We were wet and cold and exhausted—but if we had let any of it show we would have been given an extra part of an hour of practice. Endovik doesn't have to drill much with us—he's a veteran; he had survived his twenty-five years of military service. Endovik was a tough old man. He had been conscripted in 1799, before Tsar Paul I was assassinated, then served under our Tsar Alexander. He had fought against Napoleon at Borodinó in 1812, and he helped erect this military colony in 1818, almost exactly seven years ago to the date. He had survived his term of service—one of the few, for twenty-five years of discipline like Ursov's is not easy to survive—and now the army, by its own promises, was forced to take care of him, begrudgingly. Tsar Alexander doesn't know how bad things are —I am sure of it.

But, I promised I would not digress. We were standing in the fog, drilling monotonously, when we saw someone marching down the main road, spectral figures silhouetted in the fog. Now, these military colonies are isolated, and no one is allowed in—not government officials, not police—without the express permission of the commanding officer. We didn't know what to think of the strange figures in the fog, until they emerged.

A young corporal, dressed in an old, dusty uniform, marched at the head of a column of twenty peasants, all thin and covered with scanty, tattered garments in the cold and wet. Their skin was pale, and their eyes were blank and staring as if they had had their very souls wrenched from them. They made no sound—no speaking, no shuffling of feet, simply quietly stepping as they marched past the troops standing at attention in the midst of our drilling.

Ursov watched as the corporal marched up to him. The General frowned, as if he vaguely recognized the other man but could not place him. Ursov seemed troubled.

The corporal halted in front of the General, saluted, and presented himself and his column of peasants. "General Ursov," he said, "I am Corporal Belidaev. I have brought you these new recruits, as you requested, to replace some of the colonists who fell in your tragic epidemic." Belidaev gestured to the vacant-faced peasants, allowing his words to sink in. Then he spoke again. "They are from the village of Vendeévna."

Ursov's eyebrows shot up, and it seemed to me that he paled rapidly. The General fidgeted, and the expression on his face seemed not to be able to decide which final form to take, as if he could not enforce the discipline on his own emotions which he demanded of his troops.

Belidaev stood placidly, matching his stare with those of the peasants. Ursov endured it uncomfortably until he turned to Lieutenant Goliepin. Goliepin is Ursov's little servant who does everything the General tells him to. Goliepin isn't very bright and that's why the General likes him. In fact, I think I have a sharper mind than the Lieutenant—and it is very shocking, believe me, the first time you realize that you are truly more intelligent than your superiors are!

Ursov snapped to Goliepin, "Lieutenant, see to it that these new recruits are placed in the empty buildings."

"The *empty* buildings, sir?"

"You are standing right next to me, Goliepin—has the fog gotten into your ears?"

Goliepin dug a finger into his left ear, seeming to take the General's question seriously. "No, sir. But the empty buildings are—"

Ursov's temper was rising. "I know full well which buildings I am talking about! If I didn't know about them, I could hardly *suggest* them, now could I?"

"But—"

"GOLIEPIN!" Ursov roared, his face livid, all traces of his former pallor gone. "Am I not the commanding officer here? Do I not give the orders? And are you not to follow them? Without question! I leave this matter in your hands—I trust the new recruits will be settled adequately."

Ursov turned and stormed away toward his private quarters. He was very upset and did not look at Goliepin standing confused in his wake, nor at Belidaev and his peasants. We soldiers were all very mystified. Belidaev was grinning to himself.

The atmosphere of the barracks in the evening always contains a mixture of different emotions. After a long session of drilling, which encompasses most of the afternoon and all of the evening, the prevailing mood is exhaustion. And the next day we would have to labor in the fields, or out in the swamp trying to "reclaim" it.

We were crowded in the hastily erected barracks, and the

noises of many men drifted through the air, mingled with the odors of sweat and dirt. Some of the newer soldiers could be heard whimpering in their sleep, dreaming of wives or families or villages left behind for the next twenty-five years. Endovik says that the ones who whimper never survive the term of service. I wonder if I whimper in my sleep. A dim lantern stood in the center of a small wooden table, surrounded by four soldiers attempting to play a game about which no one could remember the rules precisely, but that didn't seem to bother them much. They couldn't cheat if no one knew the rules anyway.

Endovik's bunk was next to mine—technically he was a farmer-colonist now that he had retired, free to till his land and be self-sufficient. But many things had been changed in the crisis of the epidemic. Many of the men lay wide awake in their bunks, staring and trying to find whatever they wished for. That's the funny thing about exhaustion—it is harder to sleep if you're completely exhausted than it is if you aren't tired at all. By the time your muscles and nerves relax enough to permit sleep, it is time to wake up anyway. Oh well, not even the Tsar can change that.

Endovik usually stayed awake to talk with me, since he knew I wouldn't be able to sleep for some time. Those were the times when I missed you the most, and also the times when life in the military colonies was the most bearable. Endovik and I became great friends during those quiet conversations. Poor Endovik.

I told him about the new recruits, and Corporal Belidaev, and Ursov's reaction to the name of Vendeévna.

"Vendeévna?" Endovik said, and I looked at him to see that he was frowning, searching his memories. "Vendeévna was the name of the village that was here—before the colony. General Ursov had us tear it down to erect the colony...."

"Why would Belidaev say his peasants were from Vendeévna then? Could there be another village with that name near here?"

Endovik pursed his lips and scratched his cheek by the mole under his ear. "Maybe you should know more about our General Ursov, Alexis," he said to me.

I lay on my back and listened—Endovik was good at telling stories.

"Ursov was the fifth son of a nobleman and entered the army in the hope that his family name might bring him more success than the family fortunes would have. He fought against Napoleon at Borodinó under Field Marshall Kutuzov—and was the only survivor of his company because he hid in the dark corner of a ruined peasant home as soon as the heavy shooting started. Instead of being hung for cowardice as he should have been, Ursov was promoted. He had noble blood in his veins. I fought at Borodinó too—I was even shot in the arm."

Endovik fumbled with his shirt, but it was dark, and I had seen the scar before anyway. "If only the Tsar knew ..." We both sighed. Endovik continued.

"That was the time when I was half-finished with my term of service. The memories of my family were just numb spots in my mind, and the anticipation of getting out of the army was a dream, endlessly far away.

"After the wars, Ursov was given a soft administerial position in the military, right where he could embezzle money which was supposed to buy better food and uniforms for the soldiers. Then the Tsar started his program of military colonies and transferred Ursov out of his easy desk job and dropped him here in the wilderness to establish a new colony!" Endovik allowed himself a small chuckle. I was beginning to suspect that he was making much of this up, but I didn't know how much, nor did I really care.

"Tsar Alexander had selected this piece of land to be the site of Ursov's colony—out in a muddy swamp—where stood a generations-old peasant village named Vendeévna. It was common practice in erecting a military colony to raze the existing village, level it to the ground, and build a new military colony on the site, each building constructed according to a master plan. However, the peasants of Vendeévna had lived in their traditional village for as far as their memories stretched into the past—and they realized that Ursov was a lazy desk-man who had gone to fat in the previous few years.

"The peasants of Vendeévna rose up and refused to allow the construction of the colony, saying that the document of authorization from the Tsar had been forged—even though none of them could read—because the Tsar would never do such a thing.

"Then Ursov changed into a completely different person. He was like a raving, bloodthirsty general. He resented being here even more than the soldiers did and decided to make things even more miserable for the rest of us. Perhaps he saw a chance to make up for his cowardice at Borodinó—although he would probably make me run the gauntlet if he knew I had suggested he has a conscience—maybe there were other reasons. The General had us soldiers take out our weapons, fit the bayonets. We were to put the peasants in their places by violence.

"I remember one of our soldiers ... I can't remember his name ... was originally from Vendeévna, and he refused to fight against his own townspeople. Ursov shot him dead right in front of all of us and ordered the rest of us to attack—our muskets and bayonets against sticks and pitchforks ... we had seen what would have happened had we disobeyed the General's orders. What could we do? The soldiers had been worn thin from Ursov's discipline—and he unleashed them to burn and pillage. I don't know how many peasants were killed before Vendeévna surrendered. Ursov sent the survivors out into the steppe, without provisions, with orders to travel to the nearest military colony, which was about a hundred *versts* away, with no villages in between." Endovik sighed, "We never received word if any of them reached their destination...."

The old man drew a heavy breath. Many of the other soldiers had already gone to sleep. I was startled by the sudden darkness as the gameplayers extinguished their lantern and got up from their table, groping in shadows to find their bunks.

"But why would anyone claim to be from Vendeévna seven years after that village was leveled?"

Endovik was silent for a short while, then spoke. "I just tell the stories—don't ask me to explain them."

Three days a week we practiced our military drill. On alternate days we worked. Hard. Since it was springtime, most of the soldiers and peasants were out working in the fields, plowing and planting. Lt. Goliepin had taken Corporal Belidaev and his twenty peasants out into the swamp to try to "drain" it. Nobody really knew what they were doing out in the swamp—Goliepin least of all—but they were kept busy sloshing in the mud, skirting the deep and treacherous muddy pools, and digging random trenches that led nowhere.

I had been assigned to sweep the streets and sidewalks, due to the cholera-inflicted shortage of peasants. This was the first time I had done this job, but I found it much more tolerable than working in the swamp, or even in the fields. Ursov is very imaginative, I must admit, for he can find tasks which absolutely *must* be done that no one else would even think of doing. Such as sweeping the trunks of trees....

It was midmorning, and I had been working for five hours. I had swept most of the main street clean, and I was working on the walk in front of General Ursov's headquarters. I was tired, but I dared not rest so close to the General's watchful eye. I kept working, and it was very quiet.

But peace doesn't last very long in the colony. I heard a horse coming and looked up to see Goliepin galloping down the street toward the General's headquarters. Goliepin looked agitated, and his horse, covered up to its belly with globs of mud, looked angry at him for being so stupid as to bring a horse into the treacherous swamp. I watched the lumps of mud the horse left in its wake to mark its hoofprints, standing out in a bold trail down the center of the street I had just spent five hours sweeping.

"General! General!" Goliepin cried as he charged up the walk. I had to leap out of the way or be trampled. "There's been an accident!"

Ursov burst out of his office, a half-crumpled piece of paper in his hand. Goliepin tried to catch his breath, but Ursov would have none of it. "Well, what's happened? Have you—"

"One of the peasants is drowned! He fell into a deep pool of mud in the swamp and sank under! We tried to get him out, but ... the mud must be softer than I thought—we couldn't find him! Not even his body! And the other peasants just ... just stood there!"

Ursov reacted strangely to the news of the death. He appeared almost happy for a moment, or relieved may be a better word. Then he suddenly turned angry and snapped at Goliepin. "You shouldn't have left them alone out in the swamp just to tell me about the death of a peasant, you fool! They're in your *command*! You aren't a messenger boy, Goliepin! Now make the rest of them work harder for their carelessness!"

Goliepin looked confused for a moment, then seemed to think better of being confused; he saluted, turned his horse, and rode back down the clean street, laying down another set of hoofprints. I looked at the mud and sighed. One doesn't complain.

We stood rigidly in our ranks, enforcing absolute discipline on ourselves. Our faces betrayed no emotion, our bodies allowed no movement whatsoever, not even a shiver in the cold night. It was time for the final roll call before retiring to our barracks; Ursov seemed to find it helpful to our sleep that we each get a good chill before turning in. Our uniforms were old and thin and did little to keep out the cold wind.

All the colonists stood in neat lines, facing the General who stalked back and forth in front of the ranks, hands clasped behind his back. Goliepin went carefully down each column, counting with his fingers, and losing track more than once so that we had to stand in the cold longer while the Lieutenant corrected his error.

Goliepin went to the single line of the twenty silent peasants under the supervision of Corporal Belidaev. Belidaev stood serenely as Goliepin counted his charges. Once again, the

Lieutenant's voice broke out in a half-whine of surprise. "General!"

Ursov had been watching Belidaev intently, and strode over as Goliepin shouted again, abruptly lowering his voice as he realized the General had stepped closer. "The new peasants are all here!"

Ursov frowned, "And should they not be? They were under your command."

"No, sir, General! I mean they're *all* here! Even the one who drowned! Well, he didn't drown if he's here—I mean the one we *thought* had drowned! The one *I* thought—"

Ursov pushed past the babbling Lieutenant and moved slowly down the column of peasants, glaring at each one of them. He came to the man, an old man, caked with mud, his clothes, his hair —mud dried even on his eyes and lips, in his mouth and teeth. He stared at the General with unblinking eyes and made no sign that he saw anything.

It took a supreme effort for the rest of us soldiers not to break discipline and turn our heads to watch the silent conflict. We could feel the tension crawling in the air, and we were certain that much more was here than we were aware of.

"Excuse me, General." The voice startled Ursov in the silence, and he snapped his head up. Belidaev had spoken. "I did not mention this before, but I believe you knew my sister?"

It appeared as if someone had physically struck the General. Ursov stormed up to Belidaev, and his face was terrible to see, yet he also appeared helpless at the same time.

"Surely you must remember her, General?" Belidaev continued, his voice mildly taunting. "She had long brown hair in braids. And a mole on her left cheek?"

Ursov seethed, and Belidaev raised his voice, almost shouting into the General's face: *"A mole on her left cheek!"*

Something snapped in Ursov, and he let out a cry of rage as he struck Belidaev a blow across the face which would have toppled a horse. Belidaev stood firmly.

"Tomorrow morning you shall endure the *knut!*" Ursov

roared, and he stormed off to his private quarters, but it seemed almost as if he fled.

Belidaev smiled.

When we finally retired to the barracks, generally with more noise than was necessary (but then we needed some release from the amount of control Ursov's discipline forced on us), I found Endovik already in his bunk. I spoke to him, but he didn't answer. I frowned, knowing he couldn't be asleep with all the commotion the soldiers were causing, and upon bending closer to him I saw that he had a strange pallor. He was shivering.

"Endovik?"

His face had a tight expression of pain and discomfort, and when I touched him, his skin had a clammy feeling. Tears swam in front of my vision.

"Endovik?" I asked again.

He opened his eyes and sighed heavily. "I know...."

We both had seen enough of the epidemic in the past weeks that neither of us could have any doubt. We had watched the same thing happen to our peasant hosts. I wanted to run away, but I couldn't. Not from Endovik.

"Could you help me to the infirmary, please, Alexis?" Endovik looked up at me; and I helped him out of his bed.

That was the bravest thing I have ever done in my life—it required more courage than any battlefield would have. I remember stumbling across the compound, together in the darkness, Endovik leaning heavily on me, his steps uncertain. At any moment I waited for the fatal germ to cling to my clothes, to be inhaled in each breath, wondering if I had already contracted cholera, if I was already doomed. Endovik was shivering all the way, or was it me?

When I finally returned to my own bed, I lay shaking for a

long time, listening to the silence which Endovik's breathing normally filled....

A heavy feeling of tension, uneasiness, filled the air as we filed out of the barracks early the next morning to witness the punishment of Belidaev. The sun had just risen, and the air was still chill as we marched to the plaza where we normally drilled at the center of the colony.

Ursov sent a group of soldiers with bayoneted muskets to the cholera houses to bring forth Belidaev and the peasants. The General's face was bright and smiling in anticipation of the event. Ursov seemed to feel that since he was in a position of importance he was required to strike back viciously at anyone who questioned his authority, to fight back at anyone who fought against him. He knew he had not earned his rank—especially after his cowardice at the battle of Borodinó—and perhaps he felt he had to struggle harder to keep it, as he had against the insurrection of the original peasants of Vendeévna. And now Belidaev and his peasants were frustrating the General because they seemed to be taking care to do nothing Ursov could fight against. They were like ghosts from his past who had come—not to haunt the General—but to let him haunt himself.

Two of the soldiers reappeared, stiffly resting their guns on their shoulders, flanking Belidaev as he marched toward the General. Behind them came the column of twenty peasants, also closely guarded. I could see no reason for this and I am certain I wasn't the only one mystified, since neither the peasants nor Corporal Belidaev had ever shown any form of resistance whatsoever.

Belidaev, however, did not seem to be disturbed in the least when he walked up to Ursov, even pulling slightly ahead of his guards (which we found to be one of his strangest actions yet, since each of the other colonists lives in mortal terror of the *knut*).

"Good morning, General!" he said.

Ursov's face went livid with rage, and he angrily barked orders for Belidaev's two escorts to strip the Corporal of his shirt and to bind him to a sloped wooden post sticking out of the ground at an angle. Dried blood stained the post and the ground around it, for we were forbidden to scrub this reminder of past punishments while we were forced to keep the rest of the colony so meticulously clean.

Belidaev rested against the post and did not struggle as the soldiers lashed his wrists together—more tightly than they had to, but they had no wish to incur the General's rage. The peasants of Vendeévna stood silently, looking on with their staring eyes.

Ursov removed a long rawhide lash from his belt, holding the sweat-polished handle in one hand and caressing the braided leather thongs with his other. For the occasion he had added several sharp metal barbs to the end—I had not seen him do this for any other's punishment.

"Before you whip me, General, aren't you going to announce my *crime*?" Belidaev called, his voice pitched to draw the greatest irritation from Ursov. "You do remember my *crime*, don't you, General?"

This evoked a brief murmur from the onlookers, *almost* a murmur, before they caught themselves and remained silent. Indeed, none of us understood exactly what Belidaev was being punished for.

Ursov responded with a violent crack of the whip, striking across the Corporal's back. Belidaev didn't wince or show any outward sign of pain; but a thin red line of blood appeared on his back.

"Hah! So you do bleed!" the General cried out, as if this were some odd sort of victory.

"You sound as if you expected otherwise, General?" Belidaev spoke calmly. Ursov whipped him again, and again.

And again, for a full hour. The pattern of interlaced red lines on Belidaev's back had been obliterated by the flow of blood—but still the Corporal showed no pain, nor did he ask for any release from his punishment. He seemed to be drawing strength from the very ground his feet were touching, from the air he breathed, from the place that was Vendeévna.

The General too was drawing strength from his own reservoir of anger and bitterness, from some wellspring within himself which poured forth hatred for this Belidaev with a greater intensity than I have ever before seen, in any man!

At last Ursov, exhausted, had to pause for a moment. He wiped sweat off his forehead and his upper lip, reaching inside his coat for a silver flask of vodka. He filled the capful, took a small sip, then downed the rest in a gulp. The General replaced the flask and wiped his sweaty palm on his pant leg before gripping the whip handle again.

Ursov continued the beating for another hour, leaving us to wait and watch when we would normally be practicing military drill. The peasants of Vendeévna remained silent, looking on with their staring eyes. The General was trembling and seemed incapable of continuing.

Belidaev himself finally looked weakened; his eyes were closed, his back was shredded, and the flesh hung in bloody strips. As Ursov watched, the Corporal slowly slid down the post slippery with his own blood and fell to his knees.

Ursov seemed to draw strength from this and shouted for the doctor to bring smelling salts. The doctor seemed to have been waiting for this and passed the smelling salts in front of Belidaev's face, reviving him. The doctor was a particularly uncaring man, with rough patches of stubble always scattered on his chin, as if he never shaved but could not grow a beard. His eyes were dull and tired. As Belidaev struggled to get to his feet, Ursov continued the beating again until the Corporal collapsed once more.

Like a wolf pouncing on his fallen prey, the General removed some small metal spikes from his pocket and savagely branded Belidaev on the forehead and both cheeks, leaving ugly, raw wounds. Smiling, he rubbed gunpowder into the bleeding facial wounds so that the scars would be permanent; then Ursov stepped back to inspect his work.

Belidaev was silent, huddled against the post. Ursov turned smartly to glare at the peasants, as if to find some signs of despair or compassion for the Corporal. The General seemed furious when he failed to find any. He strode up to the peasants, glaring at them, slowly pacing before each one of them, gloating.

"You see, filth, I command here! My word is power in this colony, and your resistance has no effect. Belidaev is weak—you are all *nothing*! My command comes directly from the Tsar—" The General stopped before the old man who had vanished into the swamp mire; the peasant was still caked with dried mud which clung to his hair, his lips, his eyes. "And my every action is sanctioned by him!"

Abruptly, the mud-covered peasant spat full in Ursov's face. The General looked as if his throat would burst as his roar tried to charge out of his mouth.

"SOLDIERS! I want every person in this colony to form two columns! GOLIEPIN! See that *every* man has a rod or whip! Every one of these accursed peasants will run the gauntlet! With a full thousand men on a side! I will see their blood run on the ground!"

"Haven't you seen that already, General?" A hoarse voice— Belidaev struggling against the ropes that bound him to the post. Ursov stormed over to him and kicked him savagely in the left kidney.

"You seem not to care about your own pain, Belidaev; I hope you find the punishment of your peasants more enjoyable!"

The gauntlet was formed rapidly. Ursov clapped his hand on certain soldiers as he passed, indicating that they were to lead the peasants between the two lines of soldiers armed with sticks and whips. Each soldier, when chosen, went up to a peasant, bared the peasant's back, and pointed the bayonet of his musket at the other's chest, lashing the peasant's hands to the barrel of the gun. The peasants offered no resistance whatsoever.

A long stick like a broom handle was thrust into my hands, and I knew what I had to do. I stood uneasily in line, waiting for the peasants to be led past. I saw the doctor kneeling by Belidaev, and I was angry for a moment, wondering why he had left Endovik. And then the peasants began to march between the two columns of soldiers.

It is a strange thing to have to beat someone you hold nothing against, someone you don't even know. Yet with Ursov watching us, we had to strike the peasants with all the strength we could manage—or we would end up running the gauntlet ourselves. As the peasants filed by, the soldiers holding their muskets were crouched and wary, lest they be struck themselves as they moved slowly backwards.

The blows fell, and the peasants didn't seem to mind. They uttered not one sound, and I struck with all my might, for Ursov stood near me. An old peasant woman was led past me, but she did not flinch when I tried to crack her skull with my wooden rod. My arm was numb from the force of the blow, yet an *old woman* did not feel it!

The peasants were taken through the gauntlet, and none of them fell. Not one, not even the oldest and frailest among them. They waited at the end, and Ursov was livid. He stormed forward and grabbed the man who stood next to me. "*You!* You weren't striking hard enough! Send them through the gauntlet again!" the General shouted, "And you will follow them through as punishment for your laxness!"

Then Ursov pointed at me, and my blood froze in my veins as I thought I would be forced to run the gauntlet myself. But then I realized I was to lead my companion through. His hands were stiff and trembling as I lashed them to my musket, pointing the bayonet at his chest. His eyes were wide, and I could not tell if he hated me for doing this. I didn't even know his name—that made things easier.

We followed the peasants of Vendeévna through the two columns of throbbing sticks and whips. The man I led winced and cried out and stumbled as each blow fell—but the peasants made no sound. About halfway through the long column, my companion collapsed and would not get up again as his blood oozed through bruises and smashed skin. Ursov ordered for a flat sled to be brought, then made me slide the almost unconscious man on it. I then continued to drag the man through the lines as the other soldiers beat his motionless form.

I was drenched with sweat, both from exertion and anxiety, as I emerged from the end of the lines; the other soldiers who had led the peasants looked in a similar condition, far more distraught than the peasants themselves were. The peasants were unscathed. The doctor nonchalantly shuffled forward to look at the bloody man on the sled as Ursov bellowed for the peasants to run the gauntlet again.

The soldiers all groaned—not aloud, of course, as they were too afraid of the General for that—but I could sense their dismay. "Not this one, General," the doctor said, indicating the man I had led. "He won't survive it."

Ursov scowled. "Take him to the infirmary, then." He glared at the peasants, as if to say "How dare you emerge without a scratch while one of my men undergoes half what you have and almost dies." That look was so filled with hatred that I know I would have shriveled up right there if it had been directed at me.

"Belidaev, too?" the doctor mumbled, breaking Ursov's silent anger.

"No! He can lay in the barracks!" Then the General, at the peak of his frustration, dismissed the troops. He turned his back to all of us and strode off toward his office, looking for all the world like a mighty man who had just had his own impotence held out before him.

It was dark and silent in the barracks; most of us were asleep, and even the sounds of the men were muted as they went deeper into their dreams, or their nightmares, or the day's strange events. I was thinking about Endovik.

The door burst open, striking the wall to which it was hinged with a flat *crack*, waking us in an instant. Ursov stood alone, framed in the doorway, silhouetting himself with the glow from the lantern he held in his left hand. The General entered the barracks, his boots making his footsteps loud on the wooden floor. He was fully uniformed, carrying a pistol in his belt and his whip in his right hand.

"Up! *Up!*" he shouted hoarsely. Ursov strode among the bunks, rapping them with the wooden handle of his whip as the soldiers struggled to their feet. "Up, scum! You have a task to perform! Dress yourselves as quickly as you can! Hurry!"

We did so, at first muttering among ourselves in our weariness; and then, remembering our fear of the General, we placed our clothes on in silence, hastily buttoning enough buttons to make us look dressed. Then Ursov ordered us out of the barracks and into three lines.

We were marched across the compound to the three buildings where Belidaev and the peasants of Vendeévna were housed, standing next to the other cholera-emptied buildings.

"Another case of the cholera sickness has been reported," the General spoke to us. "To prevent another epidemic, the doctor has placed the victim in the strictest isolation and will not allow even the medical staff to tend him, lest they pass along the disease." Rage filled me, and I almost flung myself at Ursov. Endovik! They weren't even tending him!

"We must burn these plague buildings and everything in them to prevent another epidemic!"

Ursov ordered us to gather straw and pile it up around the buildings, so that we could set them on fire. We worked uneasily, and the General became increasingly impatient.

Finally, one of the soldiers spoke up. "General, sir, shouldn't we ... shouldn't we get the peasants out first?"

Ursov snarled and cracked his whip across the soldier's back. "You will follow my orders! Without question! I command! Do I not control this colony and everything in it? By the order of the Tsar!" The soldier was cowed and went back to work; the General turned and muttered quietly, almost to himself, "We will see if they are demons or not."

Next, we were ordered to gather up hammers, nails, and pieces of wood with which to board up the doors and windows of the three occupied buildings. Each of us worked rapidly, afraid, and the three buildings were quickly secured. The strangest thing, to me, about the entire business was that the occupants of the buildings never stirred, never shouted, never tried to break out, not with all our sounds of hammering, and Ursov's shouting. An eerie, unnatural sensation filled all of us. Perhaps the General was right—maybe the peasants of Vendeévna *were* unholy demons. Enough had happened since the new recruits had arrived that none of us was certain what to think any more.

Ursov's voice was laced with fear as he ordered the straw set on fire, as if he knew he finally had to confront Belidaev in an unearthly duel but did not know what the outcome would be. The fires were set first on one of the buildings, then the next, and finally the third building where the bleeding form of Belidaev had been taken earlier that day.

The wood burned quickly, as if eager to cleanse itself, hungry to be purged of the cholera and of the spirits within. Each of us waited, fascinated by the flames, waiting with dread to hear the first screams of the peasants within. But they never came. The wood cracked and spat as it was consumed, and the fires began to climb the walls.

Belidaev's building was in flames—and the door was suddenly flung open, the boards barricading the door shattered as if they did not exist. Belidaev stood in the doorway, framed in flames—all his lashes and bruises were healed, even the brands on his cheek and forehead had vanished. He stepped out of the burning building and turned to face Ursov, glaring at him with eyes made of shattered pain and ice.

"Good evening, General," Belidaev said.

Ah, Tania, the horror as I write this!

Ursov used a mask of rage to cover his fear, and he lashed out at Belidaev with his whip. The General gasped in pain of his own and let the whip fall, looking in astonishment at the line of torn cloth across his chest, as if he himself had been whipped. Belidaev was untouched. Ursov fingered the sticky blood on his chest.

"You see, General, you continue to bring about your own punishment."

Ursov stood speechless, his fear forming its own discipline.

Belidaev crossed his arms over his chest. "Do you know what night this is, General? This is our anniversary. Do you remember what happened seven years ago, General?"

Ursov clenched his fists into tight balls, but he seemed too much afraid to take any direct action.

"The peasants of Vendeévna rose up against you and your military colony—but you had them put down with your muskets and bayonets. You *ordered* your soldiers to pillage and burn— Vendeévna had to be razed anyway, you said, to establish the military colony here. One of your soldiers, a Corporal Belidaev, had been born and raised in Vendeévna before being drafted into the Tsar's army. When he tried to speak out to protect the people of his village, you shot him in front of the other soldiers to show them what would happen if they disobeyed the *great* General Ursov who had fought so *bravely* at the battle of Borodinó. Do you remember shooting poor Corporal Belidaev, General?"

"You are lying!" Ursov shouted.

"And after you had turned your soldiers loose on the village to rampage, you went through the people yourself like a wolf. You raped my sister Marta, General—do you even remember? She had long brown hair, braided—and a mole on her left cheek. You told her you would shoot our parents if she did not submit—and even though in her fear she cooperated with you in every way, still you rammed your bayonet into her throat when you had finished with her! Do you remember? You thought you had no conscience, General—I am here."

"You can't know! You were dead!"

"The village of Vendeévna was here for generations, General. The peasants farmed here, sweated and died here—for *generations*. You don't think you can remove all that by tearing down the buildings and erecting your own? Your military colony,

General, is like a thorn in the skin of the earth, which is being pushed outward. The time has come, General—the splinter will be removed."

Ursov turned to us with a strange, wild expression in his eyes. "Lies! They are not true!"

The building roared in flames behind Belidaev, but he didn't seem bothered by the heat. He beckoned to Ursov. "Would you care to enter the fires of Hell a few moments sooner, General?"

Ursov grabbed the pistol from his belt and pointed it at Belidaev. "You will die, demon!"

"Yes!" Belidaev hissed. "The demon will die!"

The General fired—and fell to the ground with a bullet hole in his chest, and shock on his face. His blood soaked into the soil of Vendeévna to mingle with the peasant blood he had spilled there so many years ago.

Belidaev laughed and turned to step inside the burning building, vanishing in the flames.

Just this morning, when some of the soldiers ventured into the still-smoldering wreckage of the cholera buildings—under direct orders, since no one had willingly ventured into them since the night of the fires—they found no bones or any other remains of Belidaev or the peasants of Vendeévna. Somehow, I wasn't surprised.

I went to visit Endovik this morning, but he had already died. The doctor wouldn't even let me say goodbye to the body of my friend. It was too risky, he said. However, Endovik's death is allowing me to send you this letter. Lieutenant Goliepin has the command now, and he is very confused with all the new duties thrust upon him. I have told him that Endovik had a sister, and I asked him if I could write her a letter of consolation. Goliepin was happy to have one small duty taken from him and he quickly waved me away. He won't have time to read this letter either, and so I will trust that it reaches you uncensored.

I believe that the "official" story states something to the effect that Ursov died of cholera, and the buildings were routinely burned to remove the threat of pestilence. Officially, we never received any new recruits from Vendeévna.

Give my love and greetings to Father, and I will write you again if I can, but it may not be possible for a while. Know that you are with me and that you are my strength to endure twenty-five years of military service. I love you all, and God's blessing upon you.

Alexis

For my undergraduate degree in physics and astronomy, I went to the University of Wisconsin-Madison. Despite all the movies showing wild campus life, I was a nerdy kid who lived at home with my parents to save on dorm expenses, and I didn't have a very successful dating life.

But, because I was a writer, the mystery and misery of finding the love of my life served as inspiration for stories. "Nuptials" is a short piece that I had almost forgotten. Upon rereading, I found it surprisingly creepy.

Nuptials

"Will you marry me?"

Sincerity—passion—it shouldn't be hard to say it like you mean it, because you really do mean it. Keep saying it over and over to yourself until you get it right.

"Will you *please* marry me?"

Ah, shit, Jerry thought, exasperated and alone. Maybe Shelly would think it was sweet. He stood up from the cold, stone bench outside and paced around the statue in the campus courtyard. His tennis shoes crunched on the half-melted snow. He smeared a hand on his wind-mussed brown hair, habitually trying to keep it neat, though no one else could see him.

Few other students wandered around the campus—it was too chilly for that. The courtyard in front of the Humanities building remained deserted, surrounded by the snow-covered oak and dying elm trees. He had decided to skip his acting class. This was much more important than acting anyway.

Jerry heaved a sigh and watched his breath congeal into steam, like a fire-breathing dragon. A dragon? And him too afraid to ask Shelly a simple question?

He walked back and forth, mumbling the lines to himself, but they all sounded like wooden, overused expressions. Stale dialogue, limp soliloquy.

Trying to find some deeper inspiration, Jerry looked up at the statue—a bulky Romanesque woman wrapped in a toga, reaching out pathetically with one hand. *Love Unrequited.* Her face remained fixed in the standard acting-exercise expression of yearning, wide-eyed with hope. But thick layers of mold-green goop cheapened its artistry, supposedly protecting the bronze statue from weathering.

Clumps of snow clung to the statue's hair and in the creases of the lumpy bronze toga. Streaks of meltwater found their way down the sun-warmed metal to the marble base ... like tears at a wedding.

"But how am I supposed to ask?" he had asked his drama instructor two days before. Callahan's brown teeth and sour breath came from smoking too many ragged cigar butts that looked like used teabags. The big man was gruff and cynical and had plenty of his own personal problems. But Callahan wasn't fake like the other ass-kissing drama teachers: he said what he thought, no punches pulled, but he meant it.

Thoughts of Shelly's face fluttered around Jerry, bringing a nervousness more intense than any stage fright. "I mean, what do I say? How do I ask her?"

Callahan left his ragged cigar smoldering on the desktop. "Ease up, Parkins. Plan what you're going to say, and say it. But make sure you say it right. Be forceful, or be shy—whatever works. You're the one who knows her so well—I'm not the guy who wants to marry her. But rehearse your lines. Over and over again, so it's a part of you." Callahan grinned, making some of the tufts of his gray beard stick out.

"You've gotta get it right the first time, you know. It's like opening night, and you don't get a second chance."

Outside in the cold, Jerry rubbed his hands to keep warm. *Maybe if I tried a different tack ...*

He dug into the pocket of his flannel jacket and pulled out the gold ring in its tiny plastic bag. The ring had set him back almost a hundred dollars. Jerry had saved his food money, nearly starving himself; he had given blood plasma twice, at fifteen bucks each time. He had sold half of his album collection—but now he had the ring. Like a talisman, it would mean everything. If only he asked the question right ...

Rehearse. Rehearse. Rehearse.

He'd known Shelly only a few months. They had met in art appreciation class. She was so totally, utterly captivating. Fascinating. Jerry saw it as a whirlwind courtship; Shelly seemed baffled, but pleased, by his intense devotion.

I must be a drama major, he thought. *Hopeless romantic ... or maybe just a sap.*

Rehearse. Rehearse. Rehearse.

Jerry stared up at the statue again. *Unrequited Love.* Not like Shelly and him—he knew she loved him, must love him. He looked at the greenish bronze face of *Love* and concentrated until he began to see the reflection of Shelly there. The statue's hair was wrong, but the lines of the nose, the chin, the cheek, were suggestive.

He wrenched his emotion together into a hard ball, focusing, digging deep to find depths of his own feeling—using all the powerful techniques he had learned from Callahan.

Passion! Say it like you mean it!

Jerry took the ring out of the plastic bag and stood in front of the statue. A vision of Shelly's smiling, longing face hovered before his eyes. Pretend. Imagination. "Make the reality in your mind even greater than the reality around you. That's what acting's all about," Callahan had said.

Jerry extended the ring toward the outstretched bronze fingers. Get it right the first time. He swallowed, wet his lips, and projected his voice.

"I love you. I want to spend the rest of my life with you—I really do! Will you please ... marry me?"

Like a magnetic force, something yanked the wedding band from his numb fingertips and jammed it home on the ring finger of the massive bronze statue.

Dumbfounded, Jerry couldn't blink as the statue's

outstretched hand folded its metal fingers possessively into a fist, keeping the gold wedding band and letting it gleam into the sun.

The old house Jerry rented with three other undergrads had seemed quaint before, very "college"-ish. But this night, it emanated mysterious sounds from every corner.

Jerry sat alone in the house. His three roommates went out beer guzzling together. On the Friday before Valentine's Day, they hoped to get laid, or get drunk, preferably both.

Jerry still found himself shaking and wide-eyed, but he didn't dare tell them about the statue. Brian did ask, "What's up your butt?"

He shrugged and answered helplessly, "Exams. That's all." The other roommates rolled their eyes. They had come to expect unorthodox behavior from anyone to whom they referred (in a sarcastic, nasal voice) as a "draaama major."

With shaking fingers, Jerry finally dialed Shelly's number, agonizing over how to explain it to her, how to tell her. How could he say anything without confessing that he meant to propose to her? He didn't want to give it all away like that. But Shelly's roommate answered the phone and told him, somewhat curtly, that Shelly was sick with the flu and couldn't talk to anyone. He eased the telephone receiver back on to its cradle, already distracted by his own fears.

He had seen the bronze fingers close together. *It isn't real. It isn't real.* It isn't real! But his mind never had any doubt of the reality. He had witnessed it himself—and actors weren't supposed to go crazy until after long and successful careers. He didn't dare go back to double-check what he had seen—not even to get his wedding ring back! Maybe he'd be ready for that tomorrow, under the sunlight again.

Around him the street remained quiet, with the neighboring

house mostly deserted as other students went out to party. It had seemed ideal at first to move into an old house on the outskirts of campus, away from the frat bashes, the hectic life, the noise ... infinitely better than a godawful dorm. But now Jerry felt isolated. Alone, he went upstairs and decided to go to bed.

He pulled off his socks and added them to the pile on the bedroom floor, sliding his body between the covers of his unmade bed. For a long time he lay there and then reached over to switch off the lamp beside him. An eerie blue glow from the streetlight puddled into the room. Jerry closed his eyes and waited, and waited, but insomnia ran like a whirlwind around his head. An hour crept by. Eleven thirty, on a Friday night—and here he was lying in bed, without sleeping ... what a party animal.

The other guys wouldn't be home until about two in the morning, or much later if they got lucky. Jerry opened his eyes and stared at the ceiling, then realized he was shivering. Maybe he could tell Callahan about the creepy statue ... Sure, and maybe he could throw in some stuff about UFOs and Bigfoot too—Callahan would love it.

"You're too uptight about your stinking marriage proposal!" the big man would say. "You're seeing things."

But Jerry didn't think so.

Downstairs, a resounding crash of splintered wood and broken glass made him jerk violently upright. He felt his throat dry up and shrivel, without the ability to make even a squeaking sound. Call the campus police! Jump out the window! Run your buns off! Jerry couldn't move.

Pounding thumps came down the hall, as if someone kept hitting the floor with a sledgehammer. Without a pause and with relentless determination, the heavy sounds continued up the stairs, one at a time. He could hear the boards on the steps groaning and cracking as though from an incredible weight. Jerry recognized the rhythm of the sounds slowly moving toward him— footsteps. Incredibly heavy ... footsteps.

Madly, he clawed at the light by his bed as if by switching it on he could switch off the sound. But when his eyes adjusted to the light flooding into the room, he saw a large, bulky shape approaching him from the shadows of the upstairs hall.

He waited with incredible dread as the statue of *Love* lurched ponderously into the room.

The bronze figure moved its arms and legs with careful concentration, like an automaton taking its first steps. The statue swiveled its face, turning the head on its neck so that the bronze eyes could see him. The sickly green coating still covered it in blotches like leprosy.

The statue's expression did not change, but upon seeing Jerry in the bed, it seemed to focus its purpose and took three steps toward him. The metallic footfalls echoed in the room as more than a ton of bronze came down on each foot.

Jerry found that he was shaking uncontrollably—he was going to piss on the bed in a moment. Tears of terror ran down his eyes, and a ringing sound muffled his ears. Only a small whimper came out of his throat.

The statue remained motionless, staring at him with blind polished eyes. She didn't move for almost half a minute, and then one hand reached up to the metal-cast toga wrapped around her body.

Her fingers sheared off the sculptured clasp at the shoulder and bent the outer metal, peeling it down and prying the garment away from the main body. The bronze sheet made a groaning, tearing sound, like an automobile accident. The heavy metal toga crashed to the floor with the noise of a gong.

The female statue stood in front of him. Where the metal garment had been now gleamed a bright polished bronze, showing crude, lumpily formed but ample breasts, spheres without nipples. Even a grotesque parody of a pubic area shone between her legs.

Jerry tried to slither back up against the headboard of his bed. His fingers clenched the sheets; sweat ran down his forehead, mingling with his tears. He felt his lips trembling, and his teeth actually chattering together, until finally the dam broke, and he sobbed out his words.

"What do you want!"

The statue took another step toward him and pried open her polished metal lips with a squeaking sound. She whispered in a hollow metallic voice, like ice wind through a cave.

"This is my wedding night."

The floorboards creaked as the naked statue lumbered toward the bed.

Back to Tucker's Grove. This is one of my favorite tales set in the town, a Halloween story. It evokes so much of what I remember about empty barns, blighted fields, and weird old farmers living alone with mysterious pasts (I focused on another such character in my story "Heroes Never Die" in another volume in this set.)

"Hunter's Moon" is also one of the first Tucker's Grove stories I wrote, setting the tone for the series.

Hunter's Moon

Pinfeathers spurted into the air, and the sparrow's song fell silent. The wings continued to twitch after the bird struck the ground.

Clinton Tucker cracked open the shotgun and reloaded it with birdshot. He squinted in the afternoon sunlight but couldn't find any more sparrows. Birds didn't stay much by his farm any more.

Tucker stepped off the dusty porch—no one bothered to sweep up now that Angela had left him. He carried the shotgun around back to where a few ancient trees stood around the white farmhouse. The leaves would turn color soon in the coming autumn: red and yellow and brown. As a boy, Tucker remembered jumping into mounds of colored leaves in the farmyard.

He frowned at himself, then locked away the boyhood memories where he was safe from them.

He looked down the long hill, tracing the path of the dirt road to the buildings and whitewashed fences of Tucker's Grove. Though Clinton Tucker's great-grandfather had founded the tiny town back in 1820, sixty years before, the townspeople scorned Clinton, and he scorned them right back. He didn't have much good land and not much help to farm it, though harvest time was near. The big barn stood behind the house, snoring softly in the wind through its cracked and peeling boards, empty except for some years-old straw in the loft.

Tucker spent many nights outside by himself, walking under the stars like some nocturnal predator. He had been lonely once, but now even that feeling was dead. He could remember a time when he might have asked for help from the townspeople and given it freely in return. But not anymore. He had no desire for false friendship, to be hurt again. Better to hold tight to his bitterness after what Angela had done to him.

He had tried to love her, he had let down his wall for her—but she only used that to expose his vulnerable spots. And now she had deserted him. His face flushed, and his teeth ground together. Angela. Bitch!

He fired his shotgun into the air and listened to the echoes bounce around Tucker's Grove. What had she been thinking of? How could she *dare* leave him?

Night. Angela pounds on the door to the parsonage, panicked. Where is Mrs. Litch? Why is it taking her so long to answer the door? Angela's legs tremble, unaccustomed to running.

—Why, Angela! Malcolm, it's Angela Tucker!

—Help me! He's so cruel, Mrs. Litch! He has fits! He hits me.

—Come in, Angela. Come in. We'll get you a glass of warm milk. You're in a terrible state!

She enters. The door closes. Safety. Safety? Clinton never cared for the Methodist minister personally, nor the church in general. Safety?

—Tonight, he slapped me, and I ran! He'll know where I am! You have to hide me. You don't know how he is! He thinks he's seeing wolves again.

—There, there, Angela ... Malcolm, are you getting this poor girl some milk?

The minister's wife pats her on the back. Comfort.

—You know what they say about your husband, don't you, dear? That he had a high fever when he was a boy? Made him wrong in the head. Uncontrollable.

The minister hands her a glass of hot milk.

—Wolves? he asks, then shakes his head.

She sips the milk, burns her tongue, almost drops the glass. She is trembling. Mrs. Litch takes the milk away.

—You've had a bad fright, Angela. You'll stay with us here tonight. No question about it. I'll get some blankets out right now. Don't you worry. Everything will be all right.

A pounding at the door. Loud shouts.

—Angela! I know you're in there! Get away from those people and come back home where you belong! Now!

Terror. She clutches her hands together, kneading them. Eyes wide. Her voice a high-pitched whisper.

—Hide me! Please!

Mrs. Litch rushes her to a small bedroom and closes the door. The pounding continues.

—ANGELA!

The door bursts open. Clinton Tucker storms in, glares at the minister and his wife. Death in his eyes.

—I've come for my wife.

Mrs. Litch drops the milk. Tucker looks around the room quickly. Nothing. Sees the closed door, starts toward it, pounds on it.

—Angela! You'd best come out! NOW! Before I get angry!

No answer. Pounds again. Tries to open it. Locked, from the inside. Fury. Throws himself against the door. It cracks, splinters. He breaks in.

The room is empty. The window is open. Curtains float mockingly in the breeze. The night is dark, and he can't see her. He clenches and unclenches his hands for several moments until he speaks again.

—I hope to hell the wolves got her.

Some men have good cause to bury their boyhood memories.

Young Clinton Tucker rode with his parents in the wagon, eyes drowsy after a hectic day—traveling for hours to reach neighboring Bartonville, then errand after errand, and now making ready for the long trip back. Indian summer had come and gone, leaving the mornings covered with frost and filled with white breath. Dusk came on quick and cold, making the stars shine out like ice chips.

The wooden wheels of their wagon rattled on Bartonville's one cobblestoned street, then grew muffled as the horse trotted onto the dirt road toward the forest. The end of October lit the trees in flaming colors, but darkness made the forest seem thicker, like the wide-open mouth of a monster. The air hung thin and chilly upon them, ready to trace patterns of frost on the world. Clinton could see his white breath and pretended he was smoking a cigar, as Mr. Harrison the blacksmith did.

His parents sat in a comfortable silence next to each other on the driver's board. Clinton took the seat blanket and crawled back into the wagon bed. He huddled among the packages in the corner, trying to sleep. Overhead, the ominous branches passed by in the darkening forest. The rocking wagon along with the increasing warmth of his blanket lulled him to sleep. He smelled the musty blanket, the wood and dust of the wagon, the cool dampness of the forest. Clinton lost his sense of time.

Then he heard his father shout something. The horse made a loud, frightened noise. Clinton looked up to see glinting eyes in the forest, moving shapes. "Go on! Get!" his father yelled into the trees, waving his hand. Then he cracked the whip to keep the horse moving. "Can't figure why they don't run from us."

Clinton heard a howling, and his wide eyes focused on the lurking forms, sleek gray fur, pointed muzzles. He had never seen a wolf before, but he knew from the stories his mother told him. Normal wolves shouldn't be following so close to the wagon.

"Are they sick?" his mother said, frightened. "Is it the rabies?"

The horse rolled his eyes and snorted in terror, trying to strain out of his harness. "Jeesus!" Clinton's father said, wrestling with the reins. The horse charged ahead into the gloom, away from the smell of wolves in the air.

One of the wagon's wheels smashed into a boulder, breaking the spokes. Two wolves loped beside the wagon, barely visible in the trees and the dimness. The wagon bounced violently up and down on the broken wheel. Clinton jammed his legs against the corner, trying to keep his seat. Packages jostled around him. His mother made no sound but scrambled to keep her hold on the driver's board. Clinton's father stood up, balanced precariously, and tried to throw all his weight into controlling the horse.

One wolf, its fur patchy with tangles of cockleburs and mud, stepped out of the trees onto the road directly ahead of them.

The horse reared. The wagon crashed into a tree at the side of the path, rode partway up the trunk on its broken wheel, then hung poised for an instant before toppling back, upside-down.

Clinton's mother tumbled on top of his father—and the hard and heavy edge of the wagon crunched down on top of both of them.

Dragged by the weight of the wagon and held in place by the rigid shafts on either side, the horse toppled sideways. The traces snapped, the shafts splintered and broke through into the horse's ribcage. Bright blood splashed into the murky forest.

Clinton found himself buried in packages, flour, and supplies, and trapped underneath the shelter of the overturned wagon.

In sudden and total silence.

He waited and shivered, afraid to whimper, afraid to move or to make a sound in the stifling darkness.

Finally, groping with his outstretched hands, he tried to find his parents. His mother's skirt and torso were with him under the wagon, but her neck and one arm remained outside. He felt her chest, but the rhythm of breathing had ceased.

He found his father's boot, then something wet. He could see nothing. Dirt and tears clung to his face.

Clinton waited, still silent and still shivering, wrapped in the blanket, but it gave him scant comfort. His ears burned as he listened to the quiet noise of the leaves, the settling of dust, unable to do more than breathe and blink his eyes. He wondered if the wolves were still out there. The air under the wagon bed was thick. He smelled the perfume of the packages, the oiled wood of the wagon, leather, blood. He thought he smelled wolves, but he wasn't sure.

A quiet growling sound outside made him stiffen in terror. For just a moment, his mother's body jerked rhythmically as if she were alive and struggling, then she became motionless again.

Clinton crouched down, shuddering but not daring to whimper out loud. Tears ran down his cheeks. His heartbeat thudded in his ears.

He heard something sniffing around the wagon, pacing just on the other side of the wooden walls. The wolves could smell him. Hear his breathing. Feel his trembling. They knew he was there, alone, helpless, trapped.

Seconds, minutes, hours.

He couldn't move. He sat on a sharp rock, trying to ignore the cramping in his arms and legs, too terrified to shift to a more comfortable position. He heard nothing ...

The darkness of his shelter leached away into a soft glow. Faint light seeped through cracks and knotholes in the wood. The Hunter's Moon, first full moon after the harvest, rose like a big eye into the night, lifting itself over the edge of the forest.

Clinton held his breath. He hadn't heard the wolves for hours. A knothole near his head let in just enough air to breathe. He wanted to see, but he couldn't move his head. Something in him refused, until his neck muscles felt like snapping. Finally, with painful slowness, he craned his neck to look out the tiny hole, searching for the night sky through the crowded trees. He wanted to look at the moon, to see light again. Holding his breath, he peered out.

Straight into the eye of a wolf.

Clinton sat frozen, transfixed, unable to move. They stared at each other. Then the wolf howled, alone in the night. Clinton felt the wolf's cry steal his soul—

It was dawn. He didn't know how the time had passed: his mind had refused to accept the night any longer. He heard the sound of horse hooves, then an outcry. A single shot. Clinton could hear the new horse snorting in fear at the smell of blood and wolves. A deep voice exclaimed in horror and disgust. Footsteps traced a path around the overturned wagon, just as the wolves had done all night long. Clinton could not whimper, could not cry for help. He couldn't.

He listened for a long time as the rescuer moved about; then finally the wagon lifted. Sunlight flooded into the shadows. He saw the silhouette of a large bearded man staring in.

"Well, I'll be damned!"

The man propped the wagon on its side, but still Clinton refused to move from his shelter. Outside, he saw one dead wolf, shot through the heart, whose glassy eye seemed still to stare at him ...

He remembered nothing else until days later, when his older brother Walter began taking care of him on the farm. But Walter Tucker went off to fight in the Civil War, leaving Clinton barely old enough to tend the farm by himself. And Walter never came back.

Now, years later, both Clinton Tucker and the Tucker farm were falling into decrepitude. He walked at night, hypnotized by the past and how it had cheated him, and imagined ways that he could get back at his own life.

Elizabeth Billings knew she would never make it home in time. Nightfall had come before she realized it. At fourteen years old, she claimed to be her own girl, but not too old—according to her father—to be taken across his knee and have her buttocks livened.

Her parents had left Tucker's Grove in the morning, traveling to Bartonville to visit her Uncle Henry who had been jailed for assaulting a man. They refused to let her come along, even though Uncle Henry had always been her favorite uncle—it would be a bad experience for her, they said. *Be good. Take care of yourself. We'll be back around nightfall.*

There was a boy, Tim Miller, whose father's farm lay half an hour's walk outside of town. Tim had worked hard to finish his evening chores early, had met her behind the barn. He and Elizabeth watched the sun slip under the horizon as they enjoyed a twilight stroll down the tree-bordered farm lane. The night was warm for late September. The crops stood ready for harvesting, or so said the Harvest Moon rising above the eastern horizon. They hadn't had the first frost of autumn yet, and the plants still looked healthy and green.

Elizabeth ran back home in darkness lit only by the full moon darting among patches of thin clouds. Her pale green dress wrapped around her legs as she ran, and weeds lashed her bare calves. She was going to get a whipping tonight.

Dew spattered Elizabeth's feet as she took a desperate shortcut across Clinton Tucker's back fields, through his large and weedy garden. She saw shadowy plants, blighted potatoes, beans, a huge mound of pumpkin vines. Something warned her to stop running, to move more quietly. She became uneasy, wondering if she might have been better off just to accept her punishment ... She had heard stories about crazy and mean Clinton Tucker.

"D'you know you're trespassing?"

She whirled. He stood there, outlined by the light of the Harvest Moon clambering higher into the sky. Tucker stood tall and gaunt, dressed in old clothes and clasping a rusty, wicked-looking pitchfork whose handle had been polished from years of palm-sweat.

He stepped toward her. She tried to run, but he anticipated it and reached forward to grab the shoulder of her dress, knotting his clawlike fingers into the material.

"This is private property, young lady—and I don't take kindly to people who don't respect that."

In her mind, all the stories she had ever heard about Clinton Tucker became real: the man who lived in the haunted house of Tucker's Grove, alone up on the hill, a violent man, a monster. Children dared each other to run up at night and touch the side of his house ...

Elizabeth Billings struggled to break free of the man's grip, but his fingers were entangled in the green fabric of her dress. As she jerked back, the cloth tore in a long gash, exposing one of her small breasts.

The Harvest Moon emerged from the wispy cloud cover, shining down on the garden with its wan light, sharpening the features on Tucker's face, glinting in his eyes.

Elizabeth fumbled with the torn cloth, trying to pull her dress back up to cover herself. But Tucker stopped her, grabbing the material and ripping it farther. He looked at the green print, seemed to recognize it, and smiled.

She stared down at his hand, confused and very afraid. He slapped her across the face with enough force to knock her into the billowy mountain of the pumpkin patch. Prickly leaves folded over her, seeming to swallow her up in their jaws. She thrashed, trying to stand up again. Tucker leaned over her, but he seemed to be seeing something else, as if she had walked into a nighttime reverie, a prop for him to act out his memories under the stars.

"You are my wife, Angela, and I will do with you as I please!"

The moonlight penetrated the splayed pumpkin leaves, as if eager to watch. Tucker undid his trousers, slid to his knees in front of her.

"You're lucky you came back, else I might have gotten angry at you." His breathing came rapid and shallow. "You know how I get when I feel *angry*."

She whimpered, tried to squirm away from him. Scratchy pumpkin vines clawed at her bare skin, and a round orange pumpkin pressed hard against her back. Tucker yanked her dress completely off.

"You're not being very cooperative—"

She felt the scream exploding out of her throat, but he slapped her again and settled on top of her, prying her legs apart. Then he grabbed her shoulders and brutally thrust into her, digging his dirty fingernails into her skin. She couldn't make a sound. He pushed again and again; his eyelids didn't close tightly enough to hide the line of staring white as his eyes rolled upward. He went rigid, uttering a long, low sigh. Then he opened his eyes to look at her.

And saw a fourteen-year-old girl.

Tucker withdrew quickly, backing away, stumbling and looking down in horror. She couldn't control her ragged sobs. A thin line of blood clung to the insides of her thighs, running slowly onto the ground. But he saw her for only an instant.

The light of the Harvest Moon struck the blood on the earth, and Tucker became a boy again, trapped under the wooden wagon bed as the wolves prowled about. The full Hunter's Moon shone down on his mother's blood. He saw her move again—her shoulder jerked and jerked, striking the wooden wall as the wolves tugged. Clinton's terrified heartbeats pounded in his chest. He longed for something to protect himself with, felt something hard in his hands—he wanted to strike at the wolves, kill them! But terror locked his muscles. Something called him, a compulsion, forcing him to turn, to bring his eye over to the knothole, to look directly into the demon's eye of a wolf staring back.

He screamed.

She screamed.

And the wolf's eye became the bulging eye of Elizabeth Billings. The handle of the pitchfork still quivered in his hand. By the light of the moon he saw the pitchfork thrust through her chest, one tine through her heart and two others through her lungs. Droplets of red stained the large green leaves, the orange pumpkins.

Panic tore at him with sharp teeth. What should he do now? Confess? Tell someone? Maybe they would forgive him. Forgive him? They would crucify him! Destroy his farm! Burn his house! His farm, Tucker's farm—all he had left. He couldn't lose it! He wouldn't let them take it. No—he had to hide her. Somewhere. Only temporarily. Until he could think of something else.

Think!

His barn! He had old, dry straw ten feet deep up in his loft!

He'd HAD to kill her!

He could bury her there, in the straw.

She would have told everyone!

She would keep in the dry straw. No one would ever find her.

Ruined him!

Forever.

Forever!

Someone rapped on his door, timid and yet insistent. Tucker scowled and moved through the dim kitchen. He could see through the window, recognized the pinched face of the Methodist minister, Malcolm Litch. Tucker sucked on his teeth to swallow away the bad taste in his mouth.

He pushed on the door. It flung outward, almost hitting the minister not unintentionally.

"Ah, good day, Mr. Tucker!" Litch beamed. The voice held a false tone from years of practice talking to people who didn't particularly like him.

Tucker frowned at the hawk-faced man and said nothing.

"*Um,* it's almost Hallowe'en, you know, Mr. Tucker ..."

A long pause. "So?"

"And, uh, it *is* traditional—the Hallowe'en barn dance. Of Tucker's Grove?"

"You can't use my barn this year, Mr. Litch."

The minister looked flustered. "But your wife always—"

"I have no wife, Mr. Litch. She ran off ... or don't *you* remember?"

The minister seemed to swallow his lips as he fidgeted. Then Litch steeled himself, wrenching the conversation back to his business. "Please, Mr. Tucker—yours is the only barn around that isn't being used."

Tucker narrowed his eyes, guarded. "And what makes you so sure my barn is empty, Mr. Litch? Have you been out there, snooping around?"

"Why, no!"

Tucker continued to glare at him, relentless. Litch shuffled his feet. "The dance *does* bring in some money, Mr. Tucker ... if that makes any difference to you. The town council has decided to let you keep half of it this year, for allowing us to use your barn, as usual."

Tucker snorted. The minister filled his eyes with a plea that somehow lacked sincerity.

Tucker suddenly wanted to get rid of this man, this parasite. Make him leave. "All right, Mr. Litch, but you damn well better clean up your mess! And don't let me see you around any more than I have to."

Litch beamed. "And the pumpkins?"

"What pumpkins?"

"It is also traditional for the Tuckers to donate the pumpkins for the jack-o'-lanterns. The children, you know. I'm sure your wife ... uh, I'm sure you have some planted in your garden."

"You can have the damned pumpkins! Send someone around with a wagon tomorrow and we'll load them up." Tucker drew in a deep breath of disgust. He stood in the door frame, but the minister seemed reluctant to leave.

"Is there anything *else*, Mr. Litch?"

The minister pursed his lips, as if trying to put himself at ease. "A shame about Elizabeth Billings, isn't it?"

Tucker leaned back into the shadows. "A girl from town, is she? What happened to her?"

Litch shrugged. "Nobody knows. She just vanished. Her parents came back from Bartonville one night two weeks ago, and she was gone! Young Timothy Miller is almost frantic—he says he spent time with her, secretly, at sunset. Then she left for home ... and nobody ever saw her again!"

Tucker frowned in distant thought. "Maybe the wolves got her."

"Wolves? But there haven't been wolves in these parts since —" Litch suddenly looked alarmed, uncomfortable.

"Good day, Mr. Litch." Tucker slammed the door and stepped deeper into the house, watching through the curtain as the minister stood confused for a moment, and then left.

That night the first frost of autumn struck Tucker's Grove. It crept up from the ground, snaring the fragile roots of plants. It emerged from the air, etching its signature on windowpanes. A portent. The year was nearing its end. Things would die soon.

Hauled by one old horse, the wagon creaked as it passed down the dirt path to Tucker's garden in the bright, cold morning. Pastor Litch rode with the owner of the wagon, a burly farmer named Wilson. Clinton Tucker sat in silence, gripping the wooden edge of the wagon bed. He didn't like wagons much.

The edges of the plant leaves curled together from the shock of the frost. Tomato stems drooped, potato plants looked stunned and passing into death.

Wilson drove the horse up next to the pumpkin patch. The mound of giant leaves had fallen in upon itself, a tangle of crushed, watery vines. Wilson pulled the horse to a halt and left the beast to stand placidly, looking tired, or maybe just old. The three men climbed down from the wagon and went to pick the pumpkins.

"Hey! Look here!" Wilson snapped the stem of the first pumpkin and held it up.

Splotches of bright red covered the shiny orange skin, like fresh, wet bloodstains trickling downward.

Tucker's mouth gaped. It couldn't be. He had checked, cleaned, straightened everything. It had been three weeks.

Wilson brushed through the large leaves, and Litch searched

with him. "Funny! Every *one* of 'em is stained like that! Never seen such a thing!" Wilson ran a thumbnail into the reddened skin of the pumpkin. "It goes deep, too—ain't just a stain."

Litch broke a pumpkin off the vine and handed it to Tucker, who stood motionless beside the wagon. "No matter. The children are going to carve them up anyway—they won't care if the pumpkins got blight."

Tucker took the pumpkin and set it in the wagon. He felt numb. This wasn't real. It couldn't be. He tried to rub the red off with his own hands; but the stain held its own, mocking him. All the pumpkins. The other two men began to pick, and Tucker loaded the wagon bed.

"I wonder what could have done that, though," Litch said.

Wilson grunted as he twisted a thick stem. "First frost of autumn sometimes does funny things to plants."

Tucker grasped at the explanation. "Yeah," he managed to say, "that must be it."

Tucker sat on the porch before dusk, cradling his shotgun on his lap as the sun died on the horizon. Birds sometimes came out to sing at sunset.

He watched the moon rise. Within another few days the obese Hunter's Moon would make its annual appearance.

She was still in the loft, smothered in the dry straw with the bugs and the field mice and the spiders. It had been nearly a month.

Something made him stare at the rickety, gap-toothed barn—a calling from inside, wordless, lost, some kind of perverted siren song drawing his attention. Was it her voice? He had never heard her voice, he suddenly realized, not while she was alive ... except for that final, sharp scream.

Tucker's breathing came in quicker, shallower gasps. *She* had made the pumpkins look bloodstained. Now she was calling to him.

With all the people going in and out of his barn, setting up for the Hallowe'en dance, he needed to move her soon, *soon*. But he couldn't bring himself to. He wouldn't go to her while she whispered to him in the twilight wind. He couldn't!

Tucker raised the shotgun and fired a round of birdshot at the side of the barn.

The voice stopped.

The Hunter's Moon rode high among the stars, lord of the night sky. A cold wind whistled a dirge among the trees. The night before Hallowe'en.

Tucker *had* to move her. Now.

The door slammed behind him.

He was afraid.

He took the shotgun with him and filled his pocket with shells. Not birdshot this time. He walked toward the barn, carrying his lantern.

He'd have to bury her before the Hallowe'en dance—out in the fields somewhere. Everything had been harvested. No one would notice a little more overturned earth.

As he entered the maw of the barn, his lantern blew out, plunging everything into momentary darkness. With matches in fumbling fingers he relit the flame, but this time the jerking light only sharpened the shadows.

He cursed in a trembling voice as he stood in front of the open barn door, not certain of what to do. But the interior of the barn glowed faintly with an eerie light. The wan illumination of the moon oozed through cracks and knotholes in the barn's dilapidated sides. Like moonlight shining into an overturned wagon bed ...

Setting the lantern on the floorboards, he gripped the shotgun and entered the barn. The floor had been swept clean for the upcoming dance. He reached the rickety ladder leading to the upper loft. His hands were sweaty. He climbed upward.

The floor of the loft seemed weak and flimsy, covered with straw. Tucker groped forward, feeling with his hands in the deepest part of the straw, digging around until he felt something cold and sickeningly stiff. Pushing the straw away, he grabbed what must have been her arm, lifting her out into the pale moonlight.

Her skin was splotched and desiccated, decomposing but half-mummified from the dry straw. Her hair and fingernails had grown an alarming amount. Tucker winced, but his stomach reacted more strongly. He clenched his teeth together and forced the bile back down.

As the Hunter's Moon shone beams upon her face, the bulging eyes opened wide. And she smiled at him. Her jaws were filled with canine fangs. Her eyes were green-yellow and slitted, like the wolf's staring at him through the knothole in the overturned wagon.

The scream latched onto the inside of his throat as he jerked backward, stumbling to the edge of the loft, falling. He landed roughly, twisting his ankle. His eyes were wide and dry because he had forgotten how to blink.

He looked around in the barn, but the Hunter's Moon and the lantern by the door cast strange shadows as pointed as long fangs. He saw her face in the corner, and again along the wall, and again behind him, all with eyes wide and mouth open—faces, screaming, mocking faces, *her* face. She was surrounded by the distorted faces of wolves, jagged mouths filled with fangs, slitted animal eyes in the corners of the barn, on the floor, up near the wall. Faces wild, covered with blood dripping toward the floor, screaming. Coming to get him at last, because he had escaped them so long ago.

Now he could hear the cries of pain pounding around him— her screaming face in every corner, everywhere he looked. And the howling of wolves. Everywhere.

Tucker raised the shotgun and fired at one face. It exploded into red-orange fragments of skull and flesh. He fired at another one, and another. His hand fed shells into the gun and spat the empty ones onto the floor.

He continued to fire, but heard her voice screaming louder and louder with each face he destroyed. And the howling. As he fired, he added his own screams to hers.

Malcolm Litch stepped out of his house, followed closely by his wife. In the town of Tucker's Grove, others opened their doors, gathered on the street, looking up toward Clinton Tucker's house on the hill. Gunshots sounded as if a great battle were taking place.

They listened in horrified silence to a long series of shots, then a long, long pause, then one final shot. Murmurs ran through the crowd until someone yelled, "Come on!" A few men fetched their horses and galloped down the street; the rest ran after, following as best they could.

Tucker's house stood dark and empty with the door unlocked —and they knew Tucker always locked his doors. Litch and the farmer Wilson met together, carefully entering the dark and empty house, calling Tucker's name. They heard shouts from the old barn and ran out of the house as the others converged there.

Somewhere off in the fields, a chorus of wolves howled loudly, then fell silent. Litch felt a shiver go down his spine.

Tucker's lamp stood at the entrance to the barn. Litch and Wilson entered, feeling the hush upon the others.

On the cleanly swept floor lay Clinton Tucker with the back of his head blown away and his hands still on the shotgun stock. Piles of empty shotgun shells lay strewn about him like mourning flowers.

"My Gawd," someone shouted from the upper loft. "Is Ted Billings out there? We got something he should see." Then a long pause. "Or maybe he shouldn't."

Malcolm Litch looked around the barn in a daze as they brought the body of Elizabeth Billings down from the loft. He mumbled to himself as he tried to fit the events together. Tears hovered in his eyes, and the minister's face looked baffled. "It's crazy. Just plain crazy."

Burly Wilson put a hand on Litch's shoulder, but the minister did not notice. He spoke in a very small voice. "With all this, I just don't understand why, *why* did he have to ruin them all?" He blinked his eyes and looked at the farmer. "Why did he have to shoot *all* of the children's jack-o'-lanterns?"

This is another one of my small-press gems, drawing on all my Russian history classes, the culture and dark folklore that seems so perfect for a horror story.

This time I collaborated with my small-press friend and renowned horror poet Denise Dumars. "Trophy" was an intrinsically creepy story, the idea of which made our skin crawl. Imagine the arrogant king offhandedly commanding one of his warriors, "Bring me the head of the evil wizard."

What about the warrior? Even if he succeeds in the task, imagine carrying the head of a wizard you've murdered through the dark and scary forests of the north, night after night, letting the fear and superstition eat at you. How much do you believe in the dark magic? And what can it do to you?

This was a story I had honestly forgotten about until I unearthed a copy in the archives while searching for previous publications to be included in this set. "Trophy" is a very effective psychological horror story, and I am very glad to bring it back into the light of day.

Trophy
(with Denise Dumars)

The horse's unshod hooves packed the snow down as it plodded into the village. Relav huddled deeply in his warm pelts as he rode, but the cold and wind had long ago stolen all feeling from his fingertips and cheekbones. Spring had come to Kiev.

Already, sunset smeared a glow on the brittle sky, and Relav hoped the people he knew in the village would offer him shelter for the night. As he warmed himself among them with mead and meat, he could tell them of his victorious battle against the wizard Iarik. The bloodstained sack hung on one of the brass studs of his saddle, its burden rocking gently against the horse's side, seeming heavier than it really was.

He guided the horse down the path that passed through the center of the village. Smoke moved sluggishly from narrow chimney holes in each of the underground dwellings. The air inside would be stale and smoky, but the room would be warm and filled with the smells of other people like himself.

Relav looked at the familiar cluster of homes with regret that bordered on fear. It had once been his home. But things change.

The people came out to stare silently at him. He felt a lump in his throat as he saw a few women rushing to hide their children within the dwellings. The wind whipped dark, brown strands of hair into his Viking-blue eyes, making them sting and water.

The horse plodded defiantly onward, and Relav fixed his gaze on Tardos the village elder, a squat man with reddish hair and a voluminous heart. The others looked at the bundle tied to Relav's saddle where the blood had dried and stained the leather.

"Poor Iarik ..." someone whispered.

Relav clutched the heavy gold cross hanging at his neck, holding it out like a totem in front of him. His gaze swept over the cruder crosses that stood on sticks outside each dwelling's entryway in a grudging show of support for the new religion that Grand Prince Vladimir had commanded all Russia to embrace. Relav knew that no trace of Christian paraphernalia would be found inside the homes.

"Who will shelter me for the night?" Relav searched the faces of the villagers, but no one answered him. "I offer the blessing of Grand Prince Vladimir himself." The words seemed frighteningly bleak to him, as if a part of him had gone, lost somewhere inside the cluttered dwelling of a wizard.

Several villagers turned in nervous scorn and ducked back inside their homes. Others stared at him with wooden gazes that burned but gave off no warmth.

These people were my friends, my family, Relav thought, *but with one stroke of a sword I severed them from me as well.*

"You have committed a grave sin, Relav son of Plenkhow," Tardos said as if to a stranger; his words rang out on the harp strings of the frigid wind. "You will find no shelter here."

Relav covered his shame with anger. He raised the ornate cross before him, thrusting it at Tardos. "I am your Christian brother!"

"Oh, yes, we were all *baptized*," the elder said bitterly. "But you cannot stay here." Tardos turned his back on Relav, and the rest of the villagers fled into their homes. Relav sat alone on his horse in the cold, feeling beaten.

He waited for a long moment, unwilling to believe that no one would take pity on him. He knew that when he left the village now—his home for so many years—he would never be able to return.

Relav urged the horse into motion again, hoping to find a campsite in the forest before the iceprick stars came out.

Relav sat in the whispering forest, not yet ready for sleep. He heard only the hissing of his fire trying to burn the half-frozen wood. Birch trees rattled their branches like dry bones overhead, as if anxious for the darkness to engulf him.

With morbid fascination, Relav held the stiffening sack in front of him in the firelight. He stared at the indecipherable rust-like splotches and then, before he could lose his nerve, he pulled off the thong binding the sack. Gingerly, he unfolded the cloth to expose the severed head of wizard Iarik.

Iarik's flesh had not even begun to bloat. The skin had a waxy yellow tinge, oddly soft in the freezing air. The wizard's long, gray hair had been woven into three thick braids, and a headband made of birchbark crossed his forehead. Iarik's beardless jaw, shaven closely with a wide bronze knife, set him apart from most men. Relav was certain he had closed Iarik's dragon-green eyes before stuffing the head in his sack, but now those eyes were wide open again, and they stared at him.

Stared.

The wind picked up for a moment and then dropped away, like the gasp of a dying man.

When you kill me, you forfeit part of yourself. The rest is fertile ground. Fertile ground.

Relav heard the wizard's final curse clearly in the night, startling him, but then he realized it had been only a too-vivid memory. His neck prickled with sweat in the cold air. He didn't want to be alone here.

When the pounding of his heart had slowed, Relav sat down on a cold log, wondering if Grand Prince Vladimir even remembered sending him on his mission. Vladimir had sent out many men like Relav, commanding them to bring back the heads of the *volkhvi*, the unrepentant pagan wizards who refused to accept the newly mandated Christian religion. Relav knew that many of the people resented the decreed baptisms and supported the wizards to secretly continue the old religions. Vladimir had embraced the Eastern Orthodox Church as a way to open doors of trade with the civilized world, as well as to unify the many petty clans and peoples who squabbled over their godlings and spirits. And Vladimir had ordered that the *volkhvi* must be slain if they refused to give up their pagan ways and support him.

Relav found himself unable to return the sorcerer's head to the sack. Instead, he gingerly set it on the ground, careful not to take his eyes away, and held the heavy cross, hoping to draw some comfort from it. The glassy green eyes of the dead wizard reflected the firelight.

Iarik had been a good man, somewhat odd, powerful but gentle in his own way. In the years when Relav had lived in the village, Iarik had always helped the villagers by offering the proper sacrifices for the crops to grow, for the hunt to be good, and for the winters to be easy. Occasionally, Iarik had even helped with the actual labor, although the villagers grew nervous when he did so. The wizard had never even spoken to Relav, never harmed him—but now Relav had slain him, severed his head ... because Vladimir ordered it done.

The villagers were fearful of Relav when he had returned after years of service to the Grand Prince in Kiev. He did not need to tell them his mission; they already knew. Iarik had already fled his home and hidden somewhere in the forest in anticipation that the Grand Prince would send an assassin. But no one had expected *Relav* to be the assassin ... and Relav knew all the local places where the wizard might hide. He had spent several days stalking, until he finally found Iarik's crude hut, and he had burst in the door without knocking, sword drawn ...

Relav was a Christian now, willingly baptized, and he did not take conversion lightly. Others might have converted only to save themselves from the sword, but not Relav. He feared that the gods, or the God, would know when one's worship was not sincere. And how could the defeated gods wish anything other than to wreak harm and vengeance on the land? The old gods must fall, swiftly and cleanly, with no opportunity to cause further pain. Iarik had to die.

But what powers could such a wizard have, even in death? Why hadn't Iarik fought back when Relav came to slay him? And what did his last curse mean?

When you kill me, you forfeit part of yourself. The rest is fertile ground. Fertile ground.

Suddenly, the darkness and the silence made it difficult to breathe. Relav wanted to call for help, like a child, but he had gone far from the village, and no one there would help him anyway. And how was he going to cope with the long journey back to Kiev, alone in the restless forest, carrying the head of a dead wizard?

Relav used his fingertips to close Iarik's eyes again, then quickly wrapped the head back in its stiff sack.

He traveled all the next day but saw no one, no movement on the windswept snow, no roads, no smoke, or sign of other human beings in the vast wilderness. His voice had stiffened in his throat, and he wanted to shout, to hail someone, but it was as if the wind had swept everyone away.

Relav saw the tracks of a rabbit peppered on the snow, winding one way then another, then vanishing abruptly and leaving only a drop of blood where an owl had snatched it up. Relav knew the *volkhvi* could divine many things from looking at tracks left by a rabbit in the snow. Iarik had read messages in the flights of birds passing north and south each year, or in the paths of stars that fell on winter nights. All of nature could speak its own language to the *volkhvi*.

Relav led the horse out of the hills, crossing the flat plains where nomads often camped. The grasses had been knocked down by the snow, motionless, and the silence pressed on him again. He found the refrozen slush from an abandoned camp, but the fire was long dead, and the tracks of the nomads had been erased, leaving him to guess which direction they had gone.

After noon, a thin, abandoned dog trotted toward him through the melting snow, yapping and excited at seeing a man on a horse. The dog looked as if it had recently been in a fight, but it circled Relav's horse with enthusiasm, barking. It stopped for a moment, sniffed the air, and suddenly fixed its eyes on the bloodstained bundle tied to the saddle. The dog howled, then bounded away.

That night, Relav camped by the bank of a narrow stream in the steep hills. The forest was dense around him, and he had to tie the horse farther up the hillside where it could try to graze among the frozen grasses without losing its footing. Relav took a blanket, some food, and the makings of a fire, along with the sack containing Iarik's head. He stared at the bundle as he munched a few pieces of dry pack bread. Drawn to it, he opened the sack again.

The wizard's facial muscles had tightened with rigor, spreading his lips in a wide, unsettling grin. The three thick braids looked like waiting serpents, held back only by the birchbark headband. And Iarik's cold emerald-green eyes had opened again by themselves, unblinking and staring.

Remember.

Then ask yourself if it was just.

The words rang loudly in Relav's head, on his conscience, and he fell backward into a sudden sleep as the maw of dreams gaped at him.

Heralds ran through the wooden-walled city of Kiev, shouting the Grand Prince's orders. Every man, woman, and child must take themselves to the Dnieper River at once to be baptized in the Christian manner, or else risk Vladimir's displeasure. Stone idols were smashed, wooden ones chopped down and burned. Great fires rose up, and all saw how easily the old gods fell. Zorya, Volkh, Stribog, even mighty Perun.

The muddy banks of the river were crowded with angry, frightened people. The guards rode up and down, Relav among them, watching the people. Hundreds were herded into the cold river. One indignant merchant argued that he was already a Christian, but Relav pushed him into the water anyway.

Priests dressed in the garb of Byzantium chanted in Greek, speaking the litanies that gave protection of the gentle God to all those who stood at swordpoint in the cold with dripping clothes. Relav had heard the priests in the hall of Vladimir many times. He knew the stories, the rituals, and understood them. But these people were now Christians as well, though they did not even know the name of the Son of God. Some of the people refused, and the river was baptized with their blood. Others splashed aimlessly along the banks, as the current came and washed away the old beliefs.

Relav awoke in the grim light of dawn. He had twitched in his sleep, like a dog, and rolled over on the narrow bank to trail his hand in the icy water. The stream ran westward toward Kiev; eventually it would meet and add its life to the Dnieper, where all the "sins" had been washed away. He pulled his hand from the stream as if bitten.

Feeling unclean, cast out by his old beliefs and yet trying to find empty consolation in his new God, Relav took his knife and hacked away at his beard, cutting himself badly several times, but in the end, his whiskers lay on the snow by the dead remains of the campfire, leaving his jaw naked, an affront to Kievan tradition.

He looked at the wizard's head propped up on the gravel. The eyes had closed again, as if satisfied.

Before Relav set off into dawn, he habitually muttered a prayer to Perun and made motions signifying obeisance to Stribog and Zorya. He stopped suddenly, swore in horror at himself, and spent many long minutes huddled over his golden cross, begging forgiveness from the Christian God.

Throughout the day, Relav led the horse through the dense stand of spruce and birch. The air smelled fresh, but the forest itself seemed poised, tense. Alive, and angry at him. He remembered tales of the volatile spirits, called *leshiye*, which could be indistinguishable from their surroundings if they so desired. Tall as a tree, green and tangled as vines, shaggy as moss or bark ... or small as a field mouse in order to pass through the densest thickets. Relav also heard that the *leshiye* often appeared as a whirlwind of blowing leaves and snow, or as an owl, or a wolf. Relav looked around him in the frozen forest. He felt watched.

Leshiye could produce all the sounds of the forest: the wind, the creaking of branches, the rustling of snow-laden spruce boughs—and if a mortal man paid too much attention to such sounds, he could be put into a trance and led off the path to become lost forever.

Relav's horse seemed oblivious to any change as it plodded on, thin and exhausted from walking too far and eating too little. Trembling, Relav reached into the bags of the saddle and withdrew his last lump of bread. He broke off a piece and dropped it to the ground, then opened the drawstrings of his dwindling pouch of salt and sprinkled some of the grains on the snow, signifying life and eternity. "Accept my sacrifice, *leshiye*," he called into the silent forest, then muttered another prayer to the Christian God to forgive his weakness.

A twig snapped behind him, and the horse bolted into the thinning grove of birches. From the saddle, Relav looked around fearfully. Despite the order of Grand Prince Vladimir, the old gods were not dead. How could the old gods not be vengeful against their followers who had betrayed them, as Relav had done? He spurred his horse to a faster pace.

Relav pictured Perun, the Formidable One, who wielded a thunderbolt and a giant stone axe to strike out at the world in his anger. Relav himself had seen the shards of rock scattered around a lightning-blasted tree, splinters of Perun's axe-head. And raven-haired Zorya, the goddess of warriors, rode on her black stallion beside Perun as they watched over battlefields. And great Stribog, god of the winds, struck a fierce gale laden with storms at the onset of spring, reminding everyone of his winter's wrath. And Volkh, the Werewolf King, patron god of all wizards with his fiery eyes and bristling body, protected all the *volkhvi* ... such as Iarik.

Relav had murdered Iarik.

He felt a cold, insubstantial hand at his throat, with sharp claws preparing to rake across his jugular. Black spots danced before his eyes, and he thought he could see the shadowy form of Volkh glaring at him, looking with a vengeful anger at the bloodied sack tied to the horse's saddle. Perun, Zorya, and Stribog all stared at him in their own turn, gnashing their teeth, seething with desire for revenge. Relav, traitor to his village, to his old beliefs, rode unprotected and alone through *their* forest.

With his bare hands, Relav clutched the golden cross hanging uncovered at his chest, but the bitterly cold metal seared his fingers. The string around his neck seemed to burn like a noose, and he pulled it off, tucking the cross in the saddlebag opposite Iarik's head.

The horse stumbled uncertainly as Relav tried to push it to a faster pace. They entered an ice-locked peat bog, where the lumpy blocks of earth had frozen into grotesque and difficult terrain. Tall grasses, matted by the snow, protruded in clumps like the patches of stubble from Relav's newly shaven beard. The ashen clouds above masked how close the time was to sunset. A few solitary pines and birches stood like skeletal guardians, and the air seemed to be growing even colder. Relav did not feel safe in this place.

When you kill me, you forfeit part of yourself. The rest is fertile ground. Fertile ground.

He began to hear voices in his head, whispering curses, seductive promises, threats, all growing stronger as nightfall approached. Relav closed his eyes tight and bit his lip. He began to pray to the Christian God, loudly uttering the rites he had memorized, but a rushing roar like an angry wind filled his mind, drowning out the Christian prayer, pushing through his cold-numbed ears.

Letting out a pathetic cry that sounded eerily human, Relav's horse pitched forward onto the frozen ground. Relav tumbled to the snow and scrambled to his feet, eyes wide, looking for some supernatural attacker. The horse wheezed and groaned, and the man could see the ribs rippling beneath its thin hide. Within moments, the horse shuddered and became as cold as the frozen marsh.

Relav tried to stammer something as the night closed around him, but he was completely alone. The spruce boughs grated together in the wind, in a voice like a *leshiye*'s satisfied whisper. Relav turned around and around, terrified. He hurriedly cut free one of the dead horse's saddle bags that contained a few rations and a flint. Then, after a moment's hesitation, he snatched the sack holding Iarik's head. Relav began to run into the jumbled frozen bog, fleeing the voices and the curse-stricken horse, leaving his golden cross behind.

He collapsed when darkness, exhaustion, and cold drove him to his knees. He scavenged enough wood for a small campfire and spent the night in mortal terror, staring with his watery blue eyes out beyond the flames into the frozen marsh. An inexplicable mist had risen in the bitter cold, swirling, sometimes approaching, sometimes receding, like the slow inhaling and exhaling of a vengeful god. Dancing, hypnotic marsh lights flickered just beyond the range of his vision.

The sack holding the wizard's head sat unopened on the opposite side of the fire. Relav crouched and muttered to himself, steadfastly offering prayers, but paying little heed to whom he addressed.

Unconsciously, as he sat trembling, he began playing with his long hair, but he did not notice that heavy streaks of gray had infiltrated the once-brown strands. Moving with a life of their own, his fingers gathered his hair together into clumps, absently weaving it into three thick braids.

Relav stumbled blindly through the shin-deep snow, clutching the bloodied sack with his frozen fingers. The sun seemed to be rising and setting in a different place each day, altered in its heavenly course by the sorcery of the vengeful gods. He wandered sun-blind in the day, wind-burned at night. Time became a thing of distance. His memory was the working of an internal clock, winding down.

His three thick braids flopped in front of his eyes, but soon he fashioned for himself a headband out of papery birch bark. Wearing the birch headband, he felt stronger somehow, able to see much more as he passed through the haunted wilderness.

Images and scents that Relav could never have known rose around him: philters, herbs, the differing charms for differing times of the year, spells to invoke the power of the harvest, the power of the planting. He heard chants, prayers, incantations, but now he understood them fully and knew their magic. Relav became more and more an empty husk as the days and hours passed, as he carried the chattering burden inside his skull like a cancer.

When you kill me, you forfeit part of yourself. The rest is fertile ground. Fertile ground.

He did not feel his hair turn gray, or his eyes change hue. But his own mind faded deeper and deeper into the background, blowing like a candle in the wind, burning at the end of its wick. Until finally the part that was *Relav* flickered once, and then went out.

He plodded into the village, silently emerging from the forest in the opposite direction from which he had come days before. He still clutched the bloodstained sack in his sinewy fingers. The villagers hovered by the doors of their dwellings, astonished, unable to speak.

He flipped his three long, gray braids away from his face and stared at the villagers with his dragon-green eyes. His chin was newly shaven, cleanly this time, with a wide bronze knife.

"Iarik," someone whispered, and others repeated it, muttering among themselves. Even Tardos, the red-haired elder, hung back and waited, frightened.

"I have returned," he said in a voice that sounded very old and very powerful.

He ripped open the thongs binding the sack and spilled its shriveled burden onto the half-melted snow. Relav's head stared upward with Viking-blue eyes, his brown hair matted with mud.

Iarik turned and walked back into the glistening birch forest, following the secret ways until he reached his cold and barren hut. Then he began to scrape the dark bloodstains from the floor.

I always told my mom that it was important for me to watch those black-and-white Creature Features. It was career training. Honest.

When I was asked to write a werewolf story for The Ultimate Werewolf *anthology, I didn't see any reason not to do a funny one! I've always been a fan of old monster movies, dating all the way to when I wrote "The Injection," and for this tale I drew upon my years of diligently studying* Famous Monsters of Filmland *magazine.*

Special Makeup

The second camera operator ran to fetch the clapboard. Someone else called out, "Quiet on the set! Hey everybody, shut up!" Three of the extras coughed at the same time.

"*Wolfman in Casablanca*, Scene 23. Are we ready for Scene 23?" The second camera operator held the clapboard ready.

"Ahem." The director, Rino Derwell, puffed on his long cigarette in an ivory cigarette holder, just like all famous directors were supposed to have. "I'd like to start today's shooting sometime *today*! Is that too much to ask? Where the hell is Lance?"

The boom man swiveled his microphone around; the extras on the nightclub set fidgeted in their places. The cameraman slurped a cold cup of coffee, making a noise like a vacuum cleaner in a bathtub.

"*Um*, Lance is still, *um*, getting his makeup on," the script supervisor said.

"Christ! Can somebody find me a way to shoot this picture without the star? He was supposed to be done half an hour ago. Go tell Zoltan to hurry up—this is a horror picture, not the Mona Lisa." Derwell mumbled how glad he was that the gypsy makeup man would be leaving in a day or two, and they could get someone else who didn't consider himself such a perfectionist. The director's assistant dashed away, stumbling off the soundstage and tripping on loose wires.

Around them, the set showed an exotic nightclub, with white fake-adobe walls, potted tropical plants, and Arabic-looking squiggles on the pottery. The piano in the center of the stage, just in front of the bar, sat empty under the spotlight, waiting for the movie's star, Lance Chandler. The sound stage sweltered in the summer heat. The large standup fans had to be shut off before shooting; and the ceiling fans—nightclub props—stirred the cloud of cigarette smoke overhead into a gray whirlpool, making the extras cough even when they were supposed to keep silent.

Rino Derwell looked again at his gold wristwatch. He had bought it cheap from a man in an alley, but Derwell's pride would not allow him to admit he had been swindled even after it had promptly stopped working. Derwell didn't need it to tell him he was already well behind schedule, over budget, and out of patience.

It was going to take all day just to shoot a few seconds of finished footage. "God, I hate these transformation sequences. Why does the audience need to *see* everything? Have they no imagination?" he muttered. "Maybe I should just do romance pictures? At least nobody wants to see everything *there!*"

"Oh, God! Please no! Not again! Not NOW!!!" Lance couldn't see the look of horror he hoped would show on his face.

"You must stop fidgeting, Mr. Lance. This will go much faster." Zoltan stepped back, large makeup brush in hand, inspecting his work. His heavy eastern European accent slurred out his words.

"Well, I've got to practice my lines. This blasted makeup takes so blasted long that I forget my blasted lines by the time it comes to shoot. Was I supposed to say, 'Don't let it happen *here!*' in that scene? Hand me the script."

"No, Mr. Lance. That line comes much later—it follows 'Oh, no! I'm transforming!'" Zoltan smeared shadow under Lance's eyes. This would be just the first step in the transformation, but he still had to increase the highlights. Veins stood out on Zoltan's gnarled hands, but his fingers were rock steady with the fine detail.

"How do you know my lines?"

"You may call it gypsy intuition, Mr. Lance—or it may be because you have been saying them every morning before makeup for a week now. They have burned into my brain like a gypsy curse."

Lance glared at the wizened old man in his pale blue shirt and color-spattered smock. Zoltan's leathery fingers had a real instinct for makeup, for changing the appearance of any actor. But his craft took hours.

Lance Chandler had enough confidence in his own screen presence to carry any picture, regardless of how silly the makeup made him look. His square jaw, fine physique, and clean-cut appearance made him the perfect model of the all-American hero. Now, during the War against Germany and Japan, the U.S. needed its strong heroes to keep up morale. Besides, making propaganda pictures fulfilled his patriotic duties without requiring him to go somewhere and risk getting shot. Red-corn-syrup blood and bullet blanks were about all the real violence he wanted to experience.

Lance took special pride in his performance in *Tarzan Versus the Third Reich*. Though he had few lines in the film, the animal rage on his face and his oiled and straining body had been enough to topple an entire regiment of Hitler's finest, including one of Rommel's desert vehicles. (Exactly why one of Rommel's desert vehicles had shown up in the middle of Africa's deepest jungles was a question only the scriptwriter could have answered.)

Craig Corwyn, U-Boat Smasher, to be released next month as the start of a new series, might make Lance a household name. Those stories centered on brave Craig Corwyn, who had a penchant for leaping off the deck of his Allied destroyer and swimming down to sink Nazi submarines with his bare hands, usually by opening the underwater hatches or just plucking out the rivets in the hull.

But none of those movies would compare to *Wolfman in Casablanca*. Bogart would be forgotten in a week. The timing for this picture was just perfect; it had an emotional content Lance had not been able to bring into his earlier efforts. The country was just waiting for a new hero, strong and manly, with a dash of animal unpredictability and a heart of gold (not to mention unwavering in Allied sympathies).

The story concerned a troubled but patriotic werewolf—him, Lance Chandler—who in his wanderings has found himself in German-occupied Casablanca. There he causes what havoc he can for the enemy, and he also meets Brigitte, a beautiful French resistance fighter vacationing in Morocco. Brigitte turns out to be a werewolf herself, Lance's true love. Even in the script, the final scene as the two of them howl on the rooftops above a conflagration of Nazi tanks and ruined artillery sent shivers down Lance's spine. If he could pull off this performance, Hitler himself would tremble in his sheets.

Zoltan added spirit gum to Lance's cheeks and forehead, humming as he worked. "You will please stop perspiring, Mr. Lance. I require a dry surface for this fine hair."

Lance slumped in the chair. Zoltan reminded him of the wicked old gypsy man in the movie, the one who had cursed his character to become a werewolf in the first place. "This blasted transformation sequence is going to take all day again, isn't it? And I don't even get to *act* after the first second or so! Lie still, add more hair, shoot a few frames, lie still, add more hair, shoot a few more frames. And it's so hot in the soundstage. The spirit gum burns and ruins my complexion. The fumes sting my eyes. The fake hair itches."

He winced his face into the practiced look of horror again. "Oh, God! Please no! Not again! *Um* ... oh, yeah—don't let it happen here!" Lance paused, then scowled. "Blast, that wasn't right. Would you hurry up, Zoltan! I'm already losing my lines. And I'm really tired of you dragging your feet—get moving!"

Zoltan tossed the makeup brush with a loud clink into its glass jar of solvent. He put his gnarled hands on his hips and glared at Lance. The smoldering gypsy fury in his dark eyes looked worse than anything Lance had seen on a movie villain's face.

"I lose my patience with you, Mr. Lance! It is gone! Poof! Now I must take a short cut. A special trick that only I know. It will take a minute, and it will make you a star forevermore! I guarantee that. You will no longer suffer my efforts—and I need not suffer you! The people at the new Frankenstein picture over on Lot 17 would appreciate my work, no doubt."

Lance blinked, amazed at the old gypsy's anger but ready to jump at any chance that would get him out of the makeup trailer sooner. He heard only the words, "it will make you a star. I guarantee that."

"Well, do it then, Zoltan! I've got work to do. The great Lon Chaney never had to put up with all these delays. He did all his own makeup. My audiences are waiting to see the new meaning I can bring to the portrayal of the werewolf."

"You will never disappoint them, Mr. Lance."

Without further reply, Zoltan yanked at the fine hair he had already applied. "You no longer need this." Lance yowled as the patches came free of his skin. "That is a very good sound you make, Mr. Lance. Very much like a werewolf."

Lance growled at him.

Zoltan rustled in a cardboard box in the corner of his cramped trailer, pulled out a dirty Mason jar, and unscrewed its rusty lid. Inside, a brown oily liquid swirled all by itself, spinning green flecks in internal currents. The old man stuck his fingers into the goop and brought them out dripping.

"What is—whoa, that smells like—" Lance tried to shrink away, but Zoltan slapped the goop onto his cheek and smeared it around.

"You cannot possibly know what this smells like, Mr. Lance, because you have no idea what I used to make it. You probably do not wish to know—then you would be even more upset at having it rubbed all over your face."

Zoltan reached into the jar again and brought out another handful, which he wiped across Lance's forehead. "*Ugh!* Did you get that from the lot cafeteria?" Lance felt his skin tingle, as if the liquid had begun to eat its way inside. "*Ow!* My complexion!"

"If it gives you pimples, you can always call them character marks, Mr. Lance. Every good actor has them."

Zoltan pulled his hand away. Lance saw that the old man's fingers were clean. "Finished. It has all absorbed right in." He screwed the cover of the jar back on and replaced it in the cardboard box.

Lance grabbed a small mirror, expecting to find his (soon-to-be) well-known expression covered with ugly brown, but he could see no sign of the makeup at all. "What happened to it? It still stinks."

"It is special makeup. It will work when it needs to."

The door flew open, and the red-faced director's assistant stood panting. "Lance, Mr. Derwell wants you on the set right now! Pronto! We've got to start shooting."

Zoltan nudged his shoulder. "I am finished with you, Mr. Lance."

Lance stood up, trying not to look perplexed so that Zoltan could have a laugh at his expense. "But I don't see any—"

The old gypsy wore a wicked grin on his lips. "You need not worry about it. I believe your expression is, 'Knock 'em dead.'"

Lance sat down at the nightclub piano and cracked his knuckles. The extras and other stars took their positions. Above the soundstage, he could hear men on the catwalks, positioning cool blue gels over the lights to simulate the full moon.

"*Now* are you ready, Lance?" the director said, fitting another cigarette into his ivory holder. "Or do you think maybe we should just take a coffee break for an hour or so?"

"That's not necessary, Mr. Derwell. I'm ready. Just give the word, see?" He growled for good measure.

"Places everyone!"

Lance ran his fingers over the piano keyboard, "tickling the old ivories," as real piano players called it. No sound came out. Lance couldn't play a note, of course, so the prop men had cut all the piano wires, holding the instrument in merciful silence no matter how enthusiastically Lance might bang on it. They would add the beautiful piano melody to the soundtrack during post-production.

"*Wolfman in Casablanca*, Scene 23, Take One." The clapboard cracked.

"Action!" Derwell called.

The klieg lights came on, pouring hot white illumination on the set. Lance stiffened at the piano, then began to hum and pretend to plink on the keys.

In this scene, the werewolf has taken a job as a piano player in a nightclub, where he has met Brigitte, the vacationing French resistance fighter. While playing "As Time Goes By," Lance's character looks up to see the full moon shining down through the nightclub's skylight. To keep from having to interrupt filming, Derwell had planned to shoot Lance from the back only as he played the piano, not showing his face until after he had supposedly started to transform. But now Lance didn't appear to wear any makeup at all—he wondered what would happen when Derwell noticed, but he plunged into the performance nevertheless. That would be Zoltan's problem, not his.

At the appropriate point, Lance froze at the keyboard, forcing his fingers to tremble as he stared at them. On the soundtrack, the music would stop in mid-note. The false moonlight shone down on him. Lance formed his face into his best expression of abject horror.

"Oh, God! Please no! Not again! Don't let it happen *HERE*!!!" Lance clutched his chest, slid sideways, and did a graceful but dramatic topple off the piano bench.

On cue, one of the extras screamed. The bartender dropped a glass, which shattered on the tiles.

On the floor, Lance couldn't stop writhing. His own body felt as if it were being turned inside out. He had really learned how to bury himself in the role! His face and hands itched, burned. His fingers curled and clenched. It felt terrific. It felt *real* to him. He let out a moaning scream—and it took him a moment to realize it wasn't part of the act.

Off behind the cameras, Lance could see Rino Derwell jumping up and down with delight, jerking both his thumbs up in silent admiration for Lance's performance. "Cut!"

Lance tried to lie still. They would need to add the next layer of hair and makeup. Zoltan would come in and paste one of the latex appliances onto his eyebrows, darken his nails with shoe polish.

But Lance felt his own nails sharpening, curling into claws. Hair sprouted from the backs of his hands. His cheeks tingled and burned. His ears felt sharp and stretched, protruding from the back of his head. His face tightened and elongated; his mouth filled with fangs.

"No, wait!" Derwell shouted at the cameraman. "Keep rolling! Keep rolling!"

"Look at that!" the director's assistant said.

Lance tried to say something, but he could only growl. His body tightened and felt ready to explode with anger. He found it difficult to concentrate, but some part of his mind knew what he had to do. After all, he had read the script.

Leaping up from the nightclub dance floor, Lance strained until his clothes ripped under his bulging lupine muscles. With a roar and a spray of saliva from his fang-filled jaws, he smashed the piano bench prop into kindling, knocking it aside.

Four of the extras screamed, even without their cues.

Lance heaved the giant, mute piano and smashed it onto its side. The severed piano wires jangled like a rasping old woman trying to sing. The bartender stood up and brought out a gun, firing four times in succession, but they were only theatrical blanks, and not silver blanks either. Lance knocked the gun aside, grabbed the bartender's arm, and hurled him across the stage, where he landed in a perfect stunt man's roll.

Lance Chandler stood under the klieg lights, in the pool of blue gel filtering through the skylight simulating the full moon. He bayed a beautiful wolf howl as everyone fled screaming from the stage.

"Cut! Cut! Lance, that's magnificent!" Derwell clapped his hands.

The klieg lights faded, leaving the wreckage under the normal room illumination. Lance felt all the energy drain out of him. His face rippled and contracted, his ears shrank back to normal. His throat remained sore from the long howl, but the fangs had vanished from his mouth. He brushed his hands to his cheeks but found that all the abnormal hair had melted away.

Derwell ran onto the set and clapped him on the back. "That was *incredible!* Oscar-quality stuff!"

Old Zoltan stood at the edge of the set, smiling. His dark eyes glittered. Derwell turned to the gypsy and applauded him as well. "Marvelous, Zoltan! I can't believe it. How in the world did you do that?"

Zoltan shrugged, but his toothless grin grew wider. "Special makeup," he said. "Gypsy secret. I am pleased it worked out." He turned and shuffled toward the soundstage exit.

"Do you really think that was Oscar quality?" Lance asked.

The other actors treated Lance with a sort of awe, though a few tended to avoid him. The actress playing Brigitte kept fixing her eyes on him, raising her eyebrows in a suggestive expression. Derwell, having shot a perfect take of the transformation scene he had thought would require more than a day, ordered the set crew to repair the werewolf-caused damage so they could shoot the big love scene, as a reward to everyone.

Zoltan said nothing to Lance as he added a heavy coat of pancake and sprayed his hair into place. Lance didn't know how the gypsy had worked the transformation, but he knew when not to ask questions. Derwell had said his performance was Oscar quality! He just grinned to himself and looked forward to the kissing scene with Brigitte. Lance always tried to make sure the kissing scenes required several takes. He enjoyed his work, and so (no doubt) did his female co-stars.

Zoltan added an extra-thick layer of dark-red lipstick to Brigitte's mouth, then applied a special wax sealing coat so that it wouldn't smear during the on-screen passion.

"All right you two," Derwell said, sitting back in his director's chair, "start gazing at each other and getting starry-eyed. Places everyone!"

Zoltan packed up his kit and left the soundstage. He said goodbye to the director, but Derwell waved him away in distraction.

Lance stared into Brigitte's eyes, then wiggled his eyebrows in what he hoped would be an irresistible invitation. He had few lines in this scene, only some low grunting and a mumbled "Yes, my love" during the kiss.

Brigitte gazed back at him, batting her eyelashes, melting him with her deep brown irises.

"*Wolfman in Casablanca*, Scene 39, Take One."

Lance took a deep breath, so he could make the kiss last longer.

"Action!" The klieg lights came one.

In silence, he and Brigitte gawked at each other. Romantic music would be playing on the soundtrack. They leaned closer to each other. She shuddered with her barely contained emotion. After an indrawn breath, she spoke in a sultry, sexy French accent. "You are the type of man I need. You are my soul mate. Kiss me. I want you to kiss me."

He bent toward her. "Yes, my love."

His joints felt as if they had turned to ice water. His skin burned and tingled. He kissed her, pulling her close, feeling his passion rise to an uncontrollable pitch.

Brigitte jerked away. "*Ow!* Lance, you bit me!" She touched a spot of blood on her lip.

He felt his hands curl into claws, the nails turn hard and black. Hair began to sprout all over his body. He tried to stop the transformation, but he didn't know how. He stumbled backward. "Oh, God! Please no! Not again!"

"No, Lance—that's not your line!" Brigitte whispered to him.

His muscles bulged; his face stretched out into a long, sharp muzzle. His throat gurgled and growled. He looked around for something to smash. Brigitte screamed, though it wasn't in the script. Tossing her aside, Lance uprooted one of the ornamental palms and hurled the clay pot to the other side of the stage.

"Cut!" the director called. "What the hell is going on here? It's just a simple scene!"

The klieg lights dimmed again. Lance felt the werewolf within him dissolving away, leaving him sweating and shaking and standing in clothes that had torn in several embarrassing places.

"Oh, Lance, quit screwing around!" Derwell said. "Go to wardrobe and get some new clothes, for Christ's sake! Somebody, get a new plant and clean up that mess. Get First Aid to fix Brigitte's lip here. Come on, people!" Derwell shook his head. "Why did I ever turn down that job to make Army training films?"

Lance skipped going to wardrobe and went to Zoltan's makeup trailer instead. He didn't know how he was going discuss this with the gypsy, but if all else failed he could just knock the old man flat with a good roundhouse punch, in the style of Craig Corwyn, U-Boat Smasher.

When he pounded on the flimsy door, though, it swung open by itself. A small sign hung by a string from the doorknob. In

Zoltan's scrawling handwriting, it said "FAREWELL, MY COMPANIONS. TIME TO MOVE ON. GYPSY BLOOD CALLS."

Lance stepped inside. "All right, Zoltan. I know you're in here!"

But he knew no such thing, and the cramped trailer proved to be empty indeed. Many of the bottles had been removed from the shelves, the brushes, the latex prosthetics all packed and taken. Zoltan had also carried away the old cardboard box from the corner, the one containing the jar of special makeup for Lance.

In the makeup chair, Lance found a single sheet of paper that had been left for him. He picked it up and stared down at it, moving his lips as he read.

"Mr. Lance,

"My homemade concoction may eventually wear off, as soon as you learn a little more patience. Or they may not. I cannot tell. I have always been afraid to use my special makeup, until I met you.

"Do not try to find me. I have gone with the crew of *Fraankenstein of the Farmlands* to shoot on location in Iowa. I will be gone for some time. Director Derwell asked me to leave, to save him time and money. Worry not, though, Mr. Lance. You no longer need any makeup from me.

"I promised you would become a star. Now, every time the glow of the klieg lights strikes your face, you will transform into a werewolf. You will doubtless be in every single werewolf movie produced from now on. How can they refuse?

"P.S., You should hope that werewolves are not just a passing fad! You know how fickle audiences can be."

Lance Chandler crumpled the note, then straightened it again so he could tear it into shreds, but he didn't need any werewolf anger to snarl this time.

He stared around the empty makeup trailer, feeling his career shatter around him. There would be no more Tarzan roles, no thrilling adventures of Craig Corwyn. His hopes, his dreams were ruined, and his cry of anguish sounded like a mournful wolf's howl.

"I've been typecast!"

Edgar Allan Poe's writing has haunted me for as long as I've been able to read. When I was just a boy, I struggled through "The Raven," captivated by the creepy imagery. Fascinated with scary stories, I devoured "The Tell-Tale Heart," "The Premature Burial," "The Pit and the Pendulum," "The Oblong Box," and all the others. I watched the Roger Corman movies loosely based on the works of Poe, or at least using the same titles, starring Vincent Price. In college, I read a multi-volume set of the complete works of Edgar Allan Poe.

Recently, for her thesis project, one of my Publishing graduate students at Western Colorado University chose to assemble and publish a collection of Poe's detective fiction, which reawakened my interest.

Well before Arthur Conan Doyle created Sherlock Holmes, Edgar Allan Poe invented the detective story with his Inspector Dupin, in "The Murders in the Rue Morgue," "The Purloined Letter," and "The Mystery of Marie Roget."

While working with my student on her collection, I realized that it would be a great story idea to have Poe himself in the role of a detective hunting a serial killer in Richmond, Virginia. I love how this story turned out.

The Tell-Tale Mind

T he cramped, cluttered offices of Inspector Dupin were less impressive than the Richmond chief of police warranted. The window was so narrow and fly-specked that he had to light a kerosene lamp on his desk so he could read his handwritten case ledgers. The inspector himself needed a shave and a bath, and his dark blue uniform was dotted with stains that had been brushed off but not washed.

But Edgar Allan Poe was not one to cast judgment. He cut an even less impressive figure, bedraggled and desperate, but he had to make his report. He had to expose the terrible crimes he had seen in his mind. Poe could only hope that his strident, wavering voice conveyed urgency rather than irrational agitation.

"I assure you, Inspector Dupin, I am not mad. You must believe me. I am not mad!" Poe placed both of his palms against his high forehead, stroked back his unruly raven locks of hair in a demonstration of abject misery. "Reginald Usher has murdered three people that I know of. I've seen it."

Inspector Dupin had initially taken the young writer seriously when Poe barged into his office, slapping the side of his head as if to scatter buzzing bees from his thoughts. Dupin leaned forward at his desk and rubbed his weary eyes. "Has the police department not heard your accusations before, Mr. Poe? And have they not always turned out to be false?"

"Not false! *Unproven*—as yet. I am not mad. You must believe me."

Poe realized that he came across as entirely the opposite. His eyes were bloodshot and red-rimmed from far too much drinking. It was the only way he could silence, or at least quiet, the haunting, yammering voices that barged through his head. "I am not mad," he whispered as if unsure he could convince even himself. "I *know* Usher committed the murders. My senses are heightened. My powers of observation keen."

How could he explain that he often heard the feverish thoughts of others in his own mind?

Dupin poised with a quill pen in hand, the ink pot open, the page of his case ledger still blank. "As a writer and a poet, no doubt you believe in your understanding of human nature, but your claims are preposterous. Reginald Usher is a man of high social standing, a wealthy benefactor of the town's orphanage. He prints the most reliable newspaper in Richmond, *The Epitaph*." The inspector narrowed his eyes. "Until recently were you not in the employ of Mr. Usher, writing articles and literary criticism for *The Epitaph*?"

Poe looked away. "That job proved to be ... untenable. The things I saw there, the thoughts I heard."

Dupin raised his eyebrows. "The *thoughts* you heard, Mr. Poe?"

"I am not mad," Poe insisted again.

He recalled the time he had gathered the nerve to face Usher in his newspaper office, a finely appointed room that was more a private library than a business office. Reginald Usher had many shelves of fine books, classics of Greek and Roman literature, the plays of Socrates, the lives of Ovid, the histories of Plutarch, the works of William Shakespeare, and hundreds of unmarked journals of ancient philosophers. As a philanthropist, Usher made his wealth of information available to *Epitaph* reporters should they need to look up a fact or verify a quote, and also to scholars and seekers of truth in general, but few took him up on the invitation.

With his fascination for literature, having published his own volume of poems in 1827, Poe aspired to make his living by writing. He had accepted the position with the Richmond *Epitaph*, vowing to become an important reporter. Poe had not expected such a devastating experience when he entered the editor's office, though. Instead of a quiet sanctuary of books, he found the room *loud* with Reginald Usher's violent, unshielded thoughts that rang throughout his sensitive mind. He witnessed what the man had done, heard the screams of victims, felt the blood, and experienced the sheer joy he drew from it.

"He has killed at least three people," Poe said again, resting his clenched fists on the inspector's desk. "I am here to report a crime."

"Who are these three victims? No bodies have been found, no one reported missing."

Poe wished he had a drink as he sat sweating, shuddering, trying to get his thoughts under control. He adjusted his cravat, swallowed hard. "One is an old man ... I don't know the name. He was a boarder with a vulture-like eye, a lazy eye. It obsessed Usher so much that one night he killed the old man, smothered him with a pillow. Then he cut up the body into pieces and buried it under the floorboards. You can find the body still there in Usher's home, if you look. Even his wife does not know about it."

The inspector did not look sufficiently horrified, nor convinced. "I can't send police to tear up a man's floor because you've had a nightmare." He narrowed his eyes. "Or because you are at odds with your former employer."

Not wishing to explain, not yet, Poe pushed on. "The second victim was a business rival. A wealthy man from Atlanta who made a fortune in tobacco. Malcolm ..." He struggled for the name. He'd only caught a flash in Usher's thoughts, drowned out by the hatred and smug satisfaction. "Malcolm *Fortunato*. They knew each other, disliked each other. Fortunato came to Virginia with plans to start a new newspaper that would have ruined Usher."

Poe was breathing hard, the memories as vivid inside him as if he had committed the murders himself. "Usher pretended to be jovial, invited the man to a private dinner at his home, just the two of them. He got Fortunato drunk on expensive sherry, and when the man was unconscious, Usher chained him to a wall in the cellar. He bricked Fortunato up, leaving him there to starve in the darkness, his screams unheard." His voice dropped to a whisper. "But Usher often returned to listen, pressing his ear against the fresh-laid bricks."

"Your imagination is horrific, Mr. Poe." Inspector Dupin placed the cap on the bottle of ink and set aside the quill, upset that his time was being wasted. "Again you have yet to offer a shred of proof. How do you know these things?"

Poe struggled to put the horrors into words. He tugged at the collar of his shirt. The cravat seemed constricting. "Is there no air in here, man?" The fumes of the kerosene lamp were stifling. Dupin unlatched the leaded glass window and swung it open, although the breezes did little to help. The ringing in Poe's head changed to a different, higher pitch.

He continued doggedly, "The third murder was his cousin Berenice, a beautiful young girl with perfect white teeth, like pearls. Usher was obsessed with them just as he was obsessed with the vulture eye of the old man. He and his wife took Berenice as their young ward, but the girl is gone now. You can verify that much."

"The man killed his niece because of her teeth?" Dupin asked with a long, dubious sigh.

"Because he wanted the teeth, he *needed* the teeth. He broke them out of her jaw and kept them in a jar. I think ... I think he wanted to make a necklace of them."

Dupin was repulsed. "You have tried my patience enough, Mr. Poe."

"These things can be checked. Find what happened to Malcolm Fortunato. And the old man, his boarder. And the girl

Berenice. Where are they? Surely the great Richmond police inspector can solve the crime."

"I am not convinced there is any crime," the inspector said.

"Then prove to me there isn't! If these people have indeed disappeared, will that not be enough to raise questions?"

Dupin was at least partially swayed by the writer's earnestness. "I do appreciate solving a crime." He rose from his desk and went to the office door, calling out into the busy main room. "In the meantime, I shall have you wait in a place where you'll be safe, although not comfortable. You need it for your own good." He scratched the stubble on his face. "If your assertions turn out to be false, there will also be consequences."

The nightmarish visions continued to plague him, the murders he had witnessed through the thoughts of a killer. "They are true. You'll see."

The inspector addressed the two waiting officers. "Take Mr. Poe to the holding cell. He may be drunk or disoriented. At the very least he could use a good, long rest."

Poe was alarmed and infuriated as the policemen took him by the arms. "Look into the matter and you'll see, Inspector! I will wait to be vindicated, and then I will see Reginald Usher pay for what he's done."

With a rattle of keys in the lock, the iron bars swung open, and Poe groggily rose from the hard, narrow cot. He had slept poorly in the jail cell, hearing the muddled thoughts of another drunk in the next cell. Worse, he also overheard the violent recollections of a policeman in the corridor, a man who enforced the law while he was in uniform, but went home to beat his wife because he liked her when she was terrified of him. The shuddery memories rang in his head, and Poe squeezed his eyes shut.

The frown on Dupin's face held questions, even uncertainty. Poe recognized the change, heard the doubt in the inspector's thoughts. "You've seen it!" He stepped toward the open cell door, trying to gather his composure. His body smelled of sweat, his mouth tasted of sour old wine. He looked a disgrace.

"It is enough to make me wonder, Mr. Poe. I investigated the matter, as you requested. Malcolm Fortunato is no longer in Richmond, and he has not been seen for two weeks."

Poe felt a shiver. In his mind he saw the images of the man hanging in manacles in the dark space behind the cellar wall, while Usher used trowel and mortar, brick by brick, to seal him alive. "Because he is entombed alive behind a brick wall."

Dupin said, "Fortunato apparently boarded a ship to England, where he has other business interests. He is not expected to return."

"But you can't prove that," Poe said.

"Now you're the one who asks for proof?" The inspector extended another finger. "Then there is the old man you spoke of. Some remember a boarder at the Usher's house, and one person even remarked about the man's oddly staring eye. But he has moved on, a transient—as boarders often are."

"Again, that is no proof! He is buried under the floorboards, I tell you. Tear them up, and you'll see."

Dupin was singularly unruffled. "As for the cousin Berenice, the young girl was a ward of the Ushers, but has been sent off to a boarding school in Baltimore."

"No, she is dead. Send a rider to Baltimore," Poe insisted. "You will find that the girl is not there."

"The reasoning is thin to send a courier on such an arduous journey. Rather, I'll send a letter by post, just to investigate all possibilities. That will be sufficient."

Though not satisfied, Poe couldn't force the inspector to do more. "So I'm free to go then?" Trying to regain his composure, he shuffled out of the cell and down the corridor.

Following, Dupin scolded him. "In the meantime, you are not to besmirch the honor of Reginald Usher. You'll only find yourself thrown back in jail." The inspector spoke wearily as if he knew his words would not be heeded.

When they reached the front office, a gentleman and lady entered the Richmond police station, both of them finely dressed, both looking indignant. Poe reeled back clutching Inspector Dupin's arm for support. "Reginald Usher!"

The newspaperman had a dark goatee, heavy eyebrows, and a stare like obsidian. Poe could not have described a more evil man in his most overwrought short story. Usher had a frock coat, a top hat, and a perfectly knotted purple cravat held in place with a diamond stickpin. Their eyes locked like daggers drawn.

Usher's voice boomed, "Poe, you spread vile rumors about me, and I'll have none of it! You were fired from your position for cause, and this is just some disgruntled revenge."

But Poe's gaze locked on the woman accompanying him, slightly plump with a powdered face, red hair done up in tight curls, a green velvet dress. And a necklace of perfect white, polished pearls, a string set off against her creamy throat.

Poe heard the horrified screams of victims in his mind. "The teeth. Berenice's teeth! That's what you did with them, you monster!" He broke free of Dupin's grasp and lunged forward. As Mrs. Usher shrieked and clung to her husband, Poe fell upon her. He grabbed at the necklace, yanking it free. He felt the hard, white objects in the palm of his hand, broke the strand, and they clattered and bounced on the floor of the station.

The inspector grabbed him, while other policemen rushed to help. Usher raised his walking stick and struck Poe on the shoulders. "Leave my wife alone."

"They are teeth. Berenice's teeth!" Poe howled.

As the necklace broke, the round, white objects spread apart, rattling on the floor. Just pearls ... ordinary, beautiful pearls.

"Accusing me of heinous murder, assaulting my wife! This man should be in a madhouse." Usher glared at Poe. "I gave you a chance, young man. I thought I saw talent in you, but you are a menace."

As Mrs. Usher found a seat and fanned herself, and the policemen collected the valuable pearls from the floor, Dupin dragged Poe to the side of the room, as far as possible from the newspaperman.

Usher continued, seething. "Have you looked into this man's life, his character, Inspector? Edgar Allan Poe is a disgrace to everyone who has tried to help him. He was ejected from the University of Virginia due to excessive drinking and gambling, estranged from his foster father because of enormous debts, discharged from the United States Army under questionable circumstances. I could go on at length."

Unable to deny any of it, Poe hung his head. His hand clenched, as if longing to hold a bottle of wine so he could drink himself into a stupor.

The inspector's expression changed, becoming disappointed, even disgusted. Poe didn't have to listen in on Dupin's thoughts, and he doubted the inspector would even write a letter to the boarding school to verify the whereabouts of Berenice.

"I have seen enough. You are dismissed, Mr. Poe." Dupin looked up at the newspaper owner. "Unless you wish to press charges, sir?"

"Poe is pathetic, and he hasn't a penny to his name. I'd waste no further time on him, although if he continues to sully my good character with his wild accusations, I shall be forced to respond with all the force of the law."

Usher turned with his lady, and they left the station. The policemen waited a sufficient length of time before throwing Poe out into the streets.

Even drunk enough to blot out his conscious thoughts, Poe could not entirely escape from the resounding thought-echoes buzzing around him. At night the taverns, the dancing halls, the gambling dens were a maelstrom of shouting minds that sucked him down. Poe had spent his last few coins on a bottle of cheap grog which had only dulled the uproar by a small amount.

Now he staggered through the dark streets of Richmond, leaning against the brick walls of houses, keeping himself up by holding the rough bark of a stately elm. Feeling too exposed, he walked between buildings, seeking shelter in the shadows of an alley.

Poe could not go home, not in this condition. Even with the misery and heartache he had given his aunt Maria, she would still fawn over him ... or his lovely young cousin Virginia, of whom he was quite fond, would want to mother him, though she was just a child. They both knew of Poe's illness, his passion, the clamor in his mind, but for some odd reason they excused it as the workings of a great creative mind. They knew his muse was so insistent it drove him to the verge of irrational behavior.

Poe's parents had been actors, and the spirit of drama surely lived within him. Young Virginia adored him when he told her stories, even the horrific ones that he dredged out of his nightmares. But he couldn't share all of his pain and misery, not the true horrors he had seen in the hearts of even respectable men like Reginald Usher. Neither Aunt Marie nor sweet young Virginia deserved that.

Poe didn't deserve it either, but he had been cursed with a special acuity. All his life, the ringing and droning had ricocheted through his head. Guilty memories, dark unintended confessions sloshed out of other minds like the foam from an overfilled mug of beer. He had heard the ghosts of lost loved ones, the violence of past crimes. The only way he could get a modicum of peace was by drowning those mental echoes with brandy, wine, or even cheap grog.

Lurching down the alley, he took another swig from the dark bottle. He turned into another dark street, lost and uncaring.

At the police station, Usher had deprecated him, and the man's belittlement was all true. Poe was a failure in every aspect of his life, not through lack of talent but through a weakness in his character. How could a man lead a normal life when his very existence was an inner battle with tortuous thoughts that rose like a miasma from the crowd of humanity? Poe knew the dark secrets of even the most nondescript man in the crowd. He had to live with the guilt of every sin on which he eavesdropped. How could any man be strong enough for that?

He drained the last of the grog and tossed the empty bottle aside. The breaking glass masked the sound of other footsteps, and Poe blearily made out the burly shapes of three men at the other end of the alley. He had come here hoping to find silence from all the clamorous thoughts in the city, but now he heard a roar of violent anticipation boiling from the men. These were thugs focused on hurting him, with no subtlety whatsoever. They did not even have thoughts of robbing him, although Poe would have been a disappointing mark for any cutpurse.

He tried to flee, but his body was too clumsy from the drink, and two big men were upon him in a moment. He realized the third man was a different sort altogether. His thoughts were sharper, more dangerous and black, like the wings of a raven.

"Hold him," said the voice. "Hurt him."

One thug dutifully grabbed Poe by the collar and hauled him against the alley wall. The other man pummeled him hard in the face and again in his gut. As Poe collapsed, retching, the thoughts of the third man became more distinct. Even though he couldn't see through the shadows, pain, and alcohol, he knew this man. Reginald Usher.

Poe managed to croak, "You'll kill me now, like the others?" He meant to sound defiant and challenging, but he convulsed and spewed vomit on the ground.

"You are a madman, and your accusations are maddening." Usher leaned close, grimacing at the stink of vomit and whiskey. "I should have these men cut you open and tie you with your own entrails." He paused and grinned, showing white pearly teeth that must surely have been as noteworthy as Berenice's. "Better yet, I should just bury you alive in an unmarked grave. No one would ever find you, and you would suffocate slowly, slowly. Ah, that would be fitting."

In the resonance of Usher's murderous thoughts, Poe knew that he meant to do it.

"But first you will tell me how you know." He shook Poe by the shoulders, slamming his head against the alley wall. "Were you watching? What did you see? How is that possible?"

"I saw because you saw," Poe said. "And *you* can't stop thinking about it." He laughed. "The teeth ... the teeth were so hard and white, but you didn't expect all the blood when you used the hammer to bash them out of her lifeless face, did you?"

Usher recoiled.

"And the old man with the staring eye! You could hear his heart beating, couldn't you? Even after he was dead, pounding in your head, pounding ..."

Usher kicked him in the ribs, but it was more a reflex with little strength behind it. The two thugs, though, beat him harder. Poe kept laughing as he stared up at Usher's animal eyes, saw even deeper into his mind. "I see Fortunato on the chains, sloppily begging for his life. You may be a powerful businessman, Mr. Usher, but you're a bad bricklayer."

The man was horrified and infuriated. "You can't know! You have no proof."

Poe chucked and then spat blood. "I have your guilt."

Usher stepped away, disgusted but clearly shaken.

"Should we kill him?" asked one of the thugs.

Usher shook his head. "The police know of my connection to him. If he died now, too many people might question me." He clearly hated his conclusion. "But no one will take him seriously. He's disgraced and clearly deranged."

Even through his fog of alcohol, blood, and pain, Poe found that amusing. "I am deranged? You murder people on a whim ... and *I* am deranged?"

"Let his own demons punish him," Usher sneered, then considered. "But in the meantime, you can make him hurt."

The thugs kicked and pummeled Poe, but before he fell into unconsciousness, he was smiling. He had seen even deeper into Usher's mind and found exactly what he needed.

The annoyed policemen tried to prevent Poe from seeing Inspector Dupin. He tried to break free of their tight grip, and the struggle only exacerbated the pain of his countless bruises, his cracked ribs, his split lip. His black eye was so swollen he could barely see. "I must speak with the inspector! It is a matter of utmost importance."

Dupin emerged from his dingy office and regarded the battered man with grave disappointment, though he showed a small amount of sympathy at seeing his injuries. "I see your words have gotten you into even more trouble, Mr. Poe."

Poe yanked his arms free of the policemen. "Not my words, sir —it is what I *know* that makes Usher fear me."

One of the policemen interjected sharply, "He was obviously beaten and robbed while he was in a drunken stupor."

"Do you intend to blame this on Reginald Usher?" Dupin asked.

"It was his ruffians, but he will deny it." Poe tugged on the muddied remnants of his jacket, then stripped off the mangled cravat as a lost cause. "But this assault is insignificant when compared with the heinous murders he has committed."

The policeman groaned, and Inspector Dupin turned away. "Let me never see you again, Mr. Poe. I don't know why you bothered to come."

"Because I have proof! And I can show it to you. A full confession written in Reginald Usher's own hand."

Dupin paused and turned with a skeptical frown. "Usher was quite clear that if you made false accusations against him again, he would press charges. You will be ruined."

Poe straightened his shoulders and looked the inspector in the eye. "If you should find my claims insufficient, then you may arrest me. But you will arrest Usher instead when you read what he has written. I can show you."

The policeman who had been holding Poe looked upset. "Waste of time, sir."

Poe pushed past the pain of his injuries, heard the thoughts and unanswered questions in Dupin's mind, and took hope. "Surely there must be some question in your mind, Inspector?" His eyes pleaded. "We simply need to go to his newspaper office. It'll take only a moment, and you will take a murderer off the streets of Richmond."

"I will lock someone up before this day is done, that's for certain," grumbled Dupin. "This is your last chance."

When they arrived at the offices of the Richmond *Epitaph*, Reginald Usher rose from his great mahogany desk, clearly indignant. "Inspector Dupin, I had hoped never to see you again."

The newspaperman's office was appointed like a fine withdrawing room with its own fireplace, a small side table with a cut-crystal decanter of brandy and an overstuffed leather chair. The walls were covered with fine oak shelves filled with countless books of varying sizes, fat volumes, slender volumes with embossed spines and bound in shades of leather or cloth. The books were arranged haphazardly, giving no indication as to how the books were arranged, whether by subject, author, or language.

Two policemen entered behind Dupin and stood at attention by the door. Poe remained close as the inspector spoke in a formal voice, "Police business, sir. I hope to accept your invitation to make use of the resources in your library?" He glanced at the shelves filled with more books than any one man could read. "Might I avail upon your generosity to double-check a detail?"

Usher looked witheringly at Poe, wary. "Why have you brought this ... creature? Did we not put an end to his ravings the other day?" He sniffed. "He appears to need medical attention—and a bath. Has he hurt himself?"

A flare of violent suspicions leaked out of Usher's mind, like smoke from a badly vented fireplace. He was on the edge of more violence, expecting Poe to accuse him of the assault, which he would merely laugh at.

But Poe was not so foolish. He also heard Dupin's doubts, the impatience, and his surprising dislike for Reginald Usher. Dupin was a keen inspector with an instinct for what was not right. Poe had explained what he needed from the newspaperman's office.

The inspector led the conversation. "No need to bother with that, sir. I merely need an item from your library. One quick verification, and then I can absolve you of all guilt. No one will ever give a second thought to Mr. Poe's wild stories."

"No one ever did," Usher said pointedly, then fashioned a magnanimous smile again. "I have always said that the learned men of Richmond may peruse my library. What is it you need, Inspector? A quote from Pliny the Elder? A Greek translation of the Holy Scriptures? Berlini's account of the red death in Italy?"

"Mr. Poe has a specific title in mind."

Usher frowned at the idea. "And what does he know of my library?" Poe sensed a flare of puzzlement, then unease rippling through the murderer's closely hidden thoughts. Something about the wild look on Poe's bruised expression gave him pause. "My books are very well cared for, some of them quite valuable ..."

When Usher looked about to withdraw his invitation, Dupin quickly stepped in. Poe sensed the surprise and growing suspicion in the inspector's thoughts. "Sir, I am required to complete my investigation. Now, I would not dream of tearing up your floorboards or knocking down your brick walls in search of hidden bodies. But perusing a book from your library is not too much to ask, is it?"

Taking the initiative, Poe hurried over to the nearest library shelf. "It's here, I know it is!" He squinted with his one good eye to read the titles on the spines. He moved from volume to volume, trying to match what he had seen in a flash of Usher's memories the night before. One particular volume ...

As a murderer, Usher was ruthless. He had hidden the bodies of his victims, but his greatest camouflage was to cloak himself in the guise of a respectable businessman, to hide himself in plain sight. He relished the violence he committed, and he felt frustrated that he couldn't share his bloody deeds with others who might appreciate them.

Poe scanned the next shelf, then the next, book after book, but nothing caught his attention. He didn't bother to pull any volume from its place, didn't open a single cover.

"How much longer must we endure this masquerade, Inspector?" Usher asked. "Arrest him and end this harassment." The two policemen at the door fidgeted, uncertain.

"You are a clever man," Poe muttered. "But your greatest failing is your arrogance. You simply could not resist boasting about what you had done, writing down every aspect of how you smothered the old man and then butchered his body, how you smashed out the teeth of your dear niece after you killed her, how you taunted your rival as he hung on manacles in your cellar." He glared at the newspaperman. "You wrote it all down."

Usher scoffed. "If I were guilty of such outrageous deeds, why the devil would I document them?"

"Because you were certain no one would ever find it." He ran his fingers along the volumes on the next shelf, saw Usher stiffen. Inspector Dupin looked on with keen interest.

Poe continued, "In your journal confessing to the crimes, you recorded every last violent and painful detail because you were confident in your hiding place. A perfect hiding place." He spotted several unmarked volumes in the second middle shelf, right at eye level. "If Inspector Dupin were to ransack your offices and your house looking for such a journal, he would rack his brain to find the cleverest hiding place. He would never find it, would he?"

Poe rested his finger on a drab, nondescript volume. When he smiled, his split lip ached. "But you chose to hide your bloody confession in plain sight, right here where anyone could see it, in your own personal library which you have made available to any scholar in Richmond." Triumphant, he seized the unmarked journal, a thin volume invisible among so many weightier tomes. "But why would anyone notice something like this?"

Poe held up the book and opened the cover for Dupin. "Here, Inspector, in Reginald Usher's own hand is the full account of his murders."

Dupin was fascinated by his monologue, and the two policemen pressed forward to read as Poe opened the pages to reveal a dense account in tightly efficient handwriting.

A wordless howl of inhuman rage startled him. Red faced, Usher seized the iron poker by the fireplace and rushed at him. His eyes looked like shattered glass. In that instant, Poe saw the bestial look that his other victims must have seen.

A loud shot rang out, the report from Dupin's pistol. The bullet struck Usher in the upper chest and hurled him back into his mahogany desk. The two policemen rushed forward, taken off guard. They had been prepared to grapple with *Poe* and had never assumed the newspaperman might become violent.

"I always allow for possibilities, no matter how small," said Inspector Dupin.

Usher groaned, bleeding onto his fine desktop as the policemen seized him. Poe handed the nondescript journal to Dupin without reading it, because he already knew what the pages contained. He had witnessed the crimes themselves in the haunting thoughts of Reginald Usher.

Dupin blanched as he skimmed the first several pages. "You were right. You were right all along. This is ... hideous."

"I can also show you where to find the bodies. I wager you'll be willing to knock down the bricks and tear up the floorboards now?"

The inspector was clearly shaken. "I do not doubt you anymore, Mr. Poe, but how could you know? How could you possibly know?"

"Guilty thoughts are loud and clear to those sensitive to them," he said.

The thin explanation was insufficient, but the inspector shook his head. "Whatever the reason, you have caught a killer. Usher will surely hang for it. You have done a great service, Mr. Poe."

He did not feel victorious, however. The guilty thoughts, the miserable ghosts, the haunting crimes would continue to swirl around him. Every person had secrets, and Edgar Allan Poe could hear them, whether he wanted to or not. Even though Usher would harm no one else, countless other horrors continued to emanate from the crowds in the city, from strangers he met or, worse, from people he considered friends. The whispers and screams would never stop plaguing him.

His only respite from the ghoulish din was drinking himself into a stupor, but that was its own path of self-destruction. Usher himself had gained cold satisfaction by documenting what he had done, however, confessing to an invisible audience.

Poe himself was a writer. Maybe there was another way to purge the horrors that other people placed unwillingly in his mind. He might find some personal release if he captured those awful incidents using his gift of words.

He could write them down and publish them.

The second Frankenstein-inspired story in this collection. Christopher Golden asked me to contribute to his theme anthology The Monster's Corner for HarperCollins, stories with a sympathetic perspective on classic monsters. I always found the Frankenstein monster to be far more sympathetic than his creator, so that was my natural choice.

Here, the collision idea was taking the long-lived monster to an oppressive Jewish ghetto in Nazi Germany just before Kristallnacht. The monster had always been misunderstood, persecuted, with people afraid of him because he was different— just the sort of treatment the European Jews endured. Perhaps the monster could find sanctuary among them ...

This story has always been very close to my heart.

Torn Stitches,
Shattered Glass

A tiny silver needle, sharp point. My large fingers have grown nimble over years of practice and delicate concentration, and I could glide the moistened end of the thread through the needle's eye on the first try, then pull the strand tight. I completed the first stitches, neat ones, no excuse for clumsy black sutures such as a mortician would use after an autopsy.

The needle dipped into the end of the torn arm socket, then emerged, and I pulled the strong thread through, binding the detached arm to the shoulder. I immediately saw that I should have used white thread, because it would have shown up less. I made certain the ends were neatly aligned and continued my stitching.

I sat in my dim tailor shop in the ghetto of Ingolstadt. Some called the place cramped; I found it cozy. I was accepted here, though I wasn't Jewish—what religion would accept someone like me? The people welcomed outsiders, understood them, and did not ask awkward, probing questions. It was 1938, and I'd been here for many years. I did not look forward to the day when I'd have to move on again.

I finished stitching around the stump of the arm, then snapped off the thread after tying a solid knot. I turned toward the little girl with rich brown hair and a bright mind, who sat watching me. I handed back her repaired ragdoll. "There, little Rachel—all fixed." I propped up the doll, moving both arms with my fingers. "She doesn't hurt."

Rachel Schulmann was far wiser than she appeared. "She doesn't hurt because she's just a *doll*, Franck." The child sounded as if she needed to explain to me. "She's *made*, not real."

"Of course."

In their insular ghetto, the Jews had been suspicious of me at first—a large man with rough features and a scarred face, like a boxer who had lost too many fights. I kept to myself, showing no warmth or friendship, but posing no threat. I was tired of running, and I had almost given up on humanity because of how people hated things they didn't understand, how they despised strangers and vented their anger by lighting torches, grabbing pitchforks. But here in the Ingolstadt ghetto, I was patient, helpful, with few needs or ambitions. I became a tailor because I liked to stitch things together, making certain the pieces fit. Ironic, that.

As Rachel took the doll from me, my sleeve accidentally slid up my arm. Normally, I chose to wear bulky jackets with thick cuffs, but now the girl's eyes widened as she saw the line that encircled my wrist, the still-prominent scars from the old sutures where the hand had been attached—someone else's hand, someone else's wrist, the first two pieces in becoming *me*.

"Does that hurt?" she asked, more fascinated than frightened.

I gave her a quick, reassuring shake of my head. "No, child. It's just the way I'm made."

Now that the important work was done—repairing the girl's doll—I could turn to the other work she'd brought me. Her father, the rabbi, had sent his jacket, a dark old suit that had been carefully but inexpertly patched many times over the years. Given a few days, I could have fixed flaws that the rabbi or his wife pretended not to see, tightened the stitches, trimmed the frayed cuffs and collar. But the damage was more severe, more disturbing. As soon as I looked at the torn fabric at the shoulder, the mud stains, the dried blood, I recalled what had happened. No one could keep secrets here in the ghetto.

The Nazis—three of them—had beaten Rabbi Schulmann in the streets. Laughing, they had pushed him down into the mud, and he had not challenged them, had not cursed them—but he had retained his dignity. Unwise. When the Schutzstaffel district officer Schein and two members of his Staffeln decided that the Rabbi did not look sufficiently humiliated, they had knocked him into the gutter and pummeled him with nightsticks. Some of the people gasped and moaned, helpless, while others watched in horror. Rabbi Schulmann cringed, accepted the blows, and soon enough Staffelfuhrer Schein and his two thugs grew tired of their sport and departed.

"They attack us because we're different," the Rabbi said aloud to the stunned people who rushed to help him. "To them, we're easy targets." He was bruised and bleeding, and they helped him to a doctor.

I had watched part of the incident from behind the smeared glass windows of my tailor shop. The Jews pretended that bad things didn't happen. They cleaned up all sign of the incident, erased any marks the Nazis left, as if that was the way to survive.

Now I had the Rabbi's damaged and stained jacket. I inspected it, poked my thick fingers through the tear, studied the dried blood. My dark lips formed a smile. "Tell your father I can fix this, Rachel. I promise it will be as good as new by tomorrow evening."

"Thank you, Franck." She pulled her doll close to her chest. "When you bring it over, my mother and father would like you to join us for dinner. Tomorrow night?"

"I'd be happy to, Rachel." I was genuinely pleased. The people rarely invited me into their homes.

Outside, in the street, I watched the Jews nailing boards across their shop windows, which were shattered the previous day when Schein and his entire Staffeln of ten men had hurled bricks at any business they didn't like—an accountant, a piano teacher, a baker. I knew the shopkeepers had already placed orders with a glassmaker in the city, wanting to repair the windows as quickly as possible. Within a day, the ghetto street would look just as it always had—until the next time. But inner scars did not so easily go away.

How could I not be angry?

As Rachel went to the door to leave my shop, she suddenly paused in fear. I heard the rumble of a staff car drive down the street and placed a warning hand on the girl's shoulder, holding her there to make certain she didn't run out in full view.

Staffelfuhrer Schein sat in the back of the staff car as his driver cruised slowly down the street; he glared as the people ducked into doorways or drew the shades of their windows. The staff car rolled by, wafting silence along the shops like a hushed breath.

"Why have they come back?" Rachel whispered.

"Because they like you to be afraid, child."

We watched as the Nazis drove out of sight, but they caused no damage ... today.

Ingolstadt was still a small city, far from the rest of the war, with an insignificant Jewish quarter, which made Schein and the few men in his Staffeln all the more desperate for attention. But they wouldn't get it from me. I had learned long ago not to draw attention to myself if I wished to survive.

When the typical noises began to reappear in the street and people emerged from their shops with a nervous sigh, I let the girl run back to her parents. "Tell your father I'll bring the jacket tomorrow night."

In the past century, much had changed in Ingolstadt.

Because I hadn't come alive the way a normal person did, neither did I age or die as a normal man would. Most children have only dim memories of their early childhood, but I can remember the vivid flood of images and sensations from the moment I opened my dull yellow eyes on the table, surrounded by lightning, to see the face of Victor Frankenstein, my creator ... my father ... the man who was so horrified by *me* that he had cast me out.

Victor hated me because I was different, even though he had made me that way. What choice did I have but to hate him in return?

In a hundred years, the townspeople had done their best to forget, or at least to pretend ignorance of, the history of their town. The ancient castle was gone, torn down stone by stone at the turn of the twentieth century. The old mill had burned long ago, then was rebuilt, only to be abandoned again. It was now an ancient wreck on the hill above the town.

I had traveled the world, gone to the frozen ends of the earth in pursuit of Victor, where I'd strangled him aboard a ship in an icy sea. It should have been my vengeance, my victory, after I'd leapt overboard to drift away on a detached ice floe, but I had learned much since then.

Now I had come back home to the small German city that was my birthplace. My Jewish neighbors accepted me without asking too many questions, sometimes looking at me with pity, sometimes with a hard swallow and dry throat, as they saw my scars, my lumpish features. But I have done nothing to make them fear me. I was no longer the vengeful clumsy monster, but rather just someone trying to fit in. I felt I had a chance ... but I didn't think the Nazis would let anyone live peaceably and unnoticed.

After the girl was gone, I took the Rabbi's jacket and used gentle strokes of a bristle brush to clean the mud and chemicals to soak out the bloodstains. Then, with tiny perfect stitches, I began to repair the damage.

I toiled all night long by lantern light, and I had the Rabbi's jacket cleaned, repaired, and even pressed well before sunup. But I couldn't allow myself to do things that were *too* mysterious. If I did my work too quickly, too perfectly, there might be stories about me dabbling in dark magic, being a secret outcast sorcerer hiding in the ghetto of Ingolstadt. Rumors are easy things to start.

Since the Nazis openly blame the Jews for every perceived crime, one would think the people here in the ghetto would not be so quick to cast suspicions themselves, but it is part of the way humans are made, scars they don't even see inside themselves.

Because I don't need sleep—one of the gifts that Victor forgot to include when he gave me my life, like a missed stitch—I sat up and read the newspapers until dawn, when I would be able to venture into the streets again without looking like a fearsome, hulking shadow.

I had one paper from Berlin, one from Salzburg, and even a weekly Yiddish edition (though my grasp of the language was still uncertain). The date was November 9, 1938, and the political situation in Germany was grim. By reading the slanted stories, I could sense a brewing storm on the horizon—a storm that would not bring the spark of life, like the one that had reanimated me. All of Germany—maybe even all of Europe—seemed to be full of peasants carrying torches, looking for a target....

When the ghetto began to bustle in the morning, I helped an old silversmith across the street re-hang a splintered door that the Nazis had damaged during their previous escapade, and he was grateful for my help. I had little else to do; a pair of trousers to alter, a few buttons to reattach. I walked the length of the ghetto, without any particular aim. A dark cloud seemed to hang over the people, as if they knew something terrible was about to happen, but they pretended it was just another day.

That evening I brought the repaired jacket to the rabbi's house, which was adjacent to the synagogue, and also carried a sack with four apples I had purchased from the cart on the corner. Rachel was delighted to see me, and the rabbi thanked me for my help. He tried on his repaired jacket, pronounced it perfect.

His face looked as battered and discolored as mine had once appeared, the purple bruises from his recent beating now turning yellow at the edges. When he caught me looking at them, he said, "They will heal. We must give thanks that no greater harm was done. They have had their fun. Staffelfuhrer Schein and his men are like angry, unruly children."

The rabbi's wife was furious on his behalf. "And you think because you let them beat you that they'll be satisfied now?"

"What would you have me do?" the rabbi said in frustration.

Rachel quickly held up her doll, smiling at me. "Could you make me another one, Franck? You're so good at stitching."

"Rachel, that's not a polite request to make," her father admonished.

My dark lips formed a smile. "But a perfectly reasonable one, Rabbi. I may have some scraps of old cloth left and a few rags. Would you like me to make a husband for your stitched-together woman?"

"Yes, please."

She had no idea how much that thought hurt me. If Victor had done that one thing for me, we would never have needed to become enemies. But Victor Frankenstein was a terrible man. And the peasants called *me* inhuman!

Frau Schulmann had made a fine meal with whatever was available. She even simmered the apples I had brought with a pinch of cinnamon and some sugar.

After we ate, the rabbi invited me to smoke a pipe with him as we listened to the world news on the radio. After the tubes had warmed up, he tuned to the strongest radio station, which was playing Wagner. The rabbi sat back contentedly, puffing smoke.

I felt relaxed, remembering another old man, a blind man alone in a cottage who had befriended me and taught me many things, showing me the kind side of the human heart for the first time. I missed that blind old man; I'd seen too few people like him in all of my years.

When the radio announcer read the news in a terse, incensed voice, the Rabbi and I both listened. Tensions in Germany were already strained. Many Jews, feeling displaced and victimized, had already fled the country if they had the means to do so. They lost their homes, their wealth. They tried to find someplace to hide.

But today the situation grew much worse. In Paris, a German diplomat had been assassinated by a Polish Jew, a young man incensed by how the Nazis were persecuting his people. The assassin had been driven to violence out of despair and helplessness, but as I listened to the angry news announcer, I knew that the young man's actions would only aggravate the situation for the Jews. In fact, I was certain things would rapidly get worse. The announcer added at the end, as if it were a foregone conclusion: "Investigators are certain this is part of a much larger Jewish plot to overthrow the government."

Rabbi Schulmann turned gray and shook his head. "Oh, no." He uttered a quick prayer. "This is just the excuse the Nazis have wanted for a long time."

From the kitchen where she washed the dishes, his wife looked at him with wide eyes, frightened by the news. Rachel played with her doll in the room, and she surprised us again with her perceptiveness. "Are we in danger, Papa? Will the bad men come hurt you again?"

Rabbi Schulmann heaved a long sigh, pained by what he had to admit to his daughter. "We must pray it won't happen, my dear."

The girl was grim and serious. "We should have a golem to protect us, just like in Prague. Then we can be safe."

"That's just a story, child," Rabbi Schulmann said.

But the girl was indignant. "You said it was a *true* story."

The rabbi looked up at me with weary eyes, explaining, "It is a frightening tale, my friend—a good tale, but I can't guarantee its veracity. In Prague in 1580, Rabbi Loew fashioned a large and muscular being out of clay, a *golem*, to protect our community from a Jew-hating priest who incited hatred from the Christians. When the mob came to the ghetto, Rabbi Loew's golem stood strong and protected the Jews, preventing a pogrom. But then the golem ran amok, threatening innocents, causing great damage. Rabbi Loew was forced to remove the spark of life, rendering the golem lifeless again." He turned to his daughter. "It is meant to be a lesson."

"I still think we need our own golem," said Rachel. "But without the last part of the story."

Outside, we heard growling engines, screams, gunfire ... then laughter accompanied by the sounds of shattering glass.

Fires began to start quickly. Staffelfuhrer Schein rode imperiously in his staff car with two of his men, flanked by two more Staffeln on motorcycles. His men threw rocks and bricks, smashing every intact window on the street. When some of the shopkeepers and families ran out, begging them to stop, the Nazis threw rocks at them instead.

The old silversmith whom I had helped flailed his hands and stood in front of the door we had just repaired. One of the Staffeln grinned, hefted a broken brick, and hurled it with deadly aim, smashing the center of the silversmith's forehead. He collapsed, surely dead.

The men fired their rifles into the air, but I was sure they would choose other targets soon. When the rotund baker shook his fist and cursed them, the Staffelfuhrer turned in his seat in the staff car, raised his Luger, and shot the baker in the chest.

"Burn the synagogue," Schein ordered. "That's where they plot against us!" His men tossed kerosene lanterns against the synagogue door, smashed more windows.

Rachel ran into the street, crying, screaming in her little-girl voice for the Nazis to stop. The terrified rabbi grabbed her and pulled her back, but she'd already drawn the Nazis' attention. They spotted, and recognized, the man they had beaten only days earlier.

"Please don't hurt her!" Rabbi Schulmann cried, but the Nazis raised their guns.

I had seen mob hatred before, had faced it and barely survived. The Nazis were destructive and dangerous, more organized than unruly town peasants and capable of causing far more damage. I would have preferred to stay in my tailor shop and not get involved; that would have been the smart thing to do.

I may be large, I may look ungainly, my hands and limbs stitched together from mismatched parts, but Victor had done his work well, and I could move with predatory speed and power. I lunged forward to place myself in front of the rabbi and Rachel.

The Nazis opened fire.

I felt the impact of three rifle bullets and a much smaller caliber handgun bullet. My chest caught the deadly projectiles, preventing them from harming anyone else. The hot bullets damaged skin and muscles, but my body had already been dead once and would not so easily be brought back to death.

The Nazis had fired first. Now it was my turn.

Paying no heed to the spreading fires, the astonished crowd, or the arrogant sneer on the Nazi faces, I was upon the nearest SS man. I grabbed his rifle and yanked it free with such force that three of his fingers snapped; I heard a sickening pop as his shoulder dislocated.

I brought the butt of the rifle down so hard in the center of his face that it caved in his skull, just like the old silversmith's. Then I swung the rifle hard sideways and shattered the spine of a second man.

I charged over to the two Staffeln who were now scrambling off their motorcycles. With one hand on each, I grabbed them by the lip of their helmets, yanked them up—I think one neck broke instantly. The other soldier flailed and thrashed, but I slammed them down to the street. Then I picked up one of the motorcycles, raised it high over my head, and brought it down onto them, crushing both. In moments, I had dispatched all the Staffeln, none of whom had a chance to fire another shot.

Last was Staffelfuhrer Schein. He stared at me with round eyes and gaping mouth. I think he had shot his Luger at me several times, but I hadn't even felt the bullets. I grabbed the pistol and the hand that held it and turned the weapon. I meant to bend Schein's arm at the elbow but bent the middle of his wrist instead. It didn't matter. I jammed the Luger's hot barrel up under his chin and crushed my fingers around the trigger, firing off another shot that went through the top of his head.

Only fifteen seconds had passed.

Though the fires continued to burn in the synagogue and chunks of broken glass fell out of the smashed windows, the silence around me seemed deafening. I turned. There were several bullet holes in my own garments, but they could be easily repaired with a few neat stitches.

What I could not fix, though, was the fear and horror with which Rabbi Schulmann and his people now regarded *me*.

"What have you done?" the rabbi asked softly.

"Saved you." How else could I respond?

"Maybe ... maybe not." The rabbi shook his head, as if paralyzed by a nightmare. "What are you?"

Now my own hiding of the truth, my own erasure of my unnatural past, was laid bare before them. They saw my ugliness, saw the scars, and quickly classified me as "not one of us." Even though I had helped them, stood against their enemies, saved them from the attack of these monsters, they regarded me with fear. Even Rachel.

"He's the golem," she said.

"You killed the Nazis," said the rabbi. "Now they'll come back for us and take their vengeance tenfold. They will retaliate, kill us all."

I knew, though, that Ingolstadt had only a small Nazi garrison, a minimal presence, and I had killed them all. It would take days, perhaps as much as a week before the district leader began to wonder what had happened to Schein and his men. We would have time ... if the people let me.

I glanced up at the murky dark sky. There was no moon tonight. I had to hope that the other citizens of Ingolstadt wouldn't take it upon themselves to attack the Jewish quarter in retaliation for the news of the recent assassination.

"I have an idea," I said. "We will need blankets to cover them." As if they were no more significant than the doll I had repaired for Rachel, I picked up the dead Nazis and tossed them into the staff car, piling them like cordwood. "We can dispose of the bodies, get rid of the car and motorcycles. No one ever has to know."

"We all know," the rabbi said.

"And you'll be alive to know it." I looked down at Staffelfuhrer Schein, who lay atop the pile of bodies. He reminded me too much of how Victor had looked after I'd strangled him up in the frozen sea. I felt no satisfaction, no relief, barely even a sense of justice.

Frau Schulmann was sobbing, as were several others in the street. Finally, some went to fight the spreading fires and save the synagogue. Others went to tend to the bodies of those the Nazis had killed.

"This will get much worse for us," the rabbi said, his voice hollow. "If you were a real golem, I could remove the bit of Scripture that reanimated you, the spark of life." He shook his head. "But I don't have that power. I don't know where you come from. I can only ask you to go away and leave us alone. We don't want you here—you're too dangerous."

The Jews were afraid of me, but at least they didn't have pitchforks and torches. I would do them one last favor, then I would be gone to find someplace up in the rugged mountains.

I looked once more at Rachel, but the little girl did not look back at me. Her rag doll had fallen onto the street.

I gathered every remnant of Staffelfuhrer Schein and his men, then drove away in the staff car, out of Ingolstadt and up the rutted dirt road that led to the abandoned, creaking mill where winds whistled through broken windows. I piled the bodies inside the old mill, then set fire to the old structure. I do not like dangerous, unpredictable fire, but this brought more satisfaction than terror. As the windmill blazed into the dark sky, it seemed very appropriate to me—a different sort of ending. This time, *I* had torched the place, winning my own victory against superstition, prejudice, and fear. Even though it would never end there....

I set off in the staff car, driving away into the rugged mountains, far from Ingolstadt. I never intended to return—

although I had said the same thing a century before. Hours later, when the car was nearly out of gas, I found a pull-off by a steep cliffside, tossed the motorcycles off the cliff and pushed the empty vehicle over, where it tumbled off into the darkness. Even if the wreckage was eventually found, no one would ever know the answers.

Still feeling no pain from where I'd been shot, no weariness despite the labors of the night, I trudged up into the empty high valleys and isolated crags. I didn't care about the cold glaciers or windswept basins. I just needed to find a place where I would be alone ... where I belonged.

Previous Publication Information

"Age Rings," copyright © 1988, WordFire, Inc., first published in *Grue Magazine* #7, revised 2017.

"Baggage Check," copyright © 1988, WordFire, Inc., first published in *The Horror Show*, Spring 1988.

"Bringing the Family," copyright © 1993, WordFire, Inc., first published in *The Ultimate Zombie*, ed. Byron Preiss and John Betancourt, Dell, 1993.

"The Circus," copyright © 1984, WordFire, Inc., first published in *The Horror Show*, Winter 1984.

"Cold Storage," copyright © 2019, WordFire, Inc., first published in *Short Things*, ed. John Gregory Betancourt, Wildside Press, 2019.

"Cupid's Arrow," original to this collection, copyright © 2018, WordFire, Inc.

"Family Portrait," copyright © 1989, WordFire, Inc., first published in *2AM Magazine*, Summer 1989.

"A Glimpse of the Ankou," copyright © 1987, WordFire, Inc., first published in *The Horror Show*, Winter 1987.

"Hunter's Moon," copyright © 1991, WordFire, Inc., first published in *Obsessions*, ed. Gary Raisor, Dark Harvest, 1991.

"The Injection," copyright © 2024, WordFire, Inc., first publication.

"New Recruits," copyright © 1990, WordFire, Inc., first published in *Weirdbook* 25, Autumn 1990.

"Nuptials," copyright © 1991, WordFire, Inc., first published in *Midnight Zoo*, March/April 1991.

"Role Model," copyright © 2014, WordFire, Inc., first published in *Fiction River: Fantastic Detectives*, ed. Kristine Kathryn Rusch, WMG Publishing, 2014.

Previous Publication Information

About the Author

Kevin J. Anderson has published more than 180 books, 58 of which have been national or international bestsellers. He has 24 million copies in print in 34 languages.

He has written numerous novels in the Star Wars, X-Files, and Dune universes, as well as the unique Clockwork Angels steampunk trilogy with legendary Rush drummer Neil Peart. His original works include the Saga of Seven Suns series, the Wake the Dragon and Terra Incognita fantasy trilogies, the humorous Dan Shamble, Zombie P.I. series and The Dragon Business series.

He has edited numerous anthologies, written comics and games, and the lyrics to two rock CDs as companions to his Terra Incognita trilogy.

Anderson is the director of the graduate program in Publishing at Western Colorado University, and he and his wife Rebecca Moesta are the publishers of WordFire Press.

If You Liked ...

If you liked *Horror and Dark Fantasy Stories: Volume 1*, you might also enjoy other WordFire Press titles by Kevin J. Anderson.

Our list of other WordFire Press authors and titles is always growing. To find out more and shop our selection of titles, visit us at:
wordfirepress.com